DUNGEON LIFE

BOOK 3

DUNGEON LIFE

BOOK 3

Khenal

Podium

To Aranya, who was more confident in the story than I was, and who encouraged me to start posting it in the first place.

Cover design by Istvan Straban

ISBN: 978-1-0394-5398-2

Published in 2024 by Podium Publishing
www.podiumentertainment.com

Podium

DUNGEON LIFE

BOOK 3

Official Dungeoneer Guild Primer

Dungeon Name: Thedeim
Affinity: Fate
Classification: Cooperative

Spawners: Rats *(resource)*, Spiders *(physical)*, Ants *(resource)*, Bats *(resource)*, Birds [Corvids] *(resource)*, Snakes *(magic)*, Undead [Fleshy] *(resource)*, Undead [Hands] *(magic)*, Undead [Skeletal] *(resource)*, Bees *(unspecialized)*, Elementals [Earth] *(unspecialized)*, Slimes *(resource)*, Wolves *(magic)*

Scions: Teemo *(rat, Voice)*, Tiny *(spider)*, Queen *(ant)*, Coda *(bat)*, Poe *(raven)*, Fluffles *(coatl, Conduit)*, Rocky *(zombie)*, Thing *(hand)*, Grim *(skeleton)*, Honey *(bee)*, Slash *(Earth elemental)*, Jello *(slime)*, Leo *(wolf)*

Enclaves: Ratkin *(friendly, Crypt Complex)*, Spiderkin *(friendly, Caverns)*

Residents: Aranya *(kobold)*, Yvonne *(birdkin; hawk)*

Overview: While many of Thedeim's spawners are specialized toward different resource production, all delvers should expect to engage in combat. Thedeim forgoes a rigid room structure to focus on several zones of varying difficulty and rewards, which include the Manor, the Hedge Maze, the Tunnels, the Gauntlet, the Caverns, the Cemetery, the Crypt Complex, and the Arena.

There are more in-depth primers available, and the Dungeoneer's Guild recommends purchasing those pamphlets once you decide which you wish to focus on. A brief description of each follows.

The Manor is designed for beginner delvers, and the encounters are generally made up of low-level rats, spiders, snakes, and crows. The interior has many cabinets, chests, and other locations for traditional loot, as well as several fungus nodes. The belfry has a Garden, where herbalists may discover rare seeds, though they will need to battle past a boss in the attic to get there. Outside, there are many herbalism nodes, as well as a selection of quests from the dungeon itself available on the porch.

The Hedge Maze is one of Thedeim's special attractions, and one of the few times a scion is a direct obstacle. The Spider Scion, Tiny, is a gigantic tarantula that runs the maze. Inside are several chests and rare lumber nodes, with the more valuable of each being available deeper within.

However, the longer one stays in the maze, the more likely they will be captured by Tiny or potentially picked clean by dire rat thieves. Being caught is not a hazard to one's health, but a tax of valuables will be extracted before a delver is deposited outside the maze.

The Hedge Maze is appropriate for any level of delver, though inexperienced ones should make their trip as brief as possible if they do not wish to be caught.

The Tunnels are a series of passages and small caverns below the Manor, reached either via the basement or the cave in the yard. Snakes, bats, slimes, and spiders are the most common encounters, with occasional Earth elementals. The area is a step up in difficulty from the Manor, and it is highly recommended to bring antidotes, as well as lightning resistance for the fights.

Widows are not uncommon, as the spider spawner is located in the Tunnels. Mining nodes are common, with occasional subterranean herbalism nodes as well. Delvers should be familiar with combat, and may need to flee from widows if they are not confident in defeating the potent spiders.

The Gauntlet is a special attraction in the Tunnels which consists of a series of challenges meant to test abilities besides combat. The first half is designed to test strength and agility with many unique challenges to be overcome. The second half is designed to test the mind with riddles and puzzles, with a valuable chest at the end as a reward.

There is also a version designed to test parties, with the challenges and reward increased appropriately. While there is little danger to even the newest of delvers, the challenges are tough enough that one will need moderate experience to expect to pass the entire Gauntlet.

The Caverns are below the Tunnels, and can be accessed either by exploring through them or by taking the access shaft located not far from the cave entrance in the yard. The access shaft rarely has encounters; what ones there are are generally limited to bats or slimes.

The Caverns themselves are several large caves, and the most common encounters are elementals, slimes, spiders, and snakes. This zone is another step up from the Tunnels, and should delvers wish access to the abundant mining and herbalism nodes, they should either be accomplished adventurers or hire accomplished adventurers from the guild.

Of special note are the twinsnakes, which are often alchemically enhanced with metallic scales and Lightning affinity.

The Cemetery is on the surface, separated from the Manor by a significant amount of Fourdock. It used to house a murderous dungeon, but Thedeim subsumed it and has taken over the territory. The Cemetery itself is rather quiet, though wolf encounters can be had near the back wall. For the most part, it should be treated as any mundane cemetery; a quiet place to remember the dead.

Do not attempt to engage the scion who oversees the place. Grim is an exceptionally strong Skeleton Scion with both Life and Death affinities. He maintains the grounds and endeavors to keep a quiet and peaceful atmosphere for mourners, and is not a scion who should be engaged in combat, especially not when making his rounds.

The Crypt Complex is reached either through one of the mausoleums in the Cemetery or through the Tunnels. The Dungeoneer's Guild recommends using the Cemetery entrance, as it is much simpler to access.

The Complex is full of the various types of undead available to Thedeim. Their particular resource specialization makes them highly resistant to turning and other magics meant to directly counter the energies of the undead. Should they be defeated, the corpses are effectively herbalism nodes.

There are a few herbalism and mining nodes available as well, but the Crypt Complex is generally a place designed for fighting. The challenge level is similar to the Caverns, though the denizen-type difference requires very different preparations.

The Arena is Thedeim's latest special attraction, and the only one that features combat with one of his scions: Rocky. The Zombie Scion should not be underestimated, though fights are not to the death. If one wishes to challenge the Arena, the Dungeoneer's Guild highly recommends purchasing the pamphlet on the section, which includes the rules of the place, as well as more detail on Rocky's abilities.

In addition to the fighting floor, there is ample seating to observe the fights. All challengers are welcome, and though Rocky remains undefeated, challengers are usually rewarded even for a defeat.

Aside from the zones, Thedeim also has a myriad of scions, most of whom should be allowed to continue with their duties uninterrupted. While they can be approached and questioned, they will have limited ability to answer. The exception is, of course, Teemo, the Voice of Thedeim.

The simple rat is personable and friendly, and his Spatial affinity means that, should one have a detailed question of a scion, he will not be far away to provide an answer should Thedeim be willing to give one.

Special Notes: While it is worth mentioning that no delvers have perished within Thedeim, it is also appropriate to note that that is a deliberate decision. The Dungeoneer's Guild highly recommends against attempting to provoke Thedeim or his scions, as they are numerous and powerful.

Attempting to harm any dwellers or residents is highly recommended against, as it is likely to draw Thedeim's significant ire, resulting in imprisonment within the dungeon at best.

Lastly, the Dungeoneer's Guild rightly recommends checking with them for updates on Thedeim's sections. The dungeon has shown explosive growth, and regularly has new areas or changes to old ones. While failing to keep abreast of changes is not likely to be truly dangerous, it *is* highly likely to result in being defeated and losing some or all of the loot gained from a delve.

Chapter 1

Teemo

He has to admit, he's missed doing this kind of work. He certainly doesn't dislike being the Boss's Voice. In fact, he very much enjoys getting to talk to the delvers and listen to the Boss's crazy ideas. Being able to talk to Aranya, and especially to Yvonne, is an amazing privilege, too.

He enjoys the warmth of thinking about those two for a few moments before putting the thoughts aside for now. If he dwells on them, he'll start to think of what they're doing in the Deeps and start worrying.

He could also easily worry about all the stuff going on back home. Because *of course* the Boss expanded while he was busy! Even with him giving Teemo some time and mental space to focus on scouting, he can still hear when the Boss is thinking aloud to himself.

Teemo's not the only one trying not to worry about the party exploring the Deeps, even if it takes a bit more than scouting to keep the Boss's mind off it. He's kinda surprised he's going for an Ant Enclave before a snake one, but then again, he's not wrong about there not really being a good place for one right now. It'll probably be his spring project, though.

Unless they end up needing to deal with that deep dungeon in the spring.

No, no thinking about that. Energy spent worrying is energy not spent actually doing something!

Besides, he really should focus on his actual work. These last couple days have been putting his Scout title to the test, and he's been getting a lot of levels from it. Quick little shortcuts in the Boss's domain are one thing, but these huge ones outside are something else entirely. Those small ones were practically effortless. Even the one through the woods toward Hullbreak was a breeze compared to these!

The Boss wanted him to make them as long and as short as possible, which sounded weird to him at first. After a little thought, however, it became obvious what he meant: cover lots of distance outside with minimal distance inside.

He does his best not to think too hard about how that works, remembering the crazy math abominations that use not only bits of the alphabet but *other* symbols which make his head hurt.

He'll take the Boss's word on the specifics of how they work. Having the math never helped him when making his other shortcuts, so he doubts it'll help with these. No, experience will be his teacher, and experience is definitely what he's getting.

A lot of his shortcuts back home, especially his early ones, were mostly just more direct routes, being shorter in distance simply because nobody would have to walk around all the stuff in the way.

But then he started being able to make them even shorter, just by feeling and following his Scout title and Spatial affinity. And since working with Thing and the bag of holding, he's been able to make them even shorter. His shortcuts are only about half as long inside as the distance traveled outside, and he can feel he can do even better.

He's even been able to start creating what he thinks of as camps, expanding a space without it needing to actually lead anywhere.

Doing that for the outposts has been exhausting but enlightening. Some of them are pretty simple to work on, like the one under a bramble bush. Even though he could see daylight filtering through the branches, he'd had no problem expanding the place to be more comfortable for the wolves and other denizens on expedition.

On the other hand, the collapsed cabin had been incredibly difficult for him to expand.

He's pretty sure it's because of how easily a space is defined. A small, clear patch under some brambles is pretty easy to grasp in his mind, but a cabin missing most of the roof and with some partially collapsed walls is harder for him to wrap his head around. He managed it, but only just.

The denizens stationed there are going to try to repair the cabin for him to try again, but it will be slow to progress, if it's even possible without Coda's help.

Teemo smiles as he thinks of the Bat Scion. It's almost like the bat is trying to make up for lost time with helping the Boss, though he is pretty sure Coda's also just reveling in flexing his title. It feels right to Teemo to be making the shortcuts and camps; it must be the same for Coda, especially since he has some of Thedeim's crazy stuff to work with.

Even with his aversion to math, Teemo is still sometimes drawn to try to muscle through it anyway. He only needs to look as far as Rocky to know that having some of the Boss's knowledge can let a scion do crazy things with their title and affinities.

And speaking of title, he'll probably have to lean on being the Voice soon. He's not just making the shortcuts because they're fun. The Boss intends to help the Southwood with them, sending winter wolves soon, and other stuff once spring rolls around.

Part of Teemo thinks the Boss should just subsume or vassalize the Southwood, but he ignores that part. Sure, the mana windfall would be nice, but the Boss seems like he'd prefer a competent ally who can handle themselves rather than to try to hog all the power for himself. It's been how he's run everything so far.

Besides, even with the shortcuts, the Southwood is a bit far away to be the Boss's vassal.

The reports of the Southwood's Voice also make Teemo pretty sure the forest dungeon wouldn't go for it, anyway. Leo and Honey have been patiently waiting at the last outpost for Teemo to arrive and officially get negotiations underway. The Southwood is aware of them but hasn't bothered trying to talk with them much.

That's probably a good sign, at least. If the dungeon were feeling pressured, it'd probably immediately try to get them to help without waiting for Teemo. That it's keeping polite distance makes Teemo confident they'll be able to go on the attack after the snow melts, or maybe even earlier. That white stag would probably like that, since it seems pretty stuck up to Teemo, but Leo seems to think he's pretty strong, so maybe it's warranted.

He's pretty sure Rocky could kick his ass, though. He might not have been there to see him fight the kids, but the Boss has been loudly thinking about it enough for Teemo to wonder if the zombie could give Fluffles a run for his money.

He pauses as he thinks about that. Did those two ever keep working on expanding their affinities? He's pretty sure Fluffles picked up Wind and Storm at least from dealing with Hullbreak's desperate stunt, but he hasn't really paid much attention to their sparring since. Rocky has to have picked up a few more affinities by now too, right?

He shakes his head and continues working on the shortcut, trying not to think about what Rocky has managed. Of course, his brain betrays him and focuses on his own efforts to expand his affinities.

He stamps down the feeling of shame with his lack of progress on that front, defending himself with the fact that he finally understands what the Boss was referring to when talking about him potentially getting Fire or Ice affinity.

While making the camps, the temperature inside always dips dramatically when expanding an area. He even tried to shrink it, and felt it warm up. He just can't manage to wrap his head around the why. Sure, the Boss has shown him some math for it, but that's just not how Teemo thinks.

He *has* been noticing something strange when working with space outside of his shortcuts, though. There's some kind of resistance to what he's doing, and it's not constant. Rocky's assertion that stuff is made of stuff seems to relate to it, since he feels it a lot less when expanding space that's in the middle of the air. But getting close to things, especially to the ground, makes the resistance feel a lot stronger.

He'll probably need to ask Thedeim about it once he's back. He could ask now, but one, Teemo is a bit busy, and two, it'd probably be easier for the Boss to understand if Teemo could demonstrate it within his borders. Besides, he wants to get a better feel for the resistance on his own before he asks for help with it.

He can feel some tickle in the back of his mind, like the Boss has probably mentioned something similar before, but he can't connect the dots to it just yet.

He's not worried, though. He's a Scout, and a proper Scout is all about connecting dots, no matter if they're on a map or not.

Chapter 2

I try not to listen in on Teemo's thinking. I think he's better at ignoring it than I am, but the distance makes it a little easier, even if some of the things he's thinking about get my neurons jogging.

Spatial stuff that deals with mass and densities? That's some fundamental stuff, but I don't want to dump my suspicions about what he's working toward on him. I don't even know if it's an affinity that can be claimed.

I think he'll be better served if I let him figure it out on his own. None of the other scions have gotten affinities just from me telling them stuff. They've all had to figure it out on their own.

It's difficult to tell if the blank looks I get from explaining are because the bond isn't the best for complex concepts or if they just don't have the same foundational knowledge. There's a difference between knowing and understanding, I suppose.

Either way, I'll wait until Teemo asks, if he ever does.

Kinda like the difference in saying I'll keep Rezlar more in the loop and *actually* keeping him in the loop. It's a bit more difficult with Teemo out scouting, but I really should make an effort.

Right, I should also really try to take the Quartermaster on that tour, too. Hullbreak is making an effort, but I can feel him struggling to know what to do at times. Getting him a good view of how I do things would be a big help and a good step toward guiding him, and it might even help me identify what I've missed or managed to ignore.

Maybe I should take one of Violet's scions, too. Maybe Onyx? She's probably the one who would have the easiest time of wandering around. Legs is a bit big, Cappy is a bit, uh . . . *legless*, and Nose would probably prefer to burrow than walk. I'll let her decide who she wants to send, though, and figure out how to get Rezlar to come visit. I think I actually have a few options, surprisingly.

I haven't been testing the limits of the whole "only communicate via a Voice" thing that the system scolded me for a while ago, but I think I have at least two loopholes to potentially (ab)use. The first is my ravens. I haven't told them to say anything, but most of them have picked up at least a few words here and there.

I'd be surprised if they haven't learned Tarl's name, but I'm pretty sure they have. They just prefer making a general racket to chanting his name when he shows up. I don't think I could get actual sentences out of them, at least not without upsetting the system and getting another patch upside my nonexistent head, but a word or two would probably be alright?

My other potential avenue would be my aranea and their signs. While the rules for Rocky's arena were fine, I'm pretty sure the words were checked before going through; it felt like there was a bit of lag on them. The aranea, though, seem to have carte blanche to write whatever they want, as long as it's what *they* want.

I think I'll try signs; use them as basically letters. Even the rough, direct words the aranea write would probably be better received than a couple of ravens yelling, "Come, come!" at windows. Probably should save that for emergencies.

I spend a little mana and give the aranea the vague guidelines for what I want; I can feel that little delay again. It doesn't seem to get rejected, and I don't get told off, so I release the metaphorical breath I was holding and watch what they come up with.

Come to meet
Come to learn
As was deal

The aranea seem pretty satisfied with their work. I'd like a bit more, but I think it gets the point across. I also don't think I'd be able to get much more detail in there, so it'll have to do.

With two written, I have Poe go deliver the messages while I get Hullbreak and Violet's attention. Hullbreak is pretty easy to get to understand, and I can feel his Albatross Scion's nervousness through the bond already. It takes a little more time for Violet, but she seems excited once she understands.

She first wants to send Cappy, because of course she does, but seems to understand the difficulty with that once I point out he can't really just walk around. She decides to send Nose, and I don't argue with her. She actually has reasons, which is great.

She wanted to send Cappy because he's already the one with the best knowledge of the outside, which is fair. Legs is busy in the metalworks, which I still need to try to figure out how to get, and Onyx is trying to learn better ways to fight. She heard about Rocky's fun, and I think she was inspired.

Poe

The large raven swiftly attends his duties, though perhaps not as swiftly as he could. He must admit he doesn't take to the sky as often as he potentially should. Perhaps he'll start taking some of the closer patrol expeditions himself so he can keep in proper shape yet still remain close enough to render whatever aid Lord Thedeim requests.

He soars toward the Mayoral Manor first, feeling that the Office of Dungeon Affairs is closer to Hullbreak. Flying a bit slower is different from flying inefficiently, and Poe will not excuse the latter for himself.

The duty he has is an odd one, and he ponders where it would fit in the hierarchy of strange things Lord Thedeim does. He puts it moderately high on the list simply because of the novelties involved, but it doesn't make it near the top for how unlikely it is to cause great change. Something like the hedge maze was both novel and impactful, but he expects these messages will not cause any great uproar.

His arrival seems it may have, however, as the guards point and mill once they see him. The ashen elf, Miller, greets him at the balcony with a small bow.

"Ah, Marshal Poe. To what do we owe the pleasure?"

"Agreement," answers Poe, holding out one of the small planks in his talons. The butler accepts it as he would any other missive and takes a glance at the words there.

"Ah, of course. I take it Dungeon Thedeim would like us there at our earliest convenience?" Poe nods, and the elf smiles. "I shall inform him. I expect he will be eager to attend."

With that, Miller turns and enters the mansion, and Poe takes flight again. The butler has a strange air about him—one that would usually raise Poe's suspicions—but Voice Teemo doesn't seem to mind him. Rocky seems to think he'd give a good fight, and Poe trusts his instincts, so he is content to not try to press the odd old elf as long as he continues to be respectful.

His flight to the ODA earns some points and stares, but no shouts of alarm. He even identifies looks of respect from what adventurers notice him. He nods at them as he goes, though he doubts many can make it out from the height he soars at.

Landing at the door to the ODA, he tilts his head as he ponders how to open it. The design isn't far from the doors Lord Thedeim has in the manor, but said doors are generally geared toward hands and thumbs, not his talons. He could probably knock it open with a gust of wind, but that would be rude.

With no other option, he pecks at the wood to knock.

"It's open!" comes a voice from inside. Telar, if the expedition reports are correct, and he has no reason to doubt them. He pecks again and hears a voice that, though not entirely new to him, is not one he immediately can identify.

"I'll get it," it says, and soon, the door opens to reveal a catkin. "Welcome to the . . ." He trails off as he takes in the sight of the Raven Scion of Lord Thedeim, turning slightly to speak into the building. "Uh . . . Tarl?"

The indicated elf looks up from his desk, and Poe can't help but give a loud caw at seeing him. How can he not give the traditional greeting to one of Lord Thedeim's first delvers?

Tarl stares for a few moments, then shakes his head and stands. "I'm not going to get squawked at here all the time, am I?" he asks with a wry smile. Poe shakes his head and offers the message.

Curious, Tarl takes it and reads it. He takes a few more moments to think, confusion on his face, before speaking.

"'As was deal'?"

"Mayor," answers Poe. Tarl is quicker to put the pieces together with that hint.

"Ah, right! He mentioned working closer together with Thedeim at the speech. Thedeim wants me there, too? Probably to help translate, what with Teemo out."

Poe nods, and Tarl looks over at the catkin. "Can I bring my new apprentice? Berdol could use some on-the-job experience."

Poe tilts his head at the elf, considering the request. His Lord only said to bring Tarl, but not to bring *only* Tarl. Rezlar would certainly be bringing Miller at least. He's also confident that the meeting isn't intended to be anything secret.

He nods, and the elf smiles, while the tabby catkin looks uncertain.

"Alright, Berdol! Let's get geared up! Depending on how long the meeting takes, we might go take a look at the lava tubes or fight a twinsnake and give it an actual danger rating!"

Poe takes flight before Berdol can answer, leaving the two inspectors to their preparations.

Nova will probably be happy to see Berdol, if the two have the time to delve after the meeting. Poe is glad the newest scion is developing a good rapport with him. Most of the scions have delvers they enjoy spending some time with, and Poe is certain it has helped the scions and delvers both, which in turn helps Lord Thedeim.

He circles in a thermal and builds altitude in preparation for flying to the small island in Hullbreak. Perhaps he can forgive himself a bit of inefficient flying, after all.

He remembers how different the air was over the ocean when he and the Quartermaster fought. While he doubts they'll have reason to repeat it, he still should take the chance to improve his flying. Hullbreak is probably not the only potential problem that could come from the sea.

Chapter 3

When Poe shows up to get the Quartermaster, the albatross is standing at attention and waiting. Poe imperiously inspects his form, and I'm pretty sure the only reason the scion isn't sweating is because he physically can't. Poe has mercy on him before too long, giving a caw and letting the albatross relax slightly.

I can feel a bit of nervousness from Hullbreak, too, but I do my best to calm him. Sure, change can be scary, but it'll be good for him and his dwellers. They're already changing on their own, too. Hullbreak isn't interfering in their efforts to farm and hunt outside his borders, but he's definitely keeping a close eye on them. I don't tell him to stop, or even to tone it down. At least not yet.

Not only will him keeping a close eye help keep them safe and help ease his fears but it also might help him come to understand the dwellers aren't helpless. Small steps, though, since the dwellers are still learning how to support themselves some, too.

Poe and the Quartermaster take off, pulling me from my thoughts on Hullbreak's progress, as the First Mate breaks the surface of the water to say a few words before they truly leave.

"Pay attention and look at everything you can, Quartermaster. The Captain is relying on you," she solemnly informs him. The albatross nods firmly. Despite his nervousness around me and my scions, he intends on absorbing as much information as he can about how I run things.

With nothing else needing to be said, the flying scions make their way to me. It's looking like Poe won't quite make it back before the first member for the meeting shows up, though, as I see Nose go on expedition. I gently nudge Nova to help guide him to the public war room, and she's quick to do so.

They take their time, but they still are easily the first to arrive. Nova stays well back from the table with the maps, not wanting to set anything ablaze, but Nose curiously looks around. He can't get too good a look at the model of Fourdock on the table, but he seems to be able to make out the maps on the walls without too much difficulty.

Tarl and Berdol arrive next, and I have Fluffles guide them down to the meeting area. Berdol looks pretty intimidated by my Conduit, but Tarl looks glad to get underground and away from my noisy birbs making the traditional greeting racket.

"Why do they make noise at you?" asks Berdol, much to Fluffles's amusement and Tarl's chagrin.

"Because Thedeim thinks it's funny. Or *they* think it's funny. Or both. Probably both," he replies, glancing at Fluffles, who nods in confirmation.

"Is it normal for a dungeon to joke like that?" presses Berdol. Sounds to me like Tarl chose a good apprentice, asking questions like that.

Tarl just smirks. "No, at least not at Thedeim's age. Older dungeons may develop a relationship with inspectors, but it usually takes longer for them to even understand things like jokes."

"Do they joke around once they get older?"

Tarl shakes his head. "Not often. They can understand them, but their senses of humor can be strange. The younger ones will usually manage some truly abysmal puns involving something in their domain, though I had one dungeon that liked to listen in on the conversations of delvers and have the Voice repeat the kind of crude jokes you could hear in the seediest of taverns."

Berdol smiles at the idea of a dungeon telling dirty jokes. "What about Thedeim? How's his sense of humor?"

Tarl smirks and steals a glance at Fluffles. "Not as good as he thinks it is."

You wound me, sir. Fluffles hisses and turns his nose up at Tarl in mock indignation for me, holding the act for long enough that Berdol starts to look uncomfortable. Tarl ruins it by laughing and getting Fluffles to hiss in laughter as well.

"But not bad, heh. Looks like we're about at the public war room. Probably a good place to start the meeting," Tarl says with a smile, seeming to be in a pretty good mood today.

Poe and the Quartermaster arrive only a few seconds before Rezlar and Miller—and a small entourage of guards. The birds land before the group, and Poe gives a nod of respect, causing the albatross to give almost a bow to the mayor and his butler. Rezlar pauses at that, uncertain what to do for a moment, before what I can only assume is his training kicks in.

"Greetings, Poe, Quartermaster. If you'll guide us to the meeting, I can let my honor guard stay here at the gate."

Poe motions a wing toward the house porch, a gust of wind setting the hanging quests to swaying. Rezlar considers that for a few moments before glancing at Miller, who is keeping his face in that neutral-friendly look he always wears.

"Thank you for your hospitality, Thedeim. I don't mind my guards doing some minor delving as they wait, so long as they are ready to leave once I am." Miller's eyes shine at that, and the guards all look glad to be able to do something besides just stand around.

Poe and the Quartermaster are a bit awkward as guides on the ground, but it's not that long of a walk down to the public war room. Tarl is looking at the model of the town with a small smile on his face while Nova is kind of juggling some balls of magma for Berdol, who looks a bit uncertain what to make of that. Nose is on his hind legs, his little diggers in the air making the classic motion for uppies at Fluffles, who finally relents and levitates the mole so he can get a better look at the model.

Poe gives a squawk to get everyone's attention, and soon, everyone is gathered around the table, except for Nova. She'd like to hang out some more, but she'd probably set things on fire if she tried to participate. I pat the bond and suggest she find Jello if she wants some company, but she seems to have her own idea.

She slips beneath the floor and settles in beneath the meeting, close enough to be able to hear what's going on without being close enough to immolate anyone.

That's fine by me; I have no problem with her listening in. Fluffles hisses to get everyone's attention before tapping the map with his tail tip. Tarl nods while the others lean in to look at the map, where a dot indicating Teemo is far outside my borders.

"We'll be mostly talking with Fluffles today, which is partially why I'm here: I'll be basically an interpreter. As you can see, the Voice is out on expedition to the Southwood. If you weren't aware, Mayor, the Southwood contacted Thedeim to request aid, and Thedeim is in the process of providing that."

Tarl's finger traces a trail on the map. "Thedeim is preparing to send tundra wolves to help support the Southwood over the winter, and will probably be sending more denizens and possibly scions in the spring." He pauses as he spots Leo and Honey on the map near the Southwood.

"It looks like he's already sent his Warden and . . . his Librarian?" he asks with a questioning look at Fluffles, who simply nods. "I don't know why he'd send his Librarian, but the Warden will be there to ensure the wolves are properly organized to handle the threat."

"What threat?" asks Rezlar, and Tarl's confidence wilts slightly.

"I don't specifically know just yet. I'm not sure Thedeim does, either. For the Southwood to request defensive aid, it's something trying to attack it. I'd suspect either some expansion has triggered stronger invaders, or some rival dungeon has started to cause issues for the Southwood."

Rezlar frowns at that. "Even with how remote the Southwood is, it's still a valuable source of lumber, skins, and herbs. Will . . ." He pauses, probably finding his question to be silly, but voices it anyway after the small delay. "Will Thedeim be able to help the Southwood?"

"I hope so, because I don't think we'll have much else to offer on that front if he can't. If it's invaders, some powerful delver groups could help by either fighting them off or delving to give the Southwood the mana to fight them off on its own. If it's a dungeon . . . Thedeim has some experience with fighting those, at least."

Rezlar frowns at that, but he can't seem to think of any advice to give or any other way to help. Fluffles points at a different map, one of the area below me, and Tarl starts speaking.

"Thedeim is also aggressively searching and sending expeditions to the depths. One of his residents came to him from that way, and only recently did she explain why and how. She fled from a hostile dungeon that had enslaved her tribe, using them as labor and as sacrifice.

"She escaped when a monster to be fed to the dungeon slipped its bonds and wreaked havoc. She doesn't recall exactly how long she fled, but it must have been days before she came upon Thedeim.

"He, of course, doesn't like the idea of a strong dungeon being so close, let alone one that's so actively malevolent." Tarl pauses and peers at the map. "It doesn't look like he's found any trace of it yet, but he'll probably be sending his forces against it once he does."

Rezlar nods at that. "I think we may need to step up our plans to help support him, then. We had been planning to encourage more adventurers to delve come the spring, to help with the construction of the hold outside town. If he's going to be trying to fight a hostile dungeon from the Deeps, we should help him by delving and giving him the resources to win quickly."

Tarl nods as Fluffles points his tail at my newest expansion, and the inspector chuckles. "I don't think it'll be difficult to get the delvers motivated. Thedeim's latest expansion has given him new metal nodes, including orichalcum and mythril."

Rezlar's eyes widen at that, but Tarl continues before he can say anything. "The area is still a work in progress, but it shouldn't be difficult to help him get plenty of mana to do whatever he wants in there."

Fluffles points at my two enclaves, then points at the expansion.

"You're going to be arming your dwellers with the new metals?"

Well . . . I hadn't thought of that, but that'd be a great idea, yeah. Definitely need to get a metalworks.

Fluffles slowly shakes his head as he tries to parse what feelings I can get through the bond. His tail taps the crypt complex, then the Ratkin Enclave. Then he taps the caverns, and the Spiderkin Enclave. Finally, he taps the tubes twice.

Tarl's eyes widen as he realizes what I mean. "A new enclave?" At Fluffles's nod, Tarl shakes his head. "The area is going to be incredibly busy, then." Fluffles nods once more and taps the hedge maze and the gauntlet, which encourages Tarl.

"That's fair; he's made busy areas before. Is there anything we can do to help?"

Fluffles nods as I ask Coda to come join the meeting, and to bring a couple of things too. I know he doesn't feel ready to show his plans to anyone yet, but I can see they're basically complete now.

My Conduit taps the island in Hullbreak, much to the confusion of the gathered people, who will have to stew in that confusion for a few minutes.

I'm sure it's only more confusing for them when Coda arrives with a cinder block in one foot and a roll of paper clutched in the other. The table vibrates from the thump of the heavy piece of construction material. Rezlar looks intrigued before his attention is stolen by the paper being unfurled.

The lighthouse design is laid bare before them, and I think Coda's outdone himself with it. He's finally managed to get the silk reinforcing to work properly in testing, so this will be the first real use for it.

"Build a lighthouse in the winter?" asks Berdol. Coda simply nods.

For an ordinary construction crew, it'd be a tall order indeed. It's cold, it will probably snow, there could be delays because of storms, and those are just the most obvious problems. A lot of those go away, however, with a certain Albatross Scion and his Storm affinity. It definitely won't be easy, but it will be a good investment.

"I'll contact the masons and see if any are willing to help with that construction. If Thedeim is confident it can be made in the winter, I think a lot of them will want to help just to have their names attached to such an audacious and ambitious project," says Rezlar, a gleam in his eyes. "Not a lot of crafters get a chance to work on projects in a dungeon besides adventurers. Even adventurers don't get to work on masonry during a delve. Other crafting fields have had breakthroughs because of such work. This could lead to a breakthrough for masonry."

Coda nods at that, beaming with pride, and I wonder if Rezlar is maybe underestimating what Coda could do. He's *already* made breakthroughs with the concrete and the cinder blocks. I can't wait to see what else my nerd of a bat can manage.

Chapter 4

Projects and potential problems presented, pored over, planned for, and possibly even prevented, the meeting adjourns. Rezlar looks like he's managed to get Coda to show him some more of his stuff in the public workshop, and I encourage my bat and Architect to do so. He doesn't get to show off often, and Rezlar has a deep appreciation for infrastructural advancements.

While the two nerds and Miller head for the workshop, it looks like Poe is going to have more than just the Quartermaster and Nose tagging along. Tarl eyes the other two scions and speaks up once the mayor is on his way.

"So, why are they here? Their dungeons must be vaguely aware of what Thedeim is planning and doing already," he asks my raven.

"Work. Home. How," he answers while both Tarl and Berdol think over what he means. I think Tarl figures it out first, but he waits for Berdol to come to a conclusion.

"What do you think he means, Berdol?"

"I . . . think he's trying to teach them how he works? How he builds encounters and areas?" offers the catkin, and Poe nods as Tarl smiles.

"Looks like you've got it. Can we tag along, Poe? It'd give Berdol a good chance to observe and work on a report in the field."

I don't mind, and once Poe seems satisfied that I don't object, he nods. Berdol looks a bit nervous about it, but dutifully levitates an iron quill and flask of ink, as well as a clipboard made of metal with some blank papers attached. Poe gives the arrangement a curious look, and Tarl answers for his apprentice.

"He doesn't get a recording stone until he's a full inspector, and I don't know that he'll use one even then."

Berdol nods at that. "I think better with words written down instead of trying to listen to my own voice." Poe accepts that, while the Quartermaster doesn't react at all. Nose tries to sniff at the quill and ink, but Fluffles isn't levitating him close enough for him to get a very close look.

It looks like Fluffles is going to be joining, too, as he continues to levitate Nose while Poe leads the way back to the manor entrance.

I steal a look at Berdol's notes as they go. He has impressive penmanship. I bet Telar will try to steal him from Tarl and keep him behind a desk instead of being out in the field. I doubt she'll manage it, though.

Meeting with Dungeon adjourned, Inspector Tarl acted as an interpreter. There is a certain hostile somewhere in the Deeps, and possibly one harassing the Southwood. Thedeim has plans to deal with both, and will probably require more delver activity to be able to put those plans into motion.

Currently following scions Poe and Fluffles as they escort a scion from Violet and the Quartermaster from Hullbreak. Thedeim apparently intends to teach them how to organize their territories as he does.

Berdol lets his quill rest as they get close to the surface, and Tarl casually takes the notes to read for himself.

"I need to teach you how to condense your thoughts," he says with a smirk to his apprentice, who scrunches his face at the idea.

"I have no idea how you can make sense of your voice notes. They're so . . . sparse and clipped."

Tarl laughs, letting the metal clipboard float once more. "Years of practice and pretty good visual memory. My voice notes are mostly to make sure I don't forget anything that needs to go into the actual reports. Speaking of actual reports, I'm going to have you practice writing one on what you see of Thedeim today. Once we reach the surface, get to writing like it's the first time you've been here and information is sparse at best."

Berdol nods and gives his flask of ink a shake to feel how much he has, then starts scribbling up a storm as they all exit the front door. Poe and Fluffles both point out the hanging planks with quests on them, and I make my own notes.

While it'll probably be a while before Violet maxes out any of her spawners, Hullbreak will probably get there quicker. I doubt he'll make another Merfolk Enclave, maybe not any other enclaves at all, but maxed spawners still give semi-autonomous denizens, seems like.

My ratlings and aranea both kinda do their own thing, even more than my ordinary denizens. The ratlings help make equipment for rewards, and the aranea give quests. I'm still not a hundred percent certain how the more advanced rewards work, but I'm inclined not to go rocking the boat, at least when it seems to be in tip-top shipshape.

I wonder if any of Hullbreak's advanced denizens could make bottled messages to function as quests?

I note that down for later as everyone moves on to the herbalism nodes in the yard, with Poe and Fluffles pointing out how the encounters there are probably the weakest I have. It's not like most gatherers are expert combatants. Still, I'm not giving this stuff away for free, even if I get a decent profit from them just picking the herbs. Might as well give them an encounter to get more out of them.

Ew, I sound like the people who organize stores to deliberately encourage others to buy on impulse. I swear I'm using it for good! We both benefit! Yeah, sure, I bet that's what those organizers say too! But at least I'm not trying to drain wallets. The delvers get more experience, and I get more mana, so it's actually a win-win.

I give myself one last squinty look, making sure I'm not falling to the dark side, before turning my attention to the Quartermaster and Nose, trying to see if they're learning anything. The albatross is quietly listening and looking, but through the bond, I can feel Hullbreak analyzing every speck of information he gets. I can have Teemo talk to the First Mate about stuff all day long, but actually seeing how it works can make more sense.

Nose looks a bit distracted, more curious about the surface in general rather than what Poe is trying to teach him. I get the feeling Violet is the same, but I'm not exactly surprised. She's still a young dungeon; she has time to learn the details as she grows. Hullbreak is more established, so he has a bit more context and can compare how things work for me with how they worked for him in the past.

I think, once the lighthouse is complete, I'll let him try his hand at designing the encounters and stuff there, instead of the heavier hand I've had to take with most of the rest of his territory. It'll be a good way to build his confidence. He's following my lead with the upgrades and spawns so far, seeing more mana as a result, but I need to show him he can accomplish something similar now that he knows what to do.

Once the group gets to the hedge maze, I can feel ideas percolating through the bonds with both Hullbreak and Violet. My little protégée sees it as a game, and seems to be trying to think of ways to either copy it or do something on her own with the idea of an encounter that's not just about fighting or gathering. I don't think she'll have the room to make a maze yet, but maybe she can think of something else.

Hullbreak, on the other hand, is fascinated by the unorthodox approach to the entire encounter. While he certainly has the room for a maze if he wants one, I think he's also looking for something to put his own spin on. A scavenger hunt of some kind could be cool; maybe hide keys around that delvers would need to get at some treasure.

He could practically copy the gauntlet, come to think of it. He'd probably need to upgrade his crabs to pull it off properly. The gauntlet is a bit more *Ninja Warrior*, so the only real interaction I need is to reset the obstacles. Hullbreak would probably be more like *Wipeout*, and would need someone to man the various traps that knock people off.

Oh yeah, traps. He could probably automate that stuff fully as traps. In fact . . . that gives me a good idea for what I'll do with the lava tubes.

I can use the tunnelbore ants to make the entire area into a 3D labyrinth and strew traps all over the place. Pitfalls to land people in other parts and get lost, dousing traps, stink traps, slow traps, itch traps . . . There's a lot of stuff that can be done with them that isn't just an instant loss for the delvers. I could even put in a few knockout-gas traps that *would* be an instant loss.

While I like the gauntlet, I think I kinda failed with the initial purpose for it: wanting to get people more used to dealing with traps. The tubes could be perfect for it!

Heh, Teemo's going to have his hands full with shortcuts in there once he gets back, too.

I scribble plans as I continue to watch the scions of my vassal and protégée learn how I do things. It makes me remember something I heard a lot in college with study groups: one of the best ways to learn is to teach. I might not technically be teaching them directly, but I'm still analyzing what I've done and trying to apply it to what they could do, and in turn, getting inspired for what I can do!

Which could then inspire them, and . . . I smile at the idea of that kind of vicious cycle, especially since we'll also be helping the delvers and people of Fourdock, and probably even beyond. Working together, we can deal with things like whatever is bothering the Southwood, and even that dungeon in the Deeps.

It'd be a good idea to not get too cocky, though. I can't forget that it sounded like it had its own vicious cycle with the locals sacrificing stuff to it.

The biggest difference, I think, is that *my* style of cycle is a lot more sustainable.

Chapter 5

Fluffles and Poe seem to have the tour well in . . . wing? Yeah, they both have wings, that counts. With them focusing on the tour, I focus on working the lava tubes.

At the moment, things are at a decent baseline. The interesting fiery herbs are growing well, my wyrms are wyrming through the rock, Fire elementals are being devoured at breakneck speeds, and my cinder and crucible ants are doing their things to make the entire area be a candy store for anyone who works with metals.

My tunnelbore ants are carving out various rooms, too, and I start planning out the extra routes and turns I want them to create for the labyrinth. The hedge maze was pretty simple to make, since it's really only in two dimensions. This labyrinth, though, I want to be fully three dimensional. I might even be able to have Nova and the wyrms occasionally block off certain routes like Tiny does in the hedge maze.

And I can't forget the traps. I've done that enough already. I aim to make up for lost time with the lava labyrinth. I hope to make use of all the main categories of trap I have access to: mechanical, alchemical, and magical.

The mechanical traps are mostly standard fare: pitfalls, crushing walls, rolling boulders, falling cages, and so on; things that can be accomplished with good old physical force. I'll probably see if Coda can help with them to get a discount, but I think most of his attention will be on the lighthouse. I'm not hurting for mana, so I don't mind if he works on that instead. I'm planning to use these traps to make the labyrinth really live up to its name.

Pitfalls can land people in different sections, though I might need to upgrade the slime spawner and keep some stationed underneath those particular traps. I don't need a crushing wall, but moving walls can change the layout, and I could even make sections of floor flip up to become walls and mess with people like that. I'd like to get a surprise express elevator trap going, too, but they're incredibly expensive for the ones that would be safe.

Air jets are an interesting way to move people up, but I don't like them for safety reasons. Too easy for someone to get hit off-center and just cartwheel into a ceiling.

Oh, I could do a combo trap to lift people. Combine a cage with a winch system, and I should be able to move people upward as well as downward with minimal danger. Well, physical danger. Parties are going to be split, and people will be in great danger of being lost. I'll probably have either Jello or Fluffles patrolling to remove people who are defeated by the labyrinth.

And that's just for the ones who can still walk around. The magical and alchemical traps are going to be the real way people lose, I expect. Both types focus on various debilitating effects; they just deliver them differently. Most alchemical traps have mechanical triggers, while the magical traps are . . . Well, you get the idea.

I pick out a lot of things, like slows, blinds, deafening, numbing, immobilizing, and more. Even though I don't place them just yet, I check in on Thing and Queen and see them both excitedly working in their labs to prepare what they'll need. Thing has several books out on his research table as he makes notes for what specific rune arrays he wants to use for the traps, and Queen has her workers swarming her notes as she also prepares and organizes.

I think it'll be good to give them both a big project like this. It's been a while since I had anything specific for them to do, and it looks like they're both eager to put their individual research to the test for this. They both do great work, so I'm not worried at all for how the labyrinth will turn out.

I even upgrade the anthill to get some more tunnelbores, as I'm pretty sure I'm going to need a lot of digging to make this work how I envision it. I resist maxing out the hill just yet, not wanting to adjust to the final variety of ant right now. A lot's going to be happening in the tubes, so I should wait until the dust settles a bit before maxing out the hill, let alone assigning the enclave.

Speaking of enclaves, my current ones are being busy little ants, too. The ratkin are happily playing with the new metals, seeing the efficiencies the new materials give their processing. The limestone flux seems to be working like a charm to give them better yields, and using the coke to fuel the furnaces increases their speed. Even more, they're working with the spiderkin to produce armor and weapons.

The tarantula spiderkin are getting set up with heavy plate armor and pronged spears, and Folarn has them drilling in formation. It looks like they are going to be using their own silken nets with the spears, and are more there to be defense than offense, focusing on being big tough targets and ensnaring foes in the nets.

The smaller jumping spiderkin are going to be more of the assault troops, or basic infantry? They're going to be doing damage, darting around. Vernew has her hunters training with razor-sharp short spears and showing them how to put the entire force of a jump behind the point. It looks like they'll be carrying many spears each, as that kind of stab attack can easily get them stuck.

While most of my ratkin aren't very martial, they don't intend to let my spiderkin have all the glory when we inevitably have to come to blows with that dungeon from the depths. While the spiders are very good in melee, my rats seem to prefer ranged attacks.

Throwing knives are popular enough to start becoming a sport among my ratkin. It looks a lot like darts, but the target is larger, and it plays differently.

Instead of just trying to get to three hundred and one points, players call their shot. If they make it, they get points. If they miss, they lose points equal to the number they hit. Big numbers are grouped together, so there's a lot of risk and reward built in.

Unfortunately, throwing knives are not too effective in big battles. Some of the ratkin are sneaky enough to be able to keep the daggers in their hands and slip in to slash at the training dummies, but I think most of the ones intending to participate on the front lines are going to be archers.

Archery isn't as popular as knives, but the range and power behind them already makes them the preferred weapon for the ratkin hunters. At the moment, they're using the classic bow design, and I'm wondering if I can share any of the more interesting designs from history, like the . . . I think it's a Japanese bow that's taller than the archer, so it has an asymmetrical design.

While they look cool, I'm not so sure they'll be useful in the caves. Recurves would probably be better, but they are a bit more complicated to design. The bow needs to curve forward near the ends, giving more bow to bend for power but in a compact space. The problem is, if you don't get the curves just right, the whole thing can shatter from the forces put on it.

While I'm pretty sure we can manage to get it right, there's another option: the compound bow. With pulleys, it gives the archer mechanical advantage, letting them use stiffer and stronger arms for the bow. Even better, with the proper shape for the cams of the pulley, holding a shot while aiming is a lot easier, too, as they almost lock in place and help handle some of the tension.

I'm going to need to make one for Yvonne, too. She does great work with her recurve bow, so I can only imagine what she'd manage with a compound.

I might be able to do something special for the jumping spiders, too. Watching them practice, their spears sometimes get stuck in the training targets, which is part of their training: to recognize when it's stuck and abandon it for a fresh one from what is basically a big quiver on their back.

The problem is that they can only carry so many spears because of both the weight and the size of even a short spear. It gives me two ideas, but I only start scribbling designs for the simpler one.

They get stuck because of the wide barbed head of the spears. While that design is great for ensuring a kill when hunting, it's not great for quickly removing it. While they could just change to a more leaf-shaped blade for easy in and out, I'm not certain even that will guarantee they won't need some spares.

So my idea is to make the heads easily swappable. There are a ton of different designs for quick-change heads to draw inspiration from: from simple snug fitting to more mechanical locking systems, there are a lot of options. I want something that actually locks in, though. I don't trust a snug fit to stay in place every time until the wielder wants the head free.

I think I can manage something for that. Lots of folding furniture use the little rounded spring rods that click into position when in use, then you just need to press them down to be able to fold it back up. Something like that could work, especially if I use the shape of the barb to help!

Well, maybe. More moving parts in a weapon are usually a bad thing, and this design would need to let the head basically unfold and pop off the haft when it gets stuck.

Well, that's what testing is for! My ratlings aren't as good at forging as my ratkin are . . . but I know someone who has access to a better metal crafter than I do. While I'm pretty sure I'll need to wait for Teemo to get back to be able to try to trade for a metalworks, I don't mind sharing until I get my own.

Besides, I think Legs will like having a challenge.

Chapter 6

I go through a fair few design iterations for the spearheads before I'm satisfied. While the concept itself should work fine in theory, it takes a bit more practical time to put that theory to paper, and then a bit more to put it to paper so people can actually build it. Legion are the genius, sleek designs that have to be taken back to step zero because the real world can't *no-clip* the tools into the tight spaces to turn the screws that keep it together.

While the spearheads aren't *that* complex, I do need to not only show how everything goes together but also how each piece is shaped. I have some concerns about the number of moving parts (seven, not counting the parts that bend for the locking mechanism), but I don't think I can pull anything else out. I'm certain I'll need to *add* a few more as testing happens and unexpected needs arise, but if I can keep the entire head assembly to fifteen or fewer parts, I'll be pleasantly surprised.

I'm a lot less confident in my design for the compound bow, mostly because I know there's going to need to be a lot of tuning required for the limbs and the cams. Ideally, I'd like to use some fairly mild steel for the limbs. Steel is great at the kind of constant flexing and relaxing a bow sees. We'll just have to get the thickness right.

I can run numbers for how thick to make them in theory, but this feels like the kind of thing that will really need to be hashed out with tons of variations in the lab and in the field.

Same with the pulley wheels, or cams. The cam size will have to be proportional to the draw length, since I want it to stop at the same point every time it's at full draw, and the shape will be important too. If you basically squish the typical circle into more of a weird oval, that's how you really get to leverage mechanical advantage to make it easy to hold at full draw for longer.

I get some preliminary designs set and let the ratlings carve the shapes from wood, but it'll be a bit on the back burner for now as far as actual testing goes. Thing and Queen are more preoccupied with the traps in the lava labyrinth, and Coda is ramping up production of the cinder blocks and concrete mix, so I'm kinda out of scions who are into this sort of thing.

It's probably good to come up for air on that, anyway. Teemo's about at the Southwood now, so I should probably give that my attention instead. Teemo and

Honey are both on Leo's back as he crosses the distance from the last outpost, and it's only a few minutes later that they enter the Southwood's territory.

I'm a bit relieved when *Envoy* pops up over Teemo, and my scions get comfortable to wait for the White Stag to show up. I take the chance to look around at what I can through their eyes. While outside was pretty solidly winter, inside feels a bit more like early autumn; I'm seeing a lot more trees with leaves than with needles. There's also plenty of underbrush around, and Leo can scent a lot of different prey animals in the vicinity.

I'm pretty sure Tarl mentioned something about animal and herbalism nodes, and Rezlar mentioned lumber and hides and stuff, so it's not too shocking. I wonder if he has beavers? Their pelts used to be high-end stuff back home. Magical beavers would probably be amazing.

I don't get to muse on the possibilities for long before the Stag shows up to the tinkling of bells and glow of lights. He imperiously looks at my scions for a few long seconds before speaking.

"I was under the impression you were the Warden, not the Voice, wolf."

Leo woofs in confusion before Teemo speaks up.

"He is. I'm the Voice. Teemo." My rat hops up on Leo's head to make it clearer who's the one who will be doing my talking for me.

The Stag glares at my Voice. "This is a poor jest. Drop the illusion or bring out the true Voice. My Lord has no time for frivolities."

Teemo just sits up and folds his arms at the other Voice. "I'm the only Voice Thedeim has. If you don't have time to waste, then stop wasting it and get to the point."

The Stag's nostrils flare in anger, the gentle chiming of bells from his antlers starting to sound like they're caught in a windstorm. He opens his mouth as he rears on his hind legs before his ear flicks and he lets his forehooves impact the ground without much force.

"But my Lord! He insults you with this farce! Yes, but . . . ! Please, at least let me challenge his claim to be the Voice of a dungeon strong enough to offer you even paltry aid!" My scions all exchange glances at that, and I'm wondering if I should just leave Southwood to its fate.

I mean, I won't; it still asked for my help, and if something subsumes it, I'll probably be next on the menu. Still, not a great first impression.

The Stag's pleading look shifts to a wide smile. "Thank you, my Lord! I will give you proof of the mettle of this so-called Voice!"

With that, I get a notification.

The Stag of the Southwood Challenges Your Voice to a Duel!
Accept/Deny?

Uh . . . do you see this, Teemo?

"Yeah, I see it, Boss. I got this."

You sure? I don't want you to get hurt.

Teemo smiles at that and nods. "Yeah, I'm sure. I've been getting to flex one of my affinities on the way here, but I haven't been neglecting the other. I've been wanting to try something for a while now, and I think this guy will be a great test for it."

Confident, Teemo does a few stretches while still standing on Leo before hopping off to land on a stump. "Alright, bucko, I accept. My Boss is probably going to want a bit more for helping you now, too."

The Stag snorts. "Drop the charade, rodent. My Lord will overcome this insignificant problem before you finish respawning. Now, have at you!"

Teemo grins, picking up a pebble from atop the stump and throwing it as the Stag charges. Teemo smiles and mutters to himself before he slips through a shortcut, giving the Stag a wave as he does. The Stag swats the pebble aside with contemptible ease, then slashes his antlers through the space Teemo vacated.

My Voice pops out of the shortcut next to a nearby bush, neither looking nor sounding very impressed. "Oh, you almost got me. Wanna try again?"

With a snort, a forehoof darts forward to catch Teemo, but my slippery scion whispers and vanishes through another shortcut, appearing among the roots of a nearby tree. The hoof only catches a branch of the bush.

Teemo's tone mocks as he speaks up again with a grin. "Are we dueling or dancing?"

The Stag charges and tries to trample him as he shouts, "*You're* the one fleeing like a coward! Stand and face me!"

Teemo is doing a great impression of a game of Whac-A-Mole as he vanishes and appears in rapid succession, dodging hooves as he continues to taunt.

"Me? You're the one who can't land a hit on a little ol' rat, oh great White Stag! Butterfly Effect," he adds almost as an afterthought as he continues to lead the Stag stomping around the tree, the ground shaking from the force. After almost a minute, the Stag finally seems to realize he's getting nowhere, so he dashes a short distance away, leaving Teemo smirking as he leans a hand against the trunk.

The Stag glares at him. "Fine, I admit you're a more wily foe than I expected, but you are far from victorious yet!" The tinkling of bells gives way to a deep gong, and lightning crackles around the Stag's horns as he charges an attack.

Teemo looks like he's only half-paying attention to the stag, which only seems to further enrage the scion. After a moment, my Voice holds a long stick up in triumph then jabs it under the roots of the tree. Glancing up, he adjusts the position slightly before turning another smirk on the White Stag.

"Butterfly Effect."

"Sun Lance!" shrieks the Stag as he launches a thick beam of light at Teemo. I can see the flight path, so I know it can't be actual light, but that still doesn't mean my Voice wants to be hit by it.

He darts through a shortcut, the trajectory of the beam causing it to follow him. A moment later, the beam blasts upward into the sky as Teemo tumbles across the leaves, twigs, and dirt on the forest floor. He coughs as he finds his feet, looking a little singed and roughed up—but not beaten.

"Butterfly Effect. You *actually* almost got me that time. You got another one in you, or do you want to see if I'm slowed down from that?"

"I will grind you into fertilizer for my Lord's flowers with my bare hooves!" screams the Stag, looking more than a little unhinged at how ineffective his attacks have been, charging Teemo once more.

My Voice grins as the Stag bears down on him. "Sucker. Butterfly Effect!"

As if on command, a goose—or maybe a swan—plummets from the sky, landing on the twig wedged among the roots. A bit of Spatial magic, combined with how unstable the Stag's stomping has made the ground, easily makes a long-enough lever to uproot the aged oak and fell it directly in the Stag's path.

He doesn't realize what's wrong before it's too late, and his eyes can only widen as his horns bite deep into the wood of the tree, leaving him well and truly stuck. Teemo hops through one last shortcut, popping out of a knothole in the trunk, and simply bounces onto the Stag's snout.

"Now then, are you ready to talk, or should we just go home?"

Chapter 7

Both Leo and Honey are fighting not to laugh as the Stag tries to free his antlers, Teemo still perched on his snout. It doesn't take long for his ear to flick and for him to finally sag in defeat.

"I am bested. Finish me and claim your mana, Voice of Thedeim," he says, sounding like he finally accepts that Teemo is both my Voice and someone not to trifle with. Teemo, of course, blows a raspberry at the statement.

"And wait for you to respawn before getting to have an actual conversation? You're not getting off the hook that easily. Though, speaking of off the hook . . ." He hops to the scion's horns and takes a good look at the prongs lodged in the wood. "Yeah, you got them in there good. I think I can get you out, though."

The Stag looks like he'd rather just be killed, even if it meant not respawning, than to have to suffer the indignity of being freed from the fallen tree.

While Teemo works, I take the opportunity to politely ask him what the crap that was.

"Oh, the Butterfly Effect? I've kinda had that one in my pocket for a while, just never had a chance to use it. You've thought it to yourself a few times, and it sounded like a good use of Fate affinity to me," he idly chats as he taps the various antlers, looking for the ones most seriously lodged.

Looks like it was a good use for it, yeah. I'd ask you about some of the other affinity stuff you've been playing with, but it's probably best to wait until you're on your way back for that.

Teemo turns and gives the Stag a smirk and a wink. "Can't go spilling all our secrets, right, Boss? Anyway, Stag. It feels like these ones here are the most stuck, so I'm going to expand the space around them just a hair, and you should be able to pull yourself free." He hops back to the tree and gives it a few pats before nodding. "Alright, give it a try."

The Stag gives a defeated sigh and pulls. He doesn't make much progress, but he looks hopeful as he plants his hooves and puts a bit more force into it. He stumbles back a bit as his head finally comes free, and he gives my Voice a deep bow once he recovers.

"My deepest apologies, Voice of Thedeim. I took you as an insult to my Lord, and took offense even when he didn't. Too often, outsiders come and hope to take advantage of his kindness, and I thought you were such a vulture, coming to try to take advantage of him in this delicate time."

If I could, I'd exchange a glance with Teemo, but he seems to be on the same page, at least. "That's a pretty quick turnaround on your attitude there, Stag," points out my Voice, causing the other to wince.

". . . My Lord is also displeased with my earlier attitude. He . . . mislikes violence, and so tends to leave it to my discretion after a larger invader tried to attack his core once."

"Speaking of violence, I'm told you have an invader problem?" interjects Teemo, seizing on the chance to get the conversation on the track he had been hoping for since even before the fight.

The Stag nods and leans forward, offering for Teemo to jump atop his head. "Yes, something has changed in the Green Sea Forest."

Teemo accepts the invitation, and Leo stands to follow as the Stag looks deeper into the Southwood. He takes off with a bounding leap, Leo darting after them. They travel quickly, though I get the feeling the Stag could leave Leo in the dust if he really wanted to. The Voice takes a few minutes to organize his thoughts as they move through the forest before he explains further, still on the move.

"The Green Sea is a massive ocean of stagnant mana. If there are any other dungeons further north, my Lord knows not of them. For a time, the invaders from deeper inside were manageable. My Lord's dire bears have been up to the task of handling anything that has tried to attack us—until recently.

"Before now, the invaders were more or less mirrors of what my Lord spawns: beasts with minimal elemental affinities. Kinetic affinity abounds, but even Life and Nature ones are rare, and the invaders roughly reflected this. But now . . . they are showing other affinities.

"Birds with Wind are hardly a surprise, but a sylvan wolf was. Then an igneous cobra. Then a luminous hawk. The curiosity of the new affinities came to a head with the stygian hart, a pathetic mockery of myself. At that point, I feared there was something watching, somehow spying on my Lord's works to try to pervert it to their own vile designs, but it became quickly obvious that combination was a simple coincidence."

Leo speaks up as the pace starts to slow. "A wide variety of affinities is strange, but it sounds like you have even those under control."

The Stag nods as his leaps and bounds slow toward a jog. "We did, and technically still do. But the attacks continue to slowly ramp up despite my Lord not having expanded recently. He's not even made any new varieties of node that could draw that kind of attention." He pauses as his ear flicks and slowly shakes his head. "I don't believe prismatic salmon would draw this many different invaders, my Lord."

Teemo shakes his head as well. "Yeah, whenever the boss gets a new node, the invaders are focused on getting at it. It sounds like these are acting more like expansion invaders, but without the expansion to draw them in."

The Stag nods. "Indeed. And with their strength increasing, my Lord worries he may not be able to keep up. While he has a wide variety of spawners under his command, he's starting to max them out. If the hordes continue to grow in strength . . . he may be overrun. Yet, even that may not be the most concerning thing about these invaders."

That gets everyone's attention, including my own. Something the Stag would consider more concerning than the death of his dungeon? I can't even begin to imagine what it could be.

Fortunately, I don't need to try to imagine, as the Stag brings us to a small cave—with a dead invader inside.

I have no idea what it is. It's about the size of a wolf, and even has some of the basic shape, but none of the fur. Instead, it has bulbous, segmented carapace colored a dull red. The four legs have claws like a mantis rather than feet at the end, and a strange spiky tail comes off the rear. On the front, the head looks like a giant leech.

I'd be pretty concerned if I had this thing as an invader, sheesh. Even dead, it looks wrong in ways I can't quite put my finger on. My scions also take in the corpse in their own way: Teemo looks partially disgusted and partially creeped out by it, Leo has his lips pulled back only slightly in a wolfy frown at the abomination, and Honey is frantically making notes.

"What *is* it?" asks my Voice, looking at the Stag so he doesn't have to look at the thing.

"Take a closer look. Its status is just as . . . *unsettling* as the rest of it."

Teemo does so, and I get a look at it through his eyes. Neither of us seems to notice anything too out of place—until I look at its type.

See, both invaders and denizens have types, which seem to be roughly like a biological kingdom, or maybe whatever is a step or two below that. Still not a biologist. Whatever their actual place, the categories are pretty broad. Beasts cover most of my spawners, even the ants and bees. Undead are another category, as well as elementals, slimes, and dragons. I'm pretty sure Violet's gremlins are spirits, which feel more primal than undead. I guess they'd need to be, or they'd just be undead.

I've even heard people talk about fey, even though I don't have any of those spawners. But the point is: everything has a category.

This one doesn't. Or . . . I think it does, but . . . it's hard to explain. I know there's something there, even though I can't sense it.

Teemo frowns as he picks up on my thoughts. "That's the same kind of weird void I get when you talk about some of your stuff, Boss."

"Does your Lord know what it is?" asks the Stag, looking hopeful. I'm certainly not feeling hopeful about this.

My first thought is that it's somehow human, but I seriously hope that's not the case. It'd have to take some serious transformation magic to make a human look like that. It'd probably be easier to start with some monster template and change it to look like this instead of trying to do it to a human, and that's leaving aside for the moment that humans apparently can't exist here.

While I guess it could be the result of someone trying to do it anyway, I doubt it. My gut says the angel lady would only send humans here as dungeons.

Maybe the connection here isn't as one-way as I thought? What if someone is peeking back at home?

The idea of home hits me harder than I thought it would, but I do my best to shove it aside. I died back there, and I doubt I'm going to get a pass like Lazarus.

I force my train of thought back on the tracks and give it a shove to keep going.

If someone from here can peek at home, could they make some abomination like this? It's probably better than this thing actually being a human, but not by a whole lot.

Or maybe not. While it'd be a nightmare to be turned into something like this, the restricted supply of humans would limit the numbers pretty severely. From how the Stag's been acting, there's basically an army of these things already.

Chapter 8

Honey and her small swarm move in to examine the thing as the Stag repeats his question.

"Does your Lord Thedeim know what it is?"

Oh, right. Uh . . .

"Other than something bad, nothing specific. He has a few ideas for what it could be, I think, but I get the feeling that, even if he could put a name to it, there wouldn't be much advice for actually fighting them." Teemo looks over the weird thing while Honey tries to get my attention.

Peering through her eyes at her notes so far, I'm not a big fan of what I'm seeing. The more I look at it, the more I'm starting to think it's something specifically built to kill. And I don't mean like a tiger or a lion or something, either. Yeah, they're good at killing, but they also do things like eat, make babies, and breathe. Honey is having trouble finding any orifices, which would kinda make babies, breathing, and eating a bit difficult.

She gets Leo to help with a bit of dissection, and I think the White Stag is turning a bit green. "Is that . . . necessary?"

Teemo shrugs. "If we want more information on it, yeah. Doesn't mean the two of us need to watch, though. We can leave them to it."

The Stag nods and makes for the exit, Teemo still atop his head. Out in the fresh air, the Stag seems to be regaining his composure.

"Not quite what you expected when asking for help, eh?"

The Stag sighs. "Indeed. My Lord prefers to quickly reclaim the bodies and mana, but kept this one as proof. To see some bees swarming a corpse like a field of flowers . . ." He shudders, and Teemo snorts with a smirk.

"That's Honey. I think she hungers more for knowledge than she does pollen. The Boss will probably learn a lot more than either of us really want to know about that invader, but he should get a better idea for how to fight the things. Which reminds me: he's going to be sending tundra wolves, now that I've blazed a proper trail. Probably a pack or two a day, depending on how it goes. Honey and Leo are going to be sticking around to help with the fighting, too."

The Stag bows to Teemo as well as he can with my Voice still sitting on his head. "My Lord is grateful for the timely aid. The snows beyond my Lord's borders greatly hinder these disturbing invaders, so being able to engage them in such terrain would be a great boon."

Teemo nods at that. "That's basically his reasoning for sending them: they won't be hindered by the cold. If we still haven't dealt with this problem come spring, he'll probably send some widows or twinsnakes, or both. Or maybe just stronger wolves." Teemo shrugs while the Stag gives him a curious look.

"He has stronger wolves than tundra? Why not send them immediately?"

My Voice shakes his head. "He doesn't have them yet, but they'll be one of many options by then. The Boss grows pretty quickly."

The Stag nods at that. "I imagine his location helps greatly with that. My Lord enjoys his peace and quiet. I think a city would ill-suit him. There are dangers among so many delvers, more competition from other dungeons, but there are opportunities as well."

"Yeah, that's true, but at least he has the other dungeons kinda sorted now."

The Stag eyes him with curiosity. "Oh? The last my Lord heard, Hullbreak was content to stagnate. Unless you count that as being sorted?"

Teemo somehow manages to exchange a glance with me, and I approximate a nod in return. "Hullbreak was starving, and one of his dwellers managed to ask the Dungeoneer's for help. They asked the Boss. It ended up being a bit more of a thing than expected, and the Boss Vassalized Hullbreak."

"A vassal? Not simply subsumed?"

My Voice shakes his head. "Nah, the Boss doesn't want to just eat dungeons and take over. Neverrest had it coming, but Hullbreak just needs help. It's slow going, but the Boss at least has him making enough mana to keep himself healthy, and he has a few projects in mind to help him really take off. He also has his protégée to guide, too, so his metaphorical hands are a bit full."

The Stag looks shocked at that news. "*And* a protégée?!"

"Oh yeah. She's still real young, so she hasn't needed too much yet, but he gives her little guiding nudges every so often."

The Stag shakes his head. "What sort of ally has my Lord gotten involved with," he mutters to himself as Teemo grins.

"One whom you annoyed and who expects at least some kind of payment for his help."

The Stag's ear twitches, and he tenses. "I don't believe my Lord should pledge fealty to yours," he says with a measured tone and cadence, clearly upset at the idea but also desperately trying not to let it show.

Teemo lets him stew in it for a few moments before smiling and waving the idea off.

"He has enough dungeons to watch over; he doesn't need another one to be responsible for, heh. He *would* like to get a look at your herbalism and lumber nodes, though. The Boss is always in the market for new resources to tempt delvers with."

The Stag deflates a bit in relief at that and nods. "Yes, I expect my Lord would be more than happy to assist with that. I believe his expeditions have secured many seeds that would simply not be worth the mana to grow, thanks to the climate. Your Lord Thedeim may find he can make better use of them."

I let Teemo negotiate with the Stag over what seeds and stuff to get from the Southwood. I'll still help him even if the seeds are useless to me, but Teemo's not wrong to get at least something for the rudeness earlier. Stopping whatever these invaders are will be good for the both of us.

Speaking of the invaders, I check how Honey and Leo are handling their project.

. . . Yeah, probably a good thing the Stag left when he did. Honey isn't quite going Frankenstein on this thing yet, but I think that's only because she doesn't have Lightning affinity. This thing's insides don't paint a pretty picture, and not just because insides make unpleasant art in general.

While I'm still not a biologist, I can probably name most organs; at least the ones a mammal has. You need a brain, a heart, some kind of lungs or gills, something to filter out nasty things in the various fluids, another to digest, usually a couple things to make that digestion easier, and something to get rid of the food once you're done with it.

I'm counting a lot fewer organs than I'd expect, and I poke Honey to check her notes and get me caught up on what she's discovered so far.

So far . . . the inside is looking a lot like the outside: designed for killing and not much else. The basic interior looks vaguely like what should be in something with an exoskeleton. The layout is mostly open concept, no real veins or arteries and such, with the bits more or less floating in the goo.

Honey and Leo finally found orifices, but they all seem to be for air. The invader has little holes along the sides to draw it in—and presumably push it out, too. I have no idea how the lungs actually work, but they take up a pretty good chunk of this thing's insides. They do look like they're segmented, however, so one good shot will only disable one section, not the whole thing.

And that's apparently the only intended way in or out of this thing. No stomach or anything like that, though that brings us to the other large organ. It appears to be a big sack full of some kind of fluid, which Honey says is sweet. She even has it in her notes as "invader honey." I just hope she doesn't eat too much of it. That's just . . . *ew*.

Still, that explains the thing's energy: it's born with some kind of energy sack, I guess. However, *born* might be the wrong word, as Honey and Leo haven't been able to find anything like reproductive organs. It could be something really weird, but I'm going to trust Honey to know what bug naughty bits should look like.

There are a few other organs that do organ-y things, including what seems to be a brain of sorts encased in whatever the exoskeleton is actually made of, along where the spine would be. I think this one basically died from a concussion, as Honey's notes show certain parts to be a bit mushier than others with no apparent reason. The thing probably got thrown against a tree or something.

Whatever caused its death, what caused its life was very streamlined. No reproduction and no eating, which cuts down on the number of needed organs a lot, I imagine. But with no reproductive organs, how did this thing even happen?

I probably can't discount magic, even though everything else I've seen seems to be anatomically correct. It also could be what amounts to a drone or something, relegated to only fighting.

But that doesn't quite feel right. Even specialized fighters in a hive can do more than fight. Even when surrounded by hostiles, fighting can only take up so much time, so a warrior-caste insect needs to be able to pull its weight even when not actively engaging threats. I might just be lacking in imagination, but I can't picture this thing doing anything besides fighting. All the bits are too sharp for things like moving brood or building. It might be able to dig, but it's not moving dirt very far with just those blades. If it's that specialized, I get the feeling it's specifically made for fighting; made to be a disposable warrior.

Because if you're going to make an autonomous weapon, it kinda needs to be disposable. Umbrella and other fictional weapons corporations are always making their zombie viruses or genetically engineered dinosaurs or whatever, but they never make an off switch for them.

Even if we assume their zombies are better than just giving trained soldiers guns, they'll still need to deal with a bunch of undead after hostilities die down. And if the zombies win, they've kinda proven they're better than soldiers and guns, so what's their plan to actually use the area they've conquered?

This is why Umbrella went bankrupt in the games. I think. But back to the actual point: if these things are deliberately made like I'm thinking they are, the onboard honey sack is the off switch. Once it runs out of fuel, the thing stops moving, and the boss can waltz in like they own the place because who's going to argue? Not all those corpses, that's for sure.

But if they are engineered, why is the type hidden? It could have something to do with someone peeking back home, which would be bad. Or it could be someone deliberately hiding it, either on their own or with the actual help of the system here.

I'm not sure which would be worse.

Chapter 9

Aranya

The red kobold does her best not to sigh at the lack of progress, but it's difficult to hide her frustration. At least the others seem to be enjoying the process. While training and even delving a little for Lord Thedeim helped them all grow close, it's these kinds of longer missions that really show why the trio has stuck together for so long, and it's gratifying to know she has her own part to play in the group too.

Yvonne is in her element out in the untamed reaches of the world, whether on the surface or below. The hawkwoman's eyes are not her only keen sense, and she has the experience to spot potential trouble even in the unfamiliar conditions of the depths. She was able to pick a path through the underswamps with seemingly little difficulty, and now is helping lead the way through a dense jungle of stalagmites, stalactites, and hanging moss.

Ragnar's sense of direction—and especially of depth—helps keep everyone from getting lost, and his general good humor keeps the long marches from being a slog. His stalwart presence in a fight also brings a sense of control in the chaotic shifting of battle. They haven't had anything too difficult to fight yet, but Yvonne seems to think they're in the territory of something large, so the dwarf's presence is a comfort.

Aelara, city elf that she is, is still a gifted cartographer. With Ragnar's help, she even has the rough depths tracked, too, slowly bringing an understanding to the twisting knot the Deeps can be.

And, of course, herself. With her faith in Lord Thedeim, she can help bolster her friends both against battle and against the weariness of such long forays. Poe's Uplifting Wings and Jello's Resilience make the trek much easier, and her other prayers make combats much simpler, too. Her magic is better aligned to help patch up Ragnar and the others after an injury, leaving Aelara to focus on offensive magics.

Yvonne has even been stepping into melee with the horror's mandible Lord Thedeim gifted her. While she'll never be a true frontline fighter, she can at least give Ragnar a few moments of respite when he needs them.

Speaking of respite, it's getting close to time to set up camp, so the group stops to check the map.

Ragnar is the first to speak up. "D'we e'en need tae try an' find some water? This moss is damp enough tae make a soup jus' by puttin' it in a pot!"

Yvonne smiles at that. "I don't think water will be a concern, nor do we need to worry about accidentally starting a cave fire. I think our biggest concern will be finding anything dry enough to burn for a campfire."

"I hope we get out of the humidity soon," sighs Aelara. "I'm starting to chafe."

"I think it is nice," admits Aranya, earning a few curious looks. She shrugs. "I'm probably going to shed soon, and the humidity helps make that easier." Aelara and Ragnar's curious looks only intensify as Yvonne nods.

"Ah, I was curious, but thought it might be rude to ask if you shed. I imagine it's more pleasant than molting, at least." Yvonne huffs as Ragnar and Aelara chuckle at the memory of her last molt.

"Actually, shedding is a relief, but the days leading up to it are constantly itchy. It's a bit earlier than usual for me to need to shed, but after finding Lord Thedeim, I've been getting back to a healthy weight. Getting healthy after so long makes me feel like I'm wearing clothes a size too small," she points out, and Yvonne gives her a friendly jealous look.

"Definitely better than molting. A solid week of maddening itching and soreness and looking like I have mange before old feathers are finally replaced with fresh ones. I'd love to trade," she says with a begging smile, causing the others to laugh.

"All that aside, we really should find a place to set up camp. I'm getting hungry enough that Ragnar's proposed moss soup isn't sounding so bad," says Aelara, and everyone focuses on the task at hand once more.

"I dinae ken how we'll find someplace dry . . ." grumbles Ragnar. "A day or two more'n we'll be deep enough th' rock will nae hold s'much water. Doesnae help w' our camp now . . ."

"We may need to settle for finding a clearing and having a cold camp," admits Yvonne. Nobody likes that idea, but there doesn't seem to be much other option. At least until Aranya gets an idea.

"I might be able to help with getting us a fire and some fresh water, too." Everyone looks at her, hopeful, and she tries her best to temper that hope. "Maybe. I haven't tried it before, but I think it will work. I shouldn't need anything special for the campsite, so whatever you think will be best should be fine."

The others nod, and Yvonne takes a few moments to choose a heading. "This way, I'd say. I think the cave opens up a bit in that direction. If nothing else, it will give us a bit of headroom to cut down some of the hanging moss and have a bit of space to ourselves."

With a plan set, the map is put away, and they set out. True to Yvonne's suspicion, the cave opens up a bit. Their campsite ends up being near a wall with a veritable palisade of dripstone and moss, giving them a bit of protection from the caves at large. They end up needing to clear quite a bit of moss, which plays into

Aranya's hopeful plan perfectly. Even better, Ragnar seems to spot something under the dense carpet of life and pulls a small rock hammer from his pack.

"What'd you find?" asks Aelara as the dwarf chips at the stone around some thick lichen.

"Rockbreakers, maybe," he answers, which doesn't tell Aelara much. Yvonne fills her and Aranya in as Ragnar works.

"They're . . . I don't think I'd call them a staple for dwarves, but they're easy to grow and nutritious. The lichen grows tough little tubers in the cracks of the stone, and they'll eventually break it into gravel or even sand if given enough time. Raw, they're incredibly tough, but can be very tender once boiled."

Ragnar grins as he stands, holding an armful of gray roots that almost look like dusty carrots . . . or stalagmites. "Looks like rockbreakers t'me! Yvonne?" He holds them forward for her to examine, and she soon nods.

"I think if Aranya can get us some water and some fuel, we could make rockbreaker chowder."

"So no pressure," says the kobold with a smirk before looking over the cleared moss. "I don't know how well even the dried moss will work for a fire, but I guess it's time to try a new prayer. Get the cookpot ready, and maybe an extra one for some more water?"

The others nod as camp prep gets truly underway. Aelara helps clear the ground a bit more with her Earth magic, and bedrolls are laid out as Aranya prepares a few bundles of moss. If this works like she thinks it should, she'll only really be able to manage a large handful at a time.

She soon holds one over the pot and lets the warmth of her faith wash over her, her doubts washing away as she focuses. "Queen's Extraction!"

Water flows from the moss in her hand like a wrung rag, soon leaving water in the pot and dry moss in her hands. She gives Yvonne the bundle as Ragnar examines the water.

"Will it work?"

Yvonne nods after examining the dried moss. "If nothing else, it will work for tinder and maybe a bit of padding under our bedrolls. I can gather some false stalagmites that will burn longer so we can actually cook."

Ragnar dips a finger in the water then pops it in his mouth. "Tastes like water t'me. We'll boil it, jus' t'be safe."

"Then I'll help bundle the moss for you, and Yvonne can go get the stalagmites while you make some more water. Will you be fine to fill both pots?" asks Aelara. Aranya smiles at her consideration.

"It's a very minor prayer, so I should be fine to get us plenty of water to refill our skins."

The work goes quickly, with Ragnar taking the dried bundles to where the fire will be and then spreading the extra under the bedrolls for a bit of comfort as the metal pots slowly fill with water.

Yvonne returns with an armload of the strange false stalagmites—woody fungi that mimic the cave formations. They also mimic stalactites, but the ones on the ceiling are harder to harvest than the ones on the ground. Ragnar helps her break them down a bit more for the cooking fire, and the dried moss works perfectly as tinder to get the thicker fungi to light.

The rockbreakers get diced up and tossed into the stewpot along with some shredded jerky and a bit of travel seasoning. Everyone relaxes around the fire as Ragnar tends to the stew.

"So, Aranya, do you think you'll shed before we get back?" asks the elf, making idle conversation.

She considers the question before answering. "It's hard to say. I'm not itching yet, so there's still plenty of time."

"I think we're close to having this jungle mapped out, which would be a good time to return. Will you be all right to shed out here, if it takes longer than I expect?" asks Yvonne as she reclines against the wall.

"I'd . . . prefer the privacy of Lord Thedeim's Sanctuary for it, but there shouldn't be anything out in this jungle to prevent me from doing it here, if I need to."

"How long does it take?" asks the elf as she subtly reaches a hand toward the pot. It's unclear if she means the shed or the stew, but it seems a swat on the hand is all the answer she's getting for the latter.

"If everything goes well, maybe ten minutes. If it doesn't, I'll just look a mess and be uncomfortable until we can get back home and I can scrub the stuck shed off in a bath."

Aelara sighs happily at that idea. "Ah, a good soak after a long adventure is the absolute *best*."

Even Ragnar nods at that, the dwarf pulling some wooden bowls from his bag. "Slop's on!" he declares with a grin, ladling out stew to everyone. It's surprisingly rich and hearty, and Ragnar nods at his creation.

"Could'a used some fireberries, but those're a fair ways more south." That's the closest thing to a complaint anyone has about the meal, and the stew is finished off with aplomb. A bit more water is extracted to clean the pot, and shifts are assigned, with Aranya getting the last one.

She's perfectly fine with getting to bed a bit early and rising a bit early. She's looking forward to making breakfast for everyone as well. She has some oats and dried fruit that should make a pleasant porridge.

The extra mossy padding helps her drift off to sleep quickly, her earlier frustrations with the pace of the search forgotten. She just needs patience. They'll find her old dungeon and her people eventually. While more time will mean more pain for them, trying to rush won't help anybody.

Better a proper rescue eventually than a rushed and botched attempt right now.

Chapter 10

Thing

The Crawling Hand Scion drums his fingers as he goes over his list of enchantments. The Master has not quite given him carte blanche on what to put into the planned lava labyrinth, but he does have quite a bit of leeway. Some of the suggestions are simple enough, while some will require a bit more work on Thing's part.

While he has what he would consider to be rather standard versions for most of the magical traps, he would also like to experiment with some of his own takes. He'll need to be careful and test them thoroughly on the denizens before turning them on the delvers, though. His failed attempts to dispel the Lifedrinking enchantment led him to a deep understanding of its workings. If he adjusts the spell, he could produce debilitating effects without being life-threatening.

He gives a longing look to his personal tome of enchanting before setting it aside. No, if they're going to be used on delvers, it's better to use the tried-and-true formulae and arrays from the other books he's gathered. If he's being honest with himself, it's not like that would limit his options much.

He sighs in his own way and leans back onto the stump of his wrist, letting his fingers weave the telekinesis he needs to move his books and notes. He and Queen are going to organize and plan together in the secret war room what traps to put where. Coda is hoping to join them, but it's uncertain if he actually will be able to. The Bat Scion is still putting the finishing touches on the production of the blocks for the lighthouse.

With his materials in hand, Thing jumps atop the floating pile, levitating it and himself to the war room. He's relieved to see he seems to be early, giving him time to organize himself a bit better. He has no idea how Honey manages to keep everything so neat and tidy. He'll need to ask her for pointers once she gets back.

Queen doesn't give him much time to organize, as he soon notices a trail of ants bringing in the Alchemist's own notes. Thankfully, it seems Queen herself is delayed slightly, which gives Thing a chance to get his ducks in some semblance of a row before she makes her entrance.

"Greetings, Enchanter Thing. I hope the day finds you well." While their first attempts at communication had been a bit awkward, the need to talk shop so often had given rise to their own unique sign language, with Queen using her feelers and even some workers to communicate.

"It does, and I hope it finds you similarly," he replies. Queen prefers to speak formally, though that often falls away as they get deeper into discussions of their specialties. "It seems we will have to start without Coda."

"It is unfortunate but unsurprising. The Emperor has the Architect very busy with the lighthouse project. I beli— Hmm?" She pauses midsentence as the Conduit slithers into the war room, a book in his telekinesis. Thing and Queen both give a small bow of respect, which Fluffles receives awkwardly. Much like the Master, his Conduit is not very big on formality.

"The Den Master wished me to bring this to the meeting. I believe they are his own designs for some mechanical traps. With Coda so busy, I think Thedeim wishes to provide his help with this," hisses Fluffles, much to the interest of the other two.

"With Emperor Thedeim's more direct involvement, his new lava labyrinth will be a wonder to surpass the hedge maze and gauntlets combined!" signs Queen, her formal movements starting to lose their stately grace as the prospect of working with the Master's knowledge trumps her desire for decorum.

Not that Thing can blame her. Master Thedeim's knowledge is always exciting to witness. He would have never expected the secret to dispelling Lifedrinking would lay in his knowledge of lightning, of all things, and yet it was. Even more, Thing knows it can be used to counter theoretically any magic. He's uncertain if he could ever manage it in the time frame of a fight, but it's worked every time so far in the lab.

"Will he be specifically watching our meeting, then?"

Fluffles shrugs with his wings. "I don't know. I can't track his attention as well as Teemo. I think he is more focused on meeting with the Southwood right now, as well as gently guiding the tunnelbore ants in giving the labyrinth its rough shape."

"I hope the Emperor will upgrade the anthill once more soon. I am very interested in seeing what the last form of ant will be."

"I think he'll be doing that before long," hisses the Conduit. "Once the labyrinth is shaped, he'll probably want to get the enclave in so they can attempt to get settled before delvers flock to it."

They both nod at that, finding Fluffles's reasoning to be sound. "Then let's get started. I'm sure Queen has a whole host of ideas she could use, too, depending on what is actually needed," signs Thing as he motions for her to confirm or deny.

She nods. "Indeed. And the sooner we get started, the sooner Thing and I can practice our craft and prepare to help the Emperor with the problem in the Deeps."

Fluffles looks at the two diminutive scions with mild surprise. "Oh? Did the Den Master suggest something to you two?"

Thing motions a negative. "No, this will be more on our own initiative. Depending on the specific terrain, we can greatly help in fortifying positions and securing fallbacks with our traps. We can even help offensively with Queen's potions and my enchanting equipment. I think I'll need Teemo to shortcut a tunnelbore into the secret base here to expand the enchanting lab for me, and possibly the alchemy lab for Queen. I know I'll need the room to teach the ratlings some basic enchantment."

Queen nods her agreement. "And we will both be giving the dwellers an education in our arts for them to leverage on their own as well. The Emperor will certainly give them what he can, but I fear our rate of production will not be enough on its own."

Fluffles brings his tail around to rest his head on as he thinks. "I think Rocky, Slash, and myself will need to step up our own efforts, too. We can't let the dwellers come to harm with our inaction. I wouldn't be surprised if even Jello is preparing for the fight in her own way. She is very effective in tight tunnels."

"What about Poe and Tiny?" asks Thing, curious about the two strong scions.

Fluffles rubs his chin with his tail for a few seconds before answering. "Tiny will most likely be staying behind to be a last line of defense. With him being a Guardian, he should be very good at it. I believe Poe will also be staying to ensure Den Master Thedeim won't be left unprotected. The large caverns would be a very good place for the two to work together to thwart a counteroffensive. And I suspect the delvers would be more than happy to assist, especially if Thedeim promises compensation."

"Don't forget Nova and the wyrms," points out Thing, making Fluffles slap himself with his tail.

"Ah, of course! She has been wanting to join in the spars with Rocky, too. She wants to live up to the weight of her name, and this is exactly the kind of thing she'll want to help with for that." Fluffles smirks before continuing. "And I'm sure Rocky will enjoy the challenge of trying to fight someone he might not want to physically punch. His thermal control is astonishing, but that's still a ton of heat to try to compensate for."

Thing and Queen can only nod again. They've both run the numbers on magma, but they also know just having a number doesn't paint the entire picture. "Do you think Rocky will expand his affinities before the battle comes?" asks Queen, earning a laugh from Fluffles.

"I'll eat my tail if he hasn't gained at least one more besides Fire, Ice, and Kinetic. He hasn't shown any others off in our spars yet, but I know he's been wanting to focus on each one as they come now instead of just sprinting ahead and getting as many as possible. I think the young goblin wresting control from him that one time really showed he needed to get more of a grasp on each affinity, or else risk having it turned on him in a fight."

"How about your own affinities?" presses the Alchemist. Fluffles considers before answering.

"I'm working on mastering what I have already. Dispelling that hurricane let me gain Wind, Storm, and Lightning affinities. Those three will keep my attention for some time, I expect. I'm not the savant that Rocky is. I can feel him resonating with Wind and Lightning, and he says he can feel the same for me with Fire and Ice. I'm deliberately holding back from them, but I don't know his plan for his own affinities."

The three scions sit in comfortable silence at that, pondering their affinities. Thing has Kinetic and Meta, as well as Fate, of course, and has little idea how to expand them. While he vaguely understands that Kinetic, Fire, and Ice are all closely linked, he honestly has little interest in those. He'd like to gain Knowledge affinity but doesn't know how he would actually achieve that. His hopes likely rest on Queen or Honey expanding their own Knowledge affinities to something, and hoping he can work backward from their advice.

He shakes himself to clear his mind and raps a knuckle on the table, getting their attention. "Affinities aside, we should probably work on what we have for the labyrinth. Once we know what we want to put in there, we'll know what materials we'll need to make that a reality."

Fluffles nods and coils up, intending to sit in on the planning, and possibly even give his own suggestions. Queen straightens herself and nods as well, though her attendant workers look eager to get started, mirroring her true mood.

"Indeed! The Emperor has given us much latitude in this, so we must show him his faith in us is not misplaced! So, let us compare what effects we can produce, and work from there."

Thing takes notes as Queen lists off and explains her relevant alchemical creations, noting which ones he can mirror. They even start drawing up a few joint plans to inflict the same malady in different ways, ensuring delvers can't simply create an alchemical or magical solution and expect it to work every time.

Already, their collaboration has promise, and Thing hasn't even gone over his own presentation! He can only imagine what he and Queen will come up with, not to mention what they will accomplish once Coda can truly give his own input.

Chapter 11

As enlightening as the autopsy turned out to be, there are still a lot of questions to be answered, and not just about the weird invader. Well, not *directly* about it. I still don't know who sent it, why, or from where. It seems like the Southwood doesn't know either.

I feel like this is a good example of the difference in quality between scouting with a Marshal and without. I'm a bit tempted to get Poe up here to organize a few of my own avian expeditions, but I don't think my birbs will enjoy flying in the cold like that.

Besides, they don't call it the Green Sea just because it sounds cool. From the air, it's just a dense canopy from horizon to horizon, though there's quite a bit of white on it right now, too. But the main point is: birds just aren't going to cut it to get information on what's happening on the ground.

Thankfully, I have other options for scouts.

I upgrade the wolf spawner a bit to up the spawn rate, so Leo should be getting enough wolves to send a few out to explore to the north. If we ever want to get some kind of counteroffensive going, we'll need to know where to actually go off to and *offend*.

Much as I'd like to let Teemo stick around and try to learn more from the Stag, I probably should get him home. Using Poe as a temporary messenger worked well enough, but it was little more than a Band-Aid on something that required stitches—better than nothing, but not an actual solution.

My own Voice speaks up from atop Leo's head, preferring to look the Stag in the eyes when talking together.

"Well, seems like the Boss is ready for me to come home. Honey will get first dibs on whatever seeds and such your expeditions bring back, and in exchange, the Boss will do his best to help deal with whatever's going on with those invaders."

The Stag nods. "We have an accord, then. Is there anything else my Lord can offer in return? A few handfuls of seeds seem hardly enough to offer if you can truly fight off this threat."

Oh, that actually reminds me.

Teemo tilts his head as I explain my idea to him, nodding when he realizes where I'm going with it. "Actually, what rooms do you have access to? The Boss knows of at least one he doesn't have, so he's wondering if there's a way to trade rooms or something."

The Stag looks a bit surprised at that, but he listens to his own dungeon before answering. "With each passing year, more options will open up for your dungeon. My Lord has access to everything, in theory. While something like a magma forge is available to him, it would take a lot of effort for him to actually utilize it. My Lord has few rooms actually built, as he has little use for them. To gain access to a new building yourself, you will either need to be patient or utilize a scion.

"If a friendly dungeon has a room you would like, you would need to send your scion to utilize it and gain a title, which would then give you access to the room."

Teemo's nod mimes the one I want to do. "Ah, like with Leo. He joined the Boss, and Thedeim made him a scion, but he didn't have a wolf spawner at the time, so he gained access to it."

The Stag nods. "It is quite the investment, however, to utilize a precious scion to gain something that will come with time."

My three scions there exchange glances but don't argue. I have scions coming out of my nonexistent ears! Interestingly enough, they also mostly all have their own jobs to do already, so I'm not certain I have one to suggest that to anyway.

Teemo gives a little bow to the Stag. "Thanks for the information. The Boss will be sending more wolves in the coming days, too, so you should have a bit more breathing room from the attacks."

The White Stag gives a more elaborate bow in return. "Thank you for your aid, and for your forgiveness of my . . . earlier rashness. Your unorthodox approach may be just what my Lord needs to weather this storm."

Teemo just smiles before turning his attention back to Leo and Honey. The Bee Scion has her swarm buzzing around a wolf beside Leo, the tundra wolf weighed down with saddlebags full of notes and samples.

"Is that everything you want to send back for now, Honey? Yes, I know, I won't try to shelve your notes. I'm sure the bees back home can keep them organized until you get back. Yes, and preserve the samples, too." He laughs as he hops onto the other wolf and motions for him to get going. "You can send more stuff back later, so stop fretting! There's going to be plenty of wolves in and out. Yes, I'll make sure Grim gets that flower, too, don't worry."

Honey keeps buzzing and dancing as Teemo leans into the wolf's ear and whispers, "Just run, or we'll never get out of here." The wolf eagerly takes off, with Teemo laughing and waving at Honey and the others, my Bee Scion in a bit of a huff at his sudden departure.

While I think the visit could have gone better, it certainly could have gone worse. The Southwood could have been overrun by the time we got there, for example. Still, I'm pretty happy with how it went. I'd rather have knowledge of a foe than be surprised by it, even if I'd prefer even more not to fight in the first place. I at least have an idea for how to deal with the weird invaders now.

I'm pretty sure bugs don't do well in the cold because of the open nature of their circulation, though their size definitely plays a part, too. Stagnant stuff freezes a lot easier than moving things. But I also think that's partially why poison works so well on them, too. It might just be that bugs back home are small, so a lethal dose is small, too, but the various sprays seem to work really quickly, and I think it's because of the open layout of their insides.

In a human, a poison has to follow the veins to get where it wants to go. In a bug, it can just diffuse through everything more or less at once. I'm hoping that will mean Queen can whip up some aerosol alchemical things and make fights with these invaders nice and short.

I also should consider maxing out the anthill, too. The lava labyrinth is looking like a big, tangled mess, which is exactly what I was hoping it'd be. I even made sure to put the elevation changes in places that would prevent just being able to follow a wall to get to the prize.

Or prizes—there's going to be a lot of things to entice delvers. I'm going to be spending a bit of mana to reorganize the nodes in there so the best stuff is deeper in. I'll leave one or two of the mythril and orichalcum nodes more toward the entrance, but they're going to be in sections I can easily reroute with the moving walls and other options, so even those won't be simple to get.

Yeah, I should max the anthill and give it the chance to populate the labyrinth with whatever the new ant is. If it follows the pattern of the last two, the planned Ant Enclave will claim some or all of the types that exist, and they'll start actually making the enclave. It'll take a bit of time to let them build up the numbers for that.

I spend the mana to max it out, waiting with bated breath to see what I get. One of the smaller ant holes widens from the inside, and I see my new ant isn't a gi*ant* like the tunnelbores, which is a relief. Amazons . . . *ant-azons*? might have trouble literally fitting in down here.

As it makes its entrance, it looks sleek, almost spindly, despite the glowing grooves of magma I can see at the seams in its carapace. It's rather low slung, making me think more of a wind scorpion than an ant, though the head looks like a normal ant head. It has two crude graspers on the frontmost set of legs.

It's not as ugly as the aranea are, but this magmyrm—as the little window calls it—isn't exactly going to be winning any beauty contests.

Or maybe it will. Maybe this is the Fabio of magmyrms, I dunno.

Unlike the ratling or aranea, this one doesn't seem like it has anything specific in mind as it wanders the labyrinth. I watch it as my mind wanders to the information the Stag shared about getting new rooms.

Do any of my scions have the spare time to try to pick up some kind of metalcrafting title in Violet's metalworks? Most of my scions I can dismiss pretty easily, as just about everyone is rather busy with their projects or just wouldn't fit in the small room. (Sorry, Tiny.)

In fact, I think I only have two who could even remotely have the time for it, though I'm not certain they'll have the inclination. One is Fluffles, who may not have the time for it, after all. He's been trying to train a lot more recently, and I think he's gotten to a point where he doesn't feel like he's wasting my mana when he uses it anymore. Still, it can't hurt to suggest it to him. Worst he can do is say no.

The other would be Jello. While she's definitely been keeping herself busy with keeping the tunnels clear, they wouldn't suffer if she picked up a hobby. I'm not sure she has the temperament for it, but she does like trying new things.

I mentally shrug and ask Violet for permission for my scions to use her metalworks, which she readily accepts. I think she's actually happy to have something to potentially teach *me*, which is kind of adorable.

I tap the bonds with the suggestion to give metalworking a shot, and it seems like both Fluffles and Jello are willing to at least check it out. I expect I'll probably need a new scion before I get a metalworks, or maybe hope the system or whatever it is will give it to me for my birthday.

Chapter 12

Elsewhere

Far beneath the surface, far enough that something like the surface is viewed as a myth, lay the Deeps. To those who live there, of course the surface would be a legend. A cavern so big that the top can't be seen? What would such a place even be? Some say it's a sort of promised land, a place of wealth and opportunity, or perhaps a ripe field to harvest. Others say it's a hellscape of places where someone can just fall upward forever, where a searing fire up high bakes everything in its reach.

To a certain dungeon, it is a fertile, weak place to consume and recreate in its own image. Its worshipers call it the Maw, and it enjoys the name. Its kobold residents call it Sanctuary, if they know what's good for them. They make the sweetest sacrifices; sweet enough to tempt it to consume them all at once, but it learned to resist that urge after subsuming its first rival dungeon.

If you eat something, you can't eat it again. Its next rival, the Maw consumed without taking the territory, and eventually, another one arose. While it can't eat the same dungeon a second time, a new one is not the same dungeon. So it is with the kobolds: let them make more, eat some select morsels, and it can devour them for its entire existence!

Even its emancipated enclaves are yet another source of food. With their technical freedom comes the ability to feast on their mana more effectively. No longer does it need to subsist on scraps from wild delvers. Even better, the townsfolk worship it, giving it mana that way, too.

Yet it hungered for more. It could consume the wild delvers with impunity thanks to the townsfolk, but it was too slow, since they don't show up often enough.

So it created a Voice from its metal fey. Instead of the sleek grace of the pale elves, it created a thin, tall thing, tall enough to not stand up in most tunnels, but nimble enough to be able to move quickly while hunched or squatted. Its hands had long metal claws, and the first thing it did was to slaughter one of the worshipping delvers. The Maw appreciated the mana, but was wondering how its Voice would talk if it just killed them.

"Need hat, Master," it answered the Maw. "Am Redcap, need red hat."

It fashioned a wide hat from the remains, reminiscent of the cap of a mushroom. The grisly chapeau hid most of the Voice's face in shadow, save for the eyes. The Maw felt the eyes should have been pinpricks of red light, but they were a soft blue with white sclera instead. The only outstanding thing about them was how they were so plainly visible from the dark shadows behind the brim of the hat.

The townsfolk seemed to find it possibly more disturbing for it to have such ordinary eyes, so the Maw saw no reason to force it to change. Instead, it gave them its first command:

"Bring me more to eat."

The townsfolk hurried to obey, offering livestock at first. While those gave some mana, it was . . . bland. The food for the delvers was not food for the Maw. The Redcap acquired a fresh hat from one of those with a poor offering before delivering the news:

"Delvers. Feed me delvers."

They started sending sacrificial parties to delve, each member honored to be consumed by the Maw at the end. Each party let the Redcap get a new hat and gave it new materials to ply its Metal affinity.

While the new mana was good, the Maw was concerned it may not last. It hungered for more, yet its townsfolk were already having trouble keeping up the pace of sacrifices. It was considering letting the Redcap make a new hat of its High Priest when the High Priest announced a plan to the people.

They would hunt for delvers outside to feed the mighty Maw. There were some animals that qualified as delvers, and the pale elves and dwarves were not the only people down here, either. They would feed the Maw and bask in its power and protection.

When the hunting started to bear fruit, the Maw was the happiest it had been in a while. Those hunts eventually brought it the delicacy of the kobolds, and the Maw made them dwellers; its own personal pantry to carefully manage and maintain.

And so it grew, allowing other dungeons to form before devouring them, slowly able to consume more and more, and grow more and more, allowing it to consume more . . .

Until the hunters came back from a very long and deep hunt with something the Maw had never seen before. It was big and seemed to be a mass of tentacles. It would be a perfect main course, with a kobold for dessert. But then the creature broke out and started breaking everything!

The Redcap intervened, but seemed evenly matched. Flashing and slashing steel would sever tentacles, but they would regrow as quickly as the Voice could remove them. The Redcap's blades were not so easily replaced. The two fighters disengaged, each focused on their foe, looking for an opening, something to end the stalemate, when the Maw got a notification.

Transfer Request. Accept/Deny?

Transfer? The tentacle-thing wished to join the Maw?

It told the Redcap to hold the stalemate, wanting a bit of time to consider. It would rather consume the tentacle thing, for it must have a trove of mana . . . but it may not be able to chew this particular mouthful. If it joined, however . . . the Maw could consume even more with its help!

It accepted the request, and the tentacle monster relaxed in its new home. While the Redcap left to make more blades, the Maw decided to make the new thing a scion. It was very glad it did.

While the connection was not quite as clear as with the Redcap, one concept was very clear to the Maw: to not wait to consume the invaders only when they entered. Let the townsfolk gather delvers, while the Maw consumed the invaders of the stagnant mana! If it could find a dense enough section of stagnation, the new scion could even do something interesting with it.

The Maw would very much like to have something new and interesting to consume, and so allowed the tentacle monster's plan. Expeditions were sent, invaders slaughtered, and their mana gathered. It was so effective that the invaders even started to flee, rather than blindly throwing themselves at the Maw.

And then came two discoveries at once. The first was the stagnation point the Tentacle Scion was searching for. The second was a path to the surface, opening into a dense forest. While the second was interesting, the first was the true prize.

As promised, the Tentacle Scion did . . . *something* to the knot of stagnation, presenting it to the Maw, which happily devoured it. It felt itself *twist* as it did, and suddenly, it could taste something new. It could taste the mana rolling off the delvers themselves, something that felt like the opposite of the stagnant mana. It also found the stagnant mana was not as filling as it once was.

As it attempted to figure this out, the Tentacle Scion made a suggestion: to *twist* the spawner it had come with. This surprised the Maw, as the scion had long argued the spawner should be mostly left alone, that it was useless as it was.

With the new tastes developing in the Maw, it could see now why the scion had wanted to wait. It followed the scion's instructions for how to properly *twist* the spawner and truly create something to let it devour whatever it wanted.

And it wanted to devour the surface. It could taste a dungeon on the currents of mana, taste its influence as it forced the stagnation to move. If it had an actual mouth, it would drool at the thought of the moving mana.

The scion showed it one last thing: how to properly Devour the mana it received. No more would the Maw simply nibble the edges of the mana the dwellers produced by simply living; no longer would it have to endlessly chew the stagnant mana into something more palatable. No, it could Devour it and leave only the stagnation behind.

While the stagnation may be unpleasant, Devouring the other mana is sublime, delicious, enthralling, *perfection*! That it can have a waste product from eating is not so much of a surprise, as it has seen the delvers and dwellers do the same thing.

It lets the Tentacle Scion send the newly spawned creatures to the surface, not caring that the type makes its mind hurt. It just needs to not look so hard at it. It can instead focus on Devouring, letting the Redcap focus on the delvers and townsfolk, and the Tentacle Scion exercise its new title in commanding the expeditions.

The Maw thought a Marshal was what would manage expeditions, but the Tentacle Scion became a Harbinger instead. It's not concerned about the difference, though. Time spent trying to think about that is time spent not Devouring.

Chapter 13

Coda

The Bat Scion nervously pores over his blueprints, feeling like each glance reveals a new design flaw, but any fix would require a full redesign! While he's confident the structure will hold, he wants it to be *perfect*!

As his nerves threaten to overwhelm him, he feels the soothing hand of the Foreman through the bond.

It will be fine. He ran the numbers, Queen has checked his math, and even Foreman Thedeim approves of the design. Coda is still a bit uncertain about the numbers they settled on for the force of winds against the structure, but the kinds of forces that it would take to actually topple it are . . . staggering.

He might not be so nervous about the whole thing if the leader of the local delvers wasn't so interested in the project, as well as in Coda's other experiments. It's just . . . *unsettling* to have someone from outside not only see his ideas but want to help make them a reality. It's somehow both encouraging and terrifying!

He even managed to badger a deadline out of Coda for the construction to begin, and said deadline is rapidly approaching!

Another soothing pat comes through the bond, and Coda closes his eyes, taking a breath. He's taken every precaution he could think of, and then doubled the strength on top of that. He just has to trust the math and hope his safety factor is enough to handle whatever variables he managed to miss.

He tears his focus from the plans and to the expanded workshop he was given to help with the production, where the ratlings are dutifully preparing sacks of dry mix, making the hollow blocks, and winding the chosen silk into large spools to help reinforce the structure. Other ratlings have been making simple boats and carts to help transport everything, as well as mixing troughs and buckets.

Poe tells him the masons from outside are preparing and seem to have even hired a boat to help ferry goods, but Coda is uncertain how much of their expertise he'll actually be able to use. Perhaps a stonework facade? While Coda is confident in the strength of his design, he's less confident in the looks.

Though he probably will require their help with the archways. The blocks lend themselves to square openings, which is terrible for stability. With their help, he may be able to cut the bricks into proper arches or have them make them out of stone. He'll need to run the numbers on that later. While he has the designs for the arches done in the reinforced concrete blocks, he's starting to be concerned about how to actually build them to specifications.

Probably another thing to lean on the masons for. He'd feel worse about it if the Foreman didn't seem so amused. From what he can glean from the bond, crossing the gulf between design and actually building is just part of the process. He's at least tested most of the planned methods to ensure they actually work, so he's confident his designs won't fail on that front, at least. Mostly.

The arches will be fine.

Right?

He sighs to himself and takes a closer look at his arch design. The web is set in an arc, the concrete poured, tension applied . . . His eyes widen at the final step, seeing what's been niggling at the back of his mind. When the tension is applied, the webbing will want to straighten out, not stay in the nice, smooth curve! He needs archways, not triangleways!

His rising panic is interrupted by a happy, curious voice from behind.

"What're you doing?"

He manages not to scream from being startled, though the charcoal stick in his wingclaw goes flying as he turns. He relaxes when he sees who it is.

"Oh, it's just you, Jello. I'm . . . Well, I found an issue with the design, and I don't know how to fix it."

"Can Jello help?" she asks. Though Coda doubts it, he also doubts she'd hurt anything.

"Maybe? Here, see this design?" He motions for her to examine the blueprint, and she does.

"Lines in blocks?" she asks, not quite understanding what she's looking at. Coda just nods and gets a few scrap lengths of web.

"Here, hold this one like this, this one like this . . ." He guides her through the process of aligning the webbing within herself, making a mental note to get her help with things like this more often. Paper is good for getting the numbers, but this could be invaluable for actually moving from theory to application.

Jello still doesn't seem to understand what he's doing, but she's happy to play along and hold the lines as he asks. Soon enough, Coda steps back with a nod.

"Right, so, I need these lines of web to give strength to the thing I'm building. What I'm using is like a thick mud, so it can hold the strings like that when we pour it in, but then the strings need to be tightened. Hold them at the bottom, and I'll pull at the top," he instructs.

Jello follows the directions, giggling a bit when the lines straighten out, and he sighs at that. "And that's the problem. I need them to stay in the curve when I put tension on them."

To his surprise, Jello seems to understand.

"Ah, Jello sees. She knows how hard it can be to keep a shape. Hmm . . ." The webbing twists and moves inside her as she plays with the lines for a few minutes while Coda watches, wondering if she might figure something out.

"Hmm . . . this is harder than being a cube. It reminds Jello of when she tried to be a sphere. She had to give up on that," she admits, little bubbles percolating through her as she thinks. "Maybe Tiny would know?"

"Tiny?" echoes Coda, confused what the Guardian would have to contribute.

"Yes. Tiny makes these strings; maybe he knows how to get them to behave?"

Coda stares at her for a few moments before reaching up and pulling on both of his ears. "Of course! He's a spider; he'd know!" He takes to the air but swoops back when Jello yells after him.

"Wait for Jello! She wants to help!"

It doesn't take them too long to get to Tiny's lair thanks to the shortcuts, and the gigantic spider regards his fellow scions with the detached interest with which spiders watch the entire world.

"Ah, Coda and Jello. How long has it been since we've had some time together? What brings you to my lair?" he asks as he settles himself on the thick webbing covering the ground.

"Strings!" replies Jello with excitement, showing several little bows she's managed to tie the webbing inside herself into.

"I've found a flaw in my archway design, and I was hoping you'd be able to offer some guidance with it?"

Tiny chuckles and nods. "I was wondering why the weave was suggesting I'd be needed for my skills rather than my size today. What is the problem?"

Coda and Jello quickly show him the issue, and he nods sagely. "Ah, I see. Well . . . it's been some time since I had the need to weave in a corner, but I remember the process," he says as he gets his spinnerets moving. In about a minute, he hands Jello some web. "Stretch this out inside yourself, please."

She's all too happy to oblige, and Coda is more than a little surprised to see half an arch form. He moves to test the tension, reaching into Jello to test the lines.

"A strong line from the top of the archway to the base, then other lines along that one to bring it into the desired shape," he absently notes, locking the process into his mind as he pokes and prods at the work, then he frowns. "It's only in two dimensions right now, though," he says, tapping a wingclaw to his chin as he thinks.

Tiny gives an apologetic look to the bat. "Most webs are flat, yes. I've made ones that aren't, but I don't know how structurally sound they are. I wouldn't try to hang from one."

"I think . . . Here, try this, Jello . . ." says Coda, the shape slowly taking form in his mind as he works to help it take shape in Jello too. He starts with a wide cone of webbing before quickly moving to a cylinder. A loop pinches it into an hourglass shape, and Coda grins as he adds more.

He settles into a rhythm as he guides the webbing, his mind's eye able to see the lines that would be in the full structure of the lighthouse, and how to integrate the lines of the archway to keep everything in tension without focusing too much force in any single spot.

He smiles to himself and plucks one of the strings, savoring the resonance. It takes him a moment to realize more than just the webbing is resonating. His Architect title is, too, and he feels like it's off pitch. And then it shifts.

He gasps as it corrects itself, finally clicking properly with his purpose. The weight of a new affinity—Knowledge—settles on his back, and it just feels right.

A Civil Artificer needs to know a lot of things if he doesn't want his works to collapse, after all.

Chapter 14

I'm not sure if I could be more proud of Coda than I am right now. I was kinda confused at first why he has *artificer* instead of *engineer*, but it's not too difficult to guess why: engineers are fully mundane; artificers use magic. At least that's what my current theory is.

I really like his design for the tension archway, too. It's pretty complex, but the shape tickles the engineer part of my mind for both how effective I think it'll be and just how cool it looks. It's almost a shame the web will be fully encased in concrete, but that's just how it goes sometimes. Some of the best designs are only obvious to the people who get to take a peek at how it was all put together.

Coda and Jello soon go their separate ways, with my bat looking pretty energized to build a more proper prototype than the one inside Jello, and my Purifier making her slow way toward Violet. It can be difficult to tell what Jello is thinking, even more so than with my other scions, but I think she really liked being a part of the design process with Coda, so she seems to be looking very forward to checking out the metalworks.

I nudge Fluffles to see if he wants to join her, since he didn't reject the possibility earlier. He soon uncoils from what I think was a bit of meditation and flaps his way toward my protégée. I take the opportunity to take a closer look at the room.

As it is right now, it's fairly small. Violet has been having her gremlins and moles dig into the walls of her expansion area, and she put her metalworks inside one of the walls. It's technically a secret room, though the entrance is fairly obvious.

The reason it still gets to be secret is that the entrance is a lot smaller than even the smallest delvers can fit through. They could probably reach an arm inside, but who's crazy enough to go sticking their arm into a random mole hole in a dungeon, no matter how friendly the dungeon is?

Legs is pretty long by now, but he's still easily able to slip in, and I don't think Fluffles will have any issues, either. Jello will have no problem at all. While she seems to prefer being a cube, she has no problem taking whatever shape is needed to get somewhere.

Inside, it becomes clear pretty quickly why a metalworks is different from a smithy.

For starters, there's only a single forge, and it's not a very big one. I don't even mean it's puny because of the relatively low level; I mean it just doesn't take up much of the floorspace. The metalworks is definitely more for cold working, than hot. A smithy will also usually make things that are supposed to be a single piece, but the metalworks makes things with moving parts. Lots of files, grindstones, and saws involved, not to mention pliers, screwdrivers, and so on.

Though again, *lots* is a relative term. The room simply isn't big enough for *lots* of things, but it's enough to know the kind of work that will probably be done in there. Legs is currently working on the folding spearhead, just working out a prototype from the designs so he has an idea of what it'll take to make a real one and eventually pass the designs on to the spiderkin.

Looking around in there also reminds me that my magmyrm seem to have decided what they want to focus on. Thing and Queen have started getting their projects rolling, and with Coda having his breakthrough, I think he'll be able to find the time to pick up his side of the traps, too. At the moment, it's mostly marking the tunnels for what all is planned and finalizing where the moving walls and such can be placed without having to do too much extra digging.

The magmyrm have been watching them at work, and I think they are trying to help. I would have expected them to kinda crowd Queen, but it seems Thing is actually a bit more popular among them. Thing was certainly nervous about them helping at first, especially around his books and such, but if the magmyrm are actually as hot as they look, they're good at controlling it. Not so much as a singe has appeared on Thing's things, so he's getting less and less reluctant to let them help.

Queen accepts their help readily, and even has some of them heating different mixtures as she finishes and tests a few things in the tunnel. Even if she has the perfect sleeping gas, it won't work if the airflow in a specific tunnel is wrong, so there's a lot of testing on those grounds, too.

The project with the lighthouse is getting started as well. It's probably going to be a bit awkward for the seagulls for a bit, but Hullbreak's crabs are doing their best to clean up and level the rough area. Coda did a survey a while ago, so at least the basic spot is planned out, but there are still a lot of things to do. Leveling and cleaning are simple enough to get started on, and not so much work that it can't be changed if Coda discovers the planned foundation area won't work.

In theory, foundations are simple, right? Make it solid and then build on it. The problem is, a lot of things can *look* solid when they aren't. A mechanical engineer can generally pick up whatever they're working on and give it a good whack to test how solid it is. Civil stuff is on a scale where a solid-enough whack is hard to produce, and breaking a full-scale prototype to test the strength can be a bit expensive. But that's only half the problems a civil has to deal with.

A mechanical engineer can just say the ground isn't going anywhere and design thusly, mostly because they can make the shifting parts move relative to the ground. A civil engineer needs to make sure the ground *actually* doesn't move. Everyone knows not to build a house on sand, but civil engineers need to know what patches of ground might be secret sand co-conspirators. Ground can settle a lot if you're not careful, and can make a house act more like a leaning tower than most might be comfortable with.

The other thing is drainage. Even a gentle drizzle puts out a lot of water over the area of a house, and it doesn't just vanish. It's easy to think of water erosion as a slow thing, because it *is* slow for rocks and such, but it can be shockingly quick for even seriously compacted dirt. Do the drainage wrong, and the water might like to flow down around the foundation, shifting the surrounding dirt away, and now the foundation isn't actually supported, and the house is a leaning tower again.

Thankfully, I'm pretty sure that kind of erosion won't be too much of a problem. I don't know how well the concrete will last against pounding waves, but at least those same waves have the tendency to wash away all that tricky dirt and sand patches before some enterprising dungeon decides to build a lighthouse/combat area. A fighthouse, maybe.

I should probably let Hullbreak actually name the thing.

Speaking of Hullbreak, I'm getting a bit more and more proud of him, too. The progress is still slow, but he had his first combat encounter with delvers just the other day, and it seemed to go smoothly. A group came to see what was the hubbub on the seagull island and decided to have a crack at some of the crabs.

Hullbreak had all but one scatter, which the delvers dispatched pretty quickly. He then nervously sent out two more, which were also pretty quickly defeated. I was watching the entire time, interested in seeing what he would do, doing my best not to butt in and tell him what to send. He needs to learn, not just be told what to do. I couldn't help but smile when I felt a question through the bond—if four crabs and a couple gulls would be too much—and I told him it should be fine.

The delvers were actually pressed from that attack, but they seemed satisfied—if a bit banged up—after it, soon getting back into their boat. Hullbreak's reaction to the fight was very interesting, too. I could feel him worrying about the delvers like he worries about his merfolk dwellers, and I even had to gently persuade him not to call the attack off when one of the frontliners took a claw punch to the face.

I think it's good progress. It's good he sees the delvers as something besides a threat, and maybe being able to see them get a little banged up and be no worse for wear will help him with his dwellers.

He's still a bit paranoid about their protection, but with them starting to thrive properly and mostly take care of themselves, I think he's learning to trust them with their own safety. It's still a long process, and I can feel him chewing his metaphorical fingernails when the merfolk head out past his perception, but he's improving.

Just them farming and hunting outside his borders used to send him into almost a panic, so doing the equivalent of nervous pacing is a big step up.

Chapter 15

The next few days are a weird mix of relaxing and busy; I don't know how else to describe it. Teemo returns and spends most of the first day tending to Honey's notes and the other little things she wanted him to do. Queen and Coda even take the time to go over what seeds and clippings were sent back, too, with Teemo letting them know there will be a lot more over the coming weeks.

The lighthouse gets officially underway, with Coda doing a more detailed survey and sinking some holes to give the foundation more support. The masons have a bit of adjusting to do to work with my Civil Artificer, and Teemo spends much of that day explaining what Coda wants them to do.

A few leave, thinking they know better than my scions, but most are eager to learn. The ones who left even try to return after hearing about the strange mortar that is the concrete, but the Quartermaster is happy to play bouncer.

I make sure they know they just need to give Coda a proper apology if they want to learn from him directly. We'll see if any of them swallow their pride or not.

The lava labyrinth is also getting going. The ratlings, and even some of the aranea, assist Queen and Thing with their work, with the magmyrm mostly helping Coda at night, since he can't really have the masons doing much with the sun down. And I'm pretty sure the low temperatures at night can mess with the initial set for the concrete.

I should probably ask Teemo to make some temporary shortcuts for the wyrms, in case Coda needs to warm the area up to make things work properly.

As expected, Fluffles isn't very into metalworking. I don't think he hates it, but it seems like it's a pretty passive interest. Jello, however, seems to be very into it. Whenever Legs is in there working on a new iteration of the detachable spearhead, Jello is in there, too, eager to help make it work and learn.

From what I can gather through the bond, I think the idea of shaping things appeals to her. As long as she's enjoying herself, I'm not going to complain, especially if it means I can unlock my own metalworks.

The ratkin and spiderkin continue their buildup as well. I don't know if they have the time to go through something like actual boot camp, but they're certainly not slacking on training.

Folarn and Vernew both are working their recruits hard to ensure they keep as safe as possible. The ratkin are redoubling their efforts with making weapons and armor, though I make sure Teemo lets them know there will be a new weapon for both the jumping spiders and the ratkin archers.

The ratkin still seem to prefer throwing knives, but the promise of a new kind of bow has more of them interested. I'm also curious if they could field some support classes. It's weird to think of them as kinda my priests, but if they can do the same kind of thing as Aranya, they could help turn the tide of a battle.

And speaking of Aranya: she and the rest of the party returned from their scouting mission. According to them, the swamps slowly give way to basically a mushroom rainforest or jungle. I'm not certain what the technical difference is between those, actually . . .

Anyway, it's not ringing any bells for Aranya, so they're all pretty sure they have a ways to go before we trip over her old dungeon.

Aelara and Ragnar head out to relax at the guild, while Aranya and Yvonne prepare to do the same in the secret base. Much as I'd like to let them enjoy some well-earned rest, I need to ask them both about the weird invader the Southwood is dealing with. Teemo would rather relax, too, but this problem isn't going to go away if we just ignore it.

In fact, it'll probably get worse.

I share in Teemo's sigh, but Aranya and Yvonne might know something.

"Is something wrong?" asks the birdwoman, eyeing my Voice as he relaxes on her shoulder.

"No . . . Well, yes, but not immediately. There's something the Boss wants you to look at. You too, Aranya. It's about the invaders in the Southwood. Maybe the rangers or kobold legends know about it; it's weird. I'll get Honey's notes and meet you in the base, okay?" At their nods, he hops off and slips through a shortcut. I tell him to take his time, letting them get to the base and relax a bit.

Once Teemo returns, my two residents scan the notes. At first glance, Yvonne looks confused and Aranya looks disgusted. "How does Honey know what its insides are like?" asks the kobold.

Teemo can't help but chuckle. "By dissecting one with Leo's help. Me and the Stag didn't stick around for it. I'm happy to only get the gory details rather than the actual gore. Do any of the legends have anything like this? Or anything with an unknown or maybe unknowable type?"

Aranya slowly shakes her head. "No, but if even Lord Thedeim can't discern its type, it can't be anything good."

Yvonne nods at that, grabbing the papers to get a closer look as Teemo speaks up. "Do you recognize anything about it, Yvonne?"

"No, and that's what concerns me." Teemo and Aranya exchange a glance, letting Yvonne concentrate. She takes the time to go over the notes in detail, and it's not hard to guess it's not good.

She eventually sighs and sets the notes down. "It's . . ." she takes a moment to sigh again, trying to organize her thoughts. "I've seen some insects and read about some fish that don't actually eat. For the insects, it's the final adult stage, and they spend the larval or pupal stages eating and storing energy before taking their adult form to find a mate and die to make room for the next generation.

"But if Honey's notes are correct, these aren't mating. It makes no sense . . ."

"The Boss says it does, but not a happy kind of sense. Could these be drones of some kind? Their adult stage more designed to defend a hive rather than have their own kids?"

"Maybe . . . but I doubt it. The only kind of disposable warrior I can think of would be in bees, but ordinary bees do much more than fight, and even their disposability is more as a self-sacrificial attack rather than simply starving after some amount of time."

Yvonne frowns at that for a moment. "I wonder if Aelara might know something. I've heard summoning classes often have a timer on their summons. I always assumed they would simply vanish after a time, but I've never met anyone with that kind of class. She might have met some in school . . . Can I show her these notes?"

"Yeah, he's fine with that. If she doesn't know, the Office of Dungeon Affairs is probably our last chance to get answers. Well, last chance that doesn't involve kicking down the door to this thing's nest and getting answers the old-fashioned way."

My residents smirk at that, then Aranya speaks up. "I'd like to come along, too. Not for the discussion but for a good bath. I started getting itchy this morning, so my shed won't be far away. A good, warm soak will give me some relief until it's time."

"I'll tag along, too, if you don't mind. It'll save you from having to explain it again, at least if Aelara knows anything," declares Teemo before he hops onto Yvonne's shoulder.

She rubs a finger under his chin and smiles as she nods. "Then we should go. We might be able to catch Aelara before she gets her own warm bath. Otherwise, we'll have to wait until the morning."

With the mood lightened at least a bit, they all set off to the guild. True to her prediction, they just manage to catch Aelara on her way to the baths, carrying a bag with a towel and what seems like an entire alchemist's shop worth of bottles. She doesn't play around when it comes to a good soak.

Aelara brightens at her friends. "Yvonne! Aranya! Come to join me for some luxury?"

"Perhaps, but I need to delay you first, if you don't mind?" asks the bird-woman. Aelara sends a longing look down the hall, then sighs and deflates a bit.

"I do mind, but this sounds more important." She straightens her back, laying her pout aside for now. "What do you need?"

"For you to look at this. The guild library might be the best place?" suggests Yvonne as she holds up the loose notes. The elf sends one last longing look to her original destination before nodding and following the others. I can't help but feel a pang of sympathy, as it seems the library is in exactly the opposite direction of the baths.

Once in the library and after scanning the notes, however, it seems she has a new focus.

"What . . . *is* this?" she asks, knowing she has something strange, but not knowing what.

"Maybe you should tell us what you think it is first?" suggests Aranya, earning a small frown from the elf. She folds her arms and drums her fingers on herself as she thinks, soon transitioning to voicing her inner monologue.

"Well . . . it's not a normal bug; even I can tell that. Yvonne could have told you if it was that simple. It also gives me the creeps; something about it just feels *wrong* in some way. Why do you think I might know what it is?" she asks with suspicion, her eyes falling on Teemo.

My residents exchange a look before Yvonne answers. "I thought it could be some strange kind of summon? Did any of your peers have a summoning class?"

"Hmm," hums Aelara, her brows furrowed as she chases down that line of thought. "I suppose it *could* be a summon, or maybe a golem. One of my classmates was an earth summoner. We'd talk about the differences in our magic a lot.

"There was also a demonstration once with a summoner and golemancer, both with Shadow affinity. The details went over my head, but I could maybe picture someone with Life affinity either summoning or making a golem like this? Is that what this is? Some kind of Life-affinity golem?"

"We don't know," Teemo answers simply. Aelara tries not to let her eyes bug out of her head, which gets more difficult as he continues. "It's the invader that the Southwood is having to deal with. It didn't say anything about it being a summon, and the Boss can't read the type. Neither can the Southwood."

Aelara's frown deepens at that. "I believe its type should be summon, or maybe elemental. Or golem, I suppose. I don't know much about dungeons, but I can't imagine those types would be difficult for one to comprehend . . ." Her eyes suddenly widen before she slouches, looking defeated. "We're going to go investigate, aren't we," she states, not even making it a question.

"No," answers Yvonne to the surprise of everyone, myself included.

"No?" asks Aranya, recovering quicker than the others.

Yvonne shakes her head. "While we could decide to go, I don't know that it would do us much good. Honey is already investigating these things, and there are apparently enough of them to make even an established dungeon like the Southwood ask for help. Even as a toybox, it should know how to deal with invaders. I don't know that we'd be able to stem a tide it's having trouble with, especially now that Thedeim is offering aid."

Aelara eyes her friend for a few long moments before Yvonne relents. "And I'm honestly a bit scared of these things. Even something like a tunnel horror still has the biology and instincts to do more than just kill. These things . . . seem to only exist for that purpose. One, we could handle, maybe even a dozen . . . but there are surely far more than that to deal with."

Aelara looks relieved to hear that, while Aranya looks conflicted. The elf isn't going to let my kobold stew in her thoughts for long, however, and stands, grabbing a hand of each resident.

"Then there's nothing to delay us all enjoying a nice bath after a long quest!"

Teemo hops off Yvonne's shoulder to gather up the notes. "Then I'll get these back to the Boss. You ladies enjoy yourselves," he says with a smile.

"But the invaders," tries Aranya, only to be shot down by Yvonne.

"We can decide what to do about them later. Aelara's baths are a rare treat. She swears she doesn't use any magic or alchemy in them, but I don't see how she can make them so rejuvenating otherwise."

A look of temptation crosses Aranya's face as she scratches her nose without seeming to realize. Aelara grins and pounces on the weakness.

"I bet I can whip up something to help with your shed, too!"

Teemo waves as Aranya lets the two drag her off, making his way back to me and the library.

I'm actually a bit relieved they don't want to go fight the invaders, or at least not just charge headlong into them. Even if they're not too dangerous for their size, they're still big enough to cause damage. And with the numbers the Southwood seems to be dealing with, that danger only ratchets higher.

I'm going to need to beef up what I send sooner rather than later, I think. Not only to keep them safe but to try to stay ahead of any other nasty surprises. If there was a big variety in the beginning with the invaders, there's no reason they won't spring something else new and even more dangerous.

Chapter 16

The various projects continue overnight, and I think I'm finally ready to give Yvonne the first compound bow once she and Aranya return.

I still don't know how strong to make it, but it's theoretically just a matter of swapping out the arms to adjust the strength of the draw. While that also means having to put the cams back and string it again, I'm pretty sure it's still a lot more modular than an ordinary bow. Not that I expect Yvonne will need to swap the arms around, but it's an option.

I settle on what seems like about a fifty-pound draw. I'm thinking that's pretty strong on Earth, but I have no idea what kind of strength actual soldiers used to use. Besides, the draw lessens significantly at the end, so even if it's a bit stronger than Yvonne is used to, she should be able to do it and then bring it up to aim.

I even have Tiny web a few circles on some of the trees in his lair to act as targets. I'll need to add a proper range to the list of things I'd like to make. This should work fine for now, at least.

I guess the three had a bit of a girl's-night-in last night, as Aranya and Yvonne come back well after dawn. They look more like they slept in a bit rather than staying up all night. My kobold's sleeping rhythm is probably a bit shot, but she's also been transitioning more away from being nocturnal, so maybe not as messed up as I thought.

Whatever the state of her sleep schedule, she seems to have some business with Larx, so Yvonne makes her way on her own toward the library. Teemo is more than happy to interrupt her on the way.

"Heya, Yvonne! Anything in specific you wanted to do in the library?"

The birb stops and smiles at him, offering a hand for him to hop onto. "Nothing in particular, no. Why?"

My Voice grins. "The Boss has a gift for you in the clearing around Tiny's lair."

A feathered eyebrow raises as her interest is piqued. "Oh? Did he slay another scythemaw while we were out exploring?"

Teemo laughs and shakes his head, directing her to a shortcut. "Nothing like that. He's working on helping gear up the spiderkin and ratkin, which includes a new kind of bow. Since you're a bit of an expert on the subject, he'd like your help in testing and developing them going forward."

Yvonne smirks as she follows the shortcut. "Should I be concerned? He seems to be turning Tarl's understanding of dungeons on its head. Will he do the same for my understanding of archery?"

Teemo chuckles and shrugs. "I dunno? Probably for making a bow, but he seems to think actually using it should be the same. Mostly the same. Maybe. He's not an archer."

Yvonne laughs at that as they exit the shortcut, and Tiny gives her a small bow. She responds with a cheerful wave as she looks around. Teemo then directs her attention toward the trees with webs.

"Those are going to be the targets. He'd like you to take a few shots from whatever distance you prefer—just mark your spot on the ground—and then Tiny'll give you the new bow."

Yvonne gives Teemo a curious look but sets about properly stringing her weapon. "Why does he want me to start with my usual bow?"

"He calls it a control. It's a baseline; the thing all the tests will be measured against. No fancy skills or anything, just you and the bow and the arrow . . . and the tree, I guess."

Yvonne shrugs and stands, getting a fair bit of distance away from the tree before marking a line on the ground. "Usually, I fight a bit closer than this, but for target shooting or ambushes—anything I can take my time with—I like a bit more distance," she explains as she nocks an arrow, takes aim, and lets it fly. She nails the bull's-eye, not quite dead center but definitely where she wants it.

She smiles and sinks a few more arrows in a cluster, forming a very tight group with only one outside the center. Teemo gives the impressed whistle I can't as Yvonne looks rightly proud of her skill.

"Welp, you ready for the new one?"

Yvonne nods vigorously. "Yes. I want to know just what madness he's come up with this time."

Without much ceremony, Tiny takes the compound bow from his back and holds it out to Yvonne. The archer looks at the contraption for a few moments before taking it. "*This* is a bow?"

Teemo and I both laugh. I can't blame her. A normal bow, even a recurve, looks fairly simple. At its heart, it's a string and a fancy stick. The compound bow looks like it's a piece of some complicated rigging. In a sense, it kind of is, come to think of it.

"Yep, that's it!" manages Teemo with a wide smile, and Yvonne takes her time to examine the strange weapon.

"Grip and rest are obvious enough . . ." she mutters to herself, talking through her thoughts. "The arms are strange . . . The entire contraption is made of metal?" Teemo nods, and she looks baffled as she returns to the bow in her hands. "Why are there so many strings? Why are there *wheels*?"

"The backmost string is the one that does the work. The wheels give what the Boss calls mechanical advantage. It's like a block and tackle on a ship," he explains.

Yvonne looks confused at that, looking over the arms before speaking.

"Is that why it's metal? I've seen sailors move large boxes with ease like that. That kind of force in a bow would need magical wood to not shatter."

Teemo nods. "They also give another advantage. Go ahead and pull the string all the way back."

Yvonne gives him a suspicious look but does as asked. She doesn't seem to have any trouble with the draw, so we can probably make a stronger one. Her eyes widen as she gets it most of the way back, her arm jerking as the cams do their work of making it easier to hold at full draw.

"What did you *do*?" she asks as she draws all the way, looking awed.

"The Boss says that's why the wheels are shaped like they are. They change the force needed at that point, letting you hold the draw of a much heavier bow than you might normally use."

"What an odd idea for an enchantment," she says, easing the string back into its default position.

"No magic. This bow is one hundred percent mundane. For now."

Yvonne's eyes widen again, and she takes another look at the weapon in her hands. I'm sure she's more familiar with the kinds of enchantments bows tend to have, and I can just picture her wondering what they could turn a bow like this into.

"How's the draw strength on it?"

"Hmm? Oh!" Yvonne shakes herself, remembering why I wanted her help with this. "For most of the draw, it's a little weaker than my normal bow. I'm a seasoned archer, so I prefer a heavier one than most. You said Thedeim wants to give this to his dwellers?" At Teemo's nod, she continues. "This strength should be fine. They may want a weaker draw to train with, but this trick to make holding the draw easier will let them use heavier bows than typical archers."

Teemo grins at that. "That's the idea! The Boss has another design he was going to try but decided against. He says the power puts this one to shame, but it takes a lot longer to load. Why don't you take a few shots and see how it feels?"

Yvonne nods and takes her stance. She shakes her head with a smile at the full draw before she takes a shot—and misses the entire target, the arrow embedding into the tree way above where she was aiming.

She laughs at herself and prepares another arrow. "It's so easy to forget that it still has the full draw strength. I was aiming it like it was a child's first bow instead of a standard-issue one."

Fighting her mirth, she takes a bit more time to let her giggles subside before letting the next arrow fly. This one hits dead center, and she soon sprouts an even tighter grouping than with her normal bow, each arrow within the center.

"Holding steady is so simple with the . . . what did you call them?" She points at the pulleys.

"Cams," answers Teemo.

"Yes, the cams! You're certain they're not magic?" she asks with a grin, which Teemo echoes as he nods.

"Absolutely. It's just a trick of how forces work. Oh, the Boss says he's having a ratling bring a few other arms for you to try out, to see what kind of draw you prefer. Here, I'll show you how to get this one taken apart."

It doesn't take Teemo long to show her how to take it apart, and seeing the limbs slacken as Yvonne removes them gives me an idea.

I might not need to even switch out the limbs to change the strength, at least within a certain range. If I change the angles of the limbs instead, that should adjust how hard it is to draw, and so how much force is delivered. It'd just take some kind of nut on a bolt of some sort to let people adjust the strength, like adjusting the feet of a washing machine.

I won't be able to change it for this prototype, but it's something to look into. It might not even be needed for an archery squad, or however many we end up needing, but that kind of adjustability would be great for the small-team archer that Yvonne is, and most adventurers too.

I let Teemo and Yvonne have fun as I toy with the design. The basic concept seems to have earned an enthusiastic yes from the birdwoman, so all there is now is to iterate on the design and make it more efficient. I know I'll have at least one eager tester to ensure they're up to snuff.

Chapter 17

Honey

Despite the cold, Honey is very glad she insisted on joining Leo. Not only has she had the chance to learn so many interesting new things, but she can help organize everything the scouting wolves bring back, along with the bees that nestle in their fur to provide some extra eyes.

Already, she's working to create a more accurate map for Leo to plan from, and even the Stag is more respectful of her presence after seeing her contributions.

Or Voice Teemo managed to beat some sense into his antlered head. Possibly even both.

The attacks from the invaders have not changed much since she and Leo started helping, but she has a feeling that won't last forever. Whatever is controlling those odd drones must have felt the tension ramping up in the defenders before, and so must be feeling that tension easing with the tundra wolves proving so effective.

The first battle went very well, as Leo was able to more or less just overwhelm the drones with numbers and the affinity advantage. Even with the wolves being outnumbered, the surprise counter with the Ice affinity left very few casualties for their side. Leo was even able to form a counteroffensive with some of the Southwood's stronger denizens, sallying forth past its borders to catch the drones before they could properly amass for another attack.

With that breathing room, Leo's scouts have now been able to ambush enemies before fading back into the wintery woods. From what Honey can tell, the drones aren't smart enough to be psychologically impacted by it, but simple numbers reduction makes everything easier regardless.

The downtime has also let her examine the Southwood's denizens, which has been fascinating. It appears most of the spawners are resource focused, including the deer. Their hides appear almost crystalline, and there's no *almost* about the antlers. She'd love to collect some samples to send back to Thing and Queen, but she doesn't think she'll have much chance to do so.

Most of the other spawners are familiar to her—things like birds and ants and so on—also focused toward different resources. The only two spawners she's spotted so far which are not are the bears and foxes. The bears are physical powerhouses, and the foxes are magic focused, with Illusion affinity.

That was interesting to learn, and it was interesting to watch them use illusions to deal with the more ordinary enemies. For weaker invaders, illusions seemed to work incredibly well, either to hide a stronger denizen so they could deliver a decisive blow or to outright kill them on their own.

She'd had a good discussion with a fox, learning that a lot of illusion use became rather philosophical. What is the difference between experiencing something and having that something be real? Experiencing all her black-and-yellow stripes switching was new, but not anything dangerous.

She started to understand the implications when another fox approached and asked her to warm herself in its fur. It was delightfully soft and warm, but then it vanished. The entire fox was an illusion, right down to the body heat. She could still feel the warmth on her fuzz even after it vanished.

If they can produce phantom warmth, why not phantom harm? If they can reproduce all the feelings of a severe or even mortal injury, what's the difference? If a heart is stabbed, it will stop, and it's difficult to get one beating again, even if there's no actual injury.

She declined to experiment with that level of illusion, even if the questions have some tantalizing answers. She has many experiments she'd like to try once back home to potentially expand her Knowledge affinity into Illusion. If knowledge is about learning, about taking in information, illusion is about putting that information out into the world. She just needs to figure out how to take that kind of step.

That's something she can toy with later, though. For now, her attention should be on helping the Southwood and Leo. One of the scouts just came back, so she makes her way out of the small portable hive and buzzes to land atop Leo's head so she can listen and direct her drones.

The ones with the wolves head into the hive to prepare their reports, as Honey prefers them in writing. Leo, however, likes verbal ones.

"Report," states the Warden, glancing up from the large map and the bits of twig and twine that are being used to mark out the planned scouting paths and expected enemy movements.

The small pack of wolves flick their ears in salute before the leader begins. "We were tasked with scouting to the northeast, section C, uh . . ."

"Seven. C-7," provides Honey, and the wolf nods.

"Right, C-7. The terrain is much the same, though we did find a dense copse of trees. I think the bees will be able to update the map more accurately than I can. We scented more of the drone invaders and found a trail, but I don't believe it's their main approach. It seemed to lead . . ." He pauses and looks at the map as he talks to himself. "If C-7 is . . . there . . . then . . ."

He straightens and speaks louder. "I believe into D-7 and D-8. We could smell more of their scent in that direction, but I don't think we're close to their main force." He looks like he wants to say more, but he holds his tongue for now.

Leo glances at the map and nods to himself before speaking. "What else did you want to say?"

The wolf hesitates, but soon continues. "I think they're radiating from a single place rather than marching down some main road. If they organized to a more specific path, they'd attack one part of the Southwood en masse."

Leo grins. "Why do you think they haven't focused yet?"

The other wolf tilts his head in confusion, then tilts the other way as he thinks. "Because they're stupid?"

Leo sighs and shakes his head. "Never assume an opponent is stupid. They will have a reason for everything they do, even if you can't see it. They're looking for something, most likely a weakness. If they find one they like, they'll prepare to focus on it. I want to find where they're coming from, first." He pauses for effect and grins. "Then we can see how *they* handle a siege. Go rest and recover; you'll be headed back out in the morning."

The wolves nod and make their exit, and Honey takes the chance to speak up.

"Do you think we can siege them?"

Leo considers for a few moments, then slowly shakes his head, not wanting to send Honey flying. "Not right now, at least. I want to train the bears and foxes before trying something like that. Southwood just doesn't have the temperament to prepare them for an attack on his own, so that'll be on me. I'll also want to teach the Stag a bit more about defensive tactics before we're ready to try something like that."

He chuckles and stands, pacing around the cave they've been using as their headquarters. "And we don't have nearly enough forces to try a siege, even if we had good intel and training. The Alpha has been sending more wolves, but I think it'll take a more concentrated force to do something like that. I'd love to get some wyrms to help breach whatever defenses they have, too."

"Do you think they can handle the snow?"

Leo shrugs. "I have no idea. I'll make a request," he says, and Honey can see him concentrate. She follows suit and focuses on the bond with Emperor Thedeim. While Leo may wish for a few wyrms, Honey would like some healing slimes. If they can handle the cold, they could help keep injuries down, and so keep their forces up. And the slimes tend to be rather cheerful and good for morale, too.

She can feel the attention of the Emperor upon her, and him weighing her request. It will take the slimes some time to get there . . . which only really means they should get started immediately instead of waiting. Honey buzzes in happiness when she feels the Emperor accept, and the wagging of Leo's tail says his own request went well, too.

"They'll be slow, but they're on their way. Good idea with the slimes, too. I can't forget that reinforcements are days away, so it's good to keep the denizens healthy and able to fight. Hopefully, the slimes and wyrms both will work out."

Honey nods at that, letting her attention drift to the map. "You said you think the drones are looking for a weakness? Have you found any on your own?" The first step to fixing a problem is to identify it, after all.

Leo gives a soft growl of frustration. "Yes and no. The entire northern border feels like a weakness. There's just too much area to try to actually defend on short notice. There are a few good defensive positions, so we can secure the area between them.

"If we're able to reinforce those spots, I'd expect them to make an actual effort in attacking around A-14 or so. That whole area is pretty flat and boring woodland; there's no real mountains or even hills there, nor any bodies of water or other hindrances. It'll take longer than we probably have to be able to actually make it defensible."

Honey looks at the section, and she has to agree with Leo's estimation. There's not a whole lot in the area to actually make a proper defense. Hmm.

"What about the foxes?" she asks, and Leo tilts his head in confusion at the non sequitur.

"What?"

"The foxes and their illusions. They could make the area look less vulnerable."

Leo considers that for a few moments before a grin starts to form on his muzzle.

"No . . . we'll make it look vulnerable on purpose. Even if the wyrms can't handle the snow, we can work on clearing that section, and they can prepare all sorts of nastiness that the foxes can hide. We'll put up what looks like a paltry defense of the area, like we're spread too thin and don't have the resources to fortify it, when in reality it'll be a killing field."

His grin fades as he thinks it over a bit more, and he shrugs as he continues. "Assuming the foxes can keep an illusion up over that area for as long as we need it. I'll also need to ensure the patrols closer to the borders are thick so they can't get too good a look at the area while we prepare."

Honey nods at that and returns to the small hive, both to get the reports from her bees and to update her notes. Perhaps even more interesting than the knowledge of nature and the dungeon is that of battle.

The Emperor seems to think it's more of an art than a science, and little flashes of wisdom sometimes drift through the bond. She has to admit there is a certain beauty to the wisdom of how to fight on a large scale, and she's more than happy to write every scrap down so she doesn't forget it.

Chapter 18

I had been considering not bothering Tarl with the weird invaders, since I'm pretty sure he won't know what they are either, but he should at least have a better idea of just how *bad* they are, and might have an inkling of what we might be dealing with, too.

I almost need to have Fluffles drag Teemo away from Yvonne and their playing with the arrows, but reminding them it's day now helps them figure out how long they were playing with the new toy. I think the reminder also made Yvonne aware of the soreness in her arms, which she had been ignoring, so she's back at the guild for another bath or massage.

I ask Thing to copy Honey's notes so Teemo can deliver them to Tarl and the rest of the ODA. While I'll be keeping secret the fact that the thing's type isn't the first otherworldly thing I've been involved with, I don't mind the guild at large knowing about something this potentially dangerous. If the worst happens, they have a lot more resources at their disposal than I do.

Teemo gets a lift from Poe, who I think actually enjoys visiting the various people around town. He doesn't get a chance to do it often, but it could help the big bird come out of his shell a bit.

He pecks at the door then waits, and soon, Tarl opens it.

"I thought it might have been you again, Poe. You're the only one who bothers to knock. Teemo usually just barges in."

"Hey! I'm not big enough to barge anywhere! I *slip* in, thank you very much!" declares my Voice with mock indignation, much to Tarl's amusement.

"Ah, of course. How're you doing, Teemo? Oh, please come in. Are you going to stay as well, Poe?" asks the elf, and I can feel Poe asking for direction.

You can hang out if you want. The returning expedition can wait for you. Most of the home scouting isn't in any real rush.

He's a bit conflicted, but eventually decides to stay, following Tarl in with Teemo still on his back.

"How was your trip, Teemo? I would have tried to check in on you earlier, but having an apprentice is more work than I expected."

Berdol looks up from his books and notes, giving Tarl a glower to try to hide a happy smirk. "*Being* an apprentice is a lot more work than I expected, too! I can't even remember the last time I had *homework*!"

That earns smiles from everyone, and Telar speaks up from her desk as she stands. "How do you take your tea, Marshal Poe? The kettle needs filling, so I may as well prepare some for everyone."

Poe looks a bit lost, but Teemo is there to rescue him. "I think he'd probably like it straight, but with some of those cookies. I like mine with plenty of honey, please. In a thimble, if you can manage."

Telar nods and heads into the back, already knowing how her coworkers like their tea. Tarl relaxes at his desk, motioning for Poe to take a seat. Poe looks at the chair then at Tarl with a bird smirk before simply pushing it aside to settle himself.

Tarl shakes his head. "I'm going to need to get a perch, aren't I? Anyway, what brings you both? With both the Voice and the Marshal, should I have my recording stone? Or should I very specifically *not* use my recording stone?"

"This can be as official as you'd like. The Boss has asked around a bit already, but nobody has had much in the way of answers. If your guild doesn't know about these things, they probably should start learning. Take a look," he says, hopping onto the desk, where he sets the copy of Honey's notes.

Tarl looks confused for a moment, then continues to look confused as he takes a closer look. "What is it? I'd ask if Thedeim did something weird again, but if this was one of his, he'd probably bring one along, maybe introduce his latest scion, instead of showing me these."

"Those are the invaders the Southwood is dealing with," states Teemo, not quite dropping the bombshell just yet.

"Invaders?" Tarl scans the notes more closely, even motioning for Telar to examine them when she comes with the tea.

"I'm not familiar, I'm afraid," she admits. "I've always been more focused on the paperwork and regulations rather than the fieldwork."

Tarl starts frowning as he keeps reading, soon turning his eyes back to Teemo. "This is an invader? I've never seen one like this. The closest I've ever even heard of was from a murderous dungeon that specialized in insects. But something about this one doesn't seem right."

Teemo nods. "Yvonne and Honey both say they don't have a real stomach, and no way to reproduce."

Tarl's frown deepens as Berdol looks over the notes, though he doesn't seem to have any new insight.

"That's not how dungeon spawn is supposed to work," explains Tarl. "Every other denizen has at least the parts for reproducing in their own way, even if they don't work quite right. I've heard scholars say it's because they're based on life in all its forms, and life always seeks to make more life."

"There's more," Teemo says, speaking up. "And this is the part the ODA at large will probably be the most interested in: Its type is unknown. Not that it's listed as *unknown*, either. It's a weird void, and the Southwood and the Boss are both stumped on what that actually means."

Tarl's eyes widen at that, while Berdol and Telar look confused. "Like it's been redacted?" asks Telar. Teemo shakes his head.

"It's not just a blank. There's *something* there, but it hurts to look at."

"What's Thedeim's plan to deal with them?" asks Tarl, looking a bit haunted.

Teemo shrugs. "Stop them; probably try to wipe them out. The Boss says they look like disposable warriors of some kind, and Yvonne agrees. We don't know if they're a normal invader or sent by some dungeon, but they need to be dealt with. The Boss was actually hoping you'd be able to give some insight on what could make them?"

Tarl relaxes slightly when Teemo tells him these are one of the few things I'm not willing to "live and let live" with, then grimaces when Teemo asks about their potential origin.

"I can't say for sure what could be the source. If I had to guess, I'd say they're from a dungeon. Ordinary monsters are pretty well documented, and even if it were something new, it would still have some kind of type that we could make sense of. It being from a dungeon only makes slightly more sense, and even that is just because dungeons can sometimes do weird things."

He chuckles as he meets Teemo's eyes. "Thedeim has a lot of weirdness, but he doesn't have exclusive access. If it *is* a dungeon, he should be careful."

Teemo nods at that. "That's why we're telling you, and hope you'll tell the guild at large, too. Getting the word out could be important."

Tarl looks thoughtful for a few more moments before standing. "Well, why don't I escort you back to Thedeim then, Teemo? Poe can stay and see how he likes tea and biscuits, unless he has other pressing business?"

Poe shakes his head as he eyes the tea tray, curious about the little snacks on it. Teemo shrugs. "Sure. I'll leave the notes here; they're a copy of the ones the Boss has."

With that, he hops onto Tarl's open hand, and the two start walking back to me, with Tarl speaking up once they're out on the street, though he keeps his voice lowered.

"Can I speak with you in your Sanctum, please?"

Teemo gives him a sideways look. "Sure. Got something important to talk about?"

"Yes," is his simple reply. That kind of terseness usually means something big, so we should probably get on that.

Once back inside my borders, Teemo leads him through a long series of shortcuts—not so much to disorient him but to ensure anyone following will be fully lost—before taking him to my Sanctum. Once there, Tarl doesn't mince words.

"Thedeim knows what these things are, doesn't he?"

Me and Teemo are both surprised at that, and confused. "No? What makes you think he does?"

Tarl stares at Teemo for a few long seconds, then deflates, slumping into a chair.

"That night, when I looked at his core. I saw a vision. A vision of cities the size of small nations, of potent and wondrous artifice in everyday life, of towering spires of glass that would blot out the sky just as much as they reflected it. And I saw . . . weird voids shaped like people living their lives. The way you describe the invader's type, it seems like the same kind of void.

"I was starting to think it was just some weirdness of the vision showing me some kind of lost age that Thedeim is from, maybe even of his own dwellers at some point; I don't know. But the way you describe the type . . . it's the same kind of thing, isn't it?"

I really wish I could exchange a look with Teemo right now, but even if I could, I don't think he'd have much advice for what to tell him. How would I explain where I came from? I tried once with Aranya and Yvonne, but I don't think they quite got it either.

But there's no real point in dwelling on my origin, especially when I can't explain it in any way that makes sense.

"He says the things in your vision are not the invader. At first, he thought they might be warped versions, but there's practically nothing in common aside from the weird . . . barrier, I guess? The Boss thinks they're from somewhere else. Somewhere *sideways*? It's a weird concept of his; basically, a place that's not here. And *here* doesn't want those things here either, hence why the barrier."

"Can he beat them?" asks Tarl, looking like he's not certain he wants to know the answer.

"He's sure going to try. And if he can't . . . Well, that's why he wanted to get those notes to the rest of your guild. If we can't handle them, maybe they can."

Tarl glances toward the entrance to the bedrooms and my core, and slowly shakes his head. "You have more confidence in the guild than I do."

Chapter 19

Despite Tarl's pessimism, I'm pretty confident the ODA can do *something* if things really go pear-shaped, even if it only ends up being an early warning. Of course, I'm still going to do my best to keep things under control. It's difficult to not wonder about Tarl's vision, though.

How much of Earth did he see? How much did he understand? How much detail could he glean about the voids? If they were clear silhouettes, that doesn't hide all that much, honestly.

Well, whatever he saw, he has trouble describing it, so I guess it's a moot point. Still, it nibbles at my curiosity.

I'm going to need to ignore it for now, and probably for later, too. The search for Aranya's old dungeon and the source of the weird invaders are both important enough that I should try to keep distractions to a minimum. Scouts are still scouting underground and not finding anything resembling an actual trail yet, so everything is normal on that front.

The other front, on the other hand, is turning into a proper one over with the Southwood. Honey and Leo requested some wyrms and healing slimes, which I sent pretty much immediately. They're both a bit slow to move but should get there in another day or two. The wolves should be reinforcing the lines a lot better, since I upgraded the spawner. I'm tempted to spend mana there until I get the next variety of wolf, but I hold off for now.

Instead, I decide to send a bit of everything to help reinforce too. I don't think the normal leafcutter ants will be able to do much, but I'll leave that to Leo. Maybe he'll come up with some novel use for them. Honestly, even just using them to help the Southwood's herbalism nodes probably wouldn't be a terrible idea.

Sending a bit of everything is mostly because of a good bit of wisdom I first heard in a terrible movie: I'd rather have it and not need it than need it and not have it. I don't think it saved the character in the movie, but it's still good advice.

As for what I expect Leo will use the reinforcements for, I don't know specifically, but I get the feeling the other shoe is getting ready to drop up there. Things have been progressing pretty smoothly, with the tundra wolves being great at hit-and-run kind of tactics.

I'd like to think it's just tactical expertise on Leo's part, and honestly the ease and success of what he's doing there is thanks to that, but the invaders will have to start adapting to the change eventually, right?

I dunno; I just don't like it. I don't think Leo likes it either, and even Honey seems to feel the growing tension in the air. Leo's even changing the plans for the defense, at least a little. Before, I think he was going to try to be subtle and nudge attacks and potential observers away from the planned illusory killing field, but I think he's tossing subtle out the window, at least as far as keeping the invaders well away from the border goes.

He has enough scouts and forces now to be able to project a stronger presence outside Southwood's territory, and with having pushed the invaders back a bit, he can be more proactive about keeping them away. With them not able to get close, the work can continue quicker, now that they don't need to be subtle about it.

I think speed is going to be important, too. If they're putting up less of a fight, they might be trying to gather their forces to make a more concentrated assault instead of the semirandom attacks all over the place.

. . . Maybe I should see if Rocky wants to go help. I've been keeping him and Fluffles here in case we suddenly trip over Aranya's old dungeon, but that's looking less and less likely. I want to keep Fluffles close still, just in case, but it shouldn't be too risky to send Rocky.

I could maybe try to send Slash, too, but I think I'll keep him close as well. His music would be a great way to help keep my dwellers safe if fighting erupts around here. The only other I might send would be Nova, but I think I'd like her to stick close until she's a bit more experienced. And I'm not sure she has the temperament for a long expedition and constant fighting.

Yeah, let's see if Rocky wants to head out with the sampler pack of reinforcements.

I'll need Teemo, who looks like he's just relaxing with Yvonne as she tests some more bows. The first prototype was basically all steel, which makes it a bit heavy but easily able to handle the forces. A little enchanting by Thing is enough to make it light enough to carry around, but we also have those fancy new magical metal nodes.

Right now, she's just methodically going through every combination of metals for both the body and the arms as we can think of, looking for the best mix of weight, strength, and cost. Engineering wisdom says you can pick two, but there's a bit of wiggle room as we find the balance.

Hey, Teemo, can you go talk to Rocky for me?

"Sure, Boss. The bees have all the writing handled. Hey, Yvonne!"

"Hmm?" She looks up from assembling the latest combination of body and arm.

"The Boss needs me to go talk to Rocky. You good here without me?"

She smiles and waves him off, returning her focus to the bow. "I'll be fine. Just make sure he keeps some healing ants around to help with my shoulders. I'm enjoying the process, but I'll get sore without some of their help."

I make sure to send in some more ants as Teemo heads down a shortcut. Queen would usually handle them, but she's up to her gaster in the alchemical traps in the lava labyrinth, so I can deal with it on my own.

My favorite zombie is enjoying himself in his arena, currently beating the sand out of a heavy bag. I need to have Thing enchant something to be strong enough for Rocky to punch regularly, but it'll have to be pretty low priority for now.

Teemo exits his shortcut atop a turnbuckle, shouting, "Hey, Rocky! Leave that poor bag alone! What'd it ever do to you?"

Rocky laughs and gives the bag a stay of execution as he walks over to my Voice.

"Heya, Rock. The Boss wants to know if you want to head to the Southwood and lend a hand with the defense? Nah, nothing is going particularly bad there; the Boss just wants to make sure everything will be fine."

Rocky chews on his mouthguard as he thinks, grunting a question.

"Will he be in his lich outfit?"

Eh . . . up to him, really. If he wants to, he could even go there in the disguise, and drop it if the fighting calls for it.

Teemo repeats my words, and Rocky thinks a bit more. I'm going to need to send a few extra mouthguards for him, too.

Another grunted question, which Teemo doesn't bother translating straight to me.

"Nah, everything should be safe around here. He wanted to keep you here in case we found the dungeon Aranya fled, but it's looking like that's going to take longer than expected. Besides, even if things do get dicey, we'll still have Fluffles and Slash, not to mention Tiny and Poe. Nova can probably handle a good fight, too."

Rocky nods at that, rubbing his chin with his gloved hand before giving a firm nod.

"Great! You're gonna pretend to be a lich at first, then?"

My zombie nods again and starts digging around beneath the ring, where he presumably keeps his stuff.

Don't sell yourself short when it comes to fighting, too, Teemo. You handled the Stag like a pro.

My Voice just shrugs. "Eh, maybe, but in a real fight, I don't know how well I'd do."

I think it was a real enough fight for the Stag.

Teemo grins. "Yeah, but not for me. He's strong, sure, but he's slow enough I probably could have dodged everything even without shortcuts."

That sounds to me like you'd be pretty good in a fight, then.

Teemo raises a finger to argue the point, but lets it droop as he fails to find a good argument. After a few seconds, he just huffs and folds his arms.

Hey, I'm not going to go throwing you on the front lines or anything. I'm just pointing out a fact.

"Yeah, but I'm the one who's supposed to knock *you* down a peg or two and point out what you're missing. You're not supposed to do that to me!"

Rocky grunts as he pulls his black robe out from under the ring, giving Teemo a curious look.

"Nah, not you, Rocky. The Boss is pointing out facts that I don't like."

My Boxer grunts and gets his gloves off to slip on the robe, and Teemo smirks at what he said.

"That's fair. Facts don't really care if I like them or not, and it's not a great idea to try to ignore them. You gonna practice your affinities on the way there?"

Another nod and another grunt has Teemo tapping his own chin. "A staff with an orange ball? I bet you Larx can help with that. You might be able to get Thing to do a few quick enchants on it, too."

Rocky grunts again, and Teemo laughs. "That's also fair! You gotta look the part! If you're going to rope a dope, it helps to lean into it a bit!"

Chapter 20

Rocky

The undead scion smiles as he walks with the large group of denizens. His day has been very good so far! First, Coach asked him if he wanted to help with the Southwood, which of course Rocky does. He didn't just jump at the chance, however. He had been thinking about why Coach Thedeim hadn't sent him earlier, and had decided Coach must want him to help if anything happened here.

Teemo said it was fine, though, so Rocky was happy to accept! He even got to put on a new outfit, which he finds he enjoys more than he thought he would. He remembers back when he was first spawned and given his basic boxing gear. He was so confused, not understanding why there were so many rules for how he should dress and act!

It barely took a week before he felt the changes in his movement, and though he's tried to teach some of the zombie denizens, he's pretty sure they'll never manage more than a hastened shuffle. Maybe if he gets the aranea to make some gloves and shorts for them, they might improve? Denizens grow much differently from scions.

What was he thinking about? Right, dressing up.

He also enjoyed putting on the show for Hullbreak and pretending to be a lich. He thinks he has a bad build for a lich, but if someone sees an undead with skin and fancy magic, they're not going to notice or care if he has a bit more muscle than he should. He also learned a lot about how people see liches, or at least ones dressed like he was.

Sure, he likes to cut a powerful figure, but most people are pretty scared of liches. He thinks the new staff will help soften the fear at least a little. Instead of some gnarled, blackened thing, it's a fairly simple staff, polished and stained to bring out the natural wood color, with a large orange orb affixed to the top. Thing was even able to add a few simple enchantments to it before Rocky had to go.

He'll have to strengthen it with a lot of Kinetic energy if he wants to whack anyone with it, but if anything gets that close, he'd rather just punch it.

Not that he expects much to get that close. There's no false pride in his control over Fire, Ice, and Kinetic affinities. He could probably fight with his arms folded, but that's just not as fun. Of course, to keep his lich disguise, he might need to do exactly that.

Though speaking of his lich disguise, he has another addition that the Coach cooked up: a wide hat made of aranea silk. Teemo said he looks like Rocky the White, or maybe the Wight, and he and the Coach chuckled at what Rocky can only think was a pun.

Coach has a lot of weird things in his mind, and Rocky is glad he only gets fleeting glimpses. He remembers Teemo having nosebleeds and headaches until he got used to what Coach knows, and Rocky is pretty sure his own rotten brain would have melted out his ears and then exploded.

He's fairly convinced the only reason it hasn't done that anyway is that Rocky doesn't understand a lot of what the Coach thinks, even if Teemo says he does more than anyone besides himself. Rocky just understands what the Coach thinks about magic. He even understands that Coach doesn't think of it *as* magic, which was a weird thought to wrap his mind around.

He's pretty sure it's also why he has such an easy time expanding his affinities. He suspects everyone else is still thinking of magic first. Maybe Rocky's success is because he understands what can be done without it.

Well, that's probably overstating it. Coda probably understands that even more than he does, just in a different way. The Bat Scion knows how to apply it. Rocky can move thermal energy around, but if he understands what Coda showed him on paper once, he can use that to do all sorts of weird things.

Not that Rocky is short on his own weird things. After sparring with Fluffles, he's almost certain he could dip into Sound and Lightning affinities whenever he wants. He might be able to manage actual Storm affinity too, but he'll leave that for later.

He's not quite sure what Storm actually encompasses, so he wouldn't want to have the wrong idea and have his magic picked apart by someone who knows what they're doing. Like Rhonda.

He smiles wider and lets his focus drift to the theory for sound and lightning as he remembers her stealing away his control over thermal energy and earning her class. The faceplant wasn't his most dignified moment, but her finally *getting it* was worth it. If he can get these two affinities under his belt, he'll have some more tricks to show her, too.

He lets the butt of his staff hit any rocks on the way as he walks with the others and brings his Kinetic affinity to bear. Stuff is made of stuff; even the air is some kind of stuff. Coach thinks of sound like the ocean, like how the waves move. It seems weird, but he can feel the air moving from the sound, though in a different way than how it moves for wind.

Oh, he can probably get Wind affinity too. That should be a good set to bring back, if he can figure them out.

He lets his mind drift as he feels and listens, likening the movement to how his other affinities behave. Ice and Fire move without going anywhere, like ducking and weaving while keeping his feet planted in a stable stance. Kinetic is taking a step, actually moving. He can even do both, walking and weaving, and he fights himself to not actually slip into his boxing stance as he walks.

Instead, he creates an orb of fire and of ice, and has them dance around the head of his staff as he feels out the sound and how to control it.

He's pretty sure it's closer to Kinetic affinity, but there's something more. He even puts a smidgeon of kinetic energy into the next rock, and though it makes a louder sound, he knows it's just because it had more energy behind it. So what's the difference?

Kinetic can move things. He could even transfer kinetic energy without moving . . . mostly. He's punched a rock into another rock before, and gotten the new rock to move. He's even done a chain of them, but that's still not enough to give the secret to Sonic affinity.

Remember what Coach said: ocean.

Sonic is salty? Rocky snorts and shakes his head. No, probably not that. How does the ocean move? Kinda up and down and side to side? He's seen boats bob on the waves, and even when anchored, they still move around a bit. He feels for that kind of pattern as he smacks rocks with the butt of his staff, and starts to slowly feel something.

It is a bit like the movement of the ocean, but more complicated.

Well, when things are too complicated, narrow your focus. The big picture can be overwhelming, but take it in bits, and you'll get there eventually.

He spends quite some time adjusting his sensing, looking at what he's feeling from every angle, changing how much he looks at, spending hours trying to find the ocean in the sound.

There it is! If he *flattens* his perspective, the air moves like the waves of the ocean. Is that sound?

He can feel he's onto something, and he grins once more as he recognizes the feeling of being on the verge of a new affinity. He just needs to cement his understanding. To do that, he needs to look at the big picture again.

Now that he knows how to find the ocean in the sound, it's pretty simple to see why he was having troubles when he first tried. The ocean is mostly flat, but these waves even go up instead of just out!

More hours are spent recreating the weird wiggling ball that is sound in his mind.

He doesn't manage to recreate it with his Kinetic affinity the first time, just managing to swirl some dirt and dust around. He wonders why that didn't get him Wind affinity, but quickly pushes that thought aside. He needs to focus on Sonic first, then he can try to figure out Wind.

After the dozenth failure, he at least comes to understand what might be his problem: hitting the different rocks makes slightly different sounds. He can feel the differences now, even if he still can't mimic them yet, so he picks up a stone and hits that against his staff, letting him have the same sound each time.

The denizens give him confused looks, but none bother him. If the scion wants to hit a rock against a staff as they all head for the Southwood, why stop him?

With a more consistent model to work with, Rocky feels more and more confident with his effort. As the sun starts to rise, the sound of a rock hitting a staff rings once more. This time, however, there was no contact.

Rocky smiles in satisfaction as the new affinity takes root, and he finally understands what Coach meant when he said fire and sound are inefficiencies from applying kinetic energy. He's known the explanation for fire for a while, as that moving energy gets wasted by letting the stuff wiggle more. Now that he understands the Sonic affinity, he can see more energy escaping without doing anything useful besides making noise.

Just making noise sounds fun, now that he has an affinity for that, and so that's what he does.

He starts mimicking sounds around him as he walks, just getting used to his new affinity. He'll probably want to talk with Slash about it once he gets back. He might even be able to talk to him about lightning, too. His axe uses a lot of it, and that's how he makes his music, along with using his Earth affinity to make the very ground sound like drums.

As entertaining as the new affinity is, Rocky is eager to master it and learn to apply it in a fight. He can also feel something about Sonic affinity that will help him with Wind, but he'll focus on that later.

For now, he's figured out how to mimic a fart, and he's going to get as much enjoyment out of that as he can. If Coach asks, it's an easy sound to make, so he can more easily practice his mastery with it.

That he can make it sound like all the denizens ate a bunch of beans is just a happy coincidence.

Chapter 21

Rezlar

The young noble isn't certain how he feels about paperwork. He certainly prefers it to peoplework, but that's not really saying much. He feels more confident about getting back in the ring with Rocky than he does about talking to people. His acting at being one of his own guards is helping with that a bit, but he's long come to terms with the fact that he'll never be the boisterous, outgoing type.

On the other hand, he is feeling less fond of paperwork as of late, probably because there's been more of it. Requests for funding for the small hold, reports for the proposed financial incentives to delve Thedeim more over the winter so as to help with the problem the Southwood is having, complaints from the mason's guild about certain members being barred from participating in building Hullbreak's lighthouse . . .

He has to smile a bit at that particular letter. He even got some catharsis by penning a reply telling the guild that, if they had a method to force any dungeon to allow a member to join, let alone Thedeim, he'd love to hear it. Of course, he tossed that draft into the hearth and wrote a lot of words that came to the same sentiment, just much more diplomatically.

He should see if Rhonda and Freddie would like to go see the lighthouse being built. They still need to do the follow-up delve in Hullbreak for whatever it is Rhonda needs. Bubble kelp? Bubble weed? He's pretty sure it's bubble something, and he's positive it'll be on her shoulders for them to get the correct ingredient.

The pleasant thoughts of delving with his friends fade as he looks at the letter he received from the crown. He doubts the king himself wrote it, but he may as well have for all the power Rezlar has to stop it. At least it probably won't be too much trouble; it's just a basic audit.

In hindsight, he probably should have expected something like this. Tax revenue this year was up sharply thanks to Thedeim. That kind of change in money is going to draw attention, even if everything is fully legitimate.

Which, as far as Rezlar can tell, everything is. Oh, he's sure there's some minor embezzlement and other financial wrongdoing going on, but whatever people may be doing it, they're keeping it subtle enough for him not to need to worry. He wouldn't even put it past Miller to have, if not a hand in most of it, to at least be keeping an eye on it.

Much as it irks his sensibilities, that kind of thing simply can't be fully snuffed out, so it's better to keep it manageable and not let it get obvious enough for a *real* audit to be called.

Still, he should probably put into his schedule some time to check the books himself. He can't rely on Miller to do all the work, and being able to spot accounting oddities is one of his duties as lord mayor.

But he should have plenty of time. If it's secretly a deep audit, it'll look better for him if they don't show up in a week to find him tearing through his ledgers. No, he'll take a look in a few weeks, probably after the Hullbreak delve. Any potential spies can see he's not worried, and he's more than happy to waste the time of imagined onlookers.

For the rest of today . . . he actually would like to visit the Church of the Crystal Shield. He'd like to hear their opinion on Thedeim and the fact he has worshipers, and what Rezlar should actually do about that. Not that he intends to interfere, but he doesn't want to accidentally upset someone like Thedeim even as a dungeon, let alone as a potential deity.

He misses when he could stay out of theology altogether, but at least getting involved with Thedeim earned him his two dearest friends. He can step out of his comfort zone to ensure he doesn't somehow make a mistake that turns Thedeim against them, let alone the town as a whole.

It seems pretty unlikely, but he'd rather know too much than not enough. He had sent out a message early in the morning asking if he could have some of Head Priest Torlon's time, and received a reply not long ago that he would be more than happy to receive Rezlar after lunch, or even during, should he desire.

He'd prefer the informality of a meeting after lunch, and so sent the reply. A luncheon is always so weighed down by etiquette and formality. A lunch between friends is one thing, but he doesn't think he quite knows the kindly priest well enough for an informal meal.

"Is the young master ready to go?" asks Miller as he enters the room, tidying and organizing the mess it tends to get into when Rezlar is attending to the duties of his position.

"I think so, Miller. Is my horse ready?"

If he were going as Larrez, he'd just walk, but nobles are expected to walk as little as possible. He remembers asking Miller about it when he was much younger and getting a smirk with the reply that, should a noble be in the rough position of not having a cushion upon which to rest their rear end, one should have enough padding to make do. The memory still brings a smile to his face.

"Of course, sir. White Waves is freshly brushed and awaiting you."

"Thank you, Miller," replies the young noble with a smile, looking forward to riding White Waves; he gets so little chance to take him out. His gait is incredibly smooth, better than any other horse's he's had, hence the name. Riding him—at a walk or at a gallop—is like riding gentle ocean waves.

"Why don't you have a horse?" he asks, realizing he's never seen his butler in a saddle. He thinks he actually surprised the older elf, as it takes him a few moments longer than usual to respond.

"Horses and I . . . only ever get along professionally at best, Young Master. They'll obey me when I drive the carriage or when I put them up or wipe them down, but they have never accepted carrying me. And to be frank, Young Master, I prefer my own two feet to their four," he soon answers, smirking at the end.

"Ah, that's interesting. Though that does make me wonder how you always get everywhere before me when I'm riding."

The butler gives a small smile to his charge. "That's a professional secret, I'm afraid, Young Master, only known to the most secretive ranks of the butling elite." Rezlar still isn't certain if Miller is joking when he talks like that, but at this point, he doesn't want to know either way. He wouldn't want the joke to die, nor would he like to dwell on the implications of the "butling elite."

He has enough vaguely powerful things to try to understand, which is what this whole meeting is for anyway.

It doesn't take him long to ride to the church, and the handlers there easily accept White Waves with no trouble. Before long, he enters the priest's personal rooms, finding the gnome relaxing in a plush chair with a book. He marks his place and smiles at Rezlar once he enters.

"Ah, Lord Mayor! To what do I owe the pleasure? I admit I was surprised to receive your request with my breakfast. Please, have a seat. Would you like something to drink?"

Rezlar sits down on the wide couch and politely shakes his head. "No, but thank you. And please, just Rezlar. I wanted to ask about . . . Well, a lot of things, actually."

Torlon smiles and takes his seat once more. "I take it you're not about to ask to take the initiate oaths?" he asks with a smirk, and Rezlar shakes his head.

"Uh . . . no. I mean, I appreciate what you and the church do, it's just . . ."

Torlon laughs and waves a hand. "I know, I know; it's just not for you. Honestly, it's not for most people, and a good priest needs to understand that. But I think your actual questions are along a similar vein?"

Rezlar sighs and nods. "I usually try to stay beneath the attention of any gods, but . . . did you know Thedeim is one?"

"Ah," says Torlon, like that question explains everything. "Well, you've stumbled into a question all clergy have to eventually wrestle with: what *is* a god? It's one of the few questions the gods never even acknowledge, let alone answer."

Rezlar furrows his brow at that. "What? But . . ." Torlon's laugh interrupts him again.

"Nobody knows why they don't respond, either. Some gods are more than happy to answer questions, but they all ignore that particular one, which only raises even more questions. Personally, I believe it has something to do with how Faith magic works."

Rezlar looks lost but stays quiet to let the priest continue.

"Most people think it must work like Arcane magic, or even like Martial magic, but just like those two are different, so is Faith. Arcane magic is about understanding the world and how it works, and how your affinity works in the world. From what I can tell of Martial magic, it's about understanding yourself and exemplifying your affinity in yourself. Faith magic is . . ."

He trails off for a moment, looking for the proper words, or maybe to see if Rezlar is following. The elf noble is leaning forward on the couch now, listening to every word, and Torlon smiles as he continues.

"Faith magic is more about *accepting* and striving for an ideal. Not everyone finds their ideal in a god. Even here in the church, it could be more accurate to say some people's faith is more in a concept than the Shield. But gods are the most common ideal of faith, because they encompass so many domains. That the Shield is protection is no surprise, and many paladins may be placing their faith more in that than in the Shield itself."

Rezlar is back to looking confused at that, and Torlon laughs again. "It sounds a bit heretical, doesn't it? But I think that the Shield provides guidance not just in how to protect but *why* to protect, and placing one's faith in a specific aspect of the Shield doesn't lessen anyone involved. Which brings us back to your question about Thedeim.

"I don't think he's actually a god, though as a focus of faith, the difference is a bit academic. I think he's handling it rather well, especially with how he seems to be trying his best to handle it as little as possible, heh."

"What?" escapes Rezlar's lips before he can stop it. He's handling it by not handling it at all? How does that make any sense?!

Torlon just smirks. "What would you do if it were you?"

"What?" says Rezlar again, confused to have a question aimed at him.

"What if you were suddenly the focus of someone's faith? If someone believed so utterly in what you do that their magic is focused by it." He laughs again as the elf blanches. "You couldn't even tell them to stop it! Someone with that kind of faith in you, they'd think they had done something wrong!

"So now you have quite a lot of control over someone's actions, and I think as a noble, you might understand the weight of that responsibility better than most, and the temptations of abusing that responsibility."

Rezlar slowly nods, and Torlon nods as well. "Yes, something like that can cause a lot of trouble. Dark cults and more happen when someone misuses that kind of trust and faith. But I've talked with both Aranya and Larx, and Thedeim has set really only one rule, and I think he could have done a lot worse."

"What rule?"

"To love. To care, honestly and deeply, about the well-being of others." Torlon chuckles and shakes his head. "A simple command . . . and yet, not a simple command at all, really."

Chapter 22

~~Rezlar~~ Larrez

The discussion about deities occupies Rezlar's thoughts as he returns home, making him wonder if he should try to attend some services regularly. He'll need to talk to Larx, or maybe even Lady Aranya, to see if they're willing to talk more, too. He may even try to attend to both faiths, at least to a degree.

He doubts he'll ever devote himself to anything wholly enough to change how he works his magic, but both the Shield and Thedeim aren't quite so intimidating to him anymore.

That will have to come later, however. He has the rest of the afternoon free, and he would very much like to see if Freddie and Rhonda might like to go delve Hullbreak.

The very idea makes him chuckle. If someone had suggested that just a few months ago, he'd have thought them mad! But now it's no more abnormal than any other friendly activity.

When he puts away White Waves, he wonders if he might be able to disguise the horse in some way, too, but has to regretfully abandon that idea. It would just stretch believability, and there's no simple disguise that would hide the health and breeding of the horse. No, he'll have to settle for the brief forays rather than joining Rezlar and his friends on adventures.

Besides, an ocean is no place for a horse, even if the horse is named for it.

It doesn't take long for Rezlar to get changed, and soon, Larrez is walking down the street to go meet his friends. He heads to the church first, and is relieved to hear Freddie is simply reading in his room. He always feels a bit bad interrupting the young paladin's training.

Freddie has his door open in an effort to get some of the warmth from the various hearths into his room, as he doesn't have a personal fireplace. Larrez knocks on the frame as he looks in, seeing Freddie relaxing on his bed, with Fiona fussing over his shield.

"Hello, Freddie, Fiona. I hope I'm not interrupting?"

Freddie smiles and marks his place as he shakes his head. "Nah. I'm just reading some old accounts from the archives. I think the priests like to pretend they're boring history, but they read like fantastical stories." He smirks over at Fiona as she chitters to herself, refreshing the web on his shield. "Fiona's trying a new design, but it's not coming out quite how she wants. It'll be fine, Fiona. It's not like I actually have any heraldry in the first place!"

The large spider gives him a scandalized chitter as she keeps working, and Freddie laughs as he turns his attention back to Larrez. "She says that's all the more reason to keep looking for the right one, so it'll be ready when I *do* get it."

"Do you get to design your own?" asks Larrez, honestly uncertain how that kind of thing works. He knows all about displaying and the meaning behind heraldry, but he doesn't know about making your own.

Freddie just shrugs. "Most paladins either take the symbols of the church or just use their shield. I was actually reading about Vory of the Torn Banner and his heraldry. He and his fellows would often suffer hardly a scratch in battles, but his banner would always get ruined in some way. A lance would tear a gash in it, arrows would perforate it, stray spells would singe or even melt some of it, and so on.

"So, before one battle, he took his sword and rent his banner from the center to the bottom. Some say it was out of frustration, some say it was a bit of humor to lighten the mood before the fight. Whatever the reason, no other damage happened to it in that fight. He used that same banner for the rest of his career."

"Huh." Larrez looks over at the book, wondering if he can get a copy for himself later. It sounds like an interesting tale. But he didn't come here to get distracted by stories. "Do you have the free time to go delve? Rhonda still needs to get the bubble . . . moss? From Hullbreak?"

"Bubbleweed, I think?" tries Freddie. "Whatever it is, it'll be on her to get the right stuff. And yeah, I should have plenty of time to delve today. Give me a few minutes to get ready, and I'll be right out."

"Alright. Do you think I could talk the archivist into letting me borrow some of the histories of the paladins?"

Freddie shrugs. "Maybe? I don't think they'll want to let the originals out, but there're probably some copies lying around done by the scribe acolytes. They have to practice their writing somehow, right?"

It can't hurt to ask, so Larrez does just that as Freddie prepares. As it turns out, they have some copies of shorter histories they could lend, though Larrez holds off for now; he wouldn't want to take a book into the sea. If he understands the variety of water potion Rhonda is working on, it will let them all breathe but won't keep them from getting wet. It'd be pretty rude to immediately ruin someone's work like that.

He's simply perusing the shelves when Freddie approaches. He can hear Fiona giving the orc an earful, and the orc trying not to interrupt the scribes with the noise. "Fiona, please keep it quiet at least until we're out of the archives? I know you said it's not ready, but I need my shield for this."

Larrez fails to suppress his smile as he sees Fiona fold her forelegs and humph at Freddie, but at least she's quiet for the moment. Freddie is looking a little embarrassed, so Larrez simply motions for them to exit, and soon they're on their way to Rhonda's. Fiona fusses over the shield on Freddie's back the entire time while the other two chat.

Once at the Emporium, Staiven greets the three warmly. "Ah, I was wondering when you two scoundrels would return to whisk my poor apprentice off to danger again!" Fiona chitters in response, and Staiven nods. "I know, my dear. You're the only responsible one out of the lot, and that includes Rhonda and Lucas," he says with a smile, whacking the hatch to the basement with his staff.

"Rhonda! Your friends are here!"

A muffled yell comes up, and Staiven quickly answers. "Just finish that bunch for now; I can hang them later. And bundle whatever's still loose. I think they want to go get the bubblekelp," he says before turning his attention back to the lads. "Unless you two just like to wear your full kit around town for some reason."

They shake their heads, and Staiven smiles. "Then she'll be up shortly. She's preparing some herbs for drying, and then you two can help her test her new potion."

Larrez and Freddie exchange looks at the mention of testing a new potion, but Rhonda bangs open the hatch before they can make any real movement toward the door.

"Freddie! Fiona! Larrez! Good timing! I'm pretty sure I've gotten all the kinks out of the equilibrium potion, which means we should be able to get the kelp so Master can make more proper Aqua-affinity potions! Let me get ready, and I'll explain on the way!"

Freddie's eyes follow her as she heads up the stairs, lingering for a few moments before Larrez brings his focus back to the here and now. "We could probably get away before she's done," he jokes.

Freddie smirks at his friend. "Only for a while. Fiona would probably help them catch us, too." Fiona nods and gives a no-nonsense clack of her mandibles.

"I suppose we're doomed, then," sighs the elf with mock defeat, and Freddie smiles at the stairs as he nods.

"There are worse fates."

Soon, Rhonda comes back down, but not in her typical robes. While not exactly indecent, they're much more formfitting than usual. Freddie tries not to stare as Larrez looks confused.

"Why the different robes? Are those even technically robes?"

Rhonda shrugs and heads for the door. "Technically, I think? I just know they work a lot better when wet than my normal robes, or even my adventuring ones. I haven't had a chance to enchant them with much, but Hullbreak is a lot friendlier now, so it should be fine."

Larrez elbows Freddie to get him into gear, and the orc shakes his head to clear it and focus. "When wet?"

Rhonda nods, waiting for everyone to step outside and start walking before she explains. "The Aqua-affinity potions are so great because you can basically take anything with you, and it'll be fine in the water. The water-breathing potions that Thedeim designed only let you breathe. They don't protect from all the water. With winter here now, it's especially important to get proper potions to delve Hullbreak, rather than what we'll be using."

"Then why are *we* using them?" asks Larrez. "Breathing might be fine, but that water is going to be *cold*."

Rhonda grins and pulls out an odd blueish-green potion. "That's what the equilibrium potion is for! I designed it with what I know about Fire and Ice affinities. Basically, it should keep you at a normal temperature no matter the environment!" She pauses for a moment before continuing. "Well, I don't think it'd work against something like lava or even boiling water, but it should make ordinarily dangerous temperatures feel almost pleasant!"

Freddie looks impressed. "That must have been difficult."

"It wasn— Okay, yeah, it was pretty hard, actually. The first batch was too insulating, like wearing a thick blanket next to a roaring fire. Then I made it too conductive, and even next to a fire felt like I was soaked to the bone and standing in the wind. I've made a few more batches since then, and this should be just right! We'll have to drink both a water-breathing and an equilibrium potion, and then just dive in. Make sure you don't have anything you can't get wet."

Larrez takes a few moments to go over his gear in his head. "I should be all right. With my affinity, I need to take some water into consideration anyway. I'll probably need to oil everything properly once we're done, but that should be it. How about you, Freddie?"

Freddie looks much less certain about his gear. "I don't know if my armor can stand up to being in the water for that long. But even if it can, I don't think I can swim in it anyway."

"Let's head by the church, then, and see if they have something leather or even cloth for you to wear," suggests Rhonda, to which Freddie nods.

"Probably a good idea, yeah. I might grab a short spear or something, too. I don't know how well my axe will work underwater."

Larrez speaks up almost immediately. "Swings underwater are difficult. Thrusts are the best."

"Then I think we'll be doubly reliant on you in the water, Larrez," says Rhonda with a smile. "For your affinity and your rapier. You'll probably be the best suited to any actual fighting we might need to do. If Hullbreak is learning from Thedeim, we'll probably have to overcome at least a few encounters to gather some bubblekelp, especially for the amount I want to get."

"How much do you want?" asks Freddie, looking mildly concerned.

"As much as we can carry!"

Everyone laughs at the obvious answer, and Freddie speaks up as the church comes into view.

"Then I'll also ask if they have any spare packs or maybe baskets. Something we can take underwater without too much trouble."

Chapter 23

Hullbreak

Getting used to lubbers—*delvers* again has been difficult, but Hullbreak can't act like it hasn't been better for his dwellers. Having his own mana to expand and work with has been a warm current to his mood, too. Despite his fears, his dwellers were not immediately gobbled up by some monstrosities from the deeps, nor fished up and smoked by the lubbers as a snack.

Some of his denizens have been, but that's their purpose, and it's been earning him some good mana. The gains have slowed with the cold of winter, but many lubbers still come to fish, at least. The underwater corals and clam beds don't see as much attention, but he gathers it's partially because of a shortage of potions. He's not quite certain what that has to do with it, but a lot of delvers complain about not getting to actually dive in without them.

Right, they need to breathe. And they don't move as well in the water as out. At least he can get some extra mana from the lighthouse construction. Not only does he gain a lot from the lubber masons following the directions of the Civil Artificer, but he gains a bit more with his crabs fighting what lubbers wander the island looking for fights.

He's pretty sure this is one of those mutually beneficial things Admiral Thedeim has talked about. The masons learn, he gets mana, the guards fight, he also gets mana, and he gets a lighthouse for better surface encounters. The only one who loses out is his Quartermaster, and even that is temporary. Once the lighthouse is complete, the Quartermaster can rebuild his nest at the top and maybe be a lookout, like how the Marshal watches over much of Admiral Thedeim's territory.

Speaking of the Admiral, Hullbreak can feel his attention on a dinghy just inside his borders. He follows, and curiously observes the three young lubbers.

One is green and large, while another is green and small. The third is rather tan, and seems to be dressed for delving. The other two don't seem quite as prepared, with the large green one looking uncomfortable in leathers that seem slightly too small. The small one looks ready to take a relaxing swim. There are also . . . what are the land not-crabs that make their own rigging?

Spiders! Yes, those.

He watches and listens as the large one rows, and he learns they intend to gather abundantly from his kelp fields. He's inclined to simply let them, especially with the warm feelings he can feel coming from the Admiral for the group.

Confusion seeps through the bond when Hullbreak turns his attention elsewhere, and he can only send confusion right back. After a few more volleys of mutual befuddlement, a question seeps through to Hullbreak.

Attack?

Friend? is his reply, and understanding seems to bloom in the Admiral, though Hullbreak still feels lost at sea.

Fight! Challenge! Fun!

The watery dungeon is slow to embrace the suggestion, but it makes more and more sense as the group continues to row deeper into his waters. Other delvers are expected to fight at least some. Hullbreak is still trying to wrap his mind around the idea of a fight being fun, even fights that cause injury, but the interactions with other lubbers only reinforces that concept, strange as it is.

He also gets suggestions for how to challenge this particular group. The Admiral points out many details, like how the large green one's size implies heavier armor, and the poor fit implies he's not at his best. The small green one is identified as primarily a mage, so armor isn't a priority for her in the first place.

Their stated goal also helps define how to challenge them: mostly harrying and harassing encounters on the surface, with a few stronger ones to guard each dense patch of kelp. They're a bit more than what would ordinarily be sent against gatherers, but the Admiral assures Hullbreak they can handle a good encounter. Just not *too* good. As always, test the limits and slowly ramp up.

He starts with a handful of his weakest gulls, watching as the small one and the tan one prepare for them. The large one continues to row, though he also seems to be keeping his eyes on the seas and the skies with the help of the spiders. The tan one takes some of the water and lifts it, shaping it into several thin swords, mimicking the one in his hand, and the small one creates a few small orbs of fire and lengths of ice.

"Swordfish Lunge!"

"Firebolt! Icicle!"

The water swords launch and devastate any birds they hit, and the fire and ice work to remove what gulls remain. He may need to try an actual swarm later if they're that good at dealing with the gulls. Still, it earns him mana, so he's content to keep the encounters fairly mild as a bit of a warm-up.

Eventually, the anchor is tossed over the side, and the group prepares to dive to the beds of kelp. The spiders appear to be staying on the small boat and will be hauling up baskets of the gathered plants using their strong silk. He takes a few minutes to investigate the silk rope, and while he's not very impressed with the knots, it should be serviceable enough.

Potions are drunk, and the three dive in, the tan one immediately drawing Hullbreak's attention. He's a Water affinity, and seemingly a pretty strong one.

He looks much more at ease than the other two, and Hullbreak can even feel a slight repulsion in the water.

It takes him a few moments to realize that, for some reason, he's holding the water nearest his skin still. He doesn't think it's any kind of armor, but it's not something he's seen before.

Turning his attention to the other two, he sees why the Admiral suggested slowly ramping up the difficulty instead of starting with something strong. The green ones move awkwardly, even worse than most lubbers. He can't imagine they'd be able to handle anything that can actually swim. Still, that's what his crabs are for.

After a few minutes to get acclimated, they all dive deeper, the green ones bringing the baskets with the silk trailing behind, and they all soon see the single crab fighter standing by the first kelp bed.

Strangely, the large one takes up position at the front of their small formation and slowly swims toward the guardian crustacean. The choice proves less strange as shields become visible, like ships from a fog, and move with much more grace than the green one himself has. He tries a few clumsy jabs, and the crab tries to respond, but the floating shields prove an impregnable defense.

Before the crab can think to switch targets, the tan one's rapier suddenly enters the fray, seeking the joints and other vulnerabilities in the crab's armor. Hullbreak watches the mage, wondering what she'll contribute, but she looks frustrated with her few attempts at magic.

It's no concern, though. Soon, the crab is felled, and the green one starts inspecting the corpse for anything useful to claim. He gets the two large claws, and seems to want the back carapace, but he cracks it in his inexperience, which appears to convince him he has enough from that one.

As he works on processing the crab, the smaller green one shows the tan one what to gather. It seems they're after bubblekelp, which Hullbreak has in abundance. He's more than happy to have them thin it out a bit, so he only sends a few paltry crabs as they work; nothing even as strong as the initial guardian.

When they send the baskets up full of kelp and start looking around, Hullbreak sets a few stronger encounters around the other beds. The Admiral's methods seem very effective: let them gather, but a more profitable delve should also be more difficult. Two large crabs guard the next bed, so they'll have to deal with them if they want to continue gathering.

They discuss how to tackle the two crabs as they wait for the baskets, with the small one explaining her frustration at using fire and ice under the waves. Hullbreak isn't surprised at that. He knows his water is very resistant to both types of magic, though the group seems to have an idea to try to counter it.

Their plan made, they approach the nearest bed and engage the crabs there. Once again, the large one takes the fore, but he's looking much more focused on attack than defense this time. The tan one is right beside him the whole time, too, and Hullbreak can soon feel the mana flowing around the three start to swirl in tandem.

The water around the spearhead of the large one grows still, even as Hullbreak can feel the small one heating it. The water starts to boil, yet instead of the bubbles rising to the surface, they are captured and kept around the spear tip, letting it glow with heat. At the same time, the water around the tan one's rapier grows cold . . . incredibly cold. It should freeze over, yet it refuses to.

"Creeping Frost!"

"Scalding Thrust!"

The cold water follows the strike of the rapier and freezes as it washes over the first crab, cracking the carapace and splitting its joints. The heated tip of the spear plunges into the other crab, and the boiling temperature quickly finishes it off, too.

The three whoop in victory and the success of an untested plan working, then start to gather more of the kelp. Hullbreak replays the attacks in his mind, trying to figure out how the three managed to do that. While they seem talented for their levels, it should have taken delvers much more powerful to bring that kind of elemental attack to bear beneath his waves.

He even tries to ask the Admiral about it, but all he gets is pride in those three. He probably shouldn't be surprised that the Admiral's favored lubbers have a few unique tricks.

Chapter 24

There's just something different about watching the kids delve, but not delve *me*. It's also *really* difficult to not backseat Hullbreak as he works on challenging them but not *too* much. But if I just give him the answer, he'll never figure it out on his own.

The kids are after a ton of that kelp, too. I'd probably challenge them a little harder for how much they're taking, but Hullbreak also wants to get the kelp harvested; it's a bit shaggy right now. I guess I can't fault him for taking it a bit easier so he can get a proper trim. I go easier on delvers sometimes too, if a node is past due to be gathered. It kinda chafes, if that makes any sense.

Besides, he's not just giving it away. He doubled the crabs at the third patch, and doubled again at the fourth. The third patch went pretty smoothly, but the kids got a bit banged up at the fourth. Eight crabs is probably their sweet spot. He doubled it again for the fifth, and the kids decided they had plenty of kelp for now.

Probably a good idea for them to head home, anyway—their little boat rested pretty low in the water once they all piled back into it.

I'm looking forward to Staiven processing that kelp into the fancy water potions, too. Mine only let someone breathe, but things like temperature and pressure can still be dangers. It wasn't too much of a concern in the summer, but with winter making itself at home, most delvers are content to fish instead of swim.

Speaking of making oneself at home: Rocky and the other denizens have arrived at the Southwood! My goofball Boxer spent practically half the journey making everything sound like farts, even the rockslides!

He shifted to a more dignified persona once they got close, and the Stag showed more than a little concern at the apparent lich joining the fun. I would say the fears were eased once Rocky started using his Kinetic mastery to help dig trenches and clear snow, but that'd be a lie. But however the Stag feels about Rocky, he's been polite, and I can feel Rocky resisting the urge to rip a big wet one, or at least sound like it.

I dread the day he gets some kind of Stink or Poison affinity.

I can feel him tinkering with Wind and Lightning, too. Ordinarily, I'd expect him to figure out Wind first, since it's pretty easy for him to observe and suss it out, but there are also some lightning-enhanced denizens in the big pile of reinforcements, so it's probably a toss-up as to which he'll actually embrace first.

Leo and Honey have been working hard the last couple days, too, to get all the new troops settled and integrated. They've been able to properly reinforce most of the northern border, and with the skeletons and zombies, they've been able to build some actual defenses in the big stretch of flat area. It looks like they're still going to use the illusion stuff to make it look less defended, but with the reinforcements, "less defended" still means decently defended.

I'd be feeling more confident if it weren't for the fact the invaders seem to have all but vanished. What few the scouts find and kill all seem to be scouting parties as well. I don't like it, and neither does Leo. It smells to both of us like whatever is controlling these things is preparing for something.

But there's one potential bit of good news—or maybe it's just trying to find a silver lining to a dark cloud: Leo's own scouts have started vanishing. I can find their respawn timers, but I don't think they get to keep much, if any, information from a failed scouting trip.

The good part of that is they're all vanishing around a specific area. Honey has it listed as section H-14, which is pretty far out. Right now, Leo is using some of the more subtle denizens to try to scout, but it's going to take a bit longer to get them into position. Rockslides are great at hiding in plain sight, and the wyrms can stay underground, but the slides can't report back very quickly, and the wyrms have to come up to take a look around.

Well, mostly. They can sense vibrations under the surface, but can only give a vague idea of what's actually happening up there. They can tell if something is heavier—or at least steps heavier—or if there are a lot of things, but Leo really wants more than that.

Still, some intel is better than none. He has the slides slowly making their way deeper into the Green Sea, using the wyrms to bring info back, as well as a few other wyrms to try to get at least a vague idea of the numbers in that section.

None of the wyrms have found much yet, which is starting to get concerning. If there's something *else* up there killing the scouts, this could get even more complicated.

Elsewhere

The Harbinger lets its mind wander as it follows the tide of least, trying to figure out what could be slowing their advance. The first obstacle was an oddity of the surface: it is cold. It is *very* cold. If it didn't know any better, it'd worry some Ice-affinity dungeon was already aware and trying to stop them. But as it gets closer to the surface, it can feel no signs of the kind of mana that would require.

It's hardly any wonder life flourishes so deep, if that kind of cold is common on the surface.

The second thing to slow the throngs of the least is the great number of trees. They are different from the large fungi of the Deeps, taller and more resilient.

While they keep much of the drifting ice away from the ground, they do nothing to hinder the cold.

They *do,* however, hinder movement as well as vision with their simple presence. It had ordered the least to simply destroy the obstacles, but the trees are slow to fall and great in number. It would take the full lifetime of a least to remove each tree, and though the least are legion, so too are the trees. Paths will be cut, but clearing the surface entirely will simply take too long to be worth it.

The worst thing, however, is the new slowing force. The surface dungeon had been steadily falling to the hordes of least, and then, suddenly, it wasn't. Even worse, it had forced the least back! That was ultimately what had drawn the Harbinger to journey to the surface. Its new master wished to feast on the dungeon as soon as possible, and even its true master would want to know what could have happened to counter the least so effectively.

They may be the *least* creations, but they are still His, and so should not be something easily stopped. Even worse, as it's been traveling the long way toward the surface, it has been able to receive reports of what *is* stopping the least: wolves.

Wolves, of all things, were devastating them?! The incredulity only lessened slightly when further scouting revealed them to be *tundra* wolves: wolves with Ice affinity. While the least certainly did not handle cold particularly well, a simple affinity advantage should not have resulted in such a turning of the tides.

More reports, and closer to the surface, the Harbinger has some understanding. The least are not smart. They are designed to kill, not to think. Even basic tactics are generally beyond them unless explicitly spelled out. It has always been simpler to make more of them and just bury a foe in the least.

But now, with its presence so near, it can give them more instruction.

No more raids for now. Scout and learn, leave most of the least in torpor, expand the entrance, and make a space for them to lay dormant far enough away from the freezing surface. The Harbinger must know more of this foe so it can be certain of victory.

Once it knows how and where to strike, it will be a simple matter to wake the sleeping least and turn them loose. It will be a simple matter of finding the tipping point, of finding how many least it will take to drown the foe. And if it takes too long to get enough to do it, perhaps it can get some *lessers.*

The Maw is gaining mana at a steady rate, and it would not take much temptation of the sweetness of the surface to get it to invest further into the spawner.

Its tentacles undulate in wicked glee, and its own greedy maw slavers at the thought of what a lesser would do to some wolves.

Yes . . . even a single lesser should be more than enough to handle the tundra wolves.

Chapter 25

Leo

The Wolf Scion's tail slowly waves as he ponders the map. He's hardly pleased with the reports he's getting, but he's more thoughtful than upset about them. H-14 doesn't seem to be the base of the invaders, though it does seem to be something like the tip of their territory. Unpleasant as it is to lose scouting teams, thanks to Honey's idea of dividing the area into sections, even a failed trip gives a good idea of where the danger lurks.

Sections I-13 through I-15 haven't had a successful wolf scout return yet, nor have *J* and *K*, thirteen through fifteen. That gives him a three-by-three area of information blackout; he'd put their actual base of operations in J-14, right in the center. He'll need a few more days to get the rockslides into the heart of the enemy territory, but the initial reports from H-14 give him some hope.

The rockslides have only just gotten into position in the area, but they already have important information to give: the invaders are clearing trees.

Ordinarily, that might seem like something of no real consequence, but neither he nor Honey like it. The invaders don't seem to have a need to build, so why clear trees? If they were burning them for warmth, the smoke would be easily seen, or at least scented on the wind.

Which leaves only one option in Leo's mind: they're making a road. While they're hardly setting stones for the roads like back in Fourdock, a cleared path can only mean they wish to move a *lot* more invaders at once. He takes a bit of solace in that the path seems to be headed toward the kill zone, but it's also a bit early to tell at this point.

The clearing of trees does at least give him a chance to use some of the ravens and crows to try to scout, though. He was initially uncertain how to use them when the Alpha sent them, but now he sees the wisdom in having something he may not need. He may have use of it later, and later is now.

He still needs to wait for them to return, but he's feeling confident the avians will have more information for him, even if it's just to confirm a large clearing in J-14 as their base.

The invaders haven't shown much in the way of ranged attacks yet, so the birds should be safe. Of course, if there are other types of invaders, they could be destroyed, but at least then he'll know he has to worry about more than melee.

He does have a growing concern about the potential enemy territory, however. He's sent wyrms to try to get a feel for troop numbers, and though they can feel the slow progress of the ones making the path, they can't seem to find where all the invaders went. They can sense a bit of movement in J-14, but nothing like the numbers Leo is expecting.

He's loath to have them break the surface to take an actual look and potentially ruin the element of surprise, but he might be forced to if he wants to ruin whatever surprise the invaders are hiding.

His gaze drifts back to the borders of the Southwood and what he's been having the other reinforcements get up to. The leaf cutters and fruitbats were an odd choice to send, and he honestly still isn't sure what else to do with them other than help the Southwood's own herbalism nodes.

He's placed them at the command of the Stag, who has them enriching various nodes to the south. There are no delvers to visit with the snow right now, though the Stag is confident they'll earn significant returns in the spring.

The cinder ants have probably been the biggest surprise use of the myriad of denizens. They team up very well with the slimes, helping them keep more comfortable in the cold climate beyond the Southwood's borders.

The few twinsnakes and other varieties of snake are not handling the cold so well. Even with the more autumnal feel inside the Southwood, they are sluggish. While he'd love to use them in the kill zone, they'll probably have to be more of a last line deeper within the Southwood's territory.

The denizen that he'd like to bite himself for not considering, however, are the tunnelbore ants. He only has three of the large denizens, but they've made digging trenches an act of simplicity, and the illusionist foxes are having trouble keeping up with them! A nice problem to have, in Leo's opinion.

Rocky has also been invaluable in fortifying the kill zone. With his Ice affinity to clear the snow and Kinetic to clear the trees, Leo is feeling much more confident in being able to repel whatever the invaders are building up for.

Confident doesn't mean complacent, however. He's also been drilling with the bears and foxes, along with the denizens from back home, to ensure they fight together effectively. He's even had some success with pairing the vipers and bears, as the serpents can hide in the bear's fur, nicely warm, until it's time to strike.

And the widows pair excellently with the foxes. Their natural stealth is only enhanced by the illusions, and with clever webwork, the spiders can lend even more credence to the trickery of the foxes.

Once this is all over, he should suggest Alpha Thedeim to try to trade for a fox. He's certain the Southwood would happily trade one or two for a wolf. The Alpha can easily expand out into the forest past the cemetery, and the Southwood could very much use a second scion. The Stag is practically running himself ragged trying to keep on top of everything for the forest dungeon.

Being able to see the Stag in his daily work has been an eye-opening experience for Leo. When he was a more normal spawn, back in his old dungeon, he was vaguely aware of the few scions it had. His old dungeon seemed to use them mostly as strong encounters. While the Stag is certainly the Southwood's strongest encounter, he's not really supposed to be attacked. He just tries to do what the Southwood needs.

Unfortunately for him, the Southwood needs a lot of things, and especially with the invaders, the Stag just can't do everything on his own. Even with them being mostly handled by Leo, the Stag is still constantly on the move.

He can sometimes feel the Southwood watching him and the others work, though, and thinks it will be looking into a second scion after everything calms down. A good wolf to pair with the Stag would help balance the dungeon, in Leo's unbiased opinion. Even if the Southwood doesn't want a wolf and just makes a scion from its current spawners, he thinks he and Honey have shown how good it is to have multiple scions, and Rocky can only be helping that idea along, too.

His ruminations are interrupted by the cawing of ravens and crows, and he focuses as a mixed group of them swoops into the tent and lands next to the map. They all try to speak at once, making an awful racket until Leo barks to get them to shut up.

He glares at them as Honey exits her hive and takes her spot on his head before deigning to speak to them.

"You're all the same group?"

A cacophony is the reply until another bark silences them. He points a paw at the closest raven. "You. Are you all part of the same scouting group?"

"Yeah," comes the informal reply. Leo does his best not to let his annoyance show. How the Marshal gets any semblance of order out of them, he'll never know.

"What section?" buzzes Honey.

"J-14," comes the immediate response, and Leo supposes he just needs to up his threats. The birds had, of course, mostly ignored Honey's attempts at getting them to learn the coordinate system until she had gotten that dangerous glint in her eyes.

Not a glint that promised pain—No, Honey is just not the type. It was the glint of having someone to *teach*. The looming horror of ravens and crows confined to desks so she could lecture them had been more than enough to get them to cooperate, at least on that front.

"What do you have to report, then?" follows up Leo.

"We took the direct route, over H and I-14. Like the rocks said: big path cleared of trees. We didn't see too many of those weird invaders, though. Lots at the leading edge, and a steady trickle of reinforcements as the ones chopping trees die, but not the army you said to look for. I-14 was boring, just the cleared path and the trickle of invaders."

The raven pauses and looks to his cohorts, who quietly caw and consort before the lead raven is ready to continue.

"J-14 was also quite boring, but we're pretty sure it's where the invaders are coming from. It's a big hole in the ground; some kind of cave. There's not much movement on the surface aside from the steady flow of the tree cutters. Looking into the hole, we couldn't see too much movement, either. The ant spawner back home seemed livelier. We were gonna take a closer look, but you said not to get too close, so we flew back as quick as we could."

Leo furrows his brow as he considers the report. "No obvious defenses?"

The raven shrugs. "Nothing that really stood out."

Leo thinks for a few moments before Honey speaks up from his head. "You mentioned the anthill back home. How close is the resemblance?"

The raven tilts his head at her. "The same? Just bigger? It was funny to watch them try to carry around some dirt and rocks with those weird legs of theirs."

Leo frowns at that, not liking the idea of them digging. If they can tunnel past the defenses . . . then why make the road? Is it not a road?

His tail thumps the ground as he thinks, but he can't come up with anything else the line of cleared trees could be. If they're not tunneling toward the Southwood, what are they doing?

His tail freezes as he gets an idea, and the quick buzz from Honey has Leo suspecting she thought the same thing.

"They're not tunneling—they're fortifying. They don't do well on the surface, so they're rallying beneath it, building their numbers before striking," he says with grim certainty. He looks at the map and considers his preparations, one question at the forefront of his thoughts.

Does he focus on his own fortifications and hope they dash themselves on them, or does he strike them first and hope they haven't been able to build up too much yet?

Chapter 26

I watch Leo as he and Honey seem to work on two potential plans for the situation. It's a different kind of battle than we've had to deal with before. With Neverrest, I was basically besieged, but I had an out with the surface that the other dungeon seemed to never consider, which let me sneak in a decapitating strike.

With Hullbreak, it was an infiltration mission mixed with a rescue, and though he pulled a couple good tricks, there wasn't anything outside the abilities of myself and my scions to handle.

But this one's different, I think because I knew a lot more about my opponents at the time. I could guess a lot of what Neverrest might do because of how it was attacking, trying to go slow and steady so a sudden change might work before it could really react.

Similar with Hullbreak in that he was basically limited to the water. Sure, he surprised me and mine with the Quartermaster, but my own Conduit was able to surprise him right back. Which is another big difference between this looming fight and the others: reaction time.

In the fight with Neverrest, I could react basically instantly. Even with Hullbreak, I could get reinforcements in about an hour, and I could move Poe and Fluffles to help protect the town in a matter of minutes. But with this fight, if they pull something crazy, help is days away even with the shortcuts.

It's not a fight I want, but one I have anyway. I'm sure actual military people are more used to having to deal with this kind of battle, but I'm not one of them. It's times like this when I wish I had paid a bit more attention to history. I have a vague idea of the basic flow, but I was never a battlefield historian.

I've played a lot of RTS games, but this battle is looking more like it'll be one of those scenarios where you only get a couple of units instead of being able to make your base and pump out enough to just steamroll your enemy. Even worse, I only get a couple of units, while the enemy might be getting a proper base.

I need more information, but I don't know if I have the time to wait for it. This is why actual generals are so important: they know when to seize an opportunity, and when to recognize the difference between an opportunity and a trap. I am at least pretty sure it's not a deliberate trap.

The report sounds like they're not very well established yet, and though it could be fake, I'm inclined to trust the scouts. If I can't trust my scouts to get me intel, why even send them?

Alright, let me think . . . If this was a game, I'd have some kind of scouting unit and probably something that flies and does a lot of damage.

I have scouts in the rockslides and wyrms, but an airborne assault is probably off the table. I think the closest would be having the ravens airdrop some arcane hands, but they're probably not going to be up to handling the kinds of numbers that will probably be there. And if it's only the one hole, that doesn't give me great chances for an assault. They could just hold the entrance, and we'd break upon them, especially since they probably have superior numbers.

I do have sappers, though. With the wyrms and tunnelbores, we could probably turn their fortress into a tomb. Maybe not all at once, but being able to collapse rooms and actually come out of the walls would give a nice tactical advantage.

Leo's offensive plan seems to be progressing along those lines, too. He has a lot of the forces on the surface, and looks to be organizing into . . . Is *platoons* the right word? Or is that too large? Lots of moderate groups instead of a single huge mass, in case the invaders can open up their own entrances. There's the risk of getting completely surrounded, especially with the suspected numbers, but better to plan for that than get surprised by it.

Under the surface, he'd use tunnelbores and wyrms to bring in the slimes, as well as the various snakes and a few of the Southwood's foxes. From there . . . basically everyone just makes as big of a mess as possible, with the digging team either opening a few more holes to the surface to allow strike teams in, or attacking the invaders when they make their own entrances, getting them from behind and giving the surface forces more routes deeper into the enemy stronghold.

Leo and Rocky would be part of the assault, with Honey staying behind to make sure nothing can slip in and wreak havoc in the Southwood. Leo would stay on the surface, commanding the troops, with Rocky underground, taking the fight to the enemy in close quarters like he excels in.

I like the plan in theory, but it all hinges on how many invaders there are, and how fortified the positions are beneath the surface. There'll also probably be new types in there that we can only guess at, especially if this is some kind of nest.

If it's a new nest, we should strike soon before they can get established. If it's already established, however, attacking like this will probably be a disaster.

So how about our defensive options? Well, the northern border is looking a lot more secure now than when we first got here. The kill zone is looking pretty vicious under all the illusions, as well as the more mundane snow that helps keep the various pits and such a secret.

The Southwood can also more easily leverage its own denizens in a defensive battle, though I don't know how long he can keep it up. He has a *lot* of things he can leverage to keep spawning, but if it comes down to a proper siege, that might not be enough.

I don't have to be a big history buff to know that most sieges that fail are because someone came and ran them off rather than the besieged waiting them out. If the Southwood gets into that kind of battle, there's not really a spare army to come and surprise the invaders from the rear.

Sneaking Rocky behind them could work, or maybe getting my other scions to come play. Poe and Fluffles could probably break a siege with the help of Rocky and Slash. Even Grim might help, but I'm not sure. He's not much of a fighter, despite his affinities.

Sure, I could probably order him to help, but that feels like a dick move, and it might not even work how I want it to. Trying to force Life, Death, and Fate affinities to do something might not end as well as I might hope. Better to keep Grim as a reluctant trump card and let him use his abilities as he deems fit. He understands them better than I do.

On the other hand, while the invaders will have a lot of numbers, I doubt they'll have enough to truly encircle the Southwood, so he'd just need to survive until spring, when delvers return. That's also a long time . . .

We could probably hit them with a lot of attrition by attacking the ones clearing the path through the forest, but I don't know if that'd be enough to actually make them start bleeding numbers. I think a steady drain won't be viable as a long-term solution. They have some number of reinforcements a day, and I think their new tactic is designed to let them accumulate as many as possible. With only one real group aboveground now, it's difficult to pick them off.

I think we might need to strike instead of waiting for them to attack. If we wait, they attack when they're ready. If we attack now, we at least have a chance of catching them before they can handle us.

It's fittingly ironic to zerg rush something that kinda reminds me of them. I probably shouldn't just rush off immediately with either plan, though. While it hurts a little to give the invaders another couple days to keep entrenching, I'd rather have a better idea of what their numbers are before going on an assault. It'll sting if we figure out we missed our chance, but it'll be a relief if we learn the attack would have been doomed from the start.

Either way, I'll leave the timing to Leo. I think he has a better grasp on this sort of thing. I'll work on making sure he has what he needs for whichever situation we get into. He's good at the actual fighting, so I can focus on the logistics and ensure he has what he needs to keep going. Trying to micromanage is a good way to collapse the entire thing.

Chapter 27

North of Southwood

Many underestimate what Earth elementals can do. They see the stony exterior and conclude all they can do is crush and smash, with even the clever ones only being able to add *impale* to the list of abilities.

In the defense of those who think that way, most Earth elementals would agree. Their nature suggests they should deal with problems rather directly. The rockslides may not be especially intelligent, even by low-tier spawn standards, but even they can tell Dungeon Thedeim uses them in a strange way.

An especially bright one even suggested they could respawn and find themselves listed as rock piles instead of slides, for all the movement they don't do. Still, it's hardly unpleasant work. While their nature may demand threats be neutralized quickly, it also suggests patience and a willingness to simply observe. Rocks are not the most proactive elements of nature.

And the tactic has proven effective. Their infiltration of Hullbreak showed that they can quietly slip inside a hostile dungeon and remain undetected. It's even simpler to stay hidden in the forest, as they can simply stay under the piles of needles and other detritus, gather under thick brambles, or slowly move through the loamy soil despite the extra solidity provided by the current cold.

They're also getting used to cooperating with other denizens to bring back their observations. The slimes were interesting to work with when under the waves. They're another denizen who can be easily underestimated and most often used for simple blunt work, but their similar ability to stay still and remain under notice was invaluable in the past, even if it's not especially relevant at the moment.

The rockslides feel for their fellow denizens and their inability to work well under these cold conditions, but at least there is another denizen type who can do that work here.

The wyrms are strange to work with. Even though they share the bond with Dungeon Thedeim, there is an instinctual fear of the unique variety of dragon. Magma is an odd cousin to earth, sometimes cooling to become more, sometimes heating earth and making more magma. The Librarian has even suggested wyrms could be a natural predator for living rockslides, though she thankfully never tried to get the wyrms to test that hypothesis.

Despite how uncomfortable it can be to be near the wyrms, the slides can't pretend they don't work well together. Not only do the wyrms bring their reports back to the Warden but they also can scout ahead and help guide the rockslides to more places to observe.

In fact, that is the current mission. The forward wyrms have been able to roughly map out a growing cavern around the invader's entrance, but the Warden has not allowed them to breach into the chambers to see what is going on. The reports from the wyrms make little sense, which is why the Warden is playing it very safe.

A large excavation would suggest a large force, but the wyrms report much fewer moving sources of vibrations than there should be. They are light, too, suggesting it's not simply some huge single source of the noise. The only motion can be detected at the limits of the chamber as the invaders keep digging, as well as the movement to ferry the freed stone to the surface.

Some of the slides wonder if the movement might be something large with many feet, like the centipedes of Dungeon Thedeim's protégée. So many feet could make something large sound like many smaller things, after all.

The Warden also thought of this, which is why the latest mission is to try to map the individual sources better, to see if they can rule out anything. Well, part of the latest mission, at least. The wyrms are constantly on the move, as they have to ferry back the reports, so they can't keep a precise eye on all the movement inside, just that the movement there seems much less than it should be.

Which is why several of the smaller rockslides are having the harrowing experience of being moved by the wyrms. While the slides can slowly slip through rock on their own, time is of the essence. The wyrms are the only other denizens able to move so quickly through stone without disturbing it, otherwise the tunnelbores would be used.

The unhappy rockslides would rather risk discovery than be carried in the tri-hinged jaws of the wyrms as they move through the earth. Unfortunately, they aren't making the decisions. They won't even be harmed from the experience, aside from possibly emotionally.

It is a relief for the slides once they get deposited in the rock around the growing chamber. The wyrms situate their allies above and below the excavations rather than in the way, and soon, the Earth elementals can devote their time to listening to the vibrations.

They even move themselves slowly around to get into better positions. As the wall of the cavity slowly expands, some find themselves too far away to be able to listen as well to the movements, so some repositioning is required.

The vibrations make little sense to the rockslides, which only makes them listen more intently. The walls continue to expand, which is something easily noticed even by the passing wyrms. There is a steady rumble of reinforcements, also something the wyrms can observe. The oddity comes in where the reinforcements go. They seem to simply . . . *vanish!*

They don't like giving that report, but it is all they can give, at least preliminarily. Their pride as spies pushes them to watch closer and try to think of what could possibly be happening.

Are the reinforcements dying? Is the expanding space just a mass grave? The dead don't move, after all, so they would lose track of them, but the slides don't put much stock in that theory. While it could explain the lack of movement, this is supposed to be an invading army. If they were losing so many troops, they would either fall back or launch a desperate attack, but they're doing neither.

The rockslides think as several wyrms glide through the rock, letting them know they're off to scout down the invader's trail to try to find the true source. The slides acknowledge it as politely as they can, but they are more concerned about the mystery of the reinforcements.

Perhaps they're missing something in their observations? They stopped trying to track specific movements once it became obvious they were not dealing with some huge centipede, but perhaps they should look closer and attempt to find exactly what is happening.

So, they start tracking random individuals, each slide paying careful attention as the current target comes within their range, and being ready to resume their vigil once it makes its way back. Surprisingly, they start seeing a pattern, though the purpose still eludes them.

A fresh reinforcement will start by gathering rubble and taking it to the surface, repeating this many times as the diggers work. While some of them do appear to drop dead in the work, it's not difficult to follow the sound of the body being dragged away and disposed of on the surface. As for the haulers that don't drop, they eventually take their place in the line of digging invaders.

And this is where the slides make their discovery.

Once they have their spot, the diggers don't keep moving forward to continue their excavation; instead, they claw away the earth within reach . . . and then stop. They don't simply stop digging; they seem to stop *everything.*

At first, the slides think they must die on the spot, but every other death has been accompanied by a heavy thud before the sound of dragging away the body.

The invaders are just standing there? Why? The slides continue to observe, and even track one as it drags away what must be a corpse. Once the invader returns, it takes the vacated spot and ceases all movement like its predecessor.

Perhaps they're sleeping, somehow? It doesn't feel quite right to the slides, but they at least have something more concrete to report: the invaders are filling the space as quickly as they dig it and standing still once their portion of the work is finished.

In retrospect, the rockslides suppose they should have expected something like that. Holding still and being beneath notice is what they do; they shouldn't be surprised they're not the only ones to figure out how well that works.

They flag down a group of wyrms who are moving quickly toward them from the trail and start to give their reports, only to find the wyrms a bit antsy to continue to give their own.

Why?

The answer is concerning. The movements of the invaders so far have been light *tik-tik-tik*ing of the sharp limbs jabbing into the ground to give them the grip to move. Far down the tunnel, though, there is a new sound.

Thud! Scraaaaape . . .

Something large and different is coming.

The rockslides quickly give their discovery, and the denizens don't need to be the Warden to know these two pieces of information could be very important. The wyrms take off, leaving the slides to continue their watch and try to figure out what to do.

The bright one suggests trying to prepare for the battle ahead. While they don't know many of the details, even they can figure out it'd be a bad idea to let all the invaders wake up and join the battle. So, they quietly work to subtly destabilize what they can of the large cavern. They don't think they'll be able to destroy even a significant fraction of the invaders, but every little bit helps.

And the idea appeals to their nature. Crushing a foe is not exactly elegant, but it is effective. Besides, they are living rockslides. The only arguable difference between them and a cave-in is if there is a roof.

Chapter 28

So . . . that's less than optimal. The invaders are building up their forces with each passing minute by using some kind of sleep or hibernation to conserve their internal fuel. Even worse: there's something big coming, and I get the feeling it'd be a bad idea to let it get to the group of invaders without throwing some kind of wrench into its plans.

It seems like Leo feels the same, as he pretty quickly orders just about everyone to move. Honey did some quick math for the floor space and the room an invader takes up, and it looks like we're still going to be outnumbered, but if we don't do something before the big thing shows up, we'll have missed our chance. The best time to strike would have been a couple days ago, but the second best is now.

The worst would be waiting for what I can only assume is some kind of leader to show up and organize everything properly. The defenses are pretty poor, which is heartening. There's just the one entrance at the top of a huge anthill, but that choke point is the only real defense they seem to have, aside from numbers.

Honey and Leo finalize their plans while on the move, and even Rocky seems to be taking the situation seriously. I can still feel him eager to mix it up a bit, but he understands the severity of the situation enough not to take things lightly.

Honey has her bees each carrying a cinder ant to keep them warm, and they help explain the basic plan as everyone marches. I can't keep much track of all my denizens with them outside Southwood's borders, but I can look through the eyes and other senses of my scions.

Almost all of my denizens are on the march, too, though not all of them are actually marching. The tunnelbore ants are covered in the arcane hands, with the crows, ravens, and bats all scouting ahead and reporting back to Leo. The bears and foxes all have snakes or slimes hitching rides to keep warm, though I'm not certain what Leo's going to do with them once they all arrive.

The wolves and wyrms are ahead of the column to strike the lumberjack invaders, clearing a path for everyone else to keep moving quickly toward the beachhead of the enemy. By the time any of my scions see the break in the trees, the invaders there are dead. A few tundra wolves are lost in the fight, but the double whammy of surprise wolves and surprise wyrms let them deal with the threat before they could form any real counter.

Leo sends them ahead to ambush the reinforcing logger invaders, and the army marches on. The ravens and fruitbats that return from scouting pick up a hand or two each before taking to the air again. I don't think they're going to be the best air support, but any is better than nothing, especially when all signs point toward the invaders not having much of an answer to flying foes.

Once they enter the clearing, the battle is truly on. The invaders screech, and even from so far away from the hill, Leo can faintly hear echoing screeches coming from deeper within. He howls a signal, and the army of denizens splits to do their assigned tasks.

It takes only a few moments for the slimes to hop off their rides, then the wolves and bears charge for the hill as the airborne hands rain magic down on the entrance. Bolts of electricity, spikes of ice, blades of wind, orbs of fire, and other moderate elemental attacks make it difficult for the invaders to sally forth. Even though each attack isn't too powerful, that kind of mix makes it very difficult to put up any kind of effective defense besides staying inside.

Not that the invaders seem inclined. The hordes behind shove the ones ahead, even if the leaders are no longer capable of moving under their own power. While the bodies of the invaders provide some cover, they still keep the horde from being able to spill out.

When the bears and wolves get there, their jobs become equal parts fighting and clearing. Vipers and spitting cobras riding the large mammals help with the fighting, as well as watching their backs as their rides work to shove aside each dispatched foe.

While the entrance is occupied, Leo has the back line making their own fortifications. The tunnelbores start carving trenches as the foxes obscure their positioning with a bit of mist. Rocky even gets in a bit of practice as he hammers the ground ahead of the bores with kinetic force, following a rhythm to help make it easier.

Once the ants are in a good groove, literally and metaphorically, Rocky starts heating it by pulling energy from the air and surrounding ground. The slimes and snakes are more than happy to hop in and wait for the probable counterattack, while Rocky is just trying to keep the cold where he wants it. My zombie knows the invaders don't handle cold well, so if he can keep a lot of it on hand, he can use it to devastating effect when he needs to.

All the while, Leo and Honey watch and coordinate. Healing ants nestled in the fur of the frontliners have kept minor injuries from building up, but an invader still sometimes gets lucky and injures or even kills one of the denizens.

While the bears will respawn and potentially be able to rejoin the fight in time, the wolves will spawn way back with me. Injured wolves limp back to get the more significant help the healing slimes can provide, while the bears seem more inclined to just tough out all but the worst of injuries.

So far, it's going well, but with each passing minute, it seems like the forces at the hill are more and more pressed to hold back the invaders. A wyrm pops up near Leo and rumbles at him, causing him and Honey both to freeze for a moment. It gives me a chance to absorb the report, which makes the reaction of my two scions a bit more reasonable.

The rockslides have been quietly sapping the large cavern, and though they can't collapse the entire thing, they're ready to go with what they have. They just need Leo's signal.

Leo's howl seems to pierce the entire Green Sea Forest as he embraces his title, and I'm surprised to see Honey is able to follow suit.

An air of authority settles over Leo, Leader of the Pack and Warden. The denizens move with more speed and confidence, the ones holding the top of the hill now able to shrug off all but the most serious of blows.

Honey's compound eyes glow a soft white as the Seeker of Truth surveys the battlefield, feeding Leo information and letting him direct the battle. The denizens move away from certain positions, leaving holes in the masses of the joint forces before rumbling is heard and felt.

Large holes appear in the ground, with the screeching of injured invaders sounding like music to their ears. Rocky takes the opportunity to send the freezing gale into the tunnels as well, ensuring any that might have tried to attack from the pockmarked battleground would have a hard time doing so.

Suddenly, Leo's eyes widen, and he howls once more, calling back the bears and wolves at the breech, solidifying defensive positions around the holes in the large clearing. The battlefield seems almost silent for a moment, broken only by the grinding of the tunnelbore ants still working and the whimpers and whines of the injured being treated.

A new sort of rumble comes from the ground, along with whispers of mad ideas. Skittering is heard, but without the usual screeching of the invaders. The rumbling intensifies, the loose hill slowly crumbling before it suddenly bursts in an explosion of black tentacles.

Through the dust, glowing green eyes and occasional gleaming white teeth can be seen, far too many of each to fit on a single head. Or any head, for that matter, as the settling dust eventually reveals what I can only describe as a shoggoth. I wish I had read more of the mythos to know any weaknesses.

It probably doesn't have much, come to think of it. Those stories aren't really about people triumphing over the unknowable terrors from beyond existence.

It bellows and waves most of its tentacles, slamming two into the ground to drag itself forward, and screeches echo up from the multitude of holes littering the clearing.

This probably isn't good . . .

Even worse than one of Lovecraft's nightmares walking around in front of my scions, possibly leading an army of killing machines: it seems my scions aren't the only ones with titles to embrace.

I just hope they can stand up to the **Harbinger of [illegible]**

Chapter 29

The Harbinger

The Harbinger glares across the battlefield at the opposing force. Rage threatens to overwhelm it, but it can't let itself fall to that. There are three scions arranged against it, as well as an army of mixed denizens. Seeing the opposition, it has to admit the least are not to blame for having failed to overrun everything.

It can taste the mana of the surface forces, and there may be as many as four dungeons fighting together. A large portion of the denizens are from one, along with at least two denizen types from another. The fewer numbers feel older, so it will have to be careful around them.

The scions all feel fairly young, at least. The wolf is the leader, and so probably from the oldest dungeon. Loath as it is to admit, the Harbinger is at a disadvantage when it comes to forces. With the wide variety of denizens, he can only rely on the numbers of the least, and the wolf across the field has taken great steps to limit that advantage.

For whatever reason, the wolf seems to be trying to hide its origin, but the Harbinger can feel its true source differs from everything else present.

The Bee Scion has traces of some other dungeon on it as well, perhaps as some ploy to make the Harbinger underestimate them. The Harbinger grins at the scions having to drop the facade and embrace their titles. Most of the forces are from a young dungeon, so pretending to be so inexperienced could have been a gambit that would have paid off, if not for its own presence here.

The strength of the denizens is bolstered by the wolf and guided by the information from the bee. Without those two, the denizens should fall easily. The Lich Scion also seems to be trying to hide its source, but it can't hide its weakness. The wolf and bee have embraced their titles, but the lich has not, so it must not have any.

Four dungeons: two sending only denizens, one sending two scions, and one last one sending the Wolf Scion. Destroy the wolf, and the others will follow. Without their Leader of the Pack, they will fall before the Harbinger.

It flexes its Mind affinity and starts directing the least, its affinity making it trivial to handle the immense rush of information from their senses. The cavern is a mess, and it will be more difficult to join the fray properly, but the number of openings mitigates that somewhat.

The Harbinger roars and the wolf howls, and the tides of forces rush to meet each other. But the Harbinger is capable of so much more than just directing the least.

It flexes its Mind affinity once more, seeking to confuse and disable the forces of the surface.

The leading edge of wolves and bears stumble for a moment before a soothing buzz settles over them, the Seeker of Truth girding their minds against the assault. The Harbinger may need to remove that one before it can focus on the wolf.

Searing pain pulls its focus back to itself, and it sees the denizens aren't limited to only the surface, after all. Magma wyrms harass the Harbinger and the least still in the cavern, even as the mammalian denizens clash on the surface. The least have difficulty dealing with the wyrms, as the odd dragons can burst from the earth with little warning and dive back into it just as quickly.

The Harbinger, however, can easily deal with such pests.

Minds are so simple to detect, even with the unique biology of the wyrms. Those minds the Harbinger can't crush find themselves crushed more literally in its tentacles when they try to attack.

That's not all the coalition of dungeons has to throw at it, however. Before it can truly savor the pain of the worms in its mental and physical grip, elemental attacks rain upon the tentacled scion. It roars, destroying some wyrms and tossing aside others before it regains control of itself. Even that small lapse lets the coalition drive the least back some, forcing the Harbinger to do more than simply direct them.

It drags itself toward the front, even as it snuffs the minds of the fliers and hands that get too close. It's a devious tactic of the surface dwellers to take advantage of the open space to attempt to attack with impunity, but the Harbinger is no least to be picked off from afar. Nor are the least to be underestimated in melee, especially with the Harbinger's direction and assistance.

Snuffing minds is more direct, but more difficult than simply stunning. Even with the bee bolstering the minds of the surface denizens, the Harbinger is perfectly synchronized with the least. Even a moment is enough of an opening for them to remove an opponent, and once the tentacled scion clears one of the breaches, the least can start truly pouring out to engage the enemy.

Unfortunately for it, the breaches closer to the enemy lines start to get overrun, letting the surface denizens swarm into the cavern. For a few moments, the Harbinger thinks to use it as a trap, but the coalition of dungeons is not led by a fool. Slimes literally pour in, giving the least little to actually attack, and they can't evade the slimes effectively with how tight the confines are.

Well, the surfacers aren't the only ones who can cause cave-ins. It will crush some of the least, but it will give the Harbinger more of a defensible position to collapse a long line of the cavern, as well as giving the least a much better exit to the surface. Better to lose a portion of them than to lose them all.

It guides the least in the controlled collapses even as it wades into the front line.

Its glee in destroying the defenders of the surface is interrupted for a moment by a disorientating fireball, and it takes a few moments to try to understand the attack. What kind of fireball was that? It felt like the explosion rippled through its entire being. While it is mostly unharmed by its force, it's a disconcerting thing to feel suddenly.

Its attention falls on the Lich Scion, who is casting a wide variety of spells from its simple staff, keeping the lines of the surface dwellers from being truly overrun. Its magic is odd, but after a few moments of observation, the Harbinger is not too concerned. It's clearly using an Arcane affinity to add a few little tricks to simple spells. While the effectiveness is impressive, it wouldn't have to rely on such surprises if it was actually strong.

The Harbinger keeps the pressure on the main line of the battle, buying time for its least to prepare the defensive cave-ins. It loses more than it would prefer in the fighting, but those least on the surface and on this side of the collapses are effectively lost anyway. This way, they can spend their lives to further the Harbinger's plan.

Moments before the Harbinger is ready to trigger the collapses, the wolf howls and pulls back its troops. It saves some of the surface forces, but not all, and soon, a chasm cuts a ragged wound across the entire battlefield.

The Harbinger roars in triumph, echoed by the throngs of least still under its command. They pour from the rent in the earth, slaying what denizens aren't quick enough to retreat. It spreads them out, extending living walls of death through the forest to start encircling the tenacious surface foes.

Its mouths drool at the tactical situation it has forced. The surface fools now have to try to either fight while surrounded or try to punch through the thick wave of least. It deliberately leaves the fewest of its forces near itself, daring the encircled to try to rush past it.

To their credit, the Wolf and Bee Scions make the decision quickly. The forces rush toward the breaches they've cleared to attempt to hole up, while the scions and a portion of the force charge the Harbinger.

It licks its many lips in anticipation of fighting the three scions directly. It even allows them to think their little ploy with hunkering in their half of the cavern could work and keeps the least from tearing into their flanks *too* hard. Leisurely snuffing the minds of the trapped denizens after will be the perfect way to celebrate its victory over the surface.

It puts aside the anticipation for now, as it still needs to crush these scions first. The bee rides the wolf's head, with the lich easily running beside them. The Harbinger welcomes them with bolts of mental anguish, but the Seeker of Truth intercepts and weakens the attacks so they splash uselessly against the minds of the enemy scions.

They don't take the attack lying down. The lich slams the butt of its staff against the earth, causing the dust and dirt of the torn land to rise into the air, obscuring the Harbinger's sight. The wolf seems to dance and flit around in the improvised sandstorm, launching blades of shadow from its claws at the Harbinger.

Unfortunately for them, it doesn't need to see them to know where they are. Their minds blaze their positions to it, even as the wolf slips through shadows to attack from what it hopes are awkward angles. That it hits with most of the attacks has less to do with surprise and more to do with the Harbinger's simple bulk. It loses a few of its thinner tentacles, but they are easy to replace.

It bides its time as the wolf attacks, preparing its own counter before lashing out with a thick tentacle. The wolf is blindsided as it exits a shadow, but the impact doesn't feel right to the Harbinger. The wolf is still sent flying, but it looks more like it was thrown rather than impacted with such a strong smash!

The orange glow from within the sandstorm gives the Harbinger a clue as to what happened. The lich must have dampened the blow somehow. The Harbinger grumbles to itself as it has to admit the three scions work well together—well enough that it needs to take them more seriously than it has.

Its form writhes and shifts, losing what semblance of structure it once had. It seems to change from a ball of teeth, tentacles, and eyes into a pool, spreading through the entire sandstorm. It brings more focus to the fight, letting the least handle themselves for the moment. With improved focus comes improved mental attacks.

The bee can't blunt the intrusive thoughts as thoroughly as before, and so the wolf and lich both are having their own focus tested as they try to avoid not only grasping tentacles and shrieking mouths but maddening thoughts whispering at the edge of their consciousness.

The wolf slips up first. Just a little nudge to try slipping through a few tentacles, a whisper that he's fast enough, the Harbinger has lost its focus . . . The wolf doesn't see the wide maw until it's too late.

The bee follows a few moments after, her grief giving the Harbinger all the opening it needs to capture the diminutive scion in a tentacle and crush her.

The Harbinger laughs like a chorus of the damned as the sandstorm disperses, leaving it and the lich standing alone. This battle is all but won now. It could torture the weak lich to death, but it has so much to do.

No, it's a better show of its dominance to simply snuff its mind, then move on to the denizens huddling underground now.

It reaches for the mind of the lich, only to find the attack batted aside. With a snarl, it repeats the attack, but the defenses *move*, letting the attack hit only air. Only when it turns its full attention on the lich does it realize the difference.

It has embraced its title. The Affinity Savant glares at the Harbinger, teeth grinding and fists clenching around the staff.

Very well then, little lich. Tentacles and teeth should be more than enough to remove the final obstacle in the Harbinger's path.

Whips of flesh with perversions of mouths lash at the enemy scion, yet they find no purchase. The lich almost seems to dance around the attacks, avoiding harm with little apparent effort. More attacks pile on, until one finally makes contact.

The Harbinger reels from the burst of mana. The attacking tentacle should have snapped the staff in half, yet instead it dropped to the ground, partly frozen and shattered, and partly burned to a crisp.

Not even the Redcap had ever struck a blow like that to the Harbinger! It surges forward in a tide of teeth and flailing tentacles, intending to rip the lich apart for its insolence, confident it's low on mana after an attack like that.

The very air around the lich vibrates as it proves the Harbinger wrong, raw intent giving it a name to put to the devastating attack.

Resonance Cascade.

The leading edge of the Harbinger shatters into ice as it feels a force ripple through its entire self again. It tries to regenerate the damage, but the waves of power keep on coming, keep striking and building more and more damage. The edges of the Harbinger keep shattering, and the wild movements of its entire body only keep growing more and more erratic.

It bellows in pain as a piece tears itself away from the wild undulations, and its many eyes can see the fragment get incinerated to ash a moment later.

It feels more and more of itself torn asunder by the rampaging waves rippling through its entire being. It's vaguely aware of each rent piece being burned to cinders, but it's difficult to concentrate through the pain of its body tearing itself apart. Somehow, it manages to focus on the lich, and it almost wishes it hadn't.

Heat shimmers around the lich, baffling the Harbinger for how it could have that much mana to produce an attack such as this. As the heat condenses into the final portion of the attack, the Harbinger gets only one hint as to how it could be possible: the lich had a second title to embrace.

No Kid Gloves is seared into its mind as its flesh is seared away. It will have to try to consider the meaning of the strange title after it respawns.

Chapter 30

The Maw

The dungeon watches through the many eyes of the Harbinger as it bursts onto the surface, greedily devouring the sights. It's clear immediately that the Maw made the correct decision to invade the surface. There are so many different things to savor!

Even the chaotic mana of the battlefield makes the dungeon practically drool at the idea of Devouring all of it. The Maw makes notes to itself about what things look especially tasty. The denizens arrayed against it rank high on the list, as most of the specific types are ones it has only come to understand via the many options for spawners. To see them moving around only makes it hungrier.

The top of the list belongs to the enemy scions, however. The wolf looks lean and tough, and its Shadow mana seems nicely marbled with Fate. It will be a meal to savor. The Bee Scion may need to be broken and turned instead of simply consumed. It understands the concept of honey, but the few varieties of underground bee don't produce very much.

It's uninterested in the undead scion, at least at first. Liches are not uncommon, and all the ones the Maw has consumed so far have been a distasteful mess of affinities or the bland homogeneity of Arcane. The Maw's opinion shifts as the battle continues, though.

While it enjoys the taste of the Wolf Scion via the Harbinger's senses, and finds the defeat of the bee to be a waste, it's surprised at how tenacious the lich is. And then the senses of the Harbinger go haywire, forcing the Maw back. With some distance, the dungeon witnesses its Harbinger torn apart, shattered, and obliterated.

It's the flow of mana that has the Maw's attention, not the way it's being used. With its focus pulled back, it can feel the mana blend and merge. It *yearns* to taste the lich, to consume and savor the unique bouquet of its mana.

For now, it will have to settle for the memory, though it will certainly have the Harbinger relive the experience once it respawns. The Maw generally doesn't care much for Mind affinity, but it knows the Harbinger can replay memories.

While it generally does so to harm others, the Maw has no problem ordering it to do so to itself so the dungeon can enjoy watching the mana flows and imagining how they'll taste.

But such diversions will have to wait. Not only does the Harbinger need to respawn, but the Maw needs to decide what to do next. It's not dissuaded from its mission to consume the surface, but it is forced to admit it will not be so simple as it had hoped.

It needs more food. It needs to grow. While its Metal-affinity fey and elemental spawners are maxed, it has a lot of potential growth in the spawner the Harbinger came with. The Maw is mildly confused as to why it doesn't have its Metal affinity, but that's not the first strange thing about the spawner.

Hmm. It also needs to decide what to do about the least already sent out on expedition. If it lets them go, the surface dungeons will be able to eat the mana from them. If it calls them back, it will have to spend some of its own mana to keep them functioning. Lose nothing new but feed the enemy, or recall them and lose its own food?

It would even cost some to recall them, making bringing them back even less appealing.

The Maw almost leaves them to their fate before remembering it doesn't *have* to feed the least when they return. It doesn't even need to just let them starve, though the very idea makes the dungeon shiver in horror. No, it can keep them from that particular fate and still feed itself.

It needs to inform the delvers of its new need for food, anyway.

It focuses on the Redcap, in the process of creating another new hat. The material for this one seems louder than most.

"Master, what can I do for you?"

Why is this one louder than the others?

"Master, I believe I'm working on my best piece yet. The suffering adds much."

Finish your meal, then call on the High Priest. He has new work.

"Yes, Master. I'm almost finished, if I can just put on the finishing touches?"

Yes. Don't ruin your meal, but don't delay, either.

The Maw watches in idle curiosity as the materials eventually gurgle their last breath, and the Redcap leaves to find the High Priest. Not that locating him is especially difficult. The pale elf is holding a banquet and meeting with the ranking members of the clergy. Despite the richness of the food, very few of the Priests of the Maw are overweight.

In truth, most are thinner than is strictly necessary, but they've learned that a fat priest is a tempting morsel for the Maw. Besides, with how busy they are, it's difficult to put on much weight in the first place.

The High Priest stands and bows to the Redcap. "Esteemed Voice of the Great Maw, what a pleasure! Is that Cardinal Birtyl on your head? I hope she was satisfactory for you?"

The Redcap nods, making the grisly display on its head jiggle in disturbing ways. "Yes, the traitor was an inspiration. I hope to keep this piece fresh for as long as possible. But The Great Maw did not send me to show off my latest hat."

The High Priest nods in understanding, with the others nodding and trying not to stare at the scion's latest fashion accessory. "We are all, of course, hungry to do the Great Maw's bidding."

"There will be a cull," states the Redcap plainly. While uncertainty flashes across many faces, the High Priest's is not among them.

"I'll have the guards start rounding up those who are not contributing enough."

"Not of the people. The Master has denizens returning that will be culled. Bring as many delvers as possible. The surface is more difficult to chew than expected. The Master wishes to send more denizens later, as well as dedicated delvers. Those who cull the most of the least will get more training. Those who *get* culled by the denizens will be food for the Master."

This time, curiosity flashes over the faces of those gathered, including the High Priest's. "We will be allowed to help the Great Maw to sink its teeth into the surface?"

"Yes. The Great Maw wishes to grow, and wishes to send more than just a probing attack next time. The surface has delicacies that are jealously guarded. Master will consume all."

"The Maw will consume all," agree the gathered priesthood before the High Priest speaks up.

"Will we need to send more delvers to harvest from and give to the Great Maw? I take it we'll also be stepping up our hunting parties?"

"Yes. Master needs strong teeth to eat the surface. Prepare warmth. The surface is cold. The least could not handle it, but the Master's other denizens should. The Great Maw also wishes to expand the special spawner. Much mana will be needed."

The High Priest bows again. "Of course. We will stock the pantry properly and ensure everyone is working toward the Great Maw's goal of claiming the surface."

The Redcap nods and leaves, having said what he needed to, and the Maw turns its attention elsewhere. It needs to prepare to do more than simply attack. Despite how distracting the wonders of the surface are, the dungeon can't let itself get *too* distracted. If it was on the surface and something tried to attack, it would try to consume the source, not just the few morsels that saw fit to wander too close.

Tempting as it is, upgrading the kitchen will probably not help it too much. The food can give a good boost, but the Maw can already feed all of its denizens to help fight back an attack. Though it might need to upgrade it anyway, if it wishes to feed the delvers.

It eventually decides to hold off, at least until it knows how many it will need to feed, and how often. It wouldn't want to waste the enhanced food.

It also starts moving around its denizens, expecting to need to cull more than just the returning least. They will be good training for the delvers, and are cheap to spawn. The Metal-affinity fey and elementals will need to be culled as well, to not only equip the delvers but to better outfit the Maw's own denizens.

It will give better guidelines for what to attack once the priesthood gathers the delvers. While it would cost the Maw to slay its own denizens, it suffers no penalty for processing the ones the delvers kill. They can bring back some to help outfit themselves and leave the rest for the Maw.

The Maw smiles as it thinks back to the sublime weave of the lich's mana. If the dungeon wishes to dine on such a masterpiece as that, it will need to ensure its knives are sharp and its stoves hot.

Failing to prepare it properly would almost be as much of a travesty as never getting to taste such a fine ingredient at all.

Chapter 31

I wish I could survey the entire battlefield right now, but Rocky is my last scion standing over there. My zombie Boxer is trying to get himself back under control as he stares at the smoldering remains of the Harbinger, and I can't really blame him.

That thing was a nasty piece of work, and I could actually feel its magic subtly influencing Leo and Honey both through their bonds with me. It couldn't control them, but it could give them little nudges, little suggestions, toy with their emotions. If anything, that attack of Rocky's was too nice of an end for that monster.

I just wish it was actually the end of it. I'll double check with the others, but I doubt ordinary wandering monsters get titles like that. If it's not a random invader, it's a scion, and if it's a scion, it'll respawn in its dungeon.

Oh, speaking of spawns: there's still a big chunk of army for Rocky to deal with. At least he won't have to fully deal with it on his own.

When Leo ordered the denizens into the holes for protection, he also ordered the tunnelbores in there. With them, they can dig through the collapsed section and charge back out if they need to. Rocky is their main target at the moment, as easily my strongest force on the field right now.

Thankfully, their weakness to cold gives Rocky a pretty simple solution, and even the killing machines are starting to understand charging at him is maybe not the best idea.

I ask Rocky to keep an eye on the denizens and watch for any other tricks, but I think the battle is pretty much over, even if there're a lot of invaders still to clean up. Which gives me a chance to try to go over the battle in my head.

We won, but it's easily the costliest victory since the battle with Neverrest. I wouldn't go so far as to call it a Pyrrhic victory, but we've definitely gotten a shiner or two. Leo and Honey are counting down to respawn; looks like it'll be the middle of the night before they come back. I've also lost a decent number of the denizens I sent, and I don't know if the mana from killing the invaders will offset the cost.

Worse than the possible loss of mana, though, is the simple fact this war has only just started. The other times I've had to deal with hostile dungeons, I've managed to make it nice and quick, settling it with a single battle, but it's not going to be so simple with this one. For starters, I don't even know where it is!

It's under the surface somewhere, but I don't have much else to go on. I'd wager it's a pretty good distance away, though. There's no way it only has those leech-headed things as denizens; not with the strength of that scion. That it only sent them suggests it's far enough away it couldn't react quickly to the things I sent. It could even be far enough away that it couldn't react in time to just send something that deals with cold better.

It might even be what the dungeon sees as a token force: a glorified expedition to try to bring back some mana. If that's the case . . . I think we're in trouble. My gut says it's not that bad, but I also don't have guts anymore, so I don't know how far I'm willing to trust them.

The dungeon should now have some vague idea of the forces I can bring to bear, which is definitely bad. I feel like I've done so well in battles so far because nobody knew what to expect. In terms of intelligence gathering, the unknown dungeon definitely came out of this fight better than I did.

It's not all bad, at least. Rocky didn't embrace his Boxer title, so there's still that ace up our sleeves. I'll also definitely need to bring another scion or two over if I want to make sure we can hold the line there. Slash will be a huge help with armies clashing, and it could also be an excellent chance for Nova to try to get some levels. Hopefully in a few smaller skirmishes before another big battle.

I'm also definitely going to need to focus on my own spawners a bit more. I'm going to absolutely see more than the leech-heads the next time we actually fight, so I better have a few more surprises of my own when the time comes.

From how the battle went . . . I should probably try to focus on the hands, the Earth elementals, the wyrms, and the wolves. I might work on the bird spawner, too.

The birds have the fewest upgrades to reach max; I think they'll only have one or two new things. to spawn. With them being focused on resources, however, I'm not certain how much benefit they'll provide in a battle. Or maybe I'm completely off base here, and they'll end up being the perfect logistics solution to having my denizens so far away. I'd rather not spend my mana on maybes, but it's an option.

The wolves are a pretty obvious choice to upgrade. I think they have one or two more new things before they max out as well. They're probably going to be great for scouting the tunnels past the hole, and that's without them getting any really cool new abilities with the new types.

The wyrms are also an obvious choice, as they have a ton of room left to grow with the spawner, and even the basic wyrms are perfect for scouting underground. I'm going to want some serious powerhouses eventually, and the wyrm spawner seems my best bet for it.

The only real downside is that it's pretty expensive to upgrade—enough that I'll probably only be able to get a single new type, at least for a while.

The Earth elementals should get upgraded too. They have plenty of room for new types, and I still need to choose a specialization for them. Ordinarily, I'd be inclined to go for resources; I'd probably end up effectively getting mobile mining nodes, which would be cool. But I also should look to see if the physical or magical specializations offer anything in the way of sneaky scouts.

The rockslides have been amazing for gathering intel. On the other hand, the wyrms might be able to take over that role if I get more of them, freeing the elementals to go for resources.

I could even pay through the nose to re-spec them after the battle, but even with my mana income, that feels like a waste. I'm leaning toward the resource focus for them, but I'll wait on actually deciding, at least for now.

Lastly come the hands. They were a lot more effective than I was expecting, so I shouldn't underestimate the little guys. If further upgrades can pack even more magical might into small packages, they could be a great choice. But what to choose?

I think I'll actually wait for Leo to respawn before I spend anything, but I can still come up with a few options while I wait. If I build an army like a party, there are roles to fill: heavies, lights, supports, range.

By that metric, I'd say I have light attackers and range covered, at least to a point. The wolves, in basically all their forms, are great light attackers, able to get in, do a lot of damage, and get out before retaliation hits. The hands and birds are my range attacks, and I could probably swap the birds for bats as we get back underground.

I have some support denizens, but not as much as I might have expected. While I can't forget the healing ants and slimes, I'd like to get a denizen that can put out some buffs or debuffs. With my current spawners, it's the hands who will most likely be able to provide that kind of support, though a new wolf might manage something, too.

I'm lacking in heavies right now. The twinsnakes are pretty heavy, but thanks to the winter, they're quite limited. They should do better once deeper into the earth, at least.

If I want to get more heavies, I'd expect the wyrms to be the ones to offer a new tanky denizen. The Earth elemental spawner could definitely do it, too, but I'd not only have to abandon the hope of focusing on resources, but I'd probably have to kiss subtle elementals goodbye.

So the wyrm and hand spawners are possibly the best chances at filling the gaps in my army. It looks like I'll have enough to get the dragon spawner to cough up something new, but it'll be close. I might need to try to encourage more delver activity to cover the cost . . . or try to figure out why I didn't get a boost from that battle. We did kill a *lot* of invaders, and Rocky even smoked the enemy scion, so where's my mana?

It doesn't take long to figure that out, at least. I can see Rocky has a large pile of reserved mana sitting in his proverbial pocket that neither I nor he can access.

I'm pretty sure it's because he's on expedition. Scouts don't get to keep the intel they gather if they don't come back to report in, and research expeditions have to bring the interesting things back, so why wouldn't fighters have to bring back the mana they gain, too?

I'll have Teemo check with Leo, or maybe bug Poe while we wait for my wolf to respawn. Once he's back, we can talk about what upgrades to get, and rotate out the denizens on the front line so we can get at the mana I'll need to actually afford them.

I also need to talk to everyone about what to do going forward. Aranya and Yvonne will want to know how the battle went, and Tarl will probably have advice for fighting the other dungeon. I'll also need to check in with Rezlar and see about his plans for encouraging more delving.

This campaign is going to be longer than anyone was hoping for.

Chapter 32

While I wait for Leo and Honey to respawn, there are at least some things I should do. For one: I should gather my people for a meeting. Somewhere around noon tomorrow sounds good.

Aranya and Yvonne are obvious to invite, as well as Tarl. My High Priestess and the inspector both know way more about dungeons than I do, and my favorite birb deserves to have her opinion heard on any risks I'm taking.

The spiderkin triumvirate and Larx also should hear what's going on. They've all been preparing to fight Aranya's old dungeon, but we haven't found any actual leads on it yet.

While I'm kinda tempted not to tell them about the Harbinger and its dungeon, it wouldn't really help my dwellers. They'll find out eventually, and either immediately jump in to try to make up for lost time, or think they did something to make me think they don't deserve to fight. If they want to join in, I won't stop them. It'd probably be good practice for them, anyway.

I'll also need to invite Rezlar. I don't know if he has many resources to directly offer for this fight, but I'll probably need his help to convince people to delve a bit more. I need to spend mana on a lot of upgrades if I want to bring this fight to the Harbinger's home.

And speaking of, I can't ignore my own home. It's easy to forget my projects here with the distraction of the Southwood's troubles. I only really have three ongoing right now, with one just about ready for the public.

While I've been focusing on the north, Queen and Thing have been working hard on the labyrinth. Coda's been working, too, but he's a bit more focused on the lighthouse. Still, he's gotten the main mechanical parts of the maze working. That, combined with the magical and alchemical fun, means the lava labyrinth is just about ready for business! I'm sure Rezlar will be happy to talk to the miners and whatnot and give them the official Thedeim go-ahead to run around in the new playground.

And with that project mostly ready, it'll free Coda to focus a bit more on the lighthouse. The first floor is more or less complete, so now Hullbreak needs to decide what to actually do with it. At the moment, it's mostly an open floor, though there are several rings of arches to keep it stable.

If the water dungeon doesn't have any ideas, I'll probably suggest to make the first floor a miniature maze. It doesn't have the massive footprint of my hedge maze, but there should still be room to put in some winding hallways and intersections, sprinkled with a few chests and encounters.

And the final project: to get a metalworks. I'm not really surprised that Fluffles isn't that into it. He gave it a proper try, but it just doesn't resonate with him. Even Nova gave it a try, but I think, if she's going to get into any crafting, she'll prefer actual forgework.

The real surprise is that Jello seems to be quite enjoying it. The last few days, when I could spare a couple minutes to check, I'd find her in Violet's metalworks, working away with Legs on the spearheads.

She hasn't gotten a title yet because I don't have access to the new room yet, but I'm pretty confident she'll manage it. I'm glad for her. After the whole mole/gremlin thing, I was a little worried she might take the failure to heart, but I shouldn't have worried. She's just not the type to worry about that kind of thing. Still, I'm glad she'll have a real success under her belt, something to show for all that optimism.

So . . . that puts all three of my main projects well on the road to completion. Even helping arm my dwellers is going well. Should I try to come up with another . . . something?

It only takes a quick glance around for me to see I probably shouldn't. There's not a whole lot of room for a major project right now. I could expand, but I don't know if I want to try to juggle all the fun new stuff along with the ongoing problem of the Harbinger and its dungeon.

I should probably just wait. If I'm lucky, it'll stay in its hole once it respawns, or try to subsume some other dungeon. Or maybe that wouldn't be lucky at all. I wouldn't want it to get even stronger.

No, I should expect it to try to come back, and I should also expect to be able to track down its dungeon relatively quickly. I mean, my wolves will have a pretty good scent trail to follow. I'll just want to make sure the scouts don't get spotted. A hand or two should be able to keep them hidden even in the tunnels. And once we discover the general area, the wyrms and rockslides can blend in better and get me some of that tasty, tasty intel.

And speaking of tasty intel: it looks like Leo and Honey are about ready to respawn.

I ask Teemo to get them to the war room once they're ready, and we can all get on the same page to figure out what to do next.

Leo

Teeth, darkness, pain, relief . . .

Life.

Leo gasps as his eyes open, safe and sound back in the wolf den. The relief of escaping that monstrosity of a scion is quickly crushed by the realization that it still lives! He staggers to his paws, eyes wide as he tries to warn his Alpha.

"Easy there, Leo."

"But that thing—"

"It's fine," reiterates Teemo. "Rocky literally tore it apart, shattered it, and burned what was left to ashes. The Southwood and Thedeim both are fine."

Leo takes a minute or two to get his panic back under control, though he finds it much more difficult to control his shame at his defeat. He can't even think of anything he could have done differently. That monster was utterly beyond him. Even with Honey's help, the weight of its focus was . . .

The wolf shudders and tucks his tail before feeling a weight land on his head and scratch his ear.

"Hey, none of that. You're home safe, and the Boss isn't upset. If you're ready, he wants you and Honey to tell him what happened, and then we'll all decide what to do next."

Leo does his best to stifle the whimper rising in his throat, and nods without speaking.

"Hey, I mean it when I say the Boss isn't upset with you, Leo. He was able to watch the battle through you guys' eyes, and he's got nothing but good things to say about your tactics and movements. Once you two give your reports, he's gonna want to hear your recommendations for what directions to take a few spawners in, to make sure we have what we'll need to field a formidable army the next time we fight."

The number of absurdities in what the Voice just said are . . . well, ***absurd***. The wolf is so thrown off, he can only echo the last of what he just heard. "The next time?"

Leo can feel him nod. "Yeah, the next time. That thing was definitely a scion, which means it has a dungeon to respawn in. It also probably has more spawners than just the weird leech-heads, so get that tactical brain in gear, because the Boss needs it."

Leo is feeling a lot less secure in his so-called tactical mind than the Voice and Alpha are, but if they still want his input, he refuses to let it be anything but his best. He takes a moment to focus himself, then lets Teemo lead him to the library as he thinks.

What could he have done better with what he had? He goes over the battle in his mind, looking for mistakes. While he certainly wouldn't call it flawless, there are a few glaring mistakes he can think of. The biggest one was letting his forces get surrounded. The trenches had been designed to be able to push back an assault from the single entrance, but he can't assume an enemy will only attack from the position he knows about.

He'll need to redesign the defensive positions the tunnelbore ants can dig, to ensure being encircled like that won't force a desperate gambit like charging the enemy commander to buy the denizens time to dig out a fresh escape route.

Yes . . . his major mistakes were in getting surrounded—and in dying. He'll need to try to join the spars that Fluffles likes to organize before heading back out to the lines.

He might have to settle for sparring with Rocky instead, depending on how quickly he needs to get back.

He's drawn from his thoughts as he enters the library and finds Honey simply sitting on the checkout desk, looking introspective.

"How're you holding up, Honey?" asks the Voice.

Honey jerks at the sound before giving a timid dance of apology.

"Nothing to be worried about. Respawning can be a bit disorienting, especially after a battle with stakes. Believe me, I know," speaks Teemo with gentle encouragement. Honey's reply is still a bit distracted and uncertain.

"The battle went fine. Rocky obliterated that Harbinger, and thanks to your quick thinking of getting the denizens into the holes, it wasn't too big of a deal to clean up the rest of the invaders. Are you up for a debrief? The Boss wants to hear your guys' take on the whole thing, and then your advice on how to upgrade some of his spawners. He has a few ideas, but he wants to make sure he's reading the tactical situation right first."

Honey dances an affirmative, looking a little more confident by the end, and then the three slip through a shortcut to the secret war room. Leo can't help but tuck his tail and show his belly when Teemo asks him to report, but the gentle warmth through the bond gives truth to the Voice's claims. The Alpha isn't here to lay blame or punishments. Mistakes will be acknowledged so they can be fixed.

Even with Teemo's warning, it's still a bit of a shock when he asks for Leo and Honey's opinions on what spawners to upgrade. Leo leans toward upgrading the Earth elemental one to produce some bruisers, but has to admit the dragon's would probably produce something at least as tough.

The idea of a stealthy path for the elementals is intriguing, too. The rockslides are excellent scouts even with their poor mobility. If the spawner can produce something stealthy and quick, it could be just what Leo needs to direct the forces of his Alpha properly.

He's also more inclined to leave the hands be, at least for now. If it comes to another large clash, the Alpha wants Slash to be there to bolster the army, so having further effects from the hands is less of a priority.

Leo's recommendation is to upgrade the dragon spawner and see what it produces after wyrms. While he's certainly willing to spend the time to go through the apparent multitude of options with the Earth elementals, the wyrms and slides are very good scouts already.

The biggest gap in the Alpha's forces is in heavy units that can operate in a wide variety of environments. The only place Leo can think that the wyrms can't work in would be underwater, but they've already dealt with a hostile in that situation.

Leo gets the feeling this new enemy dungeon will not be so reasonable as to surrender like Hullbreak did.

Chapter 33

Leo's probably right in that I should upgrade the dragon spawner if I want some heavies, and I'm pretty sure I *do* want some heavies. Dragons are never pushovers, and even the wyrms are pretty tough, especially for the initial spawn!

The rest of the debrief and chat takes us until dawn, when Teemo says Leo would like to do a bit of sparring with Fluffles before going back to the front line, if that's all right.

While I'd like him back quickly, I think he can take a day or two to get himself settled, and Honey too. I make sure I won't be messing with his plans if I send a few wolves with illusion hands into the tunnels, then spend the mana to do just that. Then grumble as I remember they're on expedition and I can't just give them orders.

Thankfully, I can have Rocky give them an order, even if it costs even more. It's probably because he's not a commander like Poe or Leo. Anyway, once Leo gets back to the front, I'll have him try to get Southwood to send some kitsune into the tunnel to scout, too.

All those invaders are sure to have left their scent all over the place, so the canids should be able to track them back to the source without too much difficulty. And their keen noses should hopefully warn them to head back once they find the source instead of needing to get close enough to potentially get caught.

Wyrms will be the main scouting force at that point, as well as the rockslides, so I dump a big chunk of my mana into the dragon spawner and get an upgrade, but it's going to take another two or three, I think, before it gives me something new. For now, I'll just accept more wyrms, and the boost Nova gets from me upgrading her spawner.

With that, it's not hard for Teemo to head out and give the invitations for a meeting. Noon might be a bit short notice, but I think everyone should be informed as quickly as possible. I'm also definitely going to need Rezlar's help in upping my mana income, which just feels weird to contemplate.

I'm pretty sure I make a lot more than most dungeons, period, and definitely make a lot for my size. Usually, I don't need to worry about waiting for the mana to accrue, but this hostile dungeon has me a little on edge.

At least the lava labyrinth should be a huge uptick in generation. Rezlar will probably only need to say it's ready for business, and the place will be swarmed.

Hopefully, it'll be enough of a mana boost to upgrade the dragons quickly. The wyrms are incredibly powerful for being just the first iteration, but the spawner is also incredibly hungry for mana to upgrade.

I just need to be patient, which is easier said than done with the mysterious home of that Harbinger out there. I do my best to try to relax and watch the delvers as I wait for noon. The miners in the cavern layer have started upping their production, quarrying out strong stone for the lighthouse, and it's interesting to watch them work.

They drill a line of small holes, hammer in some special wedges, and then it's like they're playing a song on the rock as they whack away, using the tone to tell where the stress is the greatest.

I would say it's nothing on what Slash can do, but he stops by to watch and listen a bit, too. I doubt he'll be playing anything like that, but it's a good example of earth and sound working together.

I feel much better as noon rolls around, and I prepare to nudge Honey and Leo to meet up in the public war room. Honey, I don't need to bother. She already has her home swarm setting everything up, including a rushed map of the area north of Southwood. She even has Teemo helping get everything set up to her liking.

I do need to remind Leo, though, as he's currently sparring and chatting with Fluffles. I think he's trying to get advice on expanding his affinities, but I don't know enough about Shadow to offer any advice.

I should try to point him toward Tiny. While the big guy hasn't expanded his affinities either, he can definitely help Leo navigate Fate a bit. That'd probably be a huge boost in commanding armies.

Anyway, I give him enough time to refresh himself some so he's not panting the entire time, and soon, people start showing up. Aranya arrives first, along with Larx, Folarn, Vernew, and Norloke.

My pretty red kobold smiles at my Voice as the group moves to the table. "Hello, Teemo. Looks like Honey is going all out for this one."

Teemo chuckles. "Heh, yeah. She and Leo have a lot of info to present, so I figure it's better to let her handle organizing it all. Where's Yvonne?"

"She's getting the party, as well as Tarl and Berdol. She would get Mayor Rezlar, too, but I believe he'll want to arrive semiofficially."

Teemo shudders. "Politics, bleh."

Larx smirks at Teemo's reaction. "Appearances help keep the people from panicking. If the mayor rushed to some emergency meeting with the weird local dungeon, people might wonder if something is wrong."

Teemo still sticks his tongue out at the idea. "People shouldn't worry so much, but yeah, I get it. Oh, feel free to have a seat, everyone. I don't think Honey has any specific places in mind . . . ?" he says uncertainly, glancing to the bee, who does a quick jig in negative. "Yeah, just have a seat while we wait. How're the enclaves doing? I haven't had a chance to take a good visit in a couple of weeks."

Larx gratefully takes a seat before replying. "We're still toying with new forge and smelter designs. It's mostly all theorycraft still. We might need to focus on some alchemy first, oddly enough. Our current firebricks wear too quickly for the new designs, so we'll need to figure something out. Jouler is looking into enchanting instead, hoping runework will be a viable alternative, but we'll see."

"Folarn's got a boyfriend!" pipes up Vernew with a wide grin. The small spiderkin deliberately chose a spot that puts Norloke between her and the larger woman, having expected reprisal for spilling the beans. Instead of a death glare, Folarn actually blushes a little and nods.

"I invited Yamik to dinner," she admits with little embellishment.

"He's the lobster wrangler, right?" asks Aranya, beaming with genuine happiness for the tarantulakin. They all happily chat and congratulate Folarn, trying to wring details from the taciturn woman. She doesn't give much, though it seems at least partially because there aren't many to give. It was a quiet meal together, and a nice talk that lasted well into the evening.

Yvonne arrives not long after with Ragnar, Aelara, Tarl, Berdol, and . . . the guildmaster of the adventurers' guild? What was his name again?

"Karn," whispers Teemo for my benefit before raising his voice. "Heya, Yvonne! Looks like you've got an extra?"

Yvonne nods. "Yes, the guildmaster managed to catch wind of us all gathering, and would like to attend."

"I don't want to force it, though," speaks up the thin orc. "If it's private, I can go."

I consider for a few moments before giving Teemo my answer.

"The Boss says that's fine. He didn't specifically invite you because he figured you'd be busy or just not interested, but he's not going to turn down some more help."

"Great! If he has anything he needs help with, I have a whole guild full of adventurers already trying not to be too bored with winter slowing things down."

They all take a seat at the table, and Tarl studies the large map. "That's the Southwood's northern border?"

Teemo nods. "Yeah, that's where the fighting has been. I'll save the details for when Rezlar gets here, though. There's a lot to get through, so I don't really wanna repeat it."

The elf nods at that and confers with his apprentice, going over notes and the basics of the Southwood in general. It quickly draws in the others as questions are asked, and soon, Tarl is practically giving his own presentation on the Southwood and the way it functions.

As he starts winding down, Rezlar and his entourage enter the front gate, and Teemo goes to greet him. His honor guard is allowed to do some delving while Miller accompanies him to the war room. He looks a lot less nervous than I would expect when everyone focuses on him, but I don't know if he's just getting better at acting or if he's genuinely getting more comfortable with attention.

Either way, it's time to get the meeting underway.

"Alright," speaks up Teemo. "Just to make sure everyone's on the same page: The Boss has been helping the Southwood with an invader problem. Leo and

Honey have been the ones mostly handling it, along with the Boss's denizens. Things had been going pretty smoothly—until yesterday."

Looks ranging from curiosity to concern are directed at Teemo, who mostly ignores them as he continues. "The invaders' movements had been strange for about a week before, so the Boss also sent Rocky as a bit of insurance. It was a good thing he did. Honey?"

My Bee Scion buzzes and dances as her bees take up positions on the map, each carrying a little picture of either one of my denizens or one of the invaders. The bees move as details are drawn on the map, and Teemo translates.

"Leo was able to direct the scouts to find the enemy base, which turned out to be more of a beachhead. They're from deep underground, as far as we can tell, and this was their exit to the surface. They were building up their forces, and if we'd waited much longer, we probably wouldn't have been able to stop them. And that's not counting the enemy scion that joined the battle.

"Yeah, Tarl, it's a scion, unless wild invaders can get titles?"

Tarl taps his fingers against the table as he thinks. "They can, in theory, but if they were building up their forces before attacking, that's definitely dungeon behavior."

Teemo nods and continues. "With its specific title, the Boss doesn't think it's wild, either. Here's what it looks like." Teemo pauses for a moment as Honey's bees start passing out drawings of the Harbinger. "It's a real nasty piece of work, with Mental affinity to boot. The leech-heads, as the Boss is calling them, aren't exactly tactical fighters, but this thing could command them like an extension of itself. It was able to defeat both Leo and Honey, though thankfully, Rocky was able to handle it."

Aranya's gasp catches Teemo's attention. It doesn't sound like she's worried about the two scions who are now at the table with her. She's looking at the picture with trembling hands, not noticing everyone's attention.

"Aranya?" asks Yvonne, voicing everyone's concern for the kobold.

Her eyes snap to Yvonne for a moment, wild and wide, before she gives a shuddering exhale and turns the paper over, hiding the image of the Harbinger. She takes a few more calming breaths before looking at Teemo.

"That was leading the force from the dungeon?"

Teemo slowly nods. "Yeah?"

"That . . . is what the hunters brought as tribute on the day I escaped. That's the thing that went berserk and smashed my cage. I fled in the confusion, and I thought the dungeon would have surely just killed the thing and absorbed its mana."

Yvonne frowns. "Do you think it subsumed your old dungeon, then?"

"I doubt it," interjects Tarl, causing all eyes to turn to him. "I've been trying to research the invader ever since you gave me those anatomical sketches. Nothing is even remotely similar to them. I've never seen anything like this monster, either. You never saw any of the weird invaders when the thing was presented?"

Aranya shakes her head, and Tarl continues.

"If it was some wild invader who subsumed the dungeon, it would almost certainly stay put. There's not a lot of information about invaders subsuming dungeons, but I haven't read any reports of the ones responsible heading out to attack more. They seem to settle down for a while, or maybe just dissipate back into the stagnant mana, maybe to guard against another dungeon forming.

"Either way, they don't go out and attack. If it was a rival dungeon, it would have sent some of these leech-heads as support, especially if this thing can wield them so effectively. You would have seen them attacking as you fled, if nothing else."

Tarl pauses and frowns, not liking where his logic is leading him, but also not having any other ideas that seem viable to him. "If they work so well together, that implies they have the same type. I don't think it killed your dungeon, nor do I think your dungeon killed it. I think it *transferred*, either away from some other dungeon, or was somehow pacified from being wild.

"Either way, if something like that became a scion, it would create a spawner. These things could be the lowest-tier creature, with hopefully the leader as the apex."

He pauses and shakes his head. "It's a lot of ifs and maybes, but . . ."

"But it fits," says Teemo with certainty, echoed by grim expressions from Aranya and Yvonne.

Even I can feel it in my affinity, despite how much I don't like it.

We've found Aranya's old dungeon, and it's somehow gotten even nastier since she last saw it.

Chapter 34

Much as I'd like to brood over the implications of the mystery dungeon being Aranya's old one, I'm not the only one considering the information. Larx is frowning as he thinks, while Folarn looks determined.

"We'll need to start marching soon," declares the large spiderwoman before turning her focus to Larx. "We will need your help in the cold, as well. Once back underground, we should be able to move fine, but even with the Scout's shortcuts, the cold will be taxing."

Vernew nods at that while Norloke looks thoughtful. She stays quiet as the ratkin elder speaks.

"I believe we can move whenever you're ready, Folarn. I think we'll both be waiting on Norloke to make some thicker winter wear, though," he says with a smirk, and the orb weaver nods absently.

"Yes . . . I haven't had to design much in the way of warm clothing. There are a few techniques that should work, but will take at least a few days to test out."

"That's fine," speaks up my Voice. "The Boss wants to get Leo in place to direct the scouting of the tunnels before we send any kind of actual force down there. From all appearances, it's probably a couple days' march from the surface to the foe, but Thedeim wants to be certain we won't get ambushed or stumble into them only a mile or two deep."

"If you need scouts," speaks up the orc, "I have a lot of adventurers who would love to stick their noses into places that may want to chop them clean off. In fact, you said it's near the Southwood? It's a great place to delve even in winter, but the snows tend to keep adventurers away this late in the year.

"Crafters are always starving for resources around this time, since most adventurers want to try to get some upgrades during the winter. I'm certain I can get some quests from them. We'd not only get the Southwood a nice mana injection but help outfit adventurers who would be more than happy to raid some hostile dungeon."

He smirks over at Ragnar, Aelara, and my residents. "After you helped take down Neverrest, I had a *lot* of complaints about missing out on that kind of quest. If Thedeim is aiming to take down a second dungeon, half the guild would leap at the chance, and the other half would go along as well just to have something to do."

That sounds great to me.

"The Boss isn't going to turn down help, and getting the Southwood some more mana would be great. And speaking of getting mana: the Boss is going to need a lot for this fight. He wants to upgrade the dragon spawner to get whatever is after wyrms, but the thing is expensive to upgrade. Thankfully, the lava labyrinth is pretty much ready. There are a few other finishing touches to add, but nothing really keeping him from letting the delvers officially in to run around and do their things."

Rezlar nods to himself at that. "I'll let the smithing and mining guilds know. They've been desperate to get at the mythril and orichalcum."

Ragnar interrupts with a low whistle. "Y'got *both*? Yer lucky they hav'nae barged in t' mine already! One or t'other's all well an' good, but *both* is enough t' cut off 'alf yer beard for."

Rezlar chuckles at that. "That might be underselling it. Bjorn looked almost possessed when he barged into the merchant's meeting and started shouting about it. From the looks of the other merchants, it's a major commodity. I'm not well-versed in the metals trade, but if a dwarf is excited about it, that's all I really need to know."

That earns some polite laughter around the table before Rezlar continues.

"I also think it shouldn't be too difficult to convince the merchants and crafters to step up their delving and trading. Winter is usually a slow season for them. It shouldn't take much to remind the crafters that Thedeim doesn't have to close for the cold, and the merchants will be more than happy to step up trade with the enclaves.

"With them moving to a bit more of a war footing, I'm sure they'll want a lot of goods. In fact, if you're going to be moving a lot of people a long distance, you might want to see about getting some wagons to help carry the supplies."

Larx and Norloke nod at that, with the spiderwoman replying, "We'll need to work with a wainwright to make a yoke for the tarantulakin. One or two should be more than enough to haul a loaded wagon."

When nobody else has anything to add, Teemo picks back up the lead. "The first floor of the lighthouse should be done soon, which should also help ease the Boss's mana load. He's been having to help shore up Hullbreak with the winter making it too cold for normal delving."

"Oh, normal delving will probably be picking up there soon," pipes up Karn, soon explaining, "The delving there was slow to start with, what with everyone still used to Hullbreak being belligerent and difficult to delve in the first place. But Old Staiven sent me a note the other day saying he should have proper aquatic potions for sale again soon. He had a bit of a supply issue that's been ironed out, so that should help Thedeim keep more of his mana, too."

Tarl nods at that. "I heard Freddie, Rhonda, and Larrez were able to delve and brought back a literal boatload of kelp. It's probably an ingredient in the potion. Do you have many adventurers who'll want to delve Hullbreak?"

Karn nods. "Definitely. I don't have anyone who was able to delve Hullbreak before the, uh . . . *incident*, but there's more than one group of sea dogs spending winter here who would love to dive in and keep the rust off."

"That'd be a big help. If the Boss can keep his mana for himself, not to mention getting new delvers in the labyrinth, he should be able to upgrade a few spawners, and maybe even get the Ant Enclave started."

That earns him a few surprised looks.

"A third enclave?" asks Rezlar.

"Yeah," says Teemo with a nod. "He's been leaning heavy into the ants for the labyrinth, and the spawner is maxed out now. If it weren't for the Southwood's trouble, he'd probably already have them progressing."

Larx and the spiderkin look happy at the idea of another enclave to live with, and Aranya looks eager to help guide their growth to be the best they can be.

"Can you support a third enclave?" asks Karn, looking a bit concerned.

Teemo shrugs. "I don't see why not. He had a spot in the labyrinth picked out, but it'll need to be expanded. It got a bit co-opted for a bit more labyrinth in there, but there's still plenty of room to dig. The Boss is expecting they'll be a bit fiery, and there's a pretty volcanic section past the labyrinth that they should be able to hunt or farm in. He should be able to do like with the ratkin and expand in a way to still give them plenty of room to hunt and grow."

"Speaking of growing," asks Tarl, "how's Violet doing?"

"She's doing well, still filling in her last expansion. The Boss worries a little about her defenses, but you haven't seemed too bothered by it?"

Tarl smiles and shakes his head. "She's shaping up to be a toybox, which is fine. I should take Berdol to do a fresh inspection, but last I saw, she had plenty to keep invaders at bay, which is honestly all she needs. If she wants to focus more on resource nodes, there's no problem with that. She'll honestly be cornering quite a niche if that's how she decides to progress."

"Yeah?" asks Teemo, voicing my own curiosity.

"Yeah. She's a deep dungeon, which are usually belligerent at best. If she can offer the kinds of resources they tend to have, but without the danger, she'll have more mana than she'll know what to do with."

I smile to myself at that, imagining Violet with a sprawling domain full of delvers happily gathering from her nodes, probably using all sorts of fancy rooms for crafting. She might even have some kind of arena like Rocky's for Onyx.

"How can we encourage more people to delve her?" asks Yvonne. "Thedeim already has a lot of similar nodes. She only really has her bunnies to stand out."

Tarl frowns slightly. "That's the hard part. While she'll be swimming in mana once she gets into more advanced things, Thedeim is already cornering the market a bit on that sort of stuff. She has simpler things right now, so not a whole lot of people are going to want to delve the young dungeon, especially with Thedeim trying to help train people for harder delves."

"Should the Boss try to up his lowest difficulty and give Violet a niche with newer delvers?"

The elf thinks for a few moments before shaking his head with a sigh. "Most are already past the point of needing the beginner challenge that Violet can provide."

Hmm.

Teemo quirks an eyebrow at my idea but decides to pass it on anyway. "What about kids?"

"What?" comes the surprised reply from many around the table, so Teemo quickly explains.

"Freddie and Rhonda are probably outliers, but kids need to get their first class *somewhere*, right? Probably with their parent's guidance or something? What about bringing a class or two of kids down to do a little delving. You know, bonk a few centipedes, see what it's like to do a little mining or rabbit hunting, help the kids figure out what they actually want to do."

Tarl gives Teemo a flat look. "I hope you're not about to make a whole generation of kids with rare classes."

Teemo just shrugs before Rezlar interjects. "I believe some towns have programs along those lines. Even artisan classes can gain a lot from knowing how to gather the raw material for their work, and dungeons are where the best materials are.

"I'll look into those programs and see if the local parents would be interested in something like that here. I think Thedeim starts well for apprentices, but could be a bit intense for most children. An actual toybox could be the kind of place a nervous parent could send their child, with adventurers' supervision, of course," he says, looking over at Karn. The orc nods.

"I'd be happy to provide security myself. If a parent isn't willing to let their kid into a toybox under the eye of the leader of the local adventurers' guild, they probably barely let them out of the house."

"Then I'll definitely need to do that inspection. She'll need to be officially categorized by the Dungeoneer's Guild if there's going to be any kind of outreach like that. Sending a child to a toybox is one thing, but into an uncategorized dungeon is another. Besides, it'll be good practice for Berdol for us to do that kind of detailed inspection."

"Then . . . I think that's about all the Boss needed to bring up? Karn, if you have any groups who want to go scout or delve Southwood, let me know. I'll show them the shortcuts that'll make it easier to get there."

Karn nods and the meeting ends, though nobody clears out just yet. They all start chatting about various details, coordinating for the plans, or just catching up on life with friends.

I can't help but smile to myself as I listen. It's easy to get caught up in my head and think I'll have to face stuff on my own, but I have my friends who can and will help. While it'll probably be on me and my scions to strike the final blow against the mystery dungeon, I'd never get there without help.

And seeing everyone working together, talking, laughing, helps keep me focused on why I'm fighting in the first place. I should make sure to never get too wrapped up in the fighting to forget what I'm fighting for.

Chapter 35

Elsewhere

Deep beneath the surface lies the dungeon known as the Maw. Just outside its territory lies the town of Silvervein. The inhabitants, almost entirely pale elves and pale dwarves, are emancipated dwellers, released from the Maw so they can better provide it with mana. The priesthood of the Great Maw holds sway over the town, with varying levels of enthusiasm by the inhabitants.

Most of them, like most people in any town, do their best to ignore politics. They simply want to live their lives as best they can, with many unaware of how off-putting their society is to outsiders. Most of them don't particularly care what the outsiders think, as most of what lives beyond the guarded tunnel entrances are monsters.

But there are some who dream of more, and are shrewd enough to consider that maybe, just maybe, it's not an opinion that should be shared with just anyone. The priesthood takes a very dim view on dissenting voices, and those who complain too loudly will often find their contributions to the Great Maw to be insufficient.

Those unlucky enough to gain the attention of the priesthood will generally find themselves offered to the Maw, as the hungry dungeon can always use more mana.

For most, it's just further encouragement to stay out of politics. For some, it's another sign that there can be something better, but one must be careful how one dreams. Dreaming in your bed at night is one thing, but dreaming out in the day will draw attention.

A loose network of dreamers carefully probes, daring to hope for something more. One such dreamer is a cheesemaker, Serd. He's an elf, born into a line of cheesemakers, and quite fond of his job; his Decay affinity also helps the process along perfectly.

In his youth, he tried to raise milkworms, hoping to be able to master the entire process, but the worms were more ornery than he'd expected. He'd had to take the worm to the butcher after it collapsed a wall in the cheese cellar, ruining an entire rack of product.

As an adult, he supposes it was a good lesson for him to learn: dream, but not recklessly. A rack of cheese is a small price to pay to learn that things are more complex than they might seem at first.

So he's left the milkworms to the wranglers, and outwardly turned his focus back to his cheeses. While he does take pride in his experiments with smoking them, his true work is in finding others who would like to have someplace better.

Like the veins running through a proper blue cheese, he's slowly built a network of fellow dreamers. He's been cautious, ensuring that people don't share names, don't meet up with others face-to-face, don't even tell *him* the details of who they might bring in.

It hasn't been perfect, but he thinks it's been working well. Some groups get discovered, but the security measures keep the tragedies to handfuls of people instead of exposing the entire network. Sometimes he wonders if he might be able to overthrow the priesthood if he went public, but that's a particular dream that is beyond even him.

He's no daring leader, and even if he somehow could scrape together enough people with enough levels to challenge the priests, there's nothing he could do against the Maw. He's seen others try, usually by attempting to sneak an invader deep into the Maw, but nobody has tried in many years. The Redcap's public haberdashery of the last offender was enough to dash any other ideas of similar plans.

He sighs as he pulls the wire frame curd cutter from the wall and sets about cutting the latest batch. If only processing guilt was so easy. He had thought it a stroke of luck to turn one of the cardinals, one of the people positioned high enough to actually be able to enact change!

It had been a long process, dropping subtle words and suggestions off with each wheel of his best work. Only, when he went to drop off this month's shipment, the cardinal wasn't there to accept it. Instead, it was an acolyte Serd wasn't familiar with, though the look of zeal in the young dwarf's eyes was unmistakable.

"Oh? Where is the cardinal? She usually collects my offering directly. Is she busy?" he asked, trying to keep it casual. It quickly became clear something was wrong, as the dwarf snarled and prepared to spit. The acolyte was forced to simply swallow the phlegm thanks to all the other food around, but he didn't need to be so concerned with his opinions.

"The cardinal has been hatted for being a traitor," growled the acolyte. Serd made no effort to keep his face from growing even paler at that. "Plans to free the kobolds were found in her room. Thankfully, the inquisitors discovered it before they could go much further," he finished with a cruel grin.

"Ah . . . uh, good to catch it so early?" he awkwardly replied, which seemed to satisfy the zealous acolyte. His cheese was accepted, with even the low-ranked dwarf seeming to be happy to have it. Serd is hardly a cheese*master*, but his successful experiments are apparently conversation pieces among the priests, and new challenges for the chefs.

He shakes the memory off as he shakes the cutter clean, then starts to drain the tub of the whey. He hadn't known he had made such an impression on the cardinal, but at least she hadn't sold him out. If so, he'd have probably been consumed by the Maw, no matter how interesting his experiments were. He almost wishes she had told him about her plans to free the kobolds, but it's probably for the best she didn't.

Still . . . it could be a good idea. The Maw losing its dwellers could be a blow to its legitimacy and power. If something so jealously guarded and cared for were to be taken from the Maw, the people might listen to calls for change.

Or they might not care. Those who believe in the Great Maw see the kobolds as its sacred delicacy. Those people would chase the kobolds to the molten abyss and beyond to get them back. Some others take pity on them, but don't dare to speak up.

Unfortunately . . . most people just try to ignore them, and with them so carefully guarded by the Maw, it's easy to do just that.

Hmm . . . could he be subtle about it? Breaking them free would probably only make a mess, but what if he tries to make it so people can't forget about the kobolds?

While he can't exactly go around giving speeches to argue for their freedom, he could try something a bit more subtle. He might even get the priesthood to endorse it, if he plays his cards right.

As he lets the whey drain, he goes over his cheese notes, looking for what seems to be the favored one for snacking directly. He'll need to get new molds made, and adjust the process for a smaller size, but it could work.

If he plays up the sacredness of the kobolds, makes them sympathetic, the people may take it more to heart, and so be more open to helping them. The priesthood would have difficulty clamping down on that kind of sentiment, too, especially if he uses the priests' own words against them.

He'll have to start slow, really emphasize the importance of the kobolds to the Maw, make it seem like a refutation of what the cardinal was doing. Once the new snack is established, it'll only take a subtle change in the message to emphasize empathizing with them. Once that's done, the priesthood will have a hard time arguing down the natural questions about how to improve the lot of the kobolds.

Yes . . . this could work.

Kobold cheese, shaped like their namesake. The molds will be difficult to make, but he has some coin to spend for his projects. The texture of a carved mold would usually invite irregularities into the cheese, but with small enough molds, it shouldn't make too much of a difference. He'll need one he can easily accelerate with his affinity, probably a softer cheese, but not a spreadable one.

Kids will love it; he has no doubt. Not all will carry the happy memories all the way to adulthood, and fewer will associate the actual kobolds with the memories, but maybe enough. It will take a long time, if it works at all, but it will still be him taking action. He'd like to do more, but what else can he do? Even something like this risks him being hatted, but he can't stand by and do nothing any longer.

He'll just have to be patient and take it slow, be prepared for the inevitable investigation.

He smiles as he pulls out his notes on the favored snacking cheese. Patience and attention to detail are the hallmarks of making cheese. Even if his affinity can speed the process, he's no stranger to letting time do the majority of the work, and he already knows he'll need to leave the brunt of the work to time.

Just as with cheese, trying to rush this will make much more of a mess than just a worm collapsing part of his cellar.

Chapter 36

The new dawn brings the first official visitors to the lava labyrinth. I've had signs at the entrance saying it's still a work in progress, but I couldn't technically force people to stay out. Still, most stayed away or were happy to harvest the metals closest to the entrance. It's one of those natural things: put a distraction out to keep attention away from what you still need to focus on.

But with the labyrinth being finished, I can seal those nodes behind long, looping corridors, so I don't even need to try to move the actual ore vein. Slash is hanging out in the area, playing some music and using his Earth affinity to smooth a few rough edges.

The magical and alchemical traps are polished to a mirror shine, metaphorically. A big shiny trap isn't something people are going to fall for, generally. The mechanical bits are a bit more rough, but I think Coda is going to have some unexpected help.

Jello has, somehow, gotten a hold of his designs for the mechanisms, and she and Legs are both working away in Violet's metalworks to make the parts. I don't know if Jello will be able to install them, but just having the parts available ought to make it a lot quicker for Coda to do it himself.

It's looking like the labyrinth is going to be a gold mine of mana, too. People don't seem as inclined to wait for official ODA approval for it, unlike with most of the other new things I've made.

I can see Berdol in the large group that's already making their way down, but I think he's here as a delver, not an inspector. The lack of Tarl is a big clue for that. The elf will probably be by in a couple of days to do an official inspection, and I'll see if I can take the opportunity to talk to him a bit more about the Harbinger.

I didn't have a good chance to do so at the meeting, and I didn't want to just blurt it out in front of everyone. The weirdness about what it's a harbinger *of* is pretty concerning, but I think only Tarl really has any context for it. Even then, it's probably just going to be another mystery to shove onto his plate. I'd like him to leverage some help from the ODA, but he might not be able to tell them about it.

Either way, it's a worry I can't do much about, so I resolve to watch the inaugural run of the lava labyrinth. The trip down is pretty uneventful, even though I toss quite a few heavy things at the large group. A twinsnake might be scary for a small party, but there's gotta be close to two dozen adventurers in the group.

I actually manage to pull a good surprise with some of the arcane hands, but once they realize there's magical manual mischief in their midst, they rally quickly and keep the miners from anything worse than a good scare.

They all gather outside the entrance and separate into half a dozen groups. Berdol speaks up to get everyone's attention.

"Alright, everyone should be familiar with the plan, so do your best to stick to it. We don't have much information about the layout inside, so make sure to keep track of where you are. Teemo has said there are supposed to be a lot of traps, as well as being the domain of the wyrms. He wouldn't pull something deliberately deadly, but he'll still keep what you've gathered if you're beaten, so don't lower your guard."

He pauses and smirks at the miners. "And the miners will probably not pay very much for missing out on all the ore in there. As long as you all keep a good map, the Dungeoneer's will pay for info, so keep that in mind, too. We'll split up once we can, and hopefully by the end of the day, we'll all have enough coin to buy something made from the special metals here. Any last-minute questions?"

Nobody seems to have any, everyone seeming eager to get started, including Berdol.

"Then let's go!"

With a cheer, everyone forms into a single large group again, but now that I've seen them split, I can see everyone is sticking close to their specific party, even while in the larger formation. The smaller groups quickly start splintering at each intersection, and soon, they're all happily exploring the labyrinth.

Most of the groups are taking it slow, going at a walking pace and keeping their eyes peeled. One is being pushed by their miners to hurry, three dwarves practically slavering at the idea of the ores hidden in the maze. Their protectors are a trio consisting of a bearkin with a large club, a changeling who looks like a fire mage, and a goblin with . . . lots of crystals? While I'd guess the bearkin is a berserker, I don't know what the goblin is.

The typical party makeup would suggest either a ranged attacker or some kind of support, but I honestly have no idea what the little guy actually does. I decide to watch them as they delve, curious about how they fight and if they'll stumble into a trap in their haste.

The bearkin and changeling lead the way, with the miners in the middle and goblin at the rear. The berserker is sniffing as they go, and I wonder how much scent can actually tell him. Can he smell the ores? If so, he's going to be a busy bear soon. With the shifting nature of the labyrinth, he'll probably be great at finding the actual path.

The changeling is drawing the map as they go, while the goblin tries to keep their impatient charges from doing anything too stupid.

"This is as fast as we can go," he says in a tone that indicates it's not the first time he's had to repeat it to these guys, and expects it won't be the last.

"We can't let the others beat us to the ore!" complains what seems to be the lead dwarf, though he has basically no accent at all. "We hired you to get us there as quickly as possible, but this isn't even a jogging pace!"

"Do you charge around blindly in a new forge?" asks the changeling, trying to keep the annoyance out of his voice. The three dwarves look scandalized at the very idea.

"Of course not! There are dangers in a forge if you're not careful!"

"What makes you think this is any less dangerous?" rumbles the bearkin, his large club resting easily on his shoulder.

"It's just a tunnel!"

"Inside a *dungeon*," points out the goblin. "Even if this one is friendlier than most, it's still a dungeon. They're never more dangerous than when exploring a new area, and even more so when it's explicitly said to be full of traps. Speaking of, have you managed to sniff any out, Wold?"

The bearkin, apparently Wold, shakes his head with a frown. "Nothing out of the ordinary yet. I can smell a lot of mana around, though. Anything magical would be hard to pick out."

The goblin nods and lets his hand glide across the crystals in his belt before selecting one. He gently taps it and speaks quietly, though I can feel mana swirling around him as he does.

"Brownie, I have need of your aid." Mana swirls around the crystal as the goblin holds his hand flat, and a small figure coalesces. It almost looks like loamy soil shaped into a pudgy humanoid form, and finishes with a little green stocking cap. Two small pebbles seem to form eyes, and it makes strange noises at the goblin, who shakes his head.

"This would be torture for nixie, you know that. We're in a new place, and there should be traps about. I need you to help us find them. I offer milk, honey, and bread as payment, once we're back at the guild."

The brownie looks like it's deliberating the offer, but there was no mistaking the look of naked desire in its pebbles once the food was mentioned. It nods and hops off the hand, the goblin keeping a hold of the crystal, as the party continues.

I watch the little fey as they go, the small thing moving around much faster than the others. It catches the first alchemy trap, which looks to be an itch bomb, and the party decides to route around it. It also catches a magical slowness trap, which has me starting to get a bit worried. It can spot my traps without too much difficulty, which could put the whole concept of the labyrinth in danger.

"I still think it's weird you have to pay your summons, Gerlfi," speaks the changeling, eyeing the brownie as it points out another magical trap. "I mean, you already convinced them to help you, why do you have to keep convincing them?"

"Because they can still say no. I don't create them; I just transport a small part of them. They still have their own motivations."

"Hard binding angers the spirits," rumbles the bearkin, and Gerlfi nods.

"Wold has the right of it. They're fey, not spirits, but it's the same principle. How would you like it, Vieds, if you were actually compelled to listen to my good advice?" asks the goblin with a smirk, which the changeling returns.

"It might not be so bad, if you managed to actually give good advice once in a while."

Wold chuckles as Gerlfi pretends to be offended. His retort is interrupted by the sound of the brownie finally missing a trap. Wold and Vieds fall through the floor as it rotates, and before they even land, the trap slams back into place and clicks, disabling it and separating the party.

Gerlfi steps forward before stopping himself, not wanting to fall into the same trap, and instead tries to raise his voice. "Vieds! Wold! Can you hear me? Are you alright?"

In the tunnel below, the two groan at the unexpected fall, but they haven't injured anything. The changeling summons a small fireball to help light the area, revealing the brownie is with them, too. Wold's ear twitches as he hears his goblin friend yelling, and he looks up as he shouts his own reply.

"We're safe in a second tunnel! I don't see an obvious way back!"

Gerlfi looks relieved that his friends are safe, but it doesn't take long for the reality of the situation to sink in. "Separated. Great. I'm releasing the brownie!" he yells to his friends before severing the connection and causing the little fey to vanish with a small pop. He somehow manages to keep from pointing out how much hurrying helped contribute to the predicament as he explains their options to the dwarves.

"With us separated, we should head back. I can call on a more powerful fey if you really want to try to continue, but I'll have to offer it a portion of what you mine. That also assumes we won't trip into another trap before then."

"But . . . the ore!" insists the leader, looking like he knows what he should do but has to fight with his greed to actually do it.

The goblin simply shrugs. "I think we're not getting it; at least not today. Right now, the decision is if you want to walk out, or be carried out."

"And if we decide to press on?"

Gerlfi shrugs again. "Then I think you'll be doing it without me. I'm not in the habit of continuing doomed contracts."

"You can't do that!" exclaims the lead dwarf, looking livid, but the goblin's slow smile stops his bluster in its tracks.

"I can't? Do you really want to argue the language of our deal with someone who contracts with *fey*?"

The lead dwarf looks like he might, but his companions seem a bit more levelheaded. They clamp their hands over the loud one's mouth and shake their heads.

"No! No, that's alright. I think getting escorted back to the front gates now would be for the best. No sense hammering burnt metal, after all."

The goblin's smile grows much more warm and much less predatory. "Ah, good! I knew you were reasonable dwarves."

Chapter 37

I don't pay too much attention to Gerlfi the summoner as he leads the miners out, instead choosing to watch the other two as they try to navigate the labyrinth without the help of the brownie to point out the traps. They do better than I would have expected. The mage is able to sense when a magical trigger is nearby, and the two take the time to carefully find each one they come across.

Most of the magical triggers are just proximity sensors, which are basically just fancy trip wires. Of course, once they find one, they still need a way to defuse them. The very first one, they actually take a seat nearby to try to think of what to do.

"Can we just throw a rock?" asks the large bearkin, which makes the changeling shake his head.

"I don't suppose it'll hurt to try, but I think it's a life sensor. I also don't know what the trap will actually do. The only magic I feel is from what I'm pretty sure is the trigger."

Wold nods and picks up a large rock. "I'll try it. Be ready to flee if it trips." He gives Vieds a few seconds to get ready, and the changeling even helps him aim for the right spot before the bearkin chucks the rock.

Vieds is proven right when nothing happens, and Wold just nods at the setback. "What do we do, then? Try to trigger it then run? Try to find a different route?"

The changeling consults the map and sighs. "I think backtracking might get us around *this* one, but there's going to be more traps. We're going to need to get a rogue or maybe even an Arcane-affinity mage for next time, to deal with all these traps. Meta would be even better, but most of them are crafters."

Wold grunts and leads his friend away from the trap. "We should tell crafters to come along for this area, then. They already want what's down here. They could more easily pick exactly what to bring back."

Vieds nods at that and makes a note on the back of the map. "Well, let's see how much we can map out before we miss a trap . . . and hope the dungeon doesn't take our map as punishment."

They wind their way through the tunnels of the labyrinth for a while, mostly backtracking around the traps, but they do find a couple that are defeated with just a thrown rock. There are a couple motion detector magical triggers, and various mechanical ones, which can be set off with a well-placed throw.

I consider trying to redesign them, but with the mana they make from just triggering, I'm happy to leave them as is. They're going slowly enough that they're definitely going to bring a trap expert next time, so that's fine by me.

They almost get defeated even trying to cheese my traps. They spot a pressure plate trigger and set it off, only for the resulting sleep gas to chase them back down the hallway. One of my wyrms even takes the chance to try to surprise attack them, too.

Wold's eyes widen a heartbeat before the wyrm bursts from the wall, shoving Vieds forward before diving backward and letting my denizen fly through the air where the bearkin was just a moment earlier. The changeling quickly gets to his feet, quietly admonishing himself as he casts a spell.

"Right, of course there are encounters in here, too. Protection from Fire!" Mana settles over the two as Wold stands there, senses alert for the next attack. I can see my denizen looking confused at the spell, uncertain what to do about it.

I spend a little mana to give it a suggestion. *Just do a little probing attack, see if it's up to handling some magma.* The wyrm still looks uncertain, but decides to try giving Wold a hotfoot, rapidly heating the stone under one of his feet.

It seems that protection spell is a good one, as he seems to notice the ground going soft before he notices the heat. Quickly stepping aside, he slams the area with his club. Even with all that stone between the impact and the wyrm, my denizen is a bit dazed from the force.

"Detect Heat!" declares Vieds, and soon, his eyes fall on the wyrm. "There you are . . ." he murmurs, clearly trying to figure out what to do with this information. Luckily for my wyrm, these delvers aren't the only ones who can sling a bit of magic.

The wyrm moves quickly and splits off a few blooms of heat inside the rock, forcing the changeling to try to track more than one heat signature.

"Gah, it's trying to trick me, Wold! I don't know exactly where it is; there are a couple fakes around us now!"

"Where?" asks the bearkin, his heavy club ready.

"There, there, and there!" he shouts as his form shifts, taking on the shape of a ratkin and using both arms and the tail to point. He does his best to track the two fakes and the real denizen. "Be ready, they're moving toward the surface!"

Wold simply nods, as that's all the time he has before my wyrm makes its move. Each of the fakes bursts from a wall and the floor, one heading for each of the delvers. Vieds dodges his as a line of fire starts to trail from his hand, while Wold swats his own magma ball out of the air with his club.

A heartbeat later, the wyrm dives from the ceiling, mandibles wide as it hopes to take a bite out of the berserker.

"Flame Lash!" shouts the pyromancer, the trail of fire from his hand quickly coalescing into a flexible line of fire. He swings it forward to catch and close the mouth of the wyrm, giving Wold the time to plant his feet properly and bring his club to bear on the momentarily immobilized wyrm.

"Rock Crusher!" he bellows as the blow hits home, and it looks to me like that attack is fine for crushing wyrms as well as rocks.

Still, good work with the decoys, little wyrm. Good way to keep them on their toes.

I also didn't expect the fire mage to be able to help that much against a wyrm. A fireball wouldn't do much, but that fire whip was pretty effective. The fire part didn't do anything, but being able to actually tangle up a wyrm with it is a use I wouldn't have expected.

The pair manage to get past a couple more traps, as well as another encounter with two wyrms this time, before their luck finally runs out. Perhaps ironically, it's a heat detector that dooms their delve. The pyromancer easily spots it and manages to trick it so they can get past, but unluckily for them, Nova is in the area.

The shy scion waits for them to be in the perfect spot before she simply surfaces near enough to the sensor for it to trip, causing bars at both ends of the section of tunnel to slam down, trapping the two.

They both stare at her for a few moments before she timidly slips back beneath the surface. I'm laughing the entire time, proud of Nova's little trick. The two delvers sigh and look at the bars.

"Can you smash them, Wold?"

The bearkin runs his hands along the thick steel bars. "Maybe, but I'd damage my club. Can you melt them?"

Vieds frowns as he considers. "Also maybe, but it'd take enough of my mana that I'd be more or less useless for the rest of the delve."

They pace and explore the impromptu cell for a few more minutes before Wold breaks the silence.

"Should we simply surrender, then?"

The changeling winces at that, but then sighs and nods. "I think so. Even if we could get out of this, the map indicates we're nowhere near the exit yet. At best, we'd just get defeated by the next trap or wyrm. We should just save the time and get out. We might be able to do a quest more toward the surface before dinner, if we're quick."

Wold nods and takes a seat, curiously looking around their prison. "How do we actually surrender?"

Vieds looks stumped, but the answer soon manifests itself at the bars. One of my magmyrm slipped out of a shortcut just out of sight and has two small vials in its arms. It reaches through the bars and sets them on the ground before backing up as the two delvers consider the situation.

"Do we drink these to surrender?" asks the changeling. My magmyrm nods. He and Wold both examine the vials for a few long seconds.

"What do you think it is?" rumbles the bearkin, looking like he's not sure the small vial will even be enough of a dose to work on him.

"I'm not an alchemist, but the color reminds me of that cloud we ran from earlier. But we don't really know what that did, either . . ." he trails off, trying to think. The magmyrm waves its arms to get their attention and tries to explain what it does.

The denizen mimes drinking the potion, then lays down and closes its eyes. It even makes an adorable snoring sound, which gets Wold to smile.

"A sleeping potion. We really will be putting ourselves at the mercy of the dungeon if we drink."

Vieds nods. "It's not like we aren't already at its mercy." He pulls the cork and raises it to Wold in a toast, which the bearkin mirrors. They each quickly drink the potion and set the vials aside. They each look like they're about to ask if it's working before Wold gives out a large yawn.

The changeling chuckles as he lies down, looking exhausted. "At least it works quickly . . ." he mutters before closing his eyes, Wold following not long after.

My magmyrm gives them a couple minutes before going to gather up about a dozen others, and they retract one of the sets of bars before taking the defeated delvers through a shortcut. They decide to take a pair of nice daggers from the duo before continuing on their way. Before long, the two are lying on the grass, just in time for Gerlfi and the miners to exit the manor.

The goblin laughs and gets the miners to help him haul the two adventurers away, and I'm enjoying the nice chunk of mana from defeating them. They're not the only ones to fall to the labyrinth today, either. Only the few groups that went for shallower journeys manage to get out with any ore.

I'll need to ask someone if I should make it a bit easier, or if this is just right. The ones who made it out successfully are looking like they just won the lottery, though, so it might be too easy.

I'll leave it as it is, at least for now. This has been quite the uptick in my mana generation, and if I can have that and also not crash the market for special metals, this will be a huge success.

Chapter 38

It's around sunset when the last of the miners either walk out or give up. It's also about the time that Tarl and Berdol enter through the main gates. Tarl looks relaxed as he follows Berdol, who looks a bit nervous. I watch them curiously for a few moments before remembering they want to inspect Violet again before giving her an official categorization and recognition.

I don't even need to ask Teemo to say anything before he hops out of a shortcut at the porch and squeaks at the two.

"Hey, guys! Inspecting Violet before bed, hmm?"

Tarl chuckles as Berdol nods. "It's generally a good idea to inspect during off hours. It helps keep interruptions to a minimum."

Teemo nods at that wisdom, then eyes Berdol. "How about you? Looking forward to your first official inspection?"

The catkin nods, trying to hide his nerves. "Y-Yeah. She's a toybox, so it shouldn't be a problem. And you can help with questions and such."

"Nope," interrupts Tarl, drawing the gaze of the other two. "You'll be doing this one without Teemo's help. Other dungeons this young won't have a Voice to talk with, so you'll have to learn how to read between the lines and interpret what she wants without being able to actually ask and be answered with words."

Berdol looks even more nervous about that, while Teemo looks a little disappointed.

"I can't come?"

Tarl shrugs. "I can't tell you what to do, but just being there shouldn't hurt anything. Just no interpreting for Violet, please."

Teemo brightens up at that. "Deal! You guys want a shortcut down to the tunnels, or want to get a few encounters for Thedeim and take the normal way?"

Tarl smirks and looks to Berdol. "What do you think, Inspector?"

The catkin's eyes widen at that for a moment before he considers his options. "Uh . . . the shortcut, please. An inspector should be as prepared as he is able for an inspection. While some encounters would be nice, I should be at top form to inspect Violet, toybox or no."

Tarl smiles at that response. "Then if you would be so kind, Voice Teemo?"

Teemo laughs at the formality and hops onto Tarl's shoulder, pointing the two down a shortcut. "That reminds me of something, Tarl, and you'd probably know the answer. Why can I hear Violet? I thought I could only hear the Boss."

"Ah, that's a bit complicated, and honestly, I don't think I have all the details. But I think I can give a brief explanation." Tarl takes a few moments to collect his thoughts as Berdol takes the chance to get out his note-taking stuff.

"Well, to start with: you can hear Thedeim clearer than the other scions, correct?" Teemo nods, so he continues. "That's part of the power of being the Voice. You need to have a better understanding of what the dungeon wants if you're supposed to communicate those desires. You've probably noticed you're not the only scion who can form words, so you have to know that's not something limited only to you."

Tarl chuckles. "Poe was actually doing his best to fill in for you when you were off to the Southwood. He still has a limited vocabulary, but he also doesn't have as clear of an idea of what Thedeim wants as you do. In short, he can tell delvers like myself that Thedeim would like a meeting, but he can't exactly give a presentation and list his concerns, point by intricate point."

"Alright, but that still doesn't explain why I can hear Violet."

"I'm getting there. You don't hear her as clearly as you do Thedeim, right? Maybe you think it's because she's so young, but that's not it. She has clear desires, but you can only hear the gist of them. It's fine for a protégée; they need to listen and learn more than they need to speak clearly.

"You can hear her about as well as her normal scions can, which is another function of the Voice. You facilitate communication. She can understand what you say, even more clearly than she can understand what Thedeim tries to tell her through the protégée bond, because that's part of your job. And once she gets a Voice of her own, you'll be able to have a real conversation."

"I mean, I can kinda do that now . . ." starts my Voice.

"But it's a lot of guessing and considering context," finishes the inspector.

"When do you think she'll get her own Voice?" asks Teemo, causing Tarl to grin.

"Worried you're slowing her development? You became the Voice when Thedeim was about her age. Well, don't worry. Most dungeons take at least a couple of years before they get a Voice. I think she'll probably be ahead of the curve, just not as far as you were. She'll be getting a lot of mana once she gets official recognition, and I'm led to believe the Voice upgrade isn't cheap."

Teemo nods at that. "Yeah, the Boss paid . . . Well, it was a lot at the time."

Tarl smirks as they exit the shortcut before turning his attention to Berdol. "There is a small section of potentially hostile territory now between you and Violet. Thedeim doesn't own all of these tunnels, so be on the lookout. You may begin when ready," he says, pulling out his own clipboard and charcoal stick to take notes.

Berdol takes a breath to focus himself before drawing a pair of . . . boomerangs? He pulls them from their sheath with his magic, and I ask Teemo to get a good look at them. I don't think he's used these ones before, or maybe I'm only just noticing them now.

It doesn't take much looking to know they're not boomerangs. The shape is all wrong, for starters. It makes me think of maybe a weird shuriken or something? They're sharp all over and look like two knife blades fastened at the hilt to each other. They're definitely something designed to go with his affinity, because I can't imagine anyone using a weapon like that with their actual hands, even for throwing.

Berdol doesn't get a chance to show them off on the walk over. With my own expeditions around, there's not a whole lot of unfriendly things between me and Violet. He keeps the blades out as he enters Violet's outer cavern, though I can see his stance loosen up a bit in the safety of her domain.

He inspects differently than Tarl. Instead of speaking his observations, he writes them on his clipboard. I can feel Violet's curiosity through the bond, but I don't send her any hints for what to do. This is all on her.

Berdol inspects the mining nodes and notes the barren patches of floor where the scythemaw eggs are buried. He then pulls out a small pick and mines a little by hand before Onyx slips out of a crack to greet her friend. The catkin smiles at her and speaks up for the first time in his official inspection.

"Hey, Onyx. I can't play just yet; I'm doing an inspection."

Onyx tilts her head curiously then looks to Teemo. My Voice smiles and shakes his head. "I'll explain later. Violet should know what that means, though."

Onyx still looks curious as she follows, and I feel understanding through the bond as Violet remembers the inspections Rhonda and Freddie used to do when she was first discovered.

I find Berdol's style of inspection kinda boring, but Violet's curiosity remains constant, so she seems engaged, at least. I can also feel her considering what he writes about her nodes and denizens, wondering if she should change anything, and mulling ideas for improvements.

When Berdol gets to the door, he pauses and looks at it, tapping the clean end of his pen on his chin as he thinks. After a few moments, he looks to Tarl.

"Would this count as a puzzle?"

"What do you mean?" he neutrally replies.

Berdol gestures at the large stone door. "From what I understand, these doors were put in as a response to the scythemaws, right? They're something that a beast wouldn't be able to get past, but most delvers will be able to simply open it by pulling. Does that count as a puzzle?"

Tarl's eyes brighten, but his reply remains neutral. "What is a puzzle?"

"A type of trap or hindrance that requires thought to bypass, rather than simply power." When Tarl doesn't continue, Berdol considers the door for a few more moments before he scribbles on his paper. "A puzzle, then. A very rudimentary one, but it still counts."

Tarl can't quite keep the prideful smile off his face as Berdol enters Violet's main chamber. Berdol hunts a few bunnies and sets about interacting with the mushrooms and other points of interest, unaware of the look Tarl is giving him.

I guess I'm not the only one with a protégé to be proud of.

Chapter 39

Nova

Nova listlessly glides through the rock near the border to the volcanic area, trying more to gather her thoughts than to hunt the Fire elementals that try to sneak into Thedeim. She feels a little guilty about that, about letting the other wyrms handle the brunt of the work there, but . . . well, it's complicated.

It's not that she feels bad for the elementals. She's seen what happens if one catches a spider or another denizen who isn't able to take the heat. Yeah, she has no problem eating them after seeing that, and they honestly taste pretty good. Her feelings get complicated when she tries to link her purpose to stopping them.

She's not going to get the power to rival stars by just eating Fire elementals. While she's not sure she wants the kind of terrible strength her name implies, she's getting more and more sure she wants more than to just deal with invaders.

She'd like to do something with the delvers, but that's a whole *different* kind of complicated. She's seen the grass smolder when she visits the surface, so it's not difficult to imagine she'd have a similar effect on the delvers as the Fire elementals have on the other denizens. Even without Guide Thedeim not wanting to hurt the delvers, Nova wouldn't want to do something like that to them. She actually likes a lot of them.

She's just bad at showing it. Like those two who got separated. She wanted to try to interact with them, but she surfaced right in front of the heat sensor and trapped them. That was just embarrassing, even if the Guide found it amusing.

She sighs as her thoughts settle on what's really bothering her: she doesn't know what she should do. She's been trying to follow the advice of the other scions, to just get settled and try to get used to everything, but she feels like she's letting Thedeim down by not pursuing a goal yet.

Just because she knows that's silly doesn't stop her from feeling that way. It's difficult to imagine Coda feeling lost like she does sometimes, considering how busy he always is. But she's heard the others say he used to worry if he had done something wrong to make the Guide abandon him. Does she just need to be patient? Probably . . . but *can* she?

She grinds her mandibles at the thought, then sighs and rolls over, trying to get comfortable. She should try talking to Coda about it. If he really was like her for a long time, maybe he'll have suggestions for how to handle it? If nothing else, it'll give her something to focus on.

She wallows in whatever it is she's wallowing in for a few more seconds before pulling on her big-girl pants and tunneling to the labyrinth. It's well past dusk, and Coda should be working on the mechanical traps by now. She's pretty sure he was working on the rotating T-intersection near the crucible ants last night, and she can't imagine something like that is a one-night job.

She takes the direct route there, though she goes a bit slower than one might expect. She's just making sure she doesn't leave obvious marks in the tunnels when she dives up through them. She's not trying to delay, nor does she have a sense of dread to overcome. He's a fellow scion, not someone she should be nervous around.

She even mostly believes that by the time she pokes her head through the floor. When she spots Jello there as well, she almost slips back under, but her gelatinous friend burbles a happy greeting before she can pretend she was never there.

"Friend Nova! How're you doing? Did you want to watch Friend Coda work? Jello has been helping make parts!"

That at least explains the pieces of metal floating around inside her. After a moment's hesitation, Nova nods and slides out of her hole.

"Yes . . . er, no, I didn't come to watch him work. It looks so complicated, and I wouldn't want to warp anything by getting too close."

"Nothing to worry about there, Nova," explains Coda as he motions her forward with a wingclaw. "Jello is keeping her parts at a stable temperature, and even once she gives them to me, they should be fine as long as you don't try to melt through the floor too close."

"What *did* you come for?" follows up Jello with a happy squelch.

"Well, uh . . . I wanted to ask him . . ." Nova trails off as she feels the attention of both of them on her, and it's all she can do to not dive into the floor. Not only would that not solve her problem, she also might mess up Coda's work. He very specifically asked her not to do something like that.

"Ask me what?" prompts Coda as he sends a pulse of sound into the wall, triggering the switch to open the access panel for the complex mechanism.

"Well . . . I heard you used to, uh . . . struggle? With, um . . . purpose?"

"Ah." Coda turns to face her properly, then gives her a gentle smile. "Yeah, I did. You're having the same problem?" Nova nods, so he continues. "Well, I would say you have to be patient, but that didn't help the feeling go away for me."

"What did?" asks Nova, trying to keep the pleading tone out of her voice.

"Finding a purpose," he replies simply, grinning at Nova's groan. "Yeah, also not a great help, is it?"

Nova sighs. "Not really, no."

"I do understand how you feel, at least. I might have even had it worse than you, if you can believe it." Nova sputters at that, but Coda doesn't let her interrupt. "I wasn't always a Civil Artificer. In fact, the Foreman first tasked me with tending the garden and the herbalism nodes on the surface. I did, but the bats didn't really need much guidance on that, and Queen is much better at nurturing that kind of growth. Not to mention she actually has specific things she wants grown.

"Then I was asked to direct the expeditions underground. The Foreman hoped to ease some of Poe's burden, but I knew I was nowhere near as good at directing them. At first, I asked Poe for help, and slowly, everyone just went to him instead of me."

Nova's mandibles hang slack as she listens, trying to imagine that. Not one, but *two* jobs from the Guide, and Coda couldn't find his purpose in them?

"Yeah, you can imagine I wasn't too happy with myself about that. Maybe the worst part was that Thedeim wasn't upset with me. I just wanted to do *something* to show his faith in me wasn't misplaced. I actually tried to get back into those two jobs, but they really were already handled."

Coda smiles as he remembers what came next.

"Then he needed some digging done. Not just any digging, either. He wanted to *build*. The access shaft to the caverns, then Rocky's arena, then the bypass between the swamps and aquifer lakes . . ." He trails off at that. "They never did take that tunnel, did they? Ah, well. Anyway, I found my purpose in building. And now I have more work than I know what to do with!" he ends with a chuckle.

Nova is a bit less jovial about it. "So I really do just need to wait for him to need something that calls to me?"

"Not really," burbles Jello, earning a surprised look from both Coda and Nova.

"What do you mean?" they ask as one.

"Well, Voice Thedeim doesn't always know what he actually needs. Like with Friend Queen."

"Queen?" echoes Nova, Coda looking just as lost.

"Oh yes, Jello and Friend Queen talk a lot, and she admitted he didn't actually plan for her to be an Alchemist. He wanted her to be his new Guardian, since Friend Tiny kinda outgrew the Sanctum. But she became an Alchemist instead on accident."

"Huh," muses Coda.

"I . . . I *don't* have to wait?" whispers Nova, trying to wrap her head around the idea.

"Nope!" confirms Jello.

Nova just sits there for a good minute, the other two watching her with patience, letting her try to parse what she's just learned, and to see what she'll do with that knowledge.

"I . . ." she starts, and the others lean in, eager to hear what she has to say. "I . . . I still don't know what to do," she starts, but she sounds more determined as she continues. "But I know I want to go to the Southwood, to help fight!"

"Then I hope you're all packed, Nova. The Boss wants us to move out in the morning," comes the unexpected voice of the Voice. Nova almost leaps through the ceiling in surprise.

"Voice Teemo! I, uh . . ."

He waves her off. "Just Teemo, Nova. If you want to go, the Boss is happy to let you. He's been giving you space so you can figure yourself out. If you want to go help fight, you can go help fight."

"Oh, can Jello come too?!"

Teemo gives the cube of slime a sideways look. "I mean, sure, but I thought you were having fun with the metalworking."

Jello starts to melt a little as she seriously thinks before her shape snaps back into focus. "Yes, Jello does like the metalworking. If they were undead, she might go fight instead, but that dungeon doesn't sound very tasty. Sorry, Friend Nova."

Teemo smiles at that, turning his attention to Coda. "How about you? You wanna go fight?"

"Nope. I have enough on my plate already, thank you." With that, the Bat Scion starts digging around in the mechanisms of the wall section. He calls back to Jello for parts as he works, which she dutifully hands over. Teemo smiles before focusing back on Nova.

"If you want to go, you should head to the caverns for now. Fluffles will be coming along to relieve Rocky, and he and Leo are sparring and comparing notes in there right now. Once dawn comes, we'll grab Honey and head out with whatever adventurers want to come help scout. That sound good?"

It does. It really does.

Chapter 40

The sense of purpose I feel from Nova is encouraging. Not for the first time, I wonder if maybe calling her Nova wasn't my best idea, but it's too late for that now. I'm just happy she seems to have found, if not her true calling, something to strive for. Fighting wouldn't be the worst thing for her to get into, either. Rocky and Fluffles are my heavy hitters for certain, but I bet Nova can work her way up to be their peer in combat prowess if she puts her mind to it.

A magma dragon is never going to be a pushover, after all. I kinda hope she finds her feet more with a mundane purpose, but if she's happy, I'll be happy. And Rocky will appreciate having someone else to spar with.

I watch her, Teemo, Fluffles, and Leo as they mostly just hang out in the caverns. Even Slash swings by, and Teemo checks if he wants to come for the first wave or wait. Slash says he'd like to stay here and hone his music until he's actually needed, which is fair.

His music will only really be needed once we find that dungeon and start actually marching. For now, he's better suited to playing for the denizens and delvers here. It's good practice for him, too. He's learning not only buffs but debuffs so he can make people a bit faster or slower, not hit quite as hard, hit exactly where they mean to, that sort of thing.

It kinda makes me curious about how buff/debuff fits into the affinity system, but I haven't really had a chance to look too hard into it. It's probably not its own affinity, but scientifically speaking, there's not a lot of reason for a song to produce the kind of effects I've seen Slash pull off. I dunno, maybe it's just magic and I shouldn't expect everything to work like physics says it should.

I should leave that kind of curiosity to Rocky, even if he probably won't get much chance to look into those kinds of questions until after we deal with that stupid weird dungeon. At least the next step for that plan is starting to gather just inside my gate now. The sky is still fully dark, but it won't take too long for things to brighten up.

I nudge Teemo, and he gets the scions moving. They go to get Honey while Aranya, Yvonne, Ragnar, and Aelara enter through the gate. I was kinda hoping they wouldn't want to join the scouting, but I'm not very surprised they're interested. Aranya and Yvonne haven't been around too much since the meeting, so they've probably been preparing as much as they can for this.

When my favorite party spots the adventurers gathering on the lawn, Yvonne takes the lead and heads over with a smile on her beak.

"I hope you're all prepared for some extended time in Teemo's shortcuts," she greets with a friendly tone. Most of the adventurers just nod, though a couple look a bit nervous about the idea. A lanky wolfkin in chain mail with a pair of swords at his hips speaks up, his nerves overcoming the typical adventurer compulsion to look and act cool and collected.

"I've never actually been down one before. Should . . . I be concerned?"

The more experienced adventurers chuckle as Yvonne shakes her head. "It will just take a little getting used to. A lot of senses can behave a bit oddly in a shortcut. Things outside will be distorted, but inside will feel like anywhere else. If you have a good nose, it'll be a bit worse."

He grimaces and nods at that. "I do have a good nose."

Yvonne gives him a sympathetic look. "You won't be able to smell *anything* outside the shortcut. Just try not to be too jumpy and keep in mind nothing outside should be able to notice us inside. Teemo is an expert at making and hiding them. It'd take someone with a similar mastery of space to get in if he doesn't want them to."

The wolfkin doesn't exactly look comforted by the thought of being nose-blind, but he does seem to be a bit less nervous. I guess he'd rather know and prepare himself than be caught by surprise. Probably a good attitude to have for a delver, really.

Yvonne answers a few more simple questions as more people show up. At one point, someone arrives with a bag of sweet rolls from the bakery across the street, and everyone enjoys the treat as the sun starts to peek over the horizon. Once it actually does, Teemo and the scions join the others.

"Alright, this everyone?" he asks, getting a mixture of curious looks and nods before Yvonne speaks up.

"I believe that's everyone. If they're not here by now, they can try to catch up. I'll be leading the guild contingent for this, and Ragnar will be giving everyone a crash course on how to write maps for the twisting underground. Thedeim's sending so many scions?" she asks, looking surprised to see both Fluffles and Nova in the group.

"Yeah. Fluffles is going to relieve Rocky; he's got a lot of mana from that last fight he needs to bring back. Leo and Honey are basically leading the whole thing; I'm mostly going to be working on the shortcuts and guiding everyone, and Nova wants to come help."

Yvonne nods at that. "Then I believe we're ready to go?"

"Yeah, let's go to the cemetery then head on out. There's also going to be a good number of reinforcements coming with us. Just make sure the adventurers leave them alone, yeah?"

Yvonne nods, and I'm surprised to see Aranya step away from the party, looking like this was part of the plan all along as she speaks, a hand at her necklace, finger and thumb holding the small orange orb.

"May Lord Thedeim bless the journey to be a peaceful one and keep from harm those who will surely face it." Subtle orange mana settles on everyone, and the party moves in to give Aranya a hug.

"You're sure you can't come with us yet?" asks Aelara. Aranya smiles as she shakes her head.

"I'll come with the ratkin and the spiderkin. They haven't ventured very far beyond Lord Thedeim, only far enough for their hunts. And . . . it'll give me a little more time to prepare myself," she admits. "I knew Lord Thedeim would confront that horrible place, but it felt like something that would happen in years, maybe decades."

Ragnar nods at that. "Dinnae worry. We'll 'ave summat to tell by th' time ye get there."

"And if they've actually found it by then, the Boss'll be sending another couple scions with you. Rocky will definitely want a round two with the Harbinger, and Slash is going to be a big help against any other big, organized attacks," assures Teemo.

Aranya smiles at the reassurances, standing a bit straighter for her friends. "I'll come see you all off. You're the ones going off into danger; you're not supposed to worry about me, I'm supposed to worry about you!" she jokingly accuses, and earns friendly smiles all around.

Everyone walks through town to get to the cemetery, and I see a few of the adventurers get a couple more of those rolls on the way. That bakery must make a killing. How many dungeons can people delve with a weapon in one hand and a donut in the other?

Grim is there to greet everyone, too. The delvers look a bit nervous about having his attention, but he just gives everyone a flower as his way of wishing them well.

Aw, don't worry, Grim, they're gonna be careful. I'm sure they love the flowers, too. As everyone climbs over the back wall, Slash comes hurrying from one of the mausoleums.

Is something wrong? Ah, changed your mind, hmm? Nah, that's fine. A road trip is always better with some music, and I imagine the Southwood will be nice and quiet to practice in.

The adventurers give Slash curious looks, but a few upbeat notes reassure them everything is fine. The music, combined with Grim's flowers, even distracts the adventurers a bit from thinking about the large group of my denizens following them as they hop the wall and enter the shortcut.

There are plenty of tundra wolves, obviously; they're just too well suited to the surface around the Southwood for me not to keep sending a bunch of them. I'll also need their noses to help sniff out the enemy dungeon in the tunnels.

There are plenty of ravens and arcane hands to reinforce the ranks, too. They were a lot more effective in the fight against the Harbinger than I was expecting. Once I get the dragon spawner high enough to spit out something besides wyrms, I might try to upgrade the hands again.

I'm also sending a group of skeletons, which probably has the adventurers most on edge. With the enclaves being on a war production footing, I've had plenty of weapons and armors offered by them. I kinda feel a bit bad about accepting the gifts, but the ratlings don't really care. They just keep stocking the warehouse and armory. Rather than letting the things rust, I've equipped a bunch of skeletons with what they can wear and wield.

For armor, it's mainly leather. It's strange to think about, but most metal stuff is built with fleshy things in mind, and my skeletons just can't wear most of that properly. It just doesn't sit right. Leather is a lot easier to adjust, so that's what they have, as well as the compound bows.

I also have some zombies that can gear up in the heavier armor, but I'm going to be merciful to the adventurers and not make them march with my zombies. The fungal ones smell a lot better than the normal ones, but that's still not saying a whole lot.

I'm also not sure if they'll handle the cold well. I think Leo kept the green skeletons and fungal zombies inside Southwood itself. I'll ask Teemo to have him test them out once they get there. It should take them a couple days, especially since Teemo wants to work on the shortcuts on the way, too.

Shortening the travel time can only help us in this fight. It'll still be too long to really react quickly to any rapid changes, but getting the travel time down to a day or two would make it a lot easier to keep up with the slower needs.

Chapter 41

Aranya sits atop the wall, waving and watching as her friends vanish into the shortcut. She sticks around to send off all the denizens, too. It's not difficult to see she has complex feelings about everyone going, and probably about the dwellers wanting to go, too. I know I do.

She stays for a few minutes longer after everyone is gone. The sun is fully up by now, but I don't think she's simply appreciating the view. Instead of letting her stew in her thoughts, Grim taps his scythe against the wall and offers her a hand down. She smiles at the quiet scion and accepts his help, giving him a long look before speaking.

"How do you do it, Grim?"

He tilts his skull at her, and she soon explains.

"I mean . . . the death. There hasn't been any in Thedeim's care, but people still die all the time . . ." She trails off as Grim nods then motions for her to follow, which she quietly does.

He leads her back toward the main gate, where he gestures at the flower garden, then back at the rows of graves. The kobold looks confused, and he lets her do so for a few seconds before he scythes a simple daisy from the patch and moves among the tombstones. He leads her to an aged and weathered grave, the grass on the cusp of being unruly.

A swipe of his scythe tames the grass, and a touch of his hand repairs the stone. It still shows its age, and the lettering is no more legible than before, but it doesn't look like it's about to crumble. He finishes by placing the flower atop the grave marker before taking a step back to quietly study his work.

Aranya watches, trying to figure out what Grim is trying to say, before she deflates with a sigh. "I don't think I'm quite ready for your wisdom yet," she voices, disappointment clear.

Grim doesn't look disappointed at all, patting her head as he turns to tend to more of his duties. For her part, Aranya looks briefly annoyed at being treated like a child before she gives a small smile at Grim's back. "I suppose I have more pressing issues to deal with, especially if I want to minimize the work you'll have to do once this is all over."

Despite not getting what she wanted, I think she might have gotten what she needed, and she heads for the Ratkin Enclave with a renewed sense of purpose.

The guards nod at her as she enters, and she takes a few peaceful moments to just enjoy seeing everyone going about their day.

Some move around with purpose, some chat, kids play . . . It's the kind of thing I want to defend, and I know Aranya does, too. She greets people as she walks, congratulating accomplishments and commiserating briefly over failures, and encourages everyone as she makes her way to Larx's home.

The elder ratkin is relaxing on a chair just outside his door, almost looking like he's meditating as he sits with a peaceful smile. He opens his eyes and smiles wider as Aranya closes in, and she waves him down as he starts to stand. He looks very tempted to stand anyway, but a flat look from my High Priestess keeps his butt planted in his chair.

"Ah, Aranya! How does the new day find you?" he asks jovially.

She does her best to match his mood. "With much to do. You?"

"With little to do immediately, which I often find to be the more trying option," he answers with a smirk. "Would you like something to drink?"

"Nothing for me, thank you," she replies, deftly cutting off his sneaky attempt to do something besides rest his bones. "The preparations to head north are going smoothly, then?"

Larx sighs in defeat, leaning back. "On our end, at least. The spiderkin are having difficulties with the gear. Norloke is still working on warmer silk, but I think their best option is going to be to trade for furs, or maybe some kind of warming enchantment."

"Weren't you working on warming enchantments for your smelters?"

Larx chuckles. "That'd be a bit too warm for them, I think. Our runesmith is still feeling out the class. From what I can gather, the forge enchantments are like using a sledgehammer on the problem. For warm clothing, it'd be like trying to thread a needle with the same sledge."

Aranya winces at that. "Ah. Is there anything else I can help with?"

Larx gives her a considering look. "I thought you said you had a lot to do already?"

The kobold freezes for a moment at that, then sputters as she tries to come up with an excuse. Whatever she might try is derailed by Larx's laughter.

"Worrying doesn't count as something to do, my dear," he admonishes with a chuckle.

Aranya folds her arms and tries—and fails—not to pout. "Yeah, well . . . I'm still doing it . . ."

Larx's smile softens. "I understand your fears. I don't even need to ask Teemo to know Lord Thedeim has the same ones." He smirks at himself before continuing. "I'd be lying if I said I didn't share them. But everyone is resolute in this. We want to help Lord Thedeim, even if he doesn't want us to be put in harm's way."

He smiles at my High Priestess. "Which is one of the reasons we want to do this, by the way. Another reason is . . . well, you," he admits, which draws Aranya's reply.

"Me?" she asks, confused. He nods.

"And your people. The thought of a Sanctuary being so abusive to its dwellers . . . it's wrong in ways I can't put into words. At least with Hullbreak, he was only trying to protect them. A mistake is one thing, but what you describe . . ." He shudders. "And it's not just us of Lord Thedeim, either. If the merfolk had the ability to march with us, they would, even if Hullbreak would have a fit."

"But . . . the danger!" she tries. "It was a place of nightmare when I left, but now, it must be even worse with those terrifying denizens and the Harbinger!"

Larx nods. "I know. We all know that we won't all come marching back. *They* won't all come marching back," he corrects with a note of bitterness. "I'm not suited to a battle like what's coming, but that doesn't make me any happier to allow the others to go marching off." He sighs as his expression softens.

"But I can't force them to stay. Lord Thedeim himself won't take the decision from their hands, so I can hardly do it myself. All I can do is try to prepare them, and try to accept the truth of the situation."

When he doesn't elaborate, Aranya prompts him to continue. "What *is* the truth of it? That they have to live their lives . . . even if it means dying their deaths, too?"

Larx smiles at that. "That's the philosophical core of it, yes, but I more meant the practical situation. This will be the strongest foe Lord Thedeim has faced yet. Even his scions will be tested, and he won't be able to quickly react to send more forces. That Fallen Sanctuary is old, too. Even with Lord Thedeim's strength, the other dungeon has had much more time to gather its own. I hope we won't be needed . . . but I fear we will."

Aranya looks uncomfortable as her unstated concerns spill from Larx's mouth. Silence reigns as Aranya struggles with how to respond, until she squeaks out her fears. "What if it's not enough? What if I doomed everyone by coming here? What if—" she starts, but Larx bonks her with his staff.

"None of that. You may be the High Priestess, but I can still try to knock some sense into you. You didn't doom anyone with your Fate affinity. Lord Thedeim has the same one, as does Lady Yvonne. I may not focus on the Weaver aspect of Lord Thedeim, but the spiderkin aren't wrong in their devotions.

"I refuse to accept the idea that he'd draw two other people tied with fate to him, only for it to lead to everyone's doom. More likely, we'll be *fighting* some doom or another, maybe even multiple ones. If it's our fate to face that, I'll not meet it without a fight."

His conviction shocks Aranya out of her worry, and maybe makes her think about what Grim was trying to tell her earlier. The cemetery isn't to commemorate people's deaths. Everyone dies eventually. If there's anything that doesn't deserve a participation trophy, it's dying.

No, the cemetery is to remember people's *lives*. Even that old, weathered grave marks someone's life. I think Grim even gives it special attention because it doesn't need to commemorate just a single person.

Not everyone gets a marker. Sometimes . . . people are just lost, their stories untold and unremembered. He keeps it blank because he can't tell their story. He keeps it *there* because he can at least remember.

Chapter 42

Freddie

In the adventurers' guildhall, a young orc and his goblin friend relax near the roaring fire. They've been friends for basically their entire lives, and that friendship has only grown stronger in the last year. They were two of the first people to delve Thedeim, where Rhonda was able to gather some mushrooms and secure an apprenticeship with her new mentor, Old Staiven, and Freddie was able to join the church and find a family that transcends mere blood.

And of course, the two gained their classes together from another delve in Thedeim. What's more, their classes are unique, or so rare that nobody around has ever heard of them.

While Freddie might entertain the idea of there being other Ice Sages out there, he doubts it. There are no other Legionnaire Paladins, he's sure of that . . . or at least, there weren't. Torlon was pretty clear that the Shield itself wanted to have more paladins like Freddie, which was an intimidating thing to hear.

He's been exploring his class and telling the Head Priest everything he can, while Torlon has mostly been encouraging him to take it slow, despite how important it seems. "Rushing will only encourage mistakes," he's said many times. It's a bit frustrating to take it slow, but it's difficult to argue the wisdom, especially with Rhonda doing exactly that.

Her Ice Sage class seems to be focused at least partially on learning, so if she can steel herself and not recklessly dive into her class, he can do the same. Besides, he's supposed to be the front line. An impatient defender puts his charges at risk.

It'd be easier to be patient if he knew what Rhonda was actually doing, though. It's not hard to understand why the two of them are here. They both have a day off, but are also both a bit too tired from their duties to want to go delve. The guildhall is not exactly quiet, but it is relaxing and friendly.

Ever since joining, the two orphans have been welcomed into the ranks of the adventurers. Even their spiders, Fiona and Lucas, are liked by their guildmates.

Rhonda's familiar, Lucas, is a jumping spider with gray-and-white coloring, short legs, and large eyes. Around the guild and the town, he's playful and curious, and Freddie is pretty sure he's part of the reason his friend has started coming out of her shell these last few months.

When on a delve, Lucas is excellent support for Rhonda, helping her weave her magic and even keeping a small collection of magical bits to help channel the energies.

Freddie's own spider, Fiona, is much more reserved, almost regal, despite her fearsome appearance. Her main eyes are even larger than Lucas's, and her large mandibles give her a long, severe face. Freddie can imagine her wielding a ruler and sharp tongue as she tries to teach a class of young spiders how to do something.

But she's not above some fun, and she and Lucas often play when Freddie and Rhonda are just hanging out. On a delve, Fiona helps Freddie keep the front line, webbing foes and ensuring threats don't get a drop on them. She'll even step up and take one of Freddie's shields when he manifests them, helping lend his phalanx a few extra sets of legs to push back against their foes.

He smiles as he glances up into the rafters and sees the two spiders chasing each other. Lucas likes to use his speed and maneuverability to his advantage, while Fiona plays the long game and leaves traps and snares in her wake. Still, spidery shenanigans can only keep Freddie's attention for so long.

His eyes wander to his favorite goblin in the entire world as he wonders what has her looking so pensive.

"Rhonda? You alright?" he asks, causing her to jerk to attention.

"Hmm? Oh, sorry, Freddie. Just . . . thinking."

"What about? I haven't seen you this distracted in a while."

"It's . . . mostly class stuff. I've been thinking about how Rocky fought in the ring."

Freddie nods at that, remembering their friendly fight with the undead scion. "He's a lot stronger than any zombie should be, even a scion."

"And his magic puts actual liches to shame!" exclaims Rhonda. "I know I've said it before, but—"

"His magic is at least as good as his footwork, I know. It feels weird to think about, but I can believe it. His punches look effortless but hit like a landslide. He just flows from move to move. It almost makes me want to try learning how to punch instead of using an axe."

Rhonda nods. "That's how his magic is, too. When I got my class, I only barely understood what he was doing. Now that I'm a little more advanced with my own magic, I still feel like I only barely understand."

"Is that what has you staring a hole into the fireplace, then? Trying to figure out how he does it?"

Rhonda shakes her head. "No . . . Well, not really. I mean, I *am* thinking about his magic, but I've been thinking about how he was moving it in the fight. I have the concept behind Fire and Ice affinity, but I think he was trying to tell me about how they relate to Kinetic."

That earns her a raised eyebrow from her friend. "Kinetic? How is that related?"

Rhonda sighs. "I don't know, but I feel like I *should*. It's like when Master Staiven asks me about something that I know I know, but I can't figure out how to express it, you know?"

Freddie nods. "Like a verse I know that I've memorized but blank on when quizzed on it."

The young goblin points at him. "Yeah, that! It's frustrating!"

He chuckles. "So, something about fire and ice makes you think about Kinetic affinity? But you don't know what?" She nods, thumping her forehead against the table. "Well, you said you understand fire and ice. What are they? I always thought they were opposites, but I see you using one to empower the other all the time."

Rhonda shakes her head before picking herself back up, and Freddie doesn't try to hide his smile as she goes into lecture mode.

"At their most basic, they're just temperature. Fire is hot, and ice is cold."

"So fire is just manifested heat, and ice is manifested cold?"

Rhonda shakes her head. "No, fire and ice themselves are . . . more side effects than the actual temperature. Make anything hot enough, and it'll burst into flames. Well, water will boil, but you get it."

"So if you make something cold enough, it'll burst into frost, too?"

Rhonda nods again and sighs. "There's something else there, too, but I don't know what."

"Have you tried asking Old Staiven about it?" asks Freddie, thinking surely Rhonda's master would know something. Her groan indicates otherwise.

"He says it's something I have to figure out. I'm pretty sure he has a few ideas, but he doesn't know how I do my magic."

"Maybe ask one of the guild mages, then? Old Staiven is mostly Meta, right? Maybe someone with Fire or Ice affinity can give you the hint you need?"

"But *they* don't know how my magic works, either!"

"But they do know how *theirs* works. Maybe focusing on one will finally jog whatever's been at the back of your mind," he suggests. Rhonda mulls it over.

"Maybe?" she admits. "It probably can't hurt, at least." She turns in her chair to look around the hall, and Freddie can see her unsteady resolve already starting to crumble as the idea of talking to a random guildmate starts to intimidate his friend.

He points at a table with a bearkin, a changeling, and another goblin. "They might be good to try. I'm pretty sure they've been helping map out the labyrinth, and I think one of them is a Fire mage."

Rhonda still looks reluctant, so Freddie gets up, causing her to follow. He doesn't mind starting engagements, be they social or martial. That's his job, really.

As they approach, they overhear the seated group talking.

"I'm not saying brownie isn't good at spotting the traps. I'm saying we need someone who can actually *disable* them," says the changeling while the bearkin nods.

"He's a fine tracker, but he can't actually take down his prey."

The goblin sighs. "I know, but he's not skilled in disabling runework, at least at a range. If he got close enough to disable the traps, he'd trigger them. I have a few who might be able to walk into them to set them off, but they're all contracted for combat, not traps. Tripping over a couple in a battle is one thing, but they won't stand being used just to trigger them."

The changeling starts to reply but notices the two approaching. "Oh, hey. Uh . . . Frankie, right?"

"Freddie," he corrects politely. "If you could, sir, my friend Rhonda wanted to ask you about Fire magic? She has the affinity but is having some trouble with it."

The changeling considers the two before shrugging. "Sure, I'll try to help some. We've been mostly arguing in circles, anyway. A break would be nice."

The bearkin scoots down the bench a bit, giving the kids room to join them at the table, and introduces himself. "I'm Wold. He's Vieds, and he's Gerlfi." The bearkin points out his friends as he names them.

Freddie nods in greeting while Rhonda gives a little curtsy before sitting across from the changeling, and they start to chat, leaving Freddie with the other two.

"So . . . you guys are having some troubles with the labyrinth?"

The goblin sighs as the bearkin chuckles. "Yeah, we're having problems dealing with the traps there. They're not deadly, but clients *really* want to go deeper. The traps are keeping everyone out so far."

Freddie glances over to his friend. "Well, Rhonda might be able to help with the magical ones, at least. Her master is Old Staiven, and he's been sure to teach her some runework."

"Yeah?" asks the goblin, looking interested. "We're able to find the magical ones, but haven't been able to disable them. There are also mechanical ones, which we've been having some troubles finding *and* disabling."

Freddie glances up at the spiders playing in the rafters. "Fiona and Lucas might be able to help with that, too. Fiona has great eyesight. I don't know if she'll be able to fully disable any mechanical traps, but she should be able to guide around them?"

Wold's eyes follow Freddie's, and he rumbles in amusement. "A wizard needs a familiar, but I don't think I've seen a paladin with one before."

Freddie looks a bit bashful at that. "Yeah, it . . . was a bit of a thing, but we're inseparable now. She's a valuable companion to me, like Lucas is to Rhonda." The bearkin nods in approval as Gerlfi speaks up.

"It sounds to me like your group might have just the skill set we need to go deeper. Hey, Vieds. Making any progress?" The goblin pauses for a moment before raising his voice slightly. "Vieds?"

"Hmm? Oh, sorry. We were talking about her affinities, and it's no wonder she's having trouble with fire. Her innate was Ice, and she got Fire because of her class."

Gerlfi just nods at that and returns his focus to Freddie. "Perhaps we can strike a deal, then? Vieds will help her with her Fire affinity, and your group will help us with the traps in the labyrinth."

Freddie considers that, noting that Rhonda looks receptive to it, so she must be already getting some understanding from the pyromancer. "Add a share of the rewards and loot, and it's a deal."

The goblin smiles wide at that. "Perfect! I take it you two won't mind participating in the fights, then?"

Freddie nods. "We're pretty good in a fight. Oh, there might be a third, too. Larrez delves with us when he has a chance to, between his duties as a guard."

Gerlfi waves that off. "That's no problem. He won't get any shares for the delves he doesn't go on, but I don't see any problem with sharing the spoils when he does." He looks to his companions to see if they have any problems with the proposed bargain, but they both seem fine with it.

"We'll be heading out at dawn tomorrow for our next attempt; we're not going to be bringing any miners along. The place is tricky enough that I'd like to get a bit more familiar with it before trying to escort another batch deeper in."

Rhonda nods at that. "I'll let Master Staiven know. He'll probably want me to gather as many herbs as I can in there. People have already been requesting Fire Resist potions, and he should have enough stock of everything else for me to make a trip into Thedeim."

"I'll make sure Torlon doesn't have anything planned for my own training tomorrow, too. I'll come back and let you know if I can't make it. Otherwise . . . I'll see you at dawn?"

The older adventurers nod as handshakes are exchanged before Freddie and Rhonda take their leave of the table and—once they gather their spiders—leave of the guildhall, too.

"Are you looking forward to tomorrow?" asks Freddie. Rhonda nods.

"Definitely. It's easy to see Vieds is very experienced with fire. Even if he can't help me with my affinity breakthrough, he'll help me with my fire. I really have been doing basic things with it so far. I'm a lot more used to ice."

"Good. I'm looking forward to it, too. My training lately has been more mental, so it'll be nice to get physical again. I'll swing by the mayor's manor on the way home and see if Larrez will be available tomorrow, too. See you in the morning?"

Rhonda nods, and Lucas waves. "See you in the morning, Freddie!"

Chapter 43

At sunrise, I see Rhonda and Freddie enter my main gate, followed by those three I watched in the labyrinth the other day. They don't seem very deterred, and the kids look pretty eager to test themselves against my tougher stuff. The wyrms can be a threat just by getting too close, but they seem to have taken precautions, and something strong like a Jacob's Ladder snake has to actually attack to potentially endanger them.

Vieds eyes a vial which looks like it contains liquid fire, looking uncertain. "Are you sure these are safe? I'm pretty sure I've thrown things like this at monsters before . . ."

Rhonda giggles while Lucas chitters an admonishment at the changeling. "I'm sure. Master Staiven himself brewed these to help us gather as many herbs in the labyrinth as possible. He's had a lot of requests for strong Fire Resist potions, so he needs good ingredients."

"I'm surprised he didn't want to join us himself. The other crafters wanted to see the materials in person," rumbles Wold, the large bearkin looking up at Poe on his perch near the chimney.

"Well, I *am* his apprentice. If he can trust anyone else to get the herbs, it'll be me," points out Rhonda, and Vieds finally accepts the truth as he slips the vial into a belt pouch.

The group moves to the porch to peruse the hanging quests, which has Gerlfi in a good mood as he browses. "It's still strange to see a dungeon handing out quests like this."

"It's the aranea, not the dungeon," points out Freddie, which earns him a chuckle from the older goblin.

"Which is why it's so strange. Usually, it's fey offering deals like this. I'm not sure if it's a shame or a relief that there's no fey to be had here." He pauses as he peers at a quest in the labyrinth to gather some fool's coal. "Should we all get an herbalism quest?"

Rhonda turns to the board he's looking at. "That one should be easy enough, even if you don't have much herbalism experience. The hardest part of gathering fool's coal is in finding it . . . and I guess in keeping it away from too much heat while we're there."

Freddie accepts a quest for a couple of wyrm mandibles, while Wold takes one for a wyrm hide.

How would he even get a hide from one of my wyrms?

Gerlfi looks uncertainly at the fool's coal quest. "I think keeping them away from heat will be a problem, don't you?"

Rhonda shrugs and accepts a quest for a more delicate fiery herb. "It takes sustained heat to set them off. A couple attacks shouldn't make them pop, but setting them on fire will get them to explode eventually."

Gerlfi gingerly accepts the quest, looking like he thinks the little board will explode, too. "If you say so. I don't have much herbalism experience. No crafting options have really captured my attention," he admits.

"He prefers to gather fey," jokes Vieds as he takes a fool's coal quest, too.

"How does that even work?" asks Freddie as they move into the manor proper, where I greet them with a small rat swarm. His question is left hanging while they deal with my warm-up encounter. They work well together, though, with Freddie, Fiona, and Wold holding off the swarm while Vieds and Rhonda send a few area attacks to deal with the foes. Gerlfi is mostly on overwatch, keeping an eye on the battle and calling out tactical advice.

Before long, the swarm is dispersed, and they resume their delve.

"You were asking about contracting with fey?" he asks the young orc as they move through the house, checking cabinets and drawers for any goodies. When Freddie nods, he continues. "The short version is that I'm a summoner. We deal with magic differently than most others you've seen, I imagine. I'm Illusion affinity, which can be a bit awkward for a summoner.

"An illusion mage can simply create their illusions and work to trick their foes, but I need an outside anchor for my magic. That anchor gives just a bit of reality to my illusions, making them true summons. There are a lot of different anchors to use and ways to get them. For me, dealing with fey has worked the best." He draws Freddie's attention to his various crystals.

"These let me communicate with the fey I've formed a deal with. I call them forth, offer a payment, and they lend a small piece of themselves to give my illusions weight."

"And their dungeons just let them do that?" further questions Freddie.

Gerlfi nods. "I don't know the specifics, but it earns mana for their dungeon; that's all I've really needed to know. You could probably ask the dungeoneers if you want the details. Of course, the fey want more than that. They want something for themselves, too. The simpler fey are usually happy with bread, milk, and honey, and they're great for support roles. Fighting fey usually want more than that, however, so I tend to save them for trouble."

I interrupt their conversation with a trio of widows in the basement. Wold and Freddie can keep two of the big arachnids busy, but Fiona is a bit out of her league to keep the third one occupied. Gerlfi quickly speaks into one of his crystals as Rhonda, Lucas, and Vieds try to keep the widow at bay.

"Sprig, please help us hold back this widow. I offer bread, milk, and honey, once we're back at the guild." I watch his mana flow and swirl, his explanation for how he summons making it all make sense, and a twiggy little bush pops through the stones of the basement, quickly resolving into a vaguely humanoid shape.

With the sprig's help, they manage to corral the widow. My spider doesn't seem to know how to bite the little bushy fey, giving Fiona the time to entangle her legs in webbing. With the breathing room that gives, Rhonda and Vieds are quick to finish that widow off, then take out the other two.

Freddie gets Rhonda's help to try to remove the venom gland from one of their fallen foes while Vieds watches with interest.

"Your magic is interesting, Rhonda. I've never seen someone weave opposing affinities like that before."

Rhonda absently nods as she works on heating the widow's head properly, trying to copy her master's technique with Freddie's guidance. I think it looks a little overdone compared to what Staiven did on his delve, but it was definitely quicker than if the orc tried to just hack the thing out.

With the other two dissipating already, Rhonda responds to the changeling as they all resume marching. "Thank you. It's part of my class. I . . . guess you could say weaving affinities is a big part of how it works."

Vieds nods as they head into the tunnels. "I can see that. I can also see what you meant about your Fire affinity needing work." Rhonda winces at that, but he gives her a reassuring smile. "That you can get opposing affinities to cooperate at all is impressive. Wold?" He looks to his fuzzy companion, who grunts in acknowledgement. "Can you try to keep a bit of distance in the next encounter? And Freddie too? Can you do that?" he honestly asks, to which Freddie nods.

"It's more effort, but I can. It sounds like you have something you want to try?"

The changeling nods, letting a bit of pride slip into his tone. "I'd like to show the Ice Sage how fire is more than just burning things to a crisp."

Gerlfi is all too happy to burst his friend's bubble with a friendly jab. "Maybe we should drink those potions." Vieds glares while the goblin grins, and the changeling is the first to look away.

"It might not be the worst idea. We're not too far from the labyrinth, anyway."

I nudge a couple rockslides to get in their path while the delvers quickly toss back their Fire Resist potions before continuing on their way. Fiona points out my denizens as the group gets close, and Freddie takes a deep breath as he prepares.

"Rockslides. They're not too dangerous, but they're tough and hard to corral. Can you follow my lead, please, Mr. Wold?"

The bearkin looks curious as he nods, taking position beside Freddie. "Shield Wall!" declares the orc, and Fiona eagerly moves to support the ethereal shields. Wold looks surprised for a moment before following suit. The rockslides rumble forward, but the shield wall holds, at least for the moment.

Vieds takes that moment, and a few more, to prepare his attack. I can feel a lot of mana moving, and Rhonda's eyes follow the flows, drinking in what the changeling is trying to show her.

"Fire is so much more than mere heat! Heatwave!" he shouts, conjuring a rolling wall of fire that pushes the rockslides back. Freddie moves to advance, but Wold places a hand on his shoulder and shakes his head. The reason why becomes apparent as Vieds' next attack lands.

"Explosion!" The piled-up rockslides suddenly fly apart with a sharp crack and fiery whoosh as their group cohesion is sundered from the force of the attack. My little denizens decide that's enough fun for today and scatter, leaving an awed Rhonda and a smug Vieds watching them go.

"There, you see? Sure, heat is a big part of fire, but you have to appreciate a good explosion every so often, too."

"Sure, *you* can appreciate them. You've never lost your eyebrows to them," snarks Gerlfi.

"Missing eyebrows is better than what that lesser chimera would have done to you," Vieds snarks right back.

The banter is lost to Rhonda, who has her notebook out and is scribbling like mad. Wold lets his friends bleed off adrenaline with their usual ribbing, staying out of it as he gives Freddie a considering look. "I've never seen a skill like that before."

Freddie looks a bit bashful. "Yeah . . . it's part of my class. I work really well with other melee fighters, like Larrez."

"It's good. I usually don't get to enjoy melee teamwork. Coordinating is difficult."

Freddie smiles at that. "That's what a phalanx is all about. Each shield supports the next, and the Shield supports us all."

"You should talk with Gerlfi—once he's done bickering, and we're ready to move on. If you work well with numbers, he can provide them." They both look over to the two, who seem to be winding down their fun, before Wold speaks again. "If we're to reach the depths of the labyrinth, we may need all the help we can get."

Chapter 44

While the kids and their new friends make their way down, I take the chance to look over the entrance to the labyrinth. I should probably do it up a bit. As it is, it's just like any other tunnel; it might look a bit twistier than usual, but that's really it.

I should design a fancy entryway; probably fancy up the area outside, too. I think the delvers are going to take a break just outside before heading in, and I can probably wring a bit more mana from them without wringing any of their HP too.

First, I should make a kiosk or something for the aranea. I can already see a group of three of them testing the walls, ceiling, and floor, looking for a good way to hide while putting out their little quest signs. There's plenty to do in the labyrinth, so I'm not surprised the aranea want to have a centralized place for people to accept quests before heading in.

I doodle a few rough ideas, starting with a normal gazebo. I think that'll be a bit too open for the aranea to really like, though. Sure, I can put in rafters, but they'd have no good sneaky way to get into them. Teemo could make a shortcut, but that feels a bit like cheating. I come up with a bunker design that might work well, however.

Slots on the floor will let them stick signposts through with their quests and pull them down to put fresh ones, all while letting the aranea keep hidden. I'll need to take some time later to actually design how to hook them so they won't fall, but that shouldn't be too hard. Probably just double hooks in the wall with a crossbar on the bottom of the sign, actually.

I should also put in a more proper rest area. Some benches or something would be good . . . maybe a few divots for healing slimes so people can recover from getting here before going deeper. I want this area to be difficult, but I also want people to face those difficulties at their best.

Oh, I should also put in a few workshops down here. Not only will I get to see how the fancy metals are handled, but I bet they'll give even more mana than mining if they smelt them here, too. I wonder if I can make little merchant stalls . . .

My musings are interrupted as the five arrive, so I shelve the ideas for now. I'll probably see what Coda thinks about them later. For now, the kids and their new friends are ready to dive deep into the bowels of the lava labyrinth.

Oh, I should make a sign for it, too.

"Alright, everyone on your toes. Once we round that bend there, we'll be in the labyrinth proper," says Gerlfi, to nods all around. Freddie mutters a little prayer, making his shield subtly glow. Rhonda digs through her pack with Lucas guiding her around the various bottles and vials.

"Swiftness, darkness, silence, thunderclap . . . I wish I could recreate that cold explosion thing Queen made a while ago. Ah! Perception!" She pulls the vial out of her pack and holds it out to Fiona, to mixed looks from the adults.

"Why for the spider?" asks Vieds. Freddie answers.

"She has great eyesight. With the potion, she should be able to spot trap triggers well before any of the rest of us."

Vieds mulls that as Wold nods. "And Gerlfi's brownie can spot the magical traps."

"Which Lucas and I can disarm!" finishes Rhonda. Gerlfi does his usual offer to the fey, and the little brownie soon hops onto Fiona like a mount. She looks tempted to web him up for his insolence, but lets it slide—this time.

Freddie and Fiona lead the way, each ready to keep the party safe in their own way. Wold takes the rear, in case anything tries to sneak up on the party as they go. Rhonda, Vieds, and Gerlfi all hang out in the middle, with the changeling keeping a close eye on the map.

It doesn't take him long to start grumbling as they pass through the multiple ways I have to mix the maze up, and he grumbles more when Fiona shows the mechanical method of doing so.

"Properly mapping the area is going to be a nightmare . . ." groans the changeling, though Gerlfi doesn't look too bothered.

"We just need to mark the sections that can be changed. I just hope they don't change while we're inside."

Tempting as it is to immediately make him eat his words, I don't plan to change it while people are in there. Eventually, people might be able to run through and get the layout down before selling the info to others waiting to get in, but I'm not worried. It'll probably still take half a day for someone to do that, and I expect a lot of them will prefer to just brave it themselves, at least once the basic layout is understood.

Their plan goes well, too. Fiona points out the mechanical triggers, and sometimes webs the traps in place for everyone to get across. Pressure plates are a little more of a challenge, but a silk rope swing is enough to get past them. The brownie points out the magical traps and triggers, letting Rhonda disable them. She even gets a vial of sleeping gas to put into her pack, after a delicate bit of work to get into the access space without tripping it and letting the vial shatter.

The Fire Resist potions show their worth, too, as my wyrms pop in to harass and test the group. Vieds shows off a bit more of what fire can do by basically hog-tying one of my wyrms with that flame lash of his. I don't think Rhonda is quite going to be able to gain Kinetic affinity yet, but learning to move and put a bit of weight behind her fire is definitely going to be a big help.

They take a break when they reach what I'm starting to think of as the melting pot. It's the area I put a bunch of nodes and crucible ants in, letting them alloy as they go. It's mostly mundane stuff, but there's an orichalcum node in there, too. I'm not sure if it actually alloys with the more normal metals, but there's one hill that looks a bit like Damascus steel, but with orichalcum and steel. It looks cool, even if I have no idea if it'll be useful.

Wold and Freddie eye the Damascus hill as everyone rests, with Vieds updating the map and Rhonda scribbling her own notes about what's there. Eventually, Wold speaks up.

"Do you think we could claim that hill?"

Freddie looks thoughtful. "Maybe? They're big for ants, but they'll still swarm. I should be able to keep them at bay with enough help."

"Help, hmm? What kind of help?" asks Gerlfi as he walks over.

"More fey," answers Wold simply as Freddie tries to give details.

"I think I'll need at least three people, besides me and Fiona, to keep the ants at bay long enough for Rhonda and Vieds to handle the ants?"

Gerlfi hums as he looks at the crucible ants wandering about. "I think it'll be mostly on Rhonda for this one. Vieds can say all he wants about explosions, but there's a good reason he doesn't get to use them too often. If he blew up the hill there, the effort would all be wasted. Brownie, would you be willing to take a shield and help with this in exchange for some beer back at the guildhouse?"

The little Earth fey stares for a few moments before nodding, hopping off Fiona as Gerlfi turns his attention back to Freddie. "He makes one, Wold will make two . . . Would I be able to help with the shields?"

Freddie considers that for a few seconds, then nods. "I think so. The Shield will guide you; you'll just have to listen."

"I don't need to swear myself to it or anything, right? No offense, but I try to stay out of the business of the gods."

Freddie laughs. "No, nothing like that. You just have to be willing to be led in this, like listening to a veteran when they give you pointers."

Gerlfi nods at that. "I can do that." He waves Rhonda and Vieds over. "We're going to try to defeat the hill with the weird alloy there. We'll all keep the ants at bay; can you two deal with them?"

Vieds looks uncomfortable, but Rhonda looks confident. "I'm sure we can, together. I can freeze them, I think, but I'll also make a lot of excess fire when I do. Can you work with that, Vieds?"

He shifts to looking more uncertain as he thinks. "Possibly. It'll take a lot of fire to overwhelm even one of those ants, but it sounds like that's exactly what you'll be providing?" At her confirmation, he nods. "Then I believe so. I won't be able to handle an actual swarm, but I should at least be able to deal with strays and stragglers."

"Then that's the plan," says Gerlfi with confidence. "We'll hold the ants; you two deal with them. Then Wold will carry the hill, and we'll head home." Everyone nods at that, moving into position.

Freddie and Fiona stride proudly toward the hill with the brownie, Wold, and Gerlfi at their side. As they get near, Freddie raises his shield, and I can see his magic settle on his friends. "Phalanx Formation! Hem them in!" Translucent shields appear on the arms of everyone involved, as well as several additional ones floating at Freddie's command. As one, they jog forward and quickly encircle their target.

The ants, of course, notice the threat, and start swarming over the hill as they prepare their answer. It comes quicker than even I expected, as tongues of flame lash out at the shield wall, but it stands strong. Gerlfi looks pretty uncomfortable, but seeing Wold and the others looking calm and collected helps him keep his cool despite the rising heat.

A few ants march forward, which seems to have been what Rhonda was waiting for. "Siphon!" she exclaims, and I can see her pulling the fire out of the marching ants, quickly cooling them past the point where they can still function and earning me a decent bit of mana for her efforts. Vieds claims the rising ball of heat and forges it into a thin needle before launching it at the last ant not on the hill.

"Searing Lancet!"

The attack is hotter than even the crucible ant can handle, and it collapses as well. Lucas jumps from Rhonda's hat to grab one of the cooled ants before jumping back to land at her feet.

"Good work, Lucas! Now, get me a good focus." He's already dismantling the ant before she's done speaking. She returns her attention to the hill as he works, stealing the heat from a few more ants.

It takes them some time, but they're doing pretty well with the ants. My denizens try to focus and unleash a torrent of fire that would make a dragon proud, but the phalanx holds strong against the attack. Finally, Lucas holds up a little shard of obsidian he got out of the crucible ant and hops onto Rhonda's hat.

"Ah, perfect! Vieds, don't take control of this heat, please, I have a plan!" The goblin girl grins wide as she works her magic. "Freddie, hunker!"

The orc lad nods and gives his own shout to the circle of shields. "Brace!" Wide stances are taken and shoulders are pressed to the shields as everyone prepares for what Rhonda has in mind. Lucas helps guide the mana as the little shard resonates, and I can see my crucible ants looking a bit uncomfortable. It doesn't last long, as Rhonda finally finishes her spell.

"Thermal Shock!" Heat is drawn from all the ants in and on the hill, rapidly cooling them, before it rushes back in. My ants shatter from the rapid change in temperature, some so violently that pieces ping off the shields. Rhonda breathes heavily and grins in triumph at the result of her spell, and Freddie soon dissipates the shields, sagging from his own efforts.

Gerlfi and Vieds both give low whistles of approval at the results while Wold steps forward to poke the hill with his weapon. "Looks empty."

Freddie gives a weak laugh as he sits down. "Good, because I'm about empty too. That many shields are hard to maintain, even with help."

Gerlfi laughs and pats him on the back. "Rest up, kid. You earned it. I didn't expect you two to be so good in a fight."

Rhonda smiles as she sits next to Freddie. "Rare classes, and we delve a lot."

"Well, you two have definitely earned your share. We'll rest up a bit more before making our way out. We might have our prize, but we still need to make sure we can *keep* it."

They all nod, and I would, too, if I could. I'm not going to throw anything too terrible at them on the way out, but they still don't get a free ride. They'll be fine to take the hill and show it off, especially after a rest. Once they do, they'll probably get the miners and smiths all in a tizzy again, too.

A bit more mana should make getting the entrance spruced up even easier. I poke Coda to come take a look at the designs once he's back from the lighthouse, wanting his input. I could probably just buy the things I want with mana, but it feels better to put in a bit of effort for it. The discount doesn't hurt, either.

Chapter 45

I doodle a few different designs for the labyrinth entrance while the group works their way back out. I could make it look like an obsidian tube, but I think it'd look a bit bland just like that. Some lava pools could spruce it up, and would even give some light, but I don't think they'd be OSHA approved. I might make the actual entrance look like delvers are walking into the mouth of a giant wyrm, though. That'd be cool, especially if I can get the mandibles to close.

For the resting area just outside, I try to blend the ideas of a park and an open-air mall. While I can't exactly get grass and trees in here, a few herbalism nodes could definitely make the area look nicer. Considering a lot of them have a little glow to them, the herbs can even help keep the place lit.

The sun eventually sets, and Coda is able to come take a look at the designs. He also likes the wyrm entrance, but practically vetoes the bunker design for the aranea quest kiosk. He's not wrong, either, when he points out that the ratlings could just dig a crawlspace in the roof and let them hang their signs like on the porch.

I like the variety that using signs stuck up from the ground would give, but it would probably be better to just let them hang them. Yet another brilliant design foiled by reality. At least Coda doesn't shoot down my basic design for merchant stalls. The two of us spend most of the rest of the night iterating on what to put in the rest area, and where.

The resource-processing areas will be near the walls, out of the way of delvers looking to head into the labyrinth, but still accessible enough to those coming out with things they'll want to process. I'm planning to start with four smelters and see if the demand is there for more. There's room for another four or so, but we'll see. I also plan out room for two smiths, and expect to put in the metalworks once I get it. Jello is definitely close to getting the title, which means I should be close to getting the room, too.

Speaking of getting close to things, I should probably let Coda work on finalizing the design while I focus on the dragon spawner. My desire to minimize the cost of sprucing up the labyrinth entrance isn't just pinching pennies for its own sake. That spawner *devours* mana for upgrades, but I think I might get a new thing with the next one.

Or I could finally pull the trigger on the Ant Enclave. I'm pretty confident I have plenty of room now. The tunnelbores have been dutifully digging to make that a possibility. The magmyrms have been integrating themselves well into the labyrinth, as well as some of my other special projects, too.

They seem very interested in the devices and mechanisms of the traps in the labyrinth. Be it mechanical, magical, alchemical, or a mix, they have taken it upon themselves to maintain them. They've even started moving into the gauntlets to reset the challenges in there, saving me a decent chunk of mana over if I had to reset them myself.

I'm not going to pretend the enclave isn't tempting me something fierce, but I should resist its siren song. As much as I'd like to spend the mana on something nice and quiet like an enclave, I really should stick to the plan and get the next version of dragon. I still need to deal with the Harbinger's dungeon, and I'd much rather send a new dragon variety than fresh dwellers.

I try to ignore the huge bite the upgrade takes from my mana and idly wonder how more ordinary dungeons afford these things. I don't get to think on that question for long before the spawner graces me with another dragon that doesn't look anything like what I'd expect one to look.

I can kinda squint and see the relationship to the wyrms. The label says BASILISK, but it doesn't look like what I'd expect that to look like, either. The head is weirdly shaped, making me think a lot of a dinner plate, but I think most of that is a bone ridge or some kind of weird horn structure. It has two eyes which resemble a tiger's to me, but that might just be how piercing they are. The mouth is what's really throwing me off.

If my wyrms have a mouth similar to a graboid, my basilisk has a mouth similar to the Predator, but hidden behind a jackal-like muzzle. A long tongue licks the lips before they creepily pull back toward the rest of the head, revealing four mandibles with webbing between them.

And I thought the spiderkin mouths were terrifying. The head sits on thick shoulders, or haunches? They definitely connect to forelegs and not actual arms. They look a lot like what a monitor lizard has, but with bulging muscles. After that, I think it has a rib cage, but it's hard to tell because the whole thing tapers into a long, thick tail. And, of course, the entire thing has the same living magma look the wyrms do. It rides that line between cool and terrifying, which probably means delvers are going to need new pants when they see it.

Speaking of delvers, I take a good, hard look at its abilities. And I'm relieved not to see anything about petrification. While that'd be great for fighting an enemy dungeon, I wouldn't have much use for it in my day-to-day.

My basilisk decides it's spent enough time getting its bearings and starts to wander down the tunnel to explore the labyrinth. Watching it move, I get a better feel for why it's shaped like it is. On the ground, it mostly pulls itself forward with those beefy forelegs, using the long tail more to steer than to help with propulsion.

It eventually notices a Fire elemental through the wall and dives into the rock as the head plate folds back against its neck. It keeps its forelegs loose at its sides and uses that long tail to swim through the rock like an eel. It's even faster than my wyrms!

In no time, it bursts into the tunnel with the elemental and grabs the invader with that freaky mouth before using those forelegs to tear it to shreds. Once the thing is dispatched, the basilisk spends a little time licking up the pieces with that long tongue before it resumes meandering around the tunnels of the labyrinth.

Yeah, that's going to give my delvers nightmares. With any luck, it'll give the Harbinger nightmares too. For bigger prey, I wonder if it'll wrap that long tail around the victim before savaging them with the claws? It seems flexible enough for that.

I leave it to wander the labyrinth as I turn my attention to Teemo.

It looks like they're making good progress through the shortcut, and my Voice is dutifully working on making it even quicker to traverse. I think it'll still be a day or two for him and the whole group to get to the Southwood, but the return will be much quicker, as will further expeditions. Teemo has to go slower to build the shortcut, but once he's done working on it, everyone else can go at their full pace.

"Heya, Boss. What was that . . . whatever it was you were thinking about just now?"

Ah, I upgraded the dragon spawner. Now we're getting basilisks as well as wyrms.

"Cool."

Yeah, I think those weird leech-heads are gonna be no match for them. We'll see if I can get enough of them to be able to send in time. How's Nova? With her spawner upgraded, I was wondering if she'd changed any.

Teemo glances around but doesn't see my youngest scion. "I dunno. Hey, Nova! You around?" he yells. A few of the adventurers give him curious looks but soon return to what they were doing. Once their attentions are redirected, Nova pops her head out of the ground near Teemo, rumbling at him.

My Voice chuckles and waves a dismissive hand. "I was hoping it'd make it easier for you. It's not difficult to add a bit of ground to the shortcut. I might need to figure out how to add a stream or water or something eventually, too. Imagine how surprised someone would be if I could have the First Mate pop out of a shortcut and eat an invader!"

Nova tilts her head a bit at that and rumbles again.

"Right. The Boss wanted to get a look at you, see if anything's different. He just upgraded your spawner and got basilisks, so he was curious if you had changed."

Nova slides out fully onto the ground and contorts herself to look, but I'm not seeing much in the way of a difference. It's more than a little adorable watching her twist and turn, though.

"Yeah, I don't see anything different either," agrees Teemo. Nova gives him a worried look. "Nah, it's not bad, Nova. The Boss was just curious."

She rumbles again, and Teemo hops onto her head, quickly moving to her cooler mandibles. "No, the Boss doesn't want you to change, Nova. He just wants you to be you."

She manages to pout and rumbles once more, earning a smirk from Teemo.

"That's something you have to figure out on your own."

Chapter 46

Rocky

Rocky has been feeling . . . *restless* since the battle with the Harbinger. He'd thought he could keep his skill set subtle, practicing his affinities and supporting Leo and Honey. But almost all the subterfuge went out the window when the Harbinger killed his fellow scions. Even knowing they'd respawn, he still felt their loss.

And with the Harbinger broadcasting its smug superiority at their defeat . . . Well, he couldn't take that lying down. He's honestly surprised he didn't lay into the monster with his fists and kept to only leveraging his affinities. For a brief moment, he got a glimpse of what they could be used for, the walls between the affinities falling away to give a glimpse of the potential behind them.

It's no wonder Coach is careful about letting those secrets out. Rocky is just glad the Harbinger was broadcasting its disbelief up until the moment it finally died. He'd hate to have given something like that a look at the secrets of Coach Thedeim.

After the Harbinger died, it was practically a workout cooldown to deal with the little demon things, especially with the help of the other denizens. The smaller monstrosities were simple enough to round up and squash thanks to Leo's tactics getting him into a good position. All Rocky had to do was sweep through the disoriented forces the Harbinger had left behind.

While he can't quite wrap his head around the aftermath, he's been working on wrapping his head around how he's changed. For starters, his Sonic affinity feels solidified now, almost as much a part of his skill set as Fire, Ice, and Kinetic. He wants to put on his gloves and work out his body to be able to use it, too, but he needs to wait until he gets back to Coach for that.

But that's not the only affinity he's feeling closer to.

He can feel Lightning calling to him, and his Sonic affinity calling back. Those two are linked by something deeper than just thunder following lightning. He'd have it backward if that was the only link between the two. Something about how sound moves . . .

But he has another affinity he can feel close to, too, though he can't figure out how it links to his others. When the Harbinger tried to attack him, he could feel it and react. He's certain it was something Honey did, though he's not sure what. He could feel her defenses taking the blows, and could feel what they were defending against, at least vaguely. Then he could feel the haymaker punch incoming, and his boxing instincts kicked in, and he ducked the blow.

He's been trying to recreate that feeling, but he hasn't had much success yet. Hopefully, he can talk with Honey about it before he heads back home. Coach knows he can't talk about it here, no matter how much the Stag probably wants him to.

The Stag had met him at the border when he returned, looking antsy. Looking back on it, Rocky can't blame him. Coach would probably be nervous if a dungeon was protecting him and lost two out of three scions. The amount of mana he was carrying probably didn't help the Stag's nerves, either.

"Is it over? What happened? The expeditions said something big came out of the hole, and then I could feel . . . whatever that was. It interrupted the report."

Rocky nodded and grunted.

"Dead? Then we're safe?"

This time, the grunt was accompanied by a shake of Rocky's rotten head.

"What do you mean?" insisted the Stag. Rocky got the feeling that, if he had hands, he'd be wringing them. A few more grunts gave a few more details, not that the Stag seemed happy to be hearing them.

"An enemy scion? A dungeon, then . . ." The stag looked off past Rocky into the distance, toward the battle, as if he could see through the trees. "I see. I'll . . . I'll confer with the returning expeditions and see what my Lord wishes to do."

That was fine by Rocky. Even though Coach seemed to be pretty proud of him, he'd like a bit of time to relax. He sat on a stump, going over everything for a while, hardly noticing when the sun set. He only realized how long he had been sitting there when the first rays of sunlight caused him to squint.

Why didn't the Stag come to talk to him? The scion has always seemed a bit of a busybody to Rocky, the type to come demanding answers as soon as he has questions. Rocky's mind might literally be rotten, but there's no way the Stag doesn't have more questions about what happened than the Southwood's denizens can answer. So why leave him be for so long?

He decides he should probably go see what's up. He asks a few denizens, and they quickly let him know the Stag will come find him in a few minutes. That seems strange to Rocky, but what can he do? The Southwood is huge. If he went stomping off to try to find the Stag, it'd take him days, if he could find him at all.

So he sits on his stump, wishing he had his mouthguard to chew on while he waits. At least he isn't waiting long. The Stag bounds into the small clearing, looking to Rocky more rushed than graceful. The situation only seems to get weirder when the Stag gives him a deep bow, his antlers brushing the ground before he straightens.

"My Lord wishes to give his deepest thanks, as well as a heartfelt apology. He knows respawning your two lost scions will likely not be recouped by the mana from your victory." He meets Rocky's eyes, and the Zombie Scion can feel the sincerity in his next words. "Please claim my head to help pay my Lord's debt. This is not a threat he can be victorious against, and you've wasted enough of your resources trying to help us."

Rocky just stares for a few seconds, utterly out of his depth. Sure, it's probably not cheap to respawn Honey and Leo, but Coach has probably already recouped the loss just from the delvers back home. He tries to get Coach's attention, but he seems to be busy. It's all up to Rocky.

He would have no problem doing as the Stag asked, but it sounds like the Southwood is almost trying to say goodbye, not just trying to give Coach more mana.

He grunts a question at the Stag, who looks a little confused.

"Why? You're . . . You're pulling out, correct? Even with my Lord's tithe of seeds and plants, you've surely spent more mana than you've gained. We . . . We'd be a burden to you in this fight, a wounded fawn in the herd while the wolves circle. We should give you what we can and hope that Harbinger and its dungeon are sated with—"

Rocky grunts a negative at that, cutting the Stag off before grinning and explaining.

"He's not? Why not?!" Rocky holds up a hand to keep the Stag from ranting about why the Coach should abandon them. Sure, it might be a smart move, but the Coach isn't one to do the sacrifice play.

"But . . . why?" asks the Stag again, looking baffled and just trying to understand.

Rocky gives a firm grunt. That Harbinger is something Coach doesn't intend to just let be. Something is wrong with it, and Coach is going to stop it before it can get too strong.

He can see the Stag is still lost, so Rocky gives him a grin and one more grunt. That was only round one. Once he can get this mana back to Coach, he's going to be back for round two.

The Stag looks lost in thought for a few minutes before shaking himself and remembering he was technically in the middle of a conversation. "Then . . . if you're certain you don't need more mana . . . would you like a few of my Lord's denizens? Some noticed your Warden was a transfer and expressed an interest in joining you, should the opportunity arise?"

Rocky can only shrug at that. He's not the Voice, so he doesn't know if Coach is in the market for more spawners, and he can't really ask. Still, it isn't difficult to guess the Voice will be coming with the reinforcements to chase down and sniff out that dungeon.

The days after that are a bit awkward. Rocky is pretty sure the Stag is just trying to come to terms with the fact that he's not the baddest on the block anymore, and that he doesn't actually have to be. It's one thing to get punched in the mouth, but it's another to have someone else take that punch and square up to take a few more.

As he watches from the southern border of the Southwood, he can feel the reinforcements coming. They'll probably get here today. He can't help but grin as he imagines the Southwood's reaction to seeing more of Coach's scions. This roster is deep and strong. That dungeon out there better have a lot more to throw at them than just the Harbinger. Otherwise, Fluffles might finish this fight before Rocky can even get back.

Chapter 47

It's a little disorienting to be able to watch the large group near the Southwood's borders from both the outside and the inside. Teemo, Slash, Leo, and Fluffles have more or less the same view. Honey is currently up in the air, getting a good vantage, while Nova's current sights are mostly rock.

The disorientating part is watching through Rocky and seeing everyone approach. The group looks like a lot more than it is. It's probably just the quiet of the Southwood making it seem so much bigger.

Rocky glances over at the Stag occasionally, who looks even more serious than usual. My Boxer has some complex feelings about the other scion, but the details are hard to pick out. At least it's easy to see he doesn't dislike the big elk.

The adventurers are looking in pretty high spirits, and more than a few point at the Stag as they approach. He does cut a pretty regal figure.

He looks a bit uncomfortable as he sees how many scions I've sent, but he doesn't get a chance to ask about them before Teemo speaks up.

"Stag! We brought some reinforcements!" declares my Voice with a wide grin, earning some chuckles from the gathered adventurers.

". . . Indeed, you have. And delvers, too?"

Teemo nods and waves at the people gathered. "The local guild wanted to have a better hand in rooting out that problem dungeon. They want to spend a day or so to resupply by delving before they head into the hole and get to exploring. That's fine, right?"

The Stag slowly nods. "Yes, that should be fine. My Lord would appreciate the mana they would give for that."

Teemo nods and looks to Yvonne, Aelara, and Ragnar. "You heard the guy. Go ahead and get ready. The Southwood probably wants some details and to talk to the Boss some about what happened."

The party nods at that and waves as the other adventurers head into the Southwood, looking around at the forest where it looks more like it's early fall, rather than solidly winter.

My scions gather before the Stag, waiting for him to decide what to do. He appears more and more concerned as he looks over my representatives before he turns and motions for them to follow. "Come. We should discuss matters with a bit more privacy."

My scions easily fall in line behind him, and it only takes a few minutes before Teemo speaks up with a concern I'm trying to ignore.

"Is everything alright?"

The Stag winces at the sound of Teemo's voice but doesn't look back as he continues to lead everyone deeper. "My Lord might ask the same question. You've committed all your scions to this? Are you not worried about reprisals or attacks from other rivals?"

Teemo looks at the gathered scions and slowly shakes his head. *I think it's time to put our cards on the table, Teemo. At least the ones about my scions.* "This isn't even half of the Boss's scions."

That statement gets the Stag to stumble and turn around, shock on his face as his disbelief wars with what he sees before him. "You, the Warden, the Librarian . . ." he pauses to look at the others, and I'm pretty sure he's peeking at their statuses. His eyes widen when he looks at Fluffles, but he continues. "The Bard, the *Conduit*, and the wyrm. These aren't even half your scions?"

Teemo shakes his head. "There's also the Guardian, the Marshal, the Purifier, the Alchemist, the Architect, the Grounds Reaper, and the Enchanter." Teemo pauses to count in his head, and I'm pretty sure we're missing one.

Oh, duh. Teemo smacks his forehead and points at Rocky. "And we can't forget the Savant! I guess that does technically mean half the Boss's scions are here, though."

The Stag looks a bit overwhelmed but doesn't try to argue as he resumes guiding everyone. "How grand is your Lord to be able to field so many?"

Teemo chuckles at that. "I'm pretty sure you have him beat in raw acreage, even if we pulled all the underground stuff to spread on the surface. He runs things different than the other dungeons we've met. It probably helps that his main entrance is smack-dab in the middle of Fourdock, though. Easy access to delvers."

The Stag nods at that and turns his head slightly to eye everyone, though he pauses on Fluffles for a few moments before continuing. "And how does he run things? My Lord has heard of a protégée and a vassal?"

"Yeah, Violet and Hullbreak. I dunno how much you know about Hullbreak, but the Boss vassalized him a couple months ago. He was starving, and one of his dwellers asked for help. It was a bit of a thing, but now Hullbreak is back to letting people delve, and his dwellers are learning to stand on their own feet . . . or swim with their own fins?" Teemo shrugs before continuing.

"Violet is basically a baby, only having her first real expansion like a month ago or so? The Boss has been helping her learn a few of his methods and such. The ODA classified her as a toybox not long ago, actually."

The Stag gives Teemo another confused look. "ODA?"

Teemo laughs and nods. "The Office of Dungeon Affairs. That's what he called them before he learned they were called the Dungeoneer's Guild. He still calls them the ODA most of the time."

The Stag seems to accept that, or at least doesn't try to argue as he resumes leading the way. As they all continue walking, Rocky falls back a little to grunt at Teemo, who's currently riding on Slash's shoulder.

"Oh? Rocky says you'd like to transfer a couple residents to the Boss as thanks?"

The Stag stiffens for a moment before nodding. He doesn't look back, nor does he slow down, as he speaks. "Yes, as a small token of my Lord's appreciation. One of the illusion foxes has expressed interest, and there is a current of curiosity among many of the other denizens."

A fox spawner would be really cool, but I should probably wait until I expand into the forest beyond the cemetery to make sure I'll have room.

"The Boss isn't against it, but he'll need to expand again to have room." Teemo eyes Rocky before continuing. "After Rocky and the denizens rotate out and bring that mana back, he might have enough to."

"Truly?"

Teemo shrugs, and I would, too, if I could. I can tell Rocky has a lot of mana, and I can also tell it'll be expensive to claim the woods outside. My gut says I'll need a bit more than just what Rocky and the returning denizens have, but if the new entrance to the labyrinth pans out like I hope it does, it shouldn't take too long.

"Maybe? The Boss still doesn't have a hard understanding of the numbers involved, but it'll be close." He snorts at an idea I have. "He might have any new Fox Scion be his accountant to help plan his budget."

The Stag shakes his head at that. "I won't presume to tell him what to do, but I believe he's been doing well enough without one so far. We're almost there," he finishes, nodding at a clearing through the trees where a yellow light can be seen.

Teemo's eyes widen, as well as the eyes of all my scions who have them. "Is that where the Southwood's core is?"

The Stag nods solemnly. "It is. Only a rare few have beheld my Lord's glory, but this is a matter that demands it." My scions quietly follow, and I try to look and listen through them as much as I can. I don't know exactly what's going on, but at least the Stag doesn't seem inclined to keep me hanging for long.

In the clearing, it looks more like the middle of spring, with a thick carpet of flowers covering the ground. A small spring rests in the middle of the clearing, a steady trickle of clear water seeping from a small rise to pool in a clear pond. In the center of the pond, hovering just above the surface, floats the core of the Southwood.

It's a large, thick, hexagonal crystal, tapered at both ends and looking like something straight out of a *Final Fantasy* game. The yellow crystal is semitransparent, reflecting and refracting the surroundings in its depths as it slowly rotates. It must be close to eight feet tall and probably three feet across. Teemo gives a low whistle, impressed at the scene, earning a small smile from the Stag as he moves to stand in the shallows, not too far from the crystal.

"My Lord has had much to consider since you first came to lend your aid, Lord Thedeim. Your methods were confusing at first . . . and are confusing even now, yet my Lord has gained some understanding of your intentions. Bringing the delvers was the last clue for him to come to understand you. You are a natural symbiont, seeking to grow and prosper together, like the leafcutter ants and their fungi. Yet your reach is much further, like an entire ecosystem.

"You integrate and adapt, seeking a balance. Some new species must be culled to allow the rest to flourish, but you seem to have successfully integrated more variety than my Lord could have dreamed. He would ask to be part of your pack, of your herd, of your forest. He has prospered in his isolation, but if not for your efforts, the Harbinger and its unnatural plague would have claimed him and feasted on his corpse. My Lord would swear fealty to you, Lord Thedeim."

Accept Vassal? Yes/No?

I stare at the notification, uncertain what to do. I mean . . . he's not wrong about the trouble he'd be in, but I'm not really looking to conquer. Can I make him a protégé?

Release Current Protégée? Yes/No?

Nope, no, nu-uh, no way, negative! Come on, work with me here! There's gotta be something like a partnership?

The notification seems to come slowly, less out of reluctance and more from disuse. I can practically see the dust on it and hear the squeaking of pulleys that need oil as it comes up. I get the feeling I should ask Aranya about this when I get the chance. For now, I look at it and consider.

Forge Alliance? Yes/No?

Chapter 48

Southwood

Forge Alliance? Yes/No?

The Southwood considers the prompt, and as he does, he finds more and more worth in considering it. While it seemed to appear as all prompts do, something about it speaks of the weight of ages behind it, like an ancient pine. Or perhaps like a cicada with a much longer cycle; something that has not been seen for a *long* time.

He considered dismissing it and trying to pressure Thedeim to accept him as a vassal, but that would plainly not work. Not only would it be a bit strange to try to force someone to take him as a vassal, but the other dungeon clearly doesn't want another vassal. The look on the rat's face made that plain enough. But why not?

The other dungeon certainly seems determined to be the symbiont that the Southwood classified him as a while ago, but even herbivores will snack on an unfortunate rodent occasionally. Why does Thedeim refuse?

Taking him as a vassal, or even just subsuming him, the other dungeon would reap many rewards. The Southwood is proud of his territory, spawners, and countless nodes. If Thedeim consumed him, the dungeon hiding in that hole would stand no chance. Proud of his progress as he is, he knows his capacity for self-defense is sorely lacking. If not for Thedeim's scions, the Southwood would have been subsumed already.

If he wanted a steady harvest, vassalizing the Southwood would be a good choice instead. Losing much of his autonomy would grate on his Voice, but even the Stag had come to understand how outmatched his Lord is.

As a vassal, he could tithe the mana to Thedeim and have his own growth guided by a mind more suited to battle. He doesn't need to be a fighter to recognize one, even if Thedeim prefers not to bare his teeth without cause.

He turns his attention back to the prompt, and has to acknowledge the real reason he hasn't accepted: fear. He doesn't fear it's a trick. If the other dungeon was somehow able to fake prompts like this, why would it bother tricking a dungeon as poor in a fight as he?

No, his fear is of himself.

He is . . . unprepared. Whatever this fight will entail, it is not something the Southwood understands how to handle. He would much prefer to just tuck his metaphorical tail and accept Thedeim's dominance—his guidance and protection—than to have to figure it out on his own.

Although . . . he wouldn't really be on his own, would he? An ally wouldn't just leave him to flounder, especially not after sending all those scions. If those truly are only half of what he has, Thedeim would be a powerful ally indeed. But what can the Southwood provide in exchange?

If this will really be a more formal symbiosis, the Southwood needs to be able to provide *something*. Even after having a lot of time to think, he hasn't been able to figure out what . . . though this alliance perhaps expands what he can offer. Even if he were a vassal, Thedeim would still need to send a scion to work in a room to gain it. The Southwood was willing to make some just for that purpose if Thedeim expressed any interest, but he hadn't.

With an alliance, would he be able to offer the rooms more freely? Offer *spawners* more freely? Thedeim would certainly need to have room to place them, but if he can give prizes like that, he could actually contribute! He might even be able to offer some of his more unique upgrades, like his weather control. He still remembers when he first got the option, after a particularly harsh winter.

He'd wanted to combat the damage to his nodes, the effect on his spawners, the suppression of delvers that the harsh winter bestowed. The upgrade had been expensive at the time, but he regards it as one of his better choices.

He could potentially make his domain as warm as summer even in the depth of winter, but the mana cost would be prohibitive. But letting fall extend its stay and convince spring to get an early start is a much more cost-effective way to keep the cold and snow mostly outside. It'd be nice to keep a corridor open to the orcs or to the town of Fourdock, but that hasn't been something available to him.

It probably still won't be, even if he accepts this alliance . . . but it's possible. It might not even be necessary, at least in the form the Southwood has been envisioning. Thedeim has blazed some kind of trail already. Could he do something similar for the orcs?

Just the possibility is enough to make him want to pounce on the offer like a squirrel on the last nut of the season, but he holds himself back and tries to think this through. What will the consequences be?

If he denies the offer . . . Thedeim will still fight the Harbinger's dungeon. A dungeon doesn't commit half their scions if they're not prepared to finish a fight.

The Southwood will still try to contribute, and though it stings his pride a little, he knows he won't be able to make much of a difference.

While he could possibly be the single snowflake that cracks the branch, he doesn't think his efforts will be so dramatic. If Thedeim wins, for there's no point contemplating what will happen should he *lose,* he will gain even more power, and the Southwood will try to stay in his good graces.

Hmm. Even if he denies the alliance, he will probably be reliant on the other dungeon. If being a vassal is still not an available path, denying the alliance is pointless. He'll still be dealing with the other dungeon in hopefully an amiable way for the foreseeable future. Whatever the alliance does, it can't hurt the options of working together.

The Southwood accepts. Immediately, he can feel the change, can feel his information expanding. New options bloom like flowers in spring, and he's relieved to see he can trade his more precious upgrades and options more freely. He can't give them away, but he can offer a trade.

There is also an alliance pool of mana, which any can contribute to and any can withdraw from. He can feel Thedeim's protégée, like a curious pup hiding behind her sire's legs. He can feel Hullbreak in the distance, a wounded predator slowly learning to accept help and recover.

And he can feel Thedeim. He's hardly more than a pup himself, but there is a cleverness there, far more cleverness than should exist in one so young. Happiness and confidence radiate through the alliance like a warm breeze in fall. Thedeim has no fear of losing this battle, but he's also not going to just charge blindly in.

There is a ruthless patience to him, a combination the Southwood would have never expected to exist. The closest is how wolves hunt, tracking and harrying their prey until the final blow can be struck. That kind of pursuit is one of hunger and focus, grim determination and desperate hope of securing victory.

The intentions of Thedeim are different. The Southwood can see him like one of the delvers, a similar shape, but no detail beyond the outline. He's pursuing a goal. The pursuit is almost casual, expending the minimal effort while still tracking the prey.

Opportunities can be taken advantage of, berries picked or smaller prey taken, but each step continues to close the distance. It can be outrun, but it can't be escaped. Following, always following, always moving at a steady pace. Even the fight with the Harbinger fits into the steady rhythm of Thedeim's advance. While the enemy dungeon scrambles to prepare, Thedeim continues his inexorable advance.

His new ally's preparations are simple and deliberate, slowly building momentum toward the goal. A wolf might go out and hope for victory, fight for its life and howl its latest victory against starvation . . . but Thedeim doesn't hope for victory. He knows what it will take and has prepared accordingly.

In his pursuit, foes are felled and allies carried until they can walk on their own. When they stumble, he's there to keep them moving, carrying them again if needed.

The vision fades, and it takes the Southwood a few moments to recognize it *was* a vision. The feelings through the alliance bond grow slightly concerned, but the Southwood quickly has his Voice reassure Teemo, and so Thedeim, that he's fine. He had been dimly aware of the dungeon's Fate affinity, but the vision has, perhaps appropriately, brought that knowledge into focus.

The alliance may be fresh and new, but the Southwood can already feel himself recommitting to the idea. Thedeim's intentions are clear: to nurture and uplift his allies to the point they can stride confidently, and to ensure their foes never enjoy a moment's rest.

Chapter 49

It feels a bit weird when the Southwood accepts the alliance. I can feel the new bond, with the old ones shuffling around a bit, and a bit more information flowing around now, too. I'm a bit surprised to see that Violet and Hullbreak are in it as well, but looking closer, it seems more of a technicality.

As Violet's mentor, I'm in charge of most outsider-related things, so while she's in the alliance, it's mostly because her mentor is in it. Similar with Hullbreak. As a vassal, he's not allowed to have much to do with diplomatic affairs, but as his . . . lord, I guess? As the guy he's a vassal to, he gets dragged into technically allying, too.

I take a few minutes to poke around the options; I'm probably going to eventually invite them both to the alliance properly. Honestly, Hullbreak has been doing great, and I'd love to give him the reins back, but I think that'd be moving a bit too quickly. He'll get there eventually, but for now, I think he needs a bit more time with fewer responsibilities so he can get his feet properly underneath him.

It'll definitely be longer for Violet. I don't think she's ready to stop being my protégée yet. I want to give her the time she needs to grow without having to worry about things like alliances and wars with crazy dungeons.

When I take a closer look at Southwood, I can feel him prodding the options, too, as well as politely tapping the bonds with the others. Violet is looking pretty curious, while Hullbreak is trying to put on a friendly face despite his aversion to outsiders. I'm not really worried about either of them.

Southwood is pretty interesting, too. I can get a better feel for his territory, and he's absolutely massive! Sure, my denizens have scouted his borders, but there's a difference between reading it on a map and being able to get a feel through the bond. I let him take a look at what I have, too. If this is an alliance, we should share what we can. That's the entire point of an alliance, right?

I can also feel that Southwood is old. I can't get a specific number, but he's easily the oldest of our little group. It's not surprising that he's the oldest, but there's a feeling of weight and wisdom that's going to take some getting used to. It feels kinda weird for him to act deferential to me, considering how much more experience he has being a dungeon.

We both explore the options for a few more minutes, and I discover the alliance mana pool. This thing is definitely cool. I set a trickle of my income to flow into it, hoping it'll be a good emergency stockpile in case anything happens. Some curiosity and nervousness slip through the bond, and the Stag looks a little awkward as he tries to figure out how to ask whatever it is the Southwood wants.

Of course, Teemo is more than happy to pounce. "What's up? You look like you want to ask something."

The Stag looks like he'd rather stay quiet, but eventually, he crumbles under the polite smile of my Voice. "My Lord is unsure how much he's expected to contribute to the alliance pool."

Teemo scoffs. "Pfft, that's easy: nothing. The Boss is planning to use it as a communal emergency fund, so just put in whatever you can whenever you can, and withdraw whatever you need for whatever you need it for. In fact . . . have you thought about getting a second scion?"

The Stag answers slowly, sounding more than a little ashamed. "My own upkeep is all my Lord is able to afford."

Teemo exchanges a glance with my gathered scions before nodding. "Lots of orders, yeah?"

The Stag nods, missing the tone in Teemo's voice.

"Well, that's easy to fix, Southwood. Just stop giving him orders. The Boss almost never does. He basically just brings something to our attention and lets us figure it out on our own."

The Stag looks flabbergasted, and I can feel a similar reaction through the bond. After a few seconds, the Stag manages to stammer a response. "But . . . But the complex plan! The intricate movement of your troops!"

"All Leo." My Warden gives a quiet *bork*, and Teemo smirks as he corrects himself. "Leo and Honey. He's the Warden, and Thedeim isn't going to second-guess him. Troop stuff is Leo's job, so the Boss mostly stays out of it and just makes sure he has what he needs to do it. That's how he does most of his stuff."

The Stag still looks lost, so Teemo tries to put it differently. "Look, even if the Southwood didn't order you to go do . . . whatever he asks you to, you'd still do whatever you can to help him, right?"

"Of course," answers the Stag, sounding a little more confident but still not seeing where this is going.

"That's how we are, too. If the Boss has something that needs doing, he points out the need to us and lets us figure it out. He supports and helps us, but it's mostly on us. Like with the shortcuts here. Reducing the travel time will be a huge help to the Boss, so I do it even without being ordered to."

It looks like the Stag is still wrapping his head around that idea, but I can feel comprehension slowly creeping up on Southwood through the bond, which only gets stronger as the Stag speaks up again.

"So if my Lord had a second scion . . . we could share the duty of carrying out his will?"

Teemo finger guns him with a smile. "Nailed it. You should try a second scion. Dip into the alliance fund if you need to and get a feel for how it works.

It's probably a bit expensive to try to get as many as the Boss has, but with the shortcuts getting shorter each time I go over them, you'll have more delvers, even in winter."

I can feel him thinking it over, which is fine for now. It's a pretty big risk to get a new scion, especially if he's used to giving orders. He could easily bankrupt himself like that, even with the group of delvers we brought doing some delving.

"Just think it over. We should probably also talk about how we're going to deal with the Harbinger's dungeon. If you do go for a new scion, it wouldn't be a bad idea to try them out as a Marshal or Warden, or something else that specializes in expeditions. Leo and Honey will be leading Thedeim's expeditions to get down there and find it.

"We're also going to be rotating out the denizens from the battle, as well as Rocky, so the Boss can get all that mana and keep working on his stuff. Fluffles and Slash will mostly be sticking around you, Southwood, to intercept anything funny the other dungeon might try. Nova is . . . probably going to join the scouts?" asks Teemo, looking over at my Wyrm Scion, who quietly rumbles her reply.

Leo *wuffs* and shrugs before Teemo continues.

"Sounds like scouting or training, then. If you're up for it, Stag, I'm sure they'd be happy to have you spar." Rocky grins wide as the Stag blanches.

"I, uh . . . appreciate the offer, though I don't know how much of a challenge I'd pose."

My zombie grunts as Teemo nods. "It's not about being a punching bag; it's about learning. Rocky will probably want to pick your brain about your affinity, but he'll need to do that when he gets back. The Boss really does need that mana, Rocky."

The Zombie Scion slumps slightly as his bubble bursts, but he doesn't look too upset. He's a good, responsible scion, Rocky. The Stag looks a bit relieved until Fluffles gives a quiet hiss, reminding the Stag that I still have my Conduit ready and willing to do some training.

The Stag's relief turns to fear as he tries to change the subject. "Ah . . . Oh! My Lord wished to ask if there are any rooms you may wish to trade for. It seems that allies can trade them directly rather than needing a scion to train and gain a title for access."

Teemo's curious tilt of his head mirrors my own curiosity. "Yeah? What rooms do you have? The Boss is working on getting a metalworks right now, so I dunno if he has room for another one just yet. Getting an idea of what to get next could be great."

The Stag smiles with confidence for the first time in a while. "My Lord has quite the comprehensive selection of rooms available. If Lord Thedeim doesn't have much room at the moment, perhaps my Lord could offer an upgrade instead?" The confident smile wavers slightly as I get a notification.

Purchase Climate Control? Yes/No?

Oof, that look makes more sense once I see the price tag associated with the purchase. The Stag nods when he sees Teemo's reaction.

"There is a minimum price, unfortunately. Even if he doesn't want it just yet, my Lord will be happy to offer it again at a later time." I select no while Teemo nods.

"Yeah, the Boss isn't ready to spend that much on anything right now. What's it actually do?"

The Stag's confidence returns as he stands a bit straighter. "It is what lets my Lord keep back even the depths of winter within his domain. With his focus on natural nodes, a hard winter can make them much less effective than they should be. With that upgrade, he can set the seasons at his whim. It can be expensive if he is too forceful, but he can practically have a long fall give way to an early spring, ignoring winter altogether should he wish."

Teemo gives a low whistle at that. I can see why that kind of upgrade is so expensive. For a dungeon like Southwood, it's an amazing option. It'd be cool for me, too.

It gives me all sorts of ideas for the expansion past the cemetery that I've been eyeing. It'd probably take at least a second expansion into those woods outside town to give me enough room, but it'd be so cool to be able to have a forest of four seasons.

"The Boss already has some ideas for that kind of upgrade. I don't think he'll be taking it until spring at the earliest, though."

The Stag nods at that. "Then simply let my Lord know, and he'll offer it again." Nobody seems to have anything else to say for the moment, so Fluffles hisses, earning a wince from the Stag. Reluctantly, he nods at my Conduit.

"Yes . . . I think I have some time to train. I fear I will need more advice than I may have hoped. I haven't forgotten my embarrassing loss to Teemo when we first met."

Teemo smirks at that, though the smirk falls when he hears my suggestion. "You sure, Boss?"

Yeah, we're allies.

Teemo slowly nods at that, accepting the logic before turning to my wing-noodle. "Show him the ropes properly, yeah? Get Rocky's help if you need to. The Boss says you should try to expand his horizons."

Fluffles and Rocky both look surprised at that, which makes the Stag very nervous.

"Is it too late to have sudden business elsewhere?" the Stag asks, looking like he might bolt anyway. Teemo shakes his head and chuckles as he hops onto Leo's back.

"Nah, you'll be fine. Rocky's just going to get a chance to pick your brains, after all."

Chapter 50

Fluffles

The serpentine scion knows he shouldn't find the Stag's concerns so humorous, but he does. While he can understand where the Southwood's scion is coming from, it's not like they're going to hurt him. He will probably be sore for a while, and likely fatigued in both mana and mind.

He effortlessly glides behind the Stag as he leads the group to a different clearing. Having a good spar in and around the core would just be a bad idea. Teemo, Honey, and Leo won't be joining them, as they want to either coordinate with the delvers or check on the denizens on expedition. There's a lot of organizing to be done with both, and Fluffles is happy to leave them to it.

Rocky and Nova are both looking excited to train, which isn't surprising at all. Rocky is *always* eager to practice, and Nova still seems determined to live up to her name. Fluffles has tried to tell her there's nothing to really live up to. It's not like he's fluffy, wings aside; they don't count. But she's still young and needs to find her place, even if it's a bit strange for him to call her young. He's not even a year old yet.

Slash seems to want to practice his music, specifically in supporting a fight, so this will be good practice for him, too. Fluffles is looking forward to it as well. It'll be a good chance to teach and to make sure he understands the way affinities interact as much as he thinks he does.

The Stag leads them all to a clearing with quite a bit of leaf litter, but it's simple enough for Fluffles to sweep it away with Wind and a bit of Kinetic. Even that earns a startled look from the Stag.

"You have Wind affinity?"

Fluffles nods and coils comfortably on a rock, glad it's modestly warm from the sunlight. "Wind, Storm, Kinetic, Lightning, and Fate." Rocky perks up at the mention of Lightning, but is polite enough not to interrupt. The Stag looks rather intimidated by the list, though. Fluffles just smiles.

"My Stormeater title earned me three of those. Maybe we can get Slash to tell you the story some time . . . or I can. I was there. I'm not as good a storyteller as he is, though. How about your affinities?"

"I . . . have Life, Kinetic, and Light."

Fluffles can feel the Den Master's interest in the Light affinity, followed by a few nonsensical flashes of association. Experience has taught him they're probably not so nonsensical after all, but he can't fathom how both fire and lightning relate to light. "Ah, we share one! I started with Kinetic, specifically telekinesis. I'd be glad to give you some pointers with it."

That has the Stag slowly nodding. "I started with Light and picked up Kinetic from becoming my Lord's Guardian. I've not practiced with it much beyond empowering my hooves."

Fluffles prepares to respond, but Rocky interrupts with a grunt. "I think I can get him into Fire from Light."

The Stag looks worried at that, but Fluffles is intrigued. "Already?"

Rocky nods and steps forward, eyeing the Stag. "He's real good with light, I can tell. You want Fire affinity?" he asks, causing the worry to shift to confusion.

"Fire affinity? What?"

"I think I can teach you to expand your light into fire. I'm missing something to turn my fire into light, but I think you can bridge your gap with a little push."

"Expand . . . Is that even possible?" The Stag looks at Rocky with a mixture of incredulity and hope, and the pretend lich nods.

"Yeah. I started with Fire and expanded it into Ice and Kinetic, then Kinetic into Sonic. I'm working on Lightning next."

It's still weird for Fluffles to hear it put like that. Part of him still wants to say that's impossible, but Rocky doesn't talk about it as a boast. It's just simple fact. The Stag looks inclined not to believe him, but if he'd seen what Rocky did to the Harbinger, it wouldn't be as unbelievable.

". . . How?" asks the Stag. Rocky grins.

"Make some light. Just some regular light. Fluffles, get a pile of dry leaves, please." Fluffles eagerly does so and watches as the Stag conjures a glowing sphere. Nova inches closer to watch, too, while Slash plays a soothing tune to help with concentration. Rocky conjures a ball of fire, forgoing the usual ball of ice for now, and scrutinizes the two orbs. The ball of flame intensifies for a few moments, waves of heat washing over the clearing before he calms it down.

"Yeah . . . I can make it hotter, but that's not what I need for light. Change the color," he grunts. The Stag sets the light to rapidly strobe for a few moments before Rocky waves a hand at him. "No, slow. Slow as you can."

The Stag obeys, and the ball of light starts shifting smoothly through the colors of the rainbow.

"Slower," comes Rocky's grunt. The Stag focuses more on the orb as the shifting colors go even slower.

"That is . . . remarkably difficult," admits the Stag as the colors continue to slow and Rocky continues to stare at the light.

"That's good. Now pay attention to what you're doing. Feel what's changing. That's the important thing: Feel what you're changing."

The Stag slowly nods as he continues to focus, and soon, his tongue lolls as he pants from the effort. "I . . . I think I can feel it. Different colors are . . . less?" he thinks aloud. While it doesn't make much sense to Fluffles, Rocky nods.

"Yeah, that's it. I haven't figured out how to change that on my own yet. Make it more less, and put more power into it at the same time."

Fluffles gives his fellow scion a bewildered look, but the Stag seems to understand. The ball starts shifting into warmer colors, from green through yellow and orange, and into red. But warmer colors should be more, not less, shouldn't they? The Stag pants harder with effort as the redness seems to both grow duller in shade yet brighter in intensity.

It takes Fluffles a moment to realize he might be the only one there who can truly appreciate the transformation as it continues. He watches the ball fade from his sight but *into* his heat sense. The transition is difficult to describe, even while watching. Rocky's excited grunt refocuses Fluffles.

"Now! Into the leaves!" The ball of heat dives into the dried pile, which quickly bursts into flame. The Stag collapses onto his belly, panting from the effort. Mixed in with the exhaustion are equal parts elation and disbelief, and Rocky grins as he takes a seat. "Make a lick of flame," he orders, and the Stag grunts as he obeys.

A small wisp of fire appears right before the Stag's snout, and the scion just stares at it while Rocky smiles.

"Coach says yer on the team, so you get in on the secret."

"How?" whispers the Stag, still staring at the small flame under his control.

Rocky just shrugs. "Coach knows a lot of stuff. I dunno how, but he does. He tries to teach us, but it's hard to get. Teemo's gotten hurt before just from getting it all without the filter we do. Just from Coach thinking."

The Stag's eyes widen at that, and he looks at his little flame with trepidation as Rocky continues. "You'll be fine. You can make the light even less if you want; I'm pretty sure Coach isn't worried about that. It'll act a lot like fire for a while, I think. Definitely be careful about making the light *more*, though. That sets off all sorts of warnings."

The Stag nods before letting the fire wink out, sighing with exhaustion. "I believe I'm satisfied for now. I never imagined I'd gain an affinity like Fire. Just changing Light that far was utterly exhausting. Now that I've done it . . . I believe trying to make the light *more* would be even more trying. I'm in no hurry to try to make it even less, either. I have a whole new affinity to explore already."

Rocky nods at that and leans back, relaxing as the Stag eyes the other scions. "Have you all done this?"

Slash nods while Nova looks away. Fluffles speaks up to explain. "Slash got to Sonic affinity from Earth. I got my title by using my Kinetic affinity to take advantage of perhaps one of the Den Master's greatest pieces of knowledge."

The Stag eyes him, head still firmly on the ground as he recovers. "Oh? Will you share it?"

Fluffles nods, fighting back a grin. "Like Rocky said: you're on the team. It's not an easy thing to understand, though. I still feel like, besides the Den Master, only Rocky really understands it. I'm pretty sure Den Master Thedeim puts it differently, but even Teemo hasn't seen fit to try to correct the phrasing Rocky uses. It sounds stupid and obvious, but it really is a vital piece of knowledge to comprehend."

Fluffles motions his tail for Rocky to continue, letting the grin onto his face as the Zombie Scion reveals the truth.

"Stuff is made of stuff."

The Stag gives a flat look to all involved while Rocky and Fluffles both laugh.

"A good joke," grumps the Stag, and Fluffles shakes his head.

"It's not a joke. Everything is made of something, even the air. I ate a storm by stealing away the kinetic energy in it. I focused it into a sphere of air I kept contained, forcing more and more energy into it until I unleashed it on one of Hullbreak's scions. I wasn't kidding about it sounding stupid, but it's true. I don't know exactly what air is made of, just like I don't know what rock is made of, but both are still made of *something*."

Rocky nods. "That's the wisdom of Coach Thedeim. Things don't just happen, and things are a lot more related than they look like at first. Take a closer look instead of just accepting it. Coach does that with a lot more than just magic."

The Stag still looks uncertain about all that, but Fluffles can at least see him chewing it over in his mind. That's good. It's not something to be understood just like that. Fluffles smiles as he sees the Stag toying with conjuring occasional wisps of flame, too. He's got a lot to think about now, so he can hardly blame the scion for focusing his attention on a new affinity. A new affinity is a lot easier to understand than a secret of creation, no matter how humorously it's worded.

Chapter 51

I watch my scions share some knowledge with the Stag, and it's an interesting experience. I can feel Rocky latching onto wavelengths and the fact that infrared is thermal. It's pretty cool watching the Stag gain the Fire affinity, and funny to feel the Southwood's reaction to it.

I think he was expecting it to take a lot longer, but Rocky isn't an Affinity Savant for nothing. From what the Stag was saying, it also helped that he's so experienced with his Light affinity. I also don't doubt Rocky will figure out Light if he wants it next. He can already change the pitch of his sounds, so he knows how to adjust wavelengths. He just needs to figure out which part of fire to stretch to do it.

I think he wants Lightning affinity first, though. He's managed to convince Fluffles to sling a lot of electricity as they start sparring. Whether he'll learn it before he has to go, I dunno, but I let them all have their fun.

I check in on Leo and Honey, and the two are already hip deep in organizing the denizens who will come home and the ones they brought to fill in the gaps. They'll probably want a day or two to debrief everyone, and not even Rocky will be able to avoid a proper debriefing once he's had his fun sparring.

Teemo is hanging out with the delvers, and they all seem in pretty good spirits. A lot of them have never been here before, and Yvonne, Aelara, and Ragnar are having to herd cats to try to keep everyone on the same page. They've already sent a few of the more ranger-y ones out to scout the clearing and the hole. Most of the adventurers are happy for now to do some low-effort delving and resupplying, and the Southwood is more than happy to let them.

All of that leaves me with very little to do in the Southwood right now, so I give my new ally an encouraging pat on the bond before turning my attention back to my own territory.

Coda hasn't been resting on his laurels while everyone is on a road trip and has managed to get a lot of progress done on the entrance to the lava labyrinth. With the first floor of the lighthouse finished, and the masons over there having more of an understanding of what Coda needs them to do, he's had to oversee them less and less, letting him oversee my ratlings more and more as they carve and work the entrance.

The stalls and other structures were easy enough for them to build, and Coda has even wrangled a few rockslides, magmyrms, wyrms, and even a basilisk to help. The slides aren't the strongest in their Earth affinity, but they still make it so much easier to properly fix the supports of the buildings into the cavern. My more fiery denizens are working on the more aesthetic aspects, including the wyrm mouth for the entrance.

For now, we're not going to try to make the mouth open and close, staying with a more traditional door in case I need to discourage people from heading inside during renovations or something. The wyrms and basilisk have been happy to spew magma where the magmyrms want, and the volcanic ants have been shaping it as it cools, slowly sculpting the open maw of a wyrm. They even infuse a bit of their affinity into their work, which has drawn Thing to investigate.

The magmyrms are using it more for lighting and because it looks cool, but Thing seems very interested in what they've done. I think it's some kind of rune-work, but I don't really understand the specifics. I just know it looks cool and doesn't make the ambient temperature feel like an oven.

Delvers have been curiously watching the work, but nobody has tried to interfere with anything, which is good. Fewer interruptions mean quicker and cleaner work, which means the entrance will be fully functional sooner!

The new quest board is already up and running. Quest web? Quest . . . dangling signs?

I'll need to give it a better name later, but whatever I end up calling it, it's already giving delvers a bit more guidance—and giving me a bit more mana. I've seen a few strange quests in there, too. "Only Turn Left" is a weird one, and I don't think anyone's taken it yet. Maybe once people are more used to the labyrinth they'll be more willing to take on a challenge like that.

Some of the ratkin have come by to help set up the smelters, and I wonder if it's as similar for them as the lighthouse is for the masons. Either way, my dwellers seem to be happy and enjoying the work, and I get more of a discount for the rooms. One is as discounted as I think it's going to get, so I go ahead and just spend the mana for it. It's cool to watch the subtle and not-so-subtle changes when making a room.

In the old days, the most basic things would just pop into existence, like the bit of parchment in my first library, way back in that small ant chamber. Now, I watch the mana shape and change things, reinforcing the oven there where it was a little thin, properly setting the basic crucibles, forming pegs on the walls for the tools to hang on, and more.

It feels nice to make a good workshop like this, and I can easily imagine the delvers working away, sometimes laughing and carrying on as they work, sometimes being deadly serious and focused.

It makes it easy to understand why a dungeon would go for the full toybox route. Lots of mana generated, hardly any mess.

Well, I'm sure my ratlings will need to clean the smelters and forges regularly, but that's a mundane, boring kind of mess. The more exciting messes can make even more mana, but all too often have a cost that I don't want my delvers to pay.

It's also easy to see why most dungeons go the more belligerent way. The mana I get for defeating a group of delvers in my labyrinth shows how lucrative that can be. But I'm glad I've been able to walk a middle path; take the road untaken. I can kinda have my cake and eat it too, which is one of those sayings that makes more logical sense if you reverse it, but eat your cake and have it too doesn't flow quite as well.

My fuzzy philosophical introspection is interrupted by Violet, who sends a sudden spike of worry through the protégée bond. I push thoughts of cake and how I probably will only ever have it and never eat it out of my mind, and focus on what she's so alarmed about. It's difficult to narrow it down, at least at first.

Her scions are all on high alert, and I can see a lot more spores in the air as Cappy does his best to defend his home. Legs is suiting up in all kinds of metal and looking pretty intimidating. Nose is buried near Violet's core, preparing to grab anything that might somehow slip past Legs and Cappy. And Onyx . . . What *is* Onyx doing?

She has two clawed gauntlets now and is slowly prowling around instead of taking a defensive position like the other scions. She notices me, or Violet does and gives her some direction. Either way, the shadowy gremlin points out the swirling mana in Violet's domain.

I've never seen that before. At first glance, it's just a huge mess. I can feel Violet getting a lot of mana from it, but I don't know why the flow is suddenly acting so weird! I take a few moments to focus and pay more attention, and I start noticing little patterns. It's not just one big mess . . . but a lot of smaller ones.

Taking a step back, it's easier to see, and I suddenly realize what's happening.

I bring my attention back into focus and try to figure out what's the best way to put it to Violet. Firstly, I try to get her to calm down, to impress on her that she's not in any danger. Sure, it's a surprise, but it's also one we probably should have seen coming. I also start shunting the mana she's getting into the alliance pool for now. I don't know if dungeons can get sick from too much mana, but I'd rather be safe than sorry.

Me taking action seems to calm her a bit, so I draw her attention to the cause of the sudden mana increase: the scythemaw nests. More specifically, the scythemaw eggs.

Even *more* specifically, the *hatching* scythemaw eggs.

Onyx scratches at the surface of one of the nests before Violet tells her to stop, and I suggest sending Nose to poke in and get a better look. I watch the mana flows as some of the eggs start wiggling and moving more, and Violet's panic shifts to an intense curiosity.

I can't really explain the complex process of hatching and how it differs from spawning, partially because I don't really understand too much about how spawning works.

Thankfully, I don't need to try to figure out how to explain the birds and the bees, as one of the leathery eggs sprouts a gash. Violet is alarmed at that for a moment before the first scythemaw baby pokes its little head out.

Oh no. They're *adorable*. While most mammal babies look a bit underdone at birth, and a lot of birds look like nightmares, most reptiles and amphibians look all shiny and adorable, and it seems like scythemaws are no exception.

The baby looks just like a baby alligator, with stubby little mandibles poking from its cheeks.

I'm not sure I've ever missed having hands more than I do right now. I just want to pick it up and hold it and pet it and call it George.

Violet seems curious about them, and my own feelings on the matter seem to have convinced her everything is fine, even if she doesn't share my opinion on how cute the things are.

She nudges me with a bit of concern and reminds me that I can't just sit here and squee at the things all day. No matter how cute, we have a pile of newborn apex predators to deal with. I don't think they'll be dangerous on their own, but if we want to keep the local scythemaw population stable, we should probably try to figure out how to get them to the water.

Chapter 52

Violet and I spend quite a bit of time just watching the babies hatch while I keep moving most of the mana into the alliance pool. I mentally label it "Violet's college fund," and hope I'll be able to designate it as officially hers later. For now, I should focus on the baby scythemaws.

The basic solution on what to do is fairly simple, at least: keep doing what we've been doing. The maws have been going through this for quite some time, and it's been working, so we should mostly just try to stay out of the way. Still, Violet wants to take a bit more of a direct approach in making sure they get to the water, so I suggest a few expeditions.

She's a bit nervous about that, too, but if she wants something done, she should do it. She should be capable of handling it. The aquifer lakes themselves are a bit beyond what she can patrol, but the passages between her and there are mostly safe. Her denizens should be able to handle anything they stumble upon.

I feel her trying to organize as I watch her scions work to do what she wants. Onyx is sticking close to the nests, even though the babies aren't trying to dig their way out just yet. I think she wants to both protect them and get a better look at them once they get moving. The other scions are being a bit more surprising.

I was expecting Cappy to be the one preparing to organize some expeditions, but I think Nose is going to be the one handling that. A little mushroom pops up in the metalworks as Legs and Jello both work to make a pair of little digging gauntlets for the mole, and Nose seems to split his attention between it and the two scions making gear for him.

I can only assume Cappy is giving him whatever intel he has available on those tunnels, and Nose is more able to focus and listen once Legs and Jello are done measuring him. They get to work, shaping and sharpening, and I notice Legs is taking a bit of a back seat to making the gloves. He does some basic work and a few fine adjustments, but most of it is being done by Jello.

I can feel her burbling away happily through the bond as she works, and her technique is a lot different from Legs's. He mostly uses an anvil and hammer, as well as the small heating forge to shape the metal. Jello seems to act almost like a hydraulic press, simply brute-forcing things into shape inside herself.

I'm glad to see her putting the shaped pieces into the heating forge once she's done bending them, too. Cold-working metals like that, especially steel, can introduce stresses. While it'll be harder, it will also tend to be more brittle. But a nice, gentle heating and cooling treatment will let it relax. The sharper pieces will need to be tempered later, but that comes mostly at the end, once you have the shape finalized.

She does do a little hot working, too, mostly in making little connecting pins and such for the joints. She grows little tentacles to grab the tongs and hammer, and she's getting good enough that she can work on bending one piece while hammering out another. She has a pretty impressive rhythm going, too. I think Legs has been teaching her how to properly multitask; I've seen him working on several pieces at once before, using all his legs to his advantage.

Nose eventually finishes listening to Cappy and goes to get a couple more moles to follow him. By the time he gets back, Jello is almost done with the gloves. I watch as she works on the last rivet, and I can imagine her sticking out her tongue in concentration as she works on flattening the hot piece of metal enough to not fall out but not so much that the joint will bind while moving.

One last tap of the hammer, and she picks up the gauntlet, looking at it with . . . whatever she uses to look. Satisfied, she dunks it in a water bucket, and I get a notification.

Metalworks Gained!

I stare at the notification for a moment, confused, before realizing what that means.

Jello! You did it!

She seems confused for a few moments, too, before I feel the bond practically explode with happiness and excitement. She does a happy dance in Violet's metalworks, and Legs looks on with pride at his student.

You did great, too, Legs! I even feel Violet's happiness at being able to contribute. *Metaphorical hugs all around!*

Nose makes a little noise to remind everyone who the gloves are for, and Jello happily gives him his new gear, which he eagerly equips. I don't think there's any special quality or anything to them yet, but they should at least make it a lot easier for him to dig around, and should be great to help defend himself, too.

I watch him go as Legs and Jello celebrate a bit more, and I wonder what kind of title he'll get. My scions have been more than happy to lead the expeditions from home rather than head out with them. I wonder if he'll get Scout like Teemo? It's definitely a cool title to have.

Either way, I should let him go do his job and get to playing with my new room!

It only takes a few moments of thinking for me to know exactly where I want to put my metalworks. There's plenty of room at the labyrinth entrance for something like this, and Jello will be delighted to watch the delvers and be watched in turn as she works. I spend a little mana to redirect my ratlings in their efforts of setting up the shops in the area.

There are only a few adjustments to be made to turn a smelter into a metalworks. It's mostly just in scaling down the things that make heat, and scaling up the things that work the metal once it's cooled. I spend the rest of the mana needed, and my first metalworks is officially a thing!

I nudge Jello with that knowledge, and she wiggles in happy excitement. She's eager to get to work, so she hugs Legs and makes her slow way back to me.

However, instead of going straight to the metalworks, she heads toward the labyrinth itself. I watch, curious, as she starts gathering my denizens. She starts by unceremoniously absorbing a whole hill of the cinder ants, organizing the coke they produce and keeping the ants together. I get the feeling they're confused, but not confused enough to actively resist one of my scions in her work.

She then heads to the melting pot chamber and stops at practically every hill there. Those ants are a bit too warm for her to comfortably grab up like the cinder ants, so they instead trail along behind her. She gets quite a collection by the time she's done, having crucible ants with bellies full of all the different metals and alloys they've discovered so far.

Her last stop before heading for the entrance is to grab one of my new basilisks. The strange denizen looks just as confused as the cinder ants but doesn't object, even when the crucible ants climb onto him for easier movement . . . or because he's more comfortably warm.

The whole strange procession soon emerges from a shortcut into the metalworks, and I'm just glad there aren't any delvers there at the moment. Jello deposits the cinder ants in a corner of the shop, and I make a note to ask Queen to encourage a few of the hills to move into the other planned smelter and forge areas.

I bet I can get a lot of mana out of the little guys. First, delvers will need to get coal or wood to feed them, then I get mana from them gathering the coke, and more mana from them using it to make whatever they want to make!

I think the labyrinth is going to be even more lucrative than I expected. I should check for coal nodes, too. While I have stones, gems, and metals, I don't think I've actually made any coal ones yet. I can probably have tunnelbores dig out an area nearby to put in some, too. I'll see about doing that after Jello gets her shop in shape.

With the cinders settled, she gets the basilisk to settle into the forge. I spend a bit of mana to expand it a bit, too, since the crucible ants also seem to want to stay in there. Jello calls them out, group by group, to start making ingots around the rim of the forge, and she takes the tongs to pluck them out and set aside to cool as they reach the size and shape she wants.

Looking at the shapes, I think stock is the technical term? There are rectangular pieces, round pieces, thick, flat pieces, and they all get cooled and sorted by material and shape by my new Metal Smith.

That thought reminds me of something, and I gently take a closer look at Jello, not wanting to disturb her but giving her a chance to ask for privacy.

I'm happy to see her new title comes with a new affinity: Metal! That's going to be all sorts of cool to work with. I think Coda is probably going to be hanging out with Jello a lot more, too. There's a lot of interesting things that metal can do, lots of tough moving parts that will just be easier to work with than stone.

I'll probably suggest she work on replacing a lot of the parts for the mechanical traps, once she's more settled. For now, I watch her work, watching the ants start heading back into shortcuts toward the melting pot to gather more materials. I can almost hear her humming through the bond as she works, going at a steady rhythm as she stocks her workshop.

You done good, Jello. I'm proud of you.

Chapter 53

The Harbinger

Existence has been . . . *unpleasant* as of late for the Harbinger. The surface was supposed to be soft and ripe for the taking, and it seemed like that was going to be the case until that lich finally made its play. The Harbinger would have happily taken the lesson of simply killing the lich first next time, but the Maw has other ideas.

The dungeon actually turned the Harbinger's own Mind affinity against it, forcing it to relive the encounter over and over. The Maw covets that lich, building up the undead as a delicacy beyond compare. The Harbinger thinks it's just a strong lich, but even it has to admit it is *very* strong for a lich.

As unpleasant as reliving being torn apart by that Resonance Cascade was, the Harbinger has come to appreciate the kind of skill and finesse that went into unmaking it. The blend of affinities utilized was as awe-inspiring as it was unpleasant, and the Harbinger wishes, deep in its core where no one can see, that it could figure out what was actually done. The necessary mana for something like this should have required the lich be a Conduit, but if it had such a title, it never embraced it.

But the memories of the battle are not the only unpleasantness of existence recently. The Redcap has been getting uppity lately, too. The nerve of the scion, to imply he'd be better at leading the least than the Harbinger! To even imply it would make a better hat than a scion! It would rend the Redcap's mind asunder if he wasn't already utterly mad.

Perhaps the Harbinger should attempt to piece the Redcap's mind back together. It'd be a much more difficult attack, but sudden onset sanity could have as devastating an effect on that scion as madness has on other minds.

The idea at least distracts it from the utter *boredom* the Harbinger is now faced with. It was quite pleased with itself for finding that traitor. It even helped the Redcap with his newest hat, keeping the mind from slipping into the relief of madness and forcing it to understand what was being taken. If only the Maw had a scion with Life affinity, they might have even been able to keep it alive for more than a few hours.

With the traitor hatted, the Harbinger had turned its attention to sniffing out others, but the Maw had refused to listen when it pointed out a cheesemaker as a possible ally of the traitor. When it insisted something was wrong with the stupid little curd slinger, the Maw had put it on its new tortuous duty: training the delvers.

It'd had fun with the assignment at first, happily throwing them into impossible situations and tearing them apart with the least, but that hadn't lasted long.

"Grow them properly before harvesting. The Great Maw will not starve because you refuse to make a decent meal," the Redcap had threatened at the time, ending the last bit of fun the Harbinger was likely to have for quite a while.

It's not even allowed to use its Mind affinity to influence them! They'd only go a little mad; they can still be directed! The Maw is utterly unreasonable in this, however, so the Harbinger must direct them in their delves.

At least it can take satisfaction in the fact the mana is being properly used. The spawner is so close to being able to produce lessers. Once it does, the effectiveness of the least will increase significantly! The Harbinger will no longer have to guide them and can instead focus on its own actions when they next assault the surface!

It looks forward to the next attack, even if more than just least will be committed to it. The Metal fey and elementals will be joining, as well as the delvers under the Harbinger's tutelage. After seeing the incredible variety of the surface's defenders, even the Harbinger has to swallow its pride and admit it needs some help to deal with certain minor vulnerabilities.

It will also be a good way to show the stubborn Maw that the Harbinger's spawner is easily the best it has. The Harbinger can try to explain all it likes, but a difference in dead denizens will speak for itself. And then . . . Oh, and then! Then mana will pour into its spawner, and it can finally get some standards! Any small vulnerabilities will vanish once they join the battle!

It allows itself some time to be distracted, imagining the destruction it could wreak with some standards, but reality soon demands its attention. While most of the delvers follow instructions well enough, this one has problems. If it were a lack of desire to listen, the Harbinger could shatter them, and the Maw wouldn't bat a metaphorical eye. But no, it's a problem of ability.

The Harbinger internally sighs as it focuses its attention back to the training room. According to the Redcap, the Maw calls it the cutting board: a place of preparation before actually getting down to business. The delvers are organized into small squads at the moment, working on mobility. While a battle line will need a wall of shields, skirmishes are a reality of war, too.

Most of the squads are doing their drills properly: shield at the front, spear behind, mage behind that, support furthest back. Shield intercepts spear, support intercepts mage, spear and mage look for openings to exploit. The movements are carefully measured and carried out, the squads going through the vital forms of combat.

Except for Lechula's group. It galls the Harbinger to even know her name, but she's forced it to learn just from repetition. The mage, support, and even spear all do their best to stick to the forms, but Lechula can't. Not *won't.* Can't. It watches the latest example as it moves forward, not even bothering to interrupt yet. Early disruption only ever makes a bigger mess.

"No escape!" shouts Lechula, as well as her spear and mage. The Harbinger would almost say she's getting better, since she didn't drag the entire squad into the attack with her; the mage and spear both look a little worried even as they contribute to the combination attack.

Lechula strides forward, shield ready and short sword raised, presenting an impassable barrier to her imagined foe. To one side of the nonexistent target, a field of flashing blades appears, the mage of the group unleashing a bladestorm to also present a blocked path. Lastly, the spear comes in from the other side, tip flashing in a flurry of thrusts as all three bear down on their imaginary target, presenting it with no option but to perish.

Or so Lechula would like to think. The Harbinger shifts its form, allowing itself to slip into the center of the group attack and dismantle it. The spear is simply snatched from the elf's hand and hurled at the mage. Even with a blunted training weapon, the Harbinger is strong enough to impale them through the shoulder. The bladestorm dissipates, leaving a surprised Lechula facing down the Harbinger.

A tentacle thrust dents her shield and compromises her footing before a second tentacle comes from the side and snares her feet. With an undignified yelp, she's hauled into the air upside down. It considers eating her, not for the first time, and not for the first time, it restrains itself. Instead, it flexes its affinity to communicate.

"Lechula."

"M-Master Harbinger!" she stammers, trying to act like she's not dangling in the air.

"What have I said about combination attacks?" it tiredly asks, putting the smallest of strains on her mind as it does.

"That they're a waste?"

"Why are they a waste?" It doubts repetition will teach the lesson, but it really would be unfortunate to just kill the delver. She's very good as a shield despite her glaring shortcomings.

"B-Because a strong foe can disrupt it and take advantage of the positioning! And a weak foe doesn't need that much energy wasted on it."

"Yet you keep doing it." With that, the Harbinger lets her fall, letting the thud of the floor punctuate his observation. She groans and staggers to her feet, a trickle of blood coming from her nose.

"I can't help it!" she exclaims in frustration before everyone's eyes on her gets her to calm down slightly. "I just . . . It feels like the right thing to do. A good meal brings the ingredients together and brings out the best of all of them at once."

The Harbinger fights a groan as it's forced to come up with a food analogy to explain it to the pale dwarf. "You are not ingredients—you are courses. If you serve the appetizer, main dish, and dessert all at once, you crowd the table and leave two courses at the wrong temperature by the time you get to them. You waste food."

She gasps and falls to a knee, both from the accusation and from the weight of the Harbinger speaking to her. "I . . . I will do . . . better . . ." she manages before she collapses. The Harbinger doubts it, but it's technically possible. It turns its attention to the support of the group.

"Take her to the kobolds for healing," it orders. "The mage will need the spear removed and the wound tended, too." The support staggers back and nods, blood dripping from his nose as he gets the rest of the team to carry Lechula.

The Harbinger fights its annoyance as it watches them go. It really does need to figure out some way to break Lechula of her bad habit. Teaming up for an attack is wasteful, a desperate gambit made by weaklings in the hopes of snatching victory from defeat.

It ignores the little seed of uncertainty in its gut, that little voice asking how it would defeat that lich without a team-up attack. The strong can do a team up to show off, to prove just how strong they are by being wasteful in disposing of a foe that thinks itself worthy.

It ignores the seed of doubt's reply as it turns back to watching the training, preferring boredom to losing an argument with itself.

Chapter 54

While I've been splitting my time between watching Jello and watching the baby scythemaws, others are still busy. For one, the few nests in the Spiderkin Enclave are starting to hatch, too, giving me a nice windfall of mana.

I mostly push it into the ally pool for now. I want to grow that emergency fund for when we need it, and to encourage the Southwood to make a second scion. Having a bit of a safety net should help him with the learning process of not really issuing orders anymore.

Poe went and got Tarl to get his opinion on the baby scythemaws. He thinks they're cute, too; I knew there was a reason I liked him. He doesn't have much advice for me about them, though. He's no ranger, but staying out of their way should be enough for them to keep doing what they do. He did say he'll ask the rangers for their opinion, but neither of us really thinks they'll have anything new to contribute.

They'll probably send someone to at least come take a look. I think the more outgoing ones already went off to the Southwood, leaving mostly the nerds, but what self-respecting nature nerd could resist seeing and recording a hatching nobody else has?

Aranya has been working with the enclaves to make sure they're all ready, and has apparently gotten help from a snakekin tailor. I've noticed him visiting the enclaves, but I've had more pressing things to pay attention to lately. He's built more like a constrictor, but he has a hood and fangs, so maybe he works out? Or tailoring is more physically demanding than I thought? Either way, he's enjoying a meeting with Aranya, Larx, Folarn, and Norloke in the public war room.

I should probably ask the Southwood if there's a more generic meeting room or something I could trade for. The war room is convenient for gathering and talking, but the maps are kinda in the way for what sounds more like a merchant meeting than battle planning.

I can see Aranya smile as she notices my attention, and soon, she speaks up. "Ah, Mr. Harlenss, would you mind repeating your proposal? Lord Thedeim is watching us right now, and I think he would like to hear what you have to say."

My dwellers perk up a bit at that, while the snakeman looks a little confused. "Does he not know already?"

Aranya shakes her head. "His attention has been turned to other matters recently."

He nods in understanding. "Ah, the trouble to the north. I probably shouldn't be surprised he's been preoccupied, then. Well . . . to get to the point, I may have a way to ensure everyone stays warm on the march."

Oh? He had my curiosity before, but now he has my attention. Aranya motions for him to continue, so he does.

"I'm a haberdasher by trade, basically a tailor specialized in men's clothing, not just hats," he says with a smile that indicates he's had to explain that many times before.

Haberdashers really deal in more than just hats? Of course, I can't exactly interrupt him with Teemo still up at the Southwood, so he continues without much pause.

"I've noticed the wonderful silks of your aranea and your spiderkin, so over the last week or so, I've been attempting to form some kind of trade deal. Imagine my surprise when I learned they have a pressing need that potentially falls under my purview."

Norloke nods at that. "While we've been able to weave thicker silks, the process is just too slow to be able to provide enough for everyone."

"But I know some sheep ranchers with an excess of wool. This winter is shaping up to be on the milder side, so they have more supply than is needed for the usual winter-clothing needs. I can buy the wool and trade it for silk, and everyone wins," he finishes with a smile.

I mentally nod at the proposition. I'm hardly an expert in cloth, but I imagine if he trades a bolt of wool for a bolt of silk, he'll be making out like a bandit, and my spiderkin will be able to be safe and warm on the journey.

"He's also at least passingly familiar with leatherworking," speaks up Larx, and the snakeman nods at that.

"I wouldn't be able to outfit an army on my own, of course, but I can also offer pointers to the ratkin in exchange for their strange mushroom fabric."

Mushroom fabric? Larx must be able to feel my confusion because he smiles like a grandfather who has had a gift to a grandchild revealed.

"Yes, Lord Thedeim. We've been experimenting with the mycelium itself, and we've managed to make a comfortable and durable fabric. I brought a sample for Mr. Harlenss, too." He lays a square yard of what looks a lot like denim on the table, and I can see the look of need in the snakeman's eyes. Yeah, he knows his stuff. If he makes men's clothing, he's going to make a killing selling mushroom jeans.

Aranya smiles as she speaks. "Lord Thedeim seems to approve of the trades, so let us discuss price."

"I believe I can get fifty bolts of woolen fabric on short notice, and possibly fifty more later, should it prove necessary. I would offer trading it, bolt for bolt, for silk. For my instruction on leatherworking, I'd like ten bolts of the mycelium fabric," comes his initial offer, which Norloke parries with a smile on her face.

"Twenty bolts of silk for fifty of wool. Our silk is of the highest quality, and rare in the market besides." Larx steps in and combos with her offer.

"Two bolts for the instruction. I would also offer some of our fabric to help our fellow dwellers, perhaps fifteen silk and ten mycelia for the fifty wool?" Norloke nods at that, and the snakeman needs to think quickly to counter their financial attack.

"Twenty-five and twenty, silk and mycelia, for fifty wool. Wool is a known demand, and there will not be any more until the spring. You would have me trade a known and stable product almost one for one for an unknown in the mycelia and in a fabric not known for retaining warmth? Insulation is valuable to my other potential clients."

He weathers the twin assault with aplomb, setting up his own counteroffensive. My dwellers are put on the back foot, but they aren't giving up the fight just yet.

"We also know little about your wool, or how to work it," points out Norloke. She and Larx exchange a look before she continues. "We could go as high as . . . twenty and fifteen, if you are willing to extend your expertise to show us how to properly clothe ourselves with the wool."

Their counter leaves Harlenss's wallet bleeding, and I can see in his eyes he can't outright reject an offer like that. Still, he will not go down without obtaining his own pound of flesh. "I agree, on the condition I also get three bolts each of silk and mycelium for each day of instruction."

It's my dwellers' turn to reel from the financial impact. They know how valuable his expertise would be, just as he does. Another glance is shared before Larx speaks up. "Two bolts of one, depending on which you teach that day." Harlenss grins at the counter, and my dwellers realize they've made a mistake as he counters and goes in for the kill.

"Two of *each*. I can teach both in a single day. We can even discuss after the first day if you want more of my instruction or not." Harlenss smiles in his victory, already knowing my dwellers will accept.

"Deal . . ." comes the inevitable reply from both Larx and Norloke, and though they can feel the sting of what they had to give, they both also know the value of what they gained. Harlenss claps his hands together in excitement and slithers back a bit from the table.

"So, shall we be off to the enclaves? I don't think either of us is quite ready to deliver that many bolts at once, but if I can get a look at your facilities and get four silk and three mycelium bolts, I can return in the morning with ten wool and begin the instruction!"

My dwellers are cheered by his enthusiasm, and soon lead him toward the Spiderkin Enclave. The snakeman toys with the sample of mycelium cloth the entire trip down, testing and planning.

Once deep in the heart of the weaving rooms, he looks like he's in paradise. The orb weaver spiders ply their trade, weaving and looming, sewing and dyeing. He just watches for a few seconds before his mouth betrays him.

"If you had shown me this place first, you could have argued me down further."

Norloke smiles and guides him deeper into the busy workplace. "Perhaps, but I'm happy with our deal as it is already." Her eyes gleam for a moment as she meets his gaze. "I'll keep that in mind for the next fifty bolts of wool, though."

Chapter 55

Aelara

The elven woman can't help but reflect on the last year or so of her life as she and her friends travel the winding tunnels, passages, crevasses, caves, caverns, and more. Born and raised in a city as she was, she'd usually find the minutiae of nature difficult to care too much about. Wild plants, for example, are obstacles, food, or dangers, and sometimes more than one, so it's difficult for her to care too much about the specifics of what each does.

She's very much aware that's an attitude that could get her killed, which only makes her appreciate Yvonne's presence all the more. But while she finds the details of plants and animals impossible to keep in her head for long, the formations of earth stick with her much easier. If asked, she'd say it's because Earth is her natural element. There's a small part of her that has to admit it's at least partially because Ragnar is happy to go on and on about them.

She doesn't allow her eyes nor her mind to linger on him for long, however. They're far from Fourdock right now, and actively searching for a hostile dungeon to boot. Being distracted could be a recipe for disaster. Instead, she does her best to focus on her magic and on the three extra companions the party has for this particular bit of scouting.

Her magic is simple enough to work. She can sense the angle and depth of their current path probably even more accurately than Ragnar can. Her feel for terrain is partially why she's the party's cartographer, with the other part being that her handwriting is easily the best of all her friends.

Aranya's handwriting is shaping up quite well, but she's not here, and she also still needs to practice if she wants this particular responsibility. Not that the kobold needs more responsibilities heaped on her shoulders.

She can't let her mind linger on her newest friend either, so she resumes tracking and feeling the earth around them, searching for dangers. Ragnar and Yvonne both seem pretty convinced any natural dangers have cleared out thanks to the army of leech-head monstrosities that recently came through, but that's a reason to *stay* vigilant, rather than to lower their guard. That enemy dungeon could have ambushes set up along the route.

Aelara hasn't spotted any just yet, but she's not willing to bet there won't be some eventually.

The new companions help with that, at least. She's been aware Thedeim has had Earth elementals for a while, but she hasn't really interacted with them much until now. Now, Ragnar has a rockslide riding him, and Aelara is using her affinity to carry another. And beyond just the slides, there's the wyrms. Most of the parties have a rockslide or two and a wyrm, but Thedeim's own scion decided to join their group.

She would have never described something that looks like Nova as timid, but there's really no other word that fits her quite so perfectly. She can feel the Wyrm Scion as she follows along, feeling the void of earth around the scion as she turns it to magma before letting it cool behind her.

She should try to get a sample of the cooled magma. Most of it seems to go back into more ordinary rock, though it's different from what it was before Nova's passing. Occasionally, however, she'll leave a bit of obsidian behind in the areas she breaches the surface.

The idea of playing with rocks reminds her they've been traveling for a while. "Are we going to make camp soon? Or are we planning to get back to the main trail first? Oh, and when should we drop one of the slides to let it do . . . whatever it is it's going to do?"

Ragnar hums at that as Yvonne considers more quietly. "It'd probably be a better idea to camp off the main trail, in case reinforcements come up it."

Ragnar nods at that wisdom. "Aye, I'd rather no' wake up ta all those spiky feet stompin' on me."

Aelara shudders at the idea. "Me neither. Should I start feeling for water pockets?"

"Yes, please," comments Yvonne as she squints down the tunnel they're traveling. "It might not be necessary, but good to do it anyway. There are signs of other things walking these tunnels, and the lichen doesn't look too desperate for moisture. I think it's going to open up pretty soon, and there'll be access to water."

"Should we leave a slide there?" asks Aelara as she glances back to the one she has floating along behind her. It's difficult to get a read on a living pile of rocks, but they seem pretty content with their current situation.

Ragnar shrugs, causing his own slide to clack and grind from the movement. "Ah, dunno. Teemo said they'd know when 'n' where ta drop them, an' they'd let us know."

"Nova would let us know, too," agrees Yvonne, though Aelara isn't so sure.

"Do you think so? She seems like she might not want to bother us."

Ragnar laughs as Yvonne smiles and answers. "She's shy, sure, but she's not going to let that stop her from doing her duty. Teemo says she's trying to live up to her name."

Aelara and Ragnar both nod at that. Aelara still doesn't quite understand the full meaning behind it, but she at least knows it's a very powerful name, another one of those weird things Thedeim thought up. She also knows a bit about the weight of a name. Still, even with that topic of conversation to potentially talk about, everyone stays quiet as they continue down the tunnel.

Yvonne's instincts are correct, and soon the tunnel opens into a very wide, yet very short cave. Ragnar shows perfectly why dwarves are so short and walks with ease, while Aelara and Yvonne have to almost double over to mind their heads. They're probably not the only ones who have had to do so, as the floor is a rough gravel and the ceiling seems to be full of the bases of stalactites that lost battles with harder heads.

Aelara can feel a lot of divots for small pools of water, as well as the snaking contour of a stream of some kind, and shares the knowledge. "We have puddles everywhere, but a stream that way."

"Let's go to the stream, if you're feeling like making us a campsite in the wall nearby?"

"That sounds good. I haven't had to cast much today, so I should be able to manage something. It'll probably need to be a cold camp, unless you want to leave the fire outside."

"Think Nova'd be willin' ta play campfire fer us?" asks Ragnar, and Aelara smiles at the image as Yvonne shrugs.

"We can ask. Otherwise, we can do a cold camp. It's not too bad down here."

Aelara nods, and soon, the cave opens up a bit for the stream. There's room to stand, but not much besides that. Still, Aelara and Yvonne take the chance to stretch as well as they can, and the elf moves to the wall.

She hollows out a section well above the floor to start, splurging a bit to give enough room to truly stretch once inside. From the new chamber, she creates a few divots in the wall big enough for bedrolls, then climbs into the new temporary space.

The others quickly join her, and she sends a pulse to let Nova know they're stopping for the night. The Wyrm Scion pokes her head up right in the center of the main chamber, looking around curiously before Yvonne gets her attention.

"Nova, would you mind being our source of heat for the camp? You'd mostly just need to stay there. You don't have to, if you don't want to," she reassures with a smile. Nova tilts her head as she considers, then nods and settles into place.

"Wonderful!" exclaims Aelara with a wide smile, moving to sit near the scion. "I have a dried soup mix I've been wanting to try, so this could be a great time to do it. I also wanted to talk with Nova, if you don't mind?"

Nova looks a little intimidated but doesn't refuse. Aelara takes that as permission and sets her rockslide down, letting it mingle with Ragnar's as Yvonne gets water from the stream. She gets as close as she can to Nova without feeling like she's sitting in an oven and gives the scion a smile.

"So, I've noticed you sometimes make obsidian."

Nova already looks confused, so Aelara points at the cooling magma around the hole she's resting in. "The smooth parts. Most of it cools back into ordinary stone, but some of it will make obsidian."

Nova turns to look at the cooling rock like she's never noticed. While Aelara partially wishes she was doing it on purpose, it just means she can explain herself fully without Nova having any preconceptions!

"Obsidian is special earth. Here." She magically breaks off a small piece of the obsidian, still too hot to handle directly. "In a fight, it can be a deadly sharp weapon." She shears a flake off and stretches out a single hair, which the flake cuts without resistance. "It's a bit fragile and not exactly common, otherwise it'd see a lot more uses. But I like to do something a little different with it."

Nova tilts her head in confusion as Aelara concentrates on the obsidian, which starts to shift and flow like it's magma again. "It's a little easier with normal stone; normal stone doesn't mind being shaped. Obsidian keeps wanting to break." She speaks as she focuses, and she even pulls up a small piece of the stone floor to attach to her project as she gets close to finishing.

She smiles once done and holds it up for Nova to see. The young scion seems absolutely mesmerized by the obsidian rose with the stone stem, seeming to almost blush when Aelara presses the stem into the softened rock around the wyrm.

"There we are. You should try it with your magma, Nova. It'll be good for your control, and it might help you to do what you want." She glances at the obsidian rose, and Nova's beady eyes follow her gaze. "Don't let your name be all that defines you, okay? It's a powerful one, so it's easy to be intimidated by. But make your name live up to *you*, not the other way around."

Nova sinks a little as she thinks. Aelara is glad to be distracted from her own thoughts by Yvonne bringing over the water. As she gets some tea going and digs out the soup mix, she can't help but think back to when she heard those words herself. She needed to hear them back then, and she can only imagine his smile if he knew she was able to maybe help someone else by passing them on.

Chapter 56

Harlenss is true to his word and shows up bright and early at the Ratkin Enclave. A pretty big portion of the enclave shows up, too, all eager to learn a bit of clothiery from an expert in the field. He looks a little intimidated by the numbers for a moment, but that's the only hint of weakness he shows the entire time he's there.

He teaches at the . . . it's still weird to call it that, but the open pulpit that Larx usually gives his sermons from. I can see his eyes linger for a few moments on the various murals around by now, but he's a pro and gives a proper lecture. He even brings groups closer when he demonstrates a particular stitch or cut, repeating for each group so they can have an example to go on.

By the end, he even has the showmanship to present Larx with a warm coat, produced as part of the class. He accepts it with grace, of course, and it's pretty obvious that my ratkin, at least, are satisfied with the lessons. He takes a break just before lunch to, I can only assume, get some lunch, before heading down to the Spiderkin Enclave to give them their share of lessons.

The turnout there is much larger. Practically everyone who's not a lobster wrangler shows up, including all three of the triumvirate. Norloke is especially interested, asking a few technical questions that would go right over my head if I still had it. Harlenss, however, gives her succinct answers that satisfy her and earn nods from the other spiderkin.

The practical example from this one is more of a group effort than with the ratkin. Vernew gets voluntold by Norloke to get measured, which she does with only minimal grumbling. She's definitely not grumbling by the end of the day, though. Harlenss makes one of the legs for a snow suit while the spiderkin make the others, and he continues on to the other pieces.

There's a ton of buttons and other old-school fasteners involved, too. Getting in and out of the suit is going to be a bit of a thing. I think it might be time to introduce zippers to the world. With Jello being a Smith now, it's even feasible!

I rub the rough idea on the bond with her, which seems to get her attention, and I work on trying to draw out the design for one. It's probably not a surprise there are no zippers here. Maybe someone like the king has them? Without automation, producing them could be a pain, and it's a weird idea in the first place anyway.

It's also a lot more complex and precise than most give it credit for. The teeth need to be designed to interlink, but also to disengage easily when the zipper passes. I never had a reason to investigate them before meeting that truck, so the geometry involved is going to have to be made up.

I give it my best shot, but I think the actual design will be on Jello to iterate on. Still, I have a ratling deliver her the basic design, and she gets to work on flexing that new Metal affinity of hers.

Oh man, I have *no* idea how to actually secure the teeth to the fabric either. I think it's some kind of sandwich of tough cloth, but after how little of Harlenss's lesson I understood, it's probably for the best if I step back and leave that mystery to my dwellers.

And *that's* going to have to wait until Teemo gets back. He'll be on his way soon, now that the adventurers are off to adventure. I've done everything I can to help keep them safe. They know more about scouting than I do, so I just have to trust them. From Leo's reports, nobody has really found anything aside from a big, obvious trail leading deeper. An army of spikey-footed things makes a pretty obvious path, so that's nice.

Nobody is charging down the trail, though. Just about everyone is checking side passages and tunnels, getting the lay of the land and making sure any forces I send down won't just get flanked, pincered, and obliterated. The other dungeon is going to have the home field advantage this time, rather than just a hole in the ground. We're going to need to know as much as possible if we want this to go smoothly.

Speaking of knowing, that seems to be what Aranya is working on. She's been spending a lot of time in town and telling me about her day when she comes back to rest. The adventurers' guild library has a lot of information on battles and dungeons, but it's not especially organized. The Office of Dungeon Affairs has better information, but she has to jump through a lot of red tape to get access to it.

I'm starting to wonder if she just likes having something to complain about. Not that I mind; she's fun to listen to.

"So then we *both* started going over the guild bylaws to see what she *can* share! I even brought up the info the Southwood is always after, and that was a whole other warren to scout!"

I chuckle as she dramatically leans back in her seat at the little study table as if I can't see she has some kind of book to look through from the guild. I chuckle to myself at her theatrics, and she can definitely feel something as my High Priestess, as she looks over to my core and smiles before straightening herself and continuing.

"Apparently, info on specific dungeons isn't difficult to get ahold of. Dungeons in good standing can even request a full packet, just like a delver, if they really want it! Southwood is more of a gossip than an actual strategist, though, so it never asked for that."

She taps the thick tome on the table and smiles. "This is technically that, but for a whole lot of dungeons the guild has come across. We abused a few loopholes to get this, too. I had to ask for specific dungeons to get detailed info, but I could also ask more vague questions to get there.

"If I, for example, wanted to know about murderous dungeons, there's a whole list of them. If I want to know about murderous dungeons that have effectively captured towns, there's a list for that too. There are also belligerent dungeons with captured towns, and it's apparently happened enough that 'captured town' is the official term for when a dungeon runs a town in all but the most technical way."

She smirks and winks at my core. "You're very close to that now, by the way. Anyhow, this is actually a book with dungeons that have or used to have captured towns, and how the guild deals with them. Telar helpfully suggested I ask about the specific dungeons in the book, and then we could pounce on that loophole.

"Considering the imminent threat to multiple dungeons in good standing with the guild by an unknown, hostile dungeon, she could let me just borrow the entire book instead of having to make up a packet with the information."

She smiles and glances in the direction of the library. "I'm going to let the bees copy it before I return it. They should be able to transcribe it quickly. They'd better, or Honey will have a fit when she gets back." My red kobold giggles at the idea of my big ol' nerd bee trying to come to terms with the idea of not getting to keep a copy, and I chuckle as well.

"So, let's see what we have, hmm?" We spend the rest of the day looking through the book, and I resist the urge to read ahead. Honestly, most of the "captured" towns aren't in any real trouble. A lot of them are historical accounts of old dungeons that aren't around anymore, most of them with their enclaves emancipated from the dungeon itself. We actually check the glossary for more details on that.

I don't know if I'll ever emancipate my own enclaves. While I'd be happy to let them go and grow on their own, it will plainly be a long time before they'll want that, if they ever do. It's a complicated feeling, that, but mostly a happy one. It's a lot happier than some of the dungeons in the book.

There're only a couple captured towns currently functioning today, including a trio of towns who have to periodically abandon and rebuild when their local dungeon gets too much mana and sends out a huge expedition. I'm surprised they don't quarantine it and let it starve, but apparently, the mana freed from adventurers killing the expedition kinda settles into the soil, and the towns make serious bank farming.

There's another belligerent one that managed to get its Voice elected mayor of the nearest town. I have no idea why, and the book doesn't have much in the way of answers. It just says the dungeon has not expanded into the town, and that the crown still gets taxes from the place, so who knows.

There are a few historical accounts of dungeons using their captives to go to war with other dungeons, but those records seem *really* old and don't offer much in the way of details. Still, it paints a pretty clear, if not very pretty, picture.

Warring with a dungeon with a captured town is messy. Rival dungeons don't understand or don't care about the difference between denizens and townsfolk. Offense or defense, dungeons will use them as they see fit.

That's going to make the eventual battle on the more unpleasant end of my expectations, then. How do you sort out an ordinary civilian from a dungeon zealot? Even worse, with the fog of war, how much does that difference really change what happens to them?

The only winning move is not to play, but even that's not an option in this case. My best move may be to set up the chessboard, watch my foe's moves, and be fully prepared to kick the table over and punch them in the mouth. It'll still be a mess, but hopefully, fewer pieces will be lost that way.

Chapter 57

Lechula

In the recovery ward of the Kobold Enclave rests the female pale dwarf, and she's not especially happy about it. That last combined attack still sticks in her mind, right alongside Master Harbinger's admonishment. Her hands worry her beard, braiding and weaving it as she wrestles with what happened.

The attack itself was perfect, at least as far as she can tell. She's pretty sure they could have handled half a dozen, at least, with that move! Six felled quickly with the combined effort of three is efficient . . . right? She's less certain now.

Glancing over at her friend on the bed beside her reaffirms her doubts. Merrik is always prickly, but he's been trying to take this particular wound in stride. Lechula doesn't know if he's distancing himself from her, or if he's trying to support her in his own way.

It's one thing when her actions land herself in the healing ward. She's been training to be a shield bearer since she was strong enough to pick one up, so she's used to taking painful blows and sometimes learning the hard way how to properly angle her shield to deflect rather than absorb a hit. Merrik, though . . . he's a proper steel mage. He's not supposed to have to suffer a broken shoulder to learn a point.

His situation isn't the only unfortunate bit of reality she's having to cope with. While she's been to the ward before, it was in times of peace, where the kobolds could tend to her quickly and send her on her way. They might leave something not quite fully healed as a bit of a reminder, but she'd still be in and out in a matter of hours, eager to return to training and not to make the same mistake.

But talking with Master Harbinger for so long has made her suffer bouts of dizziness that the kobolds can't just fix with a simple healing spell. While they're confident it will pass, she's in no condition to do much besides sit on her bed and worry her beard into knots.

She sighs and starts untying the mess she's made, almost tearing her beard clean off when Merrik speaks up.

"Are you alright?"

"Ow!" She relaxes her grip and rubs her neck and chin as Merrik chortles. It's actually a bit of a relief that his prickly attitude seems to be coming back. "I thought you were sleeping! You startled me!"

"I think maybe you needed startling. You've been staring at nothing for a while, tangling your beard the entire time. I'd call it a lost cause and say you should just shave it and start over, but you're stubborn about it."

"Of course I'm stubborn about it! It's my *beard*!" She glares at him, but that smirk tells her that's exactly what he wants. She takes a deep breath and tries to release some of the tension, but it's not that easy. "Besides, shouldn't I be asking if *you're* alright? I'm just a bit dizzy, but you can barely move your arm!"

He unintentionally proves her point with half a shrug. "The kobolds keep saying it'll just take a bit longer to fix than most. I'm almost relieved, knowing it hurt that badly for a reason." Lechula looks away at that, and he adopts a small frown when he notices. "It's not your fault."

Her gaze returns to him in a hard glare. "I'm pretty sure it is."

His frown deepens for a moment before he smirks and concedes the point. "But you still shouldn't blame yourself."

"Then who *should* I blame?" she asks, dangerously close to a whine. Merrik briefly considers a few jabs, but swallows them before speaking.

"Nobody. As a caster, I should be on the lookout for ranged attacks like that, as should Jayle. He didn't protect me with his support magic; I didn't protect me with my magic. By the Maw, Dergol let himself be *disarmed*! There were mistakes all around, so don't go hogging all the blame." He pauses and smirks. "You can have a second helping of it if you insist, but that's it."

"But I dragged you all into that combination attack!"

"You can't force a combination attack; you know that. We might have had our doubts, but we could each feel the shape it would take, and we added our efforts to it."

She folds her arms and sighs as she leans back against the wall, her beard still a tangled mess. "I know, but . . . it's my job to take the punishment, take the pain, so you guys don't have to. Bruises and scrapes happen, but . . ."

"Not shattered shoulders?" She winces when he finishes the thought out loud for her, but doesn't argue with him, so he continues. "In a real battle, they do. We have to be prepared for that . . . and for worse. You heard what happened to the first batch Master Harbinger was supposed to train, right?"

Lechula suppresses a shudder at the reminder of the rumors, and she can see Merrik's lips tighten at the idea as well. Before she can try to reply, though, a kobold enters their shared room and reminds Lechula of what else has been bothering her.

The kobold is a male and wears simple clothes. They're not torn nor threadbare, but they're nothing elaborate. In contrast, the chains and manacles stand out all the more. They're not the thick steel and heavy iron designed to physically restrain someone. No, these are thin and made of silver, or at least silver engraved.

At first glance, they could almost be taken as elaborate jewelry, as a thin chain connects the wrist manacle to one near the elbow, then to one near the shoulder, then to the neck. From the neck, thin silver chains connect to a band just under the ribs, then down to the hips, where the linkages at the arms are mirrored with the legs, connecting to bands at the knees and the odd ankle joint the kobolds have.

It's the traditional garb worn by the kobolds, a sign that they are claimed by the Great Maw. While it looks beautiful at first glance, Lechula can never shake the feeling that the kobolds are just wearing a cage. She'd never dare speak that thought aloud, though, and especially not with one in the room.

Her convoluted thoughts are interrupted when the kobold speaks a second time.

"Miss Lechula? Is the dizziness getting worse?"

"Huh? Oh, no, sorry! I was just . . . distracted."

The kobold simply nods. "Then please stand and lift one foot."

She gets out of bed and obeys, and is relieved to be able to stand without much difficulty.

"Squat down and quickly stand, then lift the other foot please."

She has a bit of dizziness from that, but the kobold keeps a neutral, clinical expression. He runs her through a few more movements before bidding her return to the bed. "You're improving, miss, but I think it will still be a day or two before I can clear you to return to your duties." She nods at that as he turns to Merrik. "Now, this will probably be sore, but please try not to move too much."

The pale elf grunts as the kobold pokes and prods at his shoulder for a few minutes. "It seems to be healing well. By tomorrow, I think we can remove the sling and test your range of movement. If you need anything before then, please ring the bell. Oh, I'm told there will be cheese delivered to the patients soon. It's supposed to be very good; the maker seems to be favored by the clergy."

Neither Lechula nor Merrik have anything else they need to say, and as the kobold turns to leave, her eyes trail the chains that continue down the tail, too. Once he's gone, she glances toward Merrik, whose eyes are on her, a small frown on his face.

"Ah."

She narrows her eyes at him. "What do you mean, *ah*?!"

He gives her a measured look before responding. "Well, either you were enjoying the view, or my shoulder isn't the only reason your beard is tied in knots."

She blushes and sputters at both implications, not sure which she should try to deny, but his wry smirk keeps her from saying anything coherent.

"It's not something I've had to think about before either, but something I find myself returning to, with not much else to do in the healing ward than think and heal." He doesn't elaborate. Lechula is thankful for that. While she's glad she's not the only one who feels like they're actually seeing the kobolds for the first time, it's also difficult to come to terms with what she's actually seeing.

She almost wishes he hadn't said anything. It'd be easier to pretend nothing is wrong if he hadn't. Her friend soon gets comfortable and takes another nap, resting to let the healing magic work without him interfering, and she takes the chance to untangle her beard. Talking has calmed her some, but the kobolds stick in her mind.

She's not the only one who feels something is off. If it was just her, she could ignore it, but with Merrik . . . She shoves the thoughts aside for now, not wanting to tie her beard into knots again.

By the time she gets it untangled and starts brushing her beard and hair, another dwarf pulls a hand cart up outside the room and comes inside with a covered basket.

"Let me see . . . two? No cheese allergies, I hope?" he asks with a smile, radiating a casual uncle kind of feeling. Lechula smiles and shakes her head.

"No, thank the Maw. Is that the cheese the kobold said would be delivered?"

"Yes, it is! Mild and soft, but not soft enough to be spread. The cheesers even got special molds made. Look!" He pulls out two from the basket, but they don't look like small wheels to Lechula. Instead, they look like kobolds! One is sitting, while the other seems to be sleeping, each looking peaceful even with the chains adorning them, the features easily recognizable in the protective wax coating.

"That's . . ." she starts, uncertain how to describe her feeling. Thankfully, the deliverer is happy to finish for her.

"Amazing, right? This is just a bit of a test batch, but if these do well, I'm told he's going to sell them as well as donate some to places like the healing ward and orphanage and such! It'll be a great way to give us all just a taste of how important the kobolds are to the Great Maw!"

She forces a smile and nods at that, accepting the sitting kobold from him, admiring the little cheese figurine as he sets the other on the table near Merrik. She *is* a bit hungry, so she peels the back off and easily extracts the cheese, looking at the kobold one more time.

While it looked peaceful and maybe a little happy in the wax, the cheese one somehow looks a little sad. Maybe those are just her own thoughts.

She goes to take a bite, but something seems wrong about eating the little cheese kobold, like biting its head off is a bit too close to what really happens to them. She tries to give her little kobold mercy and stuffs the whole thing in her mouth at once.

It really is a nice cheese, perfect for snacking on its own. Is that how the Maw sees them?

As she chews, both the cheese and her thoughts, Merrik's words echo in her head, about how he's also thinking about them. She can't help but come to a decision as she finishes the cheese: no matter how tasty, should the Maw get to eat people?

Maybe she can ask Merrik once they're both healed. They should start working on patrols and other training outside of the Maw soon. If there's anywhere she can ask a question like that, it'd be somewhere out in the tunnels.

Chapter 58

And those are the basics for my Butterfly Effect, Fluffles. Just subtle things lining up and leading to the next, like dominoes," explains Teemo. While he's specifically explaining it to Fluffles, he still has Rocky, Slash, and even the Stag listening.

The big elk looks a bit lost, but I'm pretty sure it's just because it's a Fate thing. From the bond, I think Rocky is interested in the theory, but isn't planning much in the way of application just yet.

He hasn't really practiced with his Fate affinity, so I think he'll work on things like True Strike and such before trying to do anything too fancy. Still, Butterfly Effect could be brutal in his gloved hands. Or his normal hands, since his gloves are still at home.

Slash seems to be taking it more as a general lesson on magic, though I wouldn't be surprised to see him trying to weave fate into his music. I'm still uncertain how Bardic magic even works, so he's on his own there. I don't think he'll have too much trouble.

Fluffles, on the other hand, is paying close attention, and I can feel him planning and theorizing through the bond with ways to use Fate affinity. If he wants to pull off something special, I have an idea, but I don't know if I'll be able to explain it even through Teemo before the next battle.

Partially because Teemo needs to get going if he wants to get back in time for it. The scouts, both my denizens and the adventurers, are starting to see signs of civilization. No actual people or anything yet, but little signs of booted feet moving around, curated wildlife, old campsites, and more. The kind of things found at the very outskirts of a town, where the more outdoorsy types occasionally visit.

With the dungeon's territory close to being spotted, I need Teemo to get back with Rocky and the other denizens so I can get that mana, and then double-time Rocky back to the front, maybe with some basilisks, too.

"Alright, but we really should get going. Rocky, you told Leo and Honey everything you could, yeah?"

Rocky gives a tired grunt, and I can't blame him. My Warden and Librarian have been grilling him for every scrap of information he could give them. Even Rocky, tough as he is, can only handle so much.

"Cool. The denizens should be ready to march, and the Boss wants us home and back here as quickly as we can." Teemo smirks as Rocky grins and grunts again. "Yep, round two. Fluffles, Slash, you guys just keep on top of things and hold the fort down if anything goes bad before we get back. Or do whatever Leo says; he and Honey are looking like they're going to be stepping up the expeditions now that they have that dungeon's scent."

The scions nod as Teemo hops onto Rocky's shoulder, and my Voice gives the Stag a salute. "Let your boss know Rocky will be back as soon as he can, maybe even with some of Thedeim's dwellers."

"My Lord will be happy to host them, and hopes the impending battle won't see them come to any harm," replies the Stag with a small bow. He's gotten a little less formal since the alliance, but he's still pretty big on appearances.

Teemo nods at that with a complicated smile. "Yeah . . . me too. The Boss doesn't want them to fight, but you gotta let them make their own decisions, you know?"

"I can only imagine. My Lord has yet to designate any enclaves, but I've seen how protective animals are of their progeny. A dungeon and their dwellers are surely similar."

"Yeah, a bird's gonna feed those hatchlings, but they're eventually gonna fledge and go do adult bird things. They might be safer if you clip their wings and keep them in your care, but then they'll never get to soar."

The Stag nods at that. "Indeed. Safe travels, Voice Teemo. I look forward to having this situation resolved so both of our Lords may return to more peaceful and prosperous times."

"Yeah, looking forward to that, and so's the Boss. Take care, Stag, Southwood." Rocky turns and waves over his shoulder as he heads for the denizens gathered near the outskirts of the Southwood. Sure, it'll still be probably an hour before they even get organized enough to go, but it's as good a farewell as any.

Even if it reminds me about the dangers my dwellers are putting themselves in for me.

If I could, I'd give a frustrated sigh, but I guess I'm going to have to settle for just feeling frustrated as I let my thoughts carry me in circles I usually try to ignore. But that hasn't really been solving the problem, so maybe I should examine them and try to break out of this annoying rut.

I don't need them to help. I don't even *want* them to help. This whole situation is a mess that I'd rather not expose them all to, but I can't force them to stay out of it. It's not even that I wouldn't try, if I thought it could possibly work. Even setting aside the massive hypocrisy that would be after helping Hullbreak, my dwellers are smart enough to get around whatever measures I might take to keep them here. It'd be doomed to failure, and only hurt them in the long run.

It's like what Teemo said about clipping a bird's wings. Sure, they'd be safe, but they'd never *soar*. I want them to reach heights even I think are impossible, to achieve their dreams and have the only hardship they ever face be trying to come up with some even more impossible, fantastical goal to achieve.

But that's just not life, no matter how much I'd like it to be. No matter how much I want to protect them, they need to be able to protect themselves. I've given them new spears and bows; I'm even trying to help with their winter clothing with the zippers Jello's working on, but it still needs to be them who learn how to use all of that. It has to be them who does the fighting for themselves, even if their first real fighting is for me.

And that's the real problem there, I think. I just don't want them to get hurt because of me. Maybe I'm being egocentric, and they'd march off to try to save Aranya's people even without me making my own plans to do it. Honestly . . . they probably would, or would at least try something.

I'm proud of them. That's why I don't want to lose any of them.

"Lord Thedeim?" Aranya's voice upends my thoughts, and I focus to see her standing in front of my core, worried. Her concerned look softens as I watch, and she gently rests a hand on my core.

"You're worried about the dwellers," she states. I don't even try to deny it. She smiles softly and continues. "They know. They know it troubles you, letting them go to war, but they're also glad you're not trying to stop them. They worry for you, too." She smirks and pats my core. "You've set too good of an example for them. You're always trying to help others. I don't know why you're surprised others would try to help you too."

I want to reply to that, but I can't come up with anything. It also doesn't help that Teemo is quietly snickering from Rocky's shoulder. I don't know if he can hear what Aranya's saying, but he probably knows we're talking, and that I'm not exactly winning this conversation.

"They know the stakes are high. Even combined, they're only a couple dozen people. Even with your gifts to help them, they're going to be outnumbered against a foe Rocky had to get serious against. And this time, it'll be in the dungeon's home, not a random outpost. They even know the Harbinger isn't the only scion they might have to face down.

"But they trust you. They know you won't just lead them to pointless deaths. They'll do their best to follow Leo's battle plan, using all their training, and try their best to come back alive. They don't want to die, of course, but stopping the dungeon and the Harbinger is a cause they are willing to give their all for. And should they fall in the line of battle, I know they'll be safe and protected in your embrace. You were their home once before, and the Raven will make sure you are again, in the end."

Wait, what? But . . . what? What?! I don't . . . ! I can't*!*

"Boss! You okay?"

"Lord Thedeim!"

I miss the rut my thoughts were in, because now I'm in a dangerous, uncharted territory I was trying to stay out of. I try to focus on Teemo and Aranya, not letting my thoughts sprint off into crazy assumptions and wild conclusions.

Just breathe . . . Wait, I don't breathe! Uh . . . calming thoughts! Aranya reading a book by the light of my core. Delvers gathering herbs. The adorable little murder machines that are the baby scythemaws. My scions.

Okay . . . okay, I think I'm doing better. Panic attacks are not any more fun without a body. Now . . . calm and collected.

"Boss?"

"Lord Thedeim?"

I'm . . . well, not okay, *but I'll be alright.* Just need to process a bit of existential dread. I thought dying made that moot, but apparently not.

Just focus. The Raven is basically the reaper here, taking souls to the afterlife. Could it bring a soul to me?

Stomp down that rising terror and think it through. What would I do with a soul? I don't think I have anywhere to put one.

Okay, good thought. Let's feel around, see if anything might disprove that theory.

I try to reassure Teemo, and hope Aranya gets the same, before I start carefully looking through my menus. I'd think an afterlife would be a pretty obvious section in my options, but if it's there, I'm not seeing it. I even try feeling around instead of just reading. If I had anything like that, it'd probably feel similar to the spawners? My denizens wait inside when they're "dead," so any "dead" dwellers *(calm, stay calm)* would probably need a similar space, right?

It's easy to feel my spawners even without looking, but I don't feel anything like an extra one. I don't feel an extra resident bond—or anything similar to what I feel with Yvonne—either. So . . . So she's probably wrong, right? My dwellers, if they die *(please don't)* will go to some version of Heaven here, right?

Logically, it makes sense. Unfortunately, I'm pretty sure I'm missing something, because it feels like my Fate affinity is giggling at me.

Chapter 59

I spend a bit more time trying to think through the impossibility of being in charge of the afterlife for my dwellers, but I make exactly zero progress. There's just too much I don't know, and I can't think of anywhere I could get that information.

While I think Torlon would share what the Crystal Shield knows, I don't think he has that knowledge himself. It also seems like the kind of thing that'd take a pact to get the Shield itself to share, and I don't really want to do that.

The closest thing to an actual idea I have would be to try to send them to the Pearly Gates, but there are rules to get in, even if I could send them there. It's just a whole can of worms that's probably better left unopened, and not in the way of me just trying to ignore it.

No . . . if something impossible like that happens, I'll just have to cross that bridge when I get there. Maybe I'll be lucky, and it will only be a hypothetical. It'd be nice.

But instead of focusing on a hypothetical, I should focus on more practical and real issues, like zippers. Coda and Jello have both been working on the idea, and though it's going well, I seriously doubt they're going to be much past the working prototype phase by the time my dwellers leave.

Much as I might like for them to keep training and planning and miss the whole battle, they're smart enough to recognize the list of things to prepare is dwindling quick. The bows and spears both are looking pretty solid. The training phase has been invaluable in finding those little weaknesses and flaws that always slip through the design phase.

It's so easy to forget about dirt and such, only for actual testing and use to show some glaring flaw that real life takes advantage of. I think the M16 had a problem like that. At first, troops hated it because it'd get dirty and constantly jam. But then they added some kind of coating to the receiver, I think, that made it so dirt and grime just couldn't stick, and it became the main rifle for . . . a long time.

Thankfully, bows are a bit less prone to jamming. The spears needed a bit of fine-tuning on that front, though. Considering all the things a spear is supposed to be stabbed into, there needs to be a good way to keep anything from gumming up the few moving parts. Still, it seems to be solved well enough for now, with each of the hunting spiders being given a more traditional leaf-shaped blade to go along with the telescoping barb version.

Can't have my spear spiders running out of ammo, so the leaf head will be a good option for dealing with opponents that don't need the over-engineered toy.

Armor is pretty easy for my dwellers to produce, especially since I haven't tried to reinvent any wheels there. Some kind of magical power armor would be cool, but I don't think I'm ready to drop some kind of project like that on Thing just yet.

Most of the heavy armor is basically a clamshell chest plate with lighter coverings for the limbs. A clamshell is one of the simplest yet most effective bits of body armor, if also one of the heaviest. It's basically two metal pieces that connect with various latches, ties, and whatnot, which practically become a single piece. It's great for resisting most kinds of blows, and as long as the metal holds, the person behind it should hold up pretty well.

The main downside is that it's heavy, and if you go too light, make the clamshell too thin, it'll just buckle when hit and be pointless.

The tarantulakin are strong enough to have not only a clamshell on their torso and abdomen but similar pieces on the first section of their legs, too. Ring mail covers the joints to the body, designed to tangle any weapons that try to swing at the weakness. A spear or pick might be able to get through, but anything else would have to have enough force to break the loose mail to do any damage.

The jumping spiderkin wear lighter padded chain on their torso and abdomen, and have metallic bracerlike sections covering their legs and arms. They aren't designed to take damage like the tarantulas, and instead focus on mobility and protection from indirect and ranged blows.

My ratkin are mostly in leather and silk, lighter armor that should protect from enemy arrows. If it comes down to them being in melee, armor isn't really going to save them at that point, anyway.

Still, they also have daggers and are quick and nimble enough to potentially attack the joints of anything that gets too close. And, of course, they'll have my denizens around as well. I don't know what Leo will keep close to keep them safe, but I trust he won't leave them flapping in the breeze during the battle.

I watch, trying not to let my nerves get the better of me, as dozens of ratkin and spiderkin go through some drills in their armor. The enclaves are about two hundred strong each, but they've still managed to field almost three dozen fighters apiece. They're all doing their last checking and speed drills, getting armor on, getting it off, getting the warm clothing on and off, loading the carts, making camps, breaking camps.

They're going to leave soon. Not today, probably not tomorrow, but maybe the day after. I think they're wanting to set out with Rocky and Teemo, so they'll need to wait for them to get back before they can all go. It's not just for the pomp and circumstance of a big send off, either. If something happens and they end up having to fight while still on the surface, my dwellers would be in serious trouble, thanks to the cold.

While there's every indication that the enemy fares even worse in that weather, nobody is willing to bet their life that the dungeon won't have some other denizens to try to engage on the surface with. So they'll wait and march in their snow gear, and suit up once far enough underground to not be bothered by the winter chill.

I could probably try to convince them to wait longer, but then again, maybe I couldn't. If something unexpected happens, they're going to want to be close enough to respond instead of having to march all the way from home. Sure, right now, I don't have anywhere for them to try to assault, but that could change by the time they get there. And if it doesn't, they'll still be in a position to respond when something does happen.

With the reports coming in, something will definitely happen eventually. One of the scouting adventurers actually spotted some of the dwellers. Well, not technically dwellers, but close enough. As far as the scout could tell, the pale elf was more or less a ranger, just checking the area around to see if the wildlife is still doing well. It doesn't seem like the dungeon is aware I'm coming down to get it yet.

We'll see how long that lasts. My own scouts are slowly yet surely making their way closer and closer. The rockslides are careful, and can even use the torn-up pathway as cover, hiding themselves among the destroyed floor as just more rubble. It's still possible the path is being watched, though, so they're not rushing. My wyrms are staying deep as they do their own explorations, staying far from any surfaces as they go.

I think they've found the main cavern, unless there's some other dungeon down there. There are no details yet, and even the location is pretty vague and could be a false positive for a lot of reasons, but I think we finally have a place to focus our attention on.

Still, that just means we have to be all the more careful. Mistakes out in the wilds of the underground are fine, but making too much noise while close could draw attention. We need to gaze long into this abyss without it noticing. It'll start gazing back eventually, but we need to do our best to be prepared to only show it what we want.

I'm also a bit nervous about what we'll see when we get a better look, too. From what Aranya was saying, the dungeon is worshiped by the pale elves and pale dwarves. If it's a situation similar to mine, it'll be mostly just a matter of them getting a morale boost and having a focus for faith casters. But if it's actually a deity . . . can we handle something like that?

Those questions are enough to make my head spin. On the one hand, I'd love for me and this other dungeon to just both be ordinary dungeons. I mean, I beat Hullbreak, and his dwellers worship him too. It'll be fine, right?

On the other hand, Hullbreak doesn't inspire the kind of insane zeal in his dwellers that this other dungeon seems to do. Hullbreak didn't and doesn't get sacrificial offerings, but this one does. Hopefully, it just means mana for the dungeon, which is already a pretty good bit of power.

If it's more than that . . . I don't know.

The idea of fighting a god is pretty scary, but it also ignites my defiance. There's only one I'll bow to, and this other dungeon is not Him. I don't know specifically what I'll do to beat a god, but I know I'll do my best. I know my scions will, too. My denizens, my residents, my dwellers, my *friends*, all of us will.

If that dungeon wants to put itself on a pedestal, to be above everyone and demand anything of us, we'll show it just how precarious of a position that can be, just how much more distance there is to fall from up there, and how much more painful the landing will be.

Chapter 60

Though I'm feeling a bit better and more motivated to go kick this dungeon's butt, reality forces me to cool my heels. I pretty much spend the entire rest of the day going over the vague plans and tricks, and have to grudgingly admit there's not a whole lot extra for me to do at the moment. There are a couple things I could do, but I think it'd be better to keep that mana for reacting to whatever the dungeon throws at us.

Upgrading the dragon spawner, for example, would get me more of the basilisks, but I doubt it'll get me enough to let them take the role of foot soldier rather than the role of a cavalry or tank: a big scary thing on the battlefield that you don't want to ignore but you also don't want to be the one to go over and try to stop it.

I could finally make the Ant Enclave, but I think I need to just accept that's not going to be a thing until after this situation with the other dungeon is handled. It's like I'm staring at a present under the tree, wanting what it has without having to wait for the proper time to open it. No, I need to just leave it be until after this war is done, and possibly until after spring arrives, too. Hard to say with underground stuff, especially if they take after the magmyrm and are all magma-y.

The only other things I have to do are smaller upgrades to the labyrinth. It's pretty much down to just fine-tuning now, I think. The entrance is still not quite as busy as I might hope, but it's getting more use every day. I'd say the reason is about evenly split between people just discovering the facilities there, and people watching Jello work.

Coda gave her a few shapes for possible zipper teeth, but she's gotten distracted by toying with how metals can be interlocked. I don't try to discourage her, either, as she basically makes little blacksmith puzzles, among other trinkets.

She actually stumbles on something I probably should have tried before zippers, but I got kinda hung up on them: snap buttons. They're certainly a lot easier to fasten than normal buttons, and a lot easier to manufacture than zippers, so I think the next iteration of the winter wear for my denizens will feature them, once Jello gets them just how she wants.

I spend my time waiting for Teemo and Rocky to return by mostly watching delvers and making small changes. I could start another big project, but the labyrinth was basically my way to fund the fight with the other dungeon. I need to bank the mana from it instead of spending it on another thing.

If I still didn't know where the dungeon was, I might spend some to get even more income, but with the scouting reports getting more details by the day, I want to keep that war chest full to bursting. And I'm curious if the ally pool has a limit.

As I watch through Teemo and Rocky's eyes while they exit the shortcut not far from the cemetery wall, I know it'll soon be time to test that out. If I still had a mouth, I'd be drooling at the idea of all that mana they're bringing.

As they approach the wall, I can feel Teemo and Rocky's satisfaction at coming home via the bond, and my Voice speaks up as Rocky comes to a stop just outside.

"Alright, Rocky, you ready? How about you, Boss? This is gonna be a lot of mana."

Definitely. I don't think it'll be too itchy to get what Rocky has for me, and I don't feel the pressure to use it if it's in the ally pool, so I'm probably going to put it mostly there.

Rocky grunts as Teemo nods. "Sounds like we're as ready as we're gonna get then. After you, Rocky." My Boxer smiles and hops the wall, and as his feet hit the cold soil, I get hit with a sledgehammer blow of mana. I quickly shunt it over to the ally pool, and am surprised at how much is in it now.

That almost doubled the pool there, wow. That Harbinger really wasn't a joke, huh.

Rocky smirks and heads for the mausoleum so he can get to his ring. I think he wants to do a bit of punching before he has to head back out, and I don't really blame him. Teemo perches on a gravestone near the wall and helps direct my returning denizens, chatting with me as I keep moving the mana into the ally pool.

"So, things have been mostly good while I was gone?" he asks, and I try to approximate a nod as I reply.

Yeah, that little panic attack aside. The scythemaw eggs are hatching, and the babies are painfully cute. They've been scurrying to the water in small groups, and me and Violet have both mostly been letting them go. There are a couple of rangers watching, and they grab one every so often to check on it. Nobody's tried to tame one yet.

"How about that panic? Everything alright?"

I think "alright" is a bit too strong of a word, but I'm at least okay. I was just a bit blindsided, is all. How about you? Southwood seemed pretty happy with everything, but I think you're better at judging that kind of thing.

"Yeah, Southwood is fine. I think he's still trying to come to terms with having an ally instead of a liege." Teemo smirks before continuing. "I'm kinda surprised you let Rocky teach the Stag about fire, though. It's a good move. I think the Southwood really will designate a second scion, hopefully before the espionage turns to outright fighting with the dungeon."

Have you been paying attention to the reports as I get them from Leo?

Teemo grimaces a bit at that. "A little? I worry about Yvonne and the others, so while I want to hear they're doing fine, I'm also afraid of hearing they're not."

Well, they seem to be doing just fine. The last report Leo got from them was that they've dropped off their last rockslide and are carefully probing closer to the dungeon. They sound confident, and I don't blame them.

Yvonne knows how rangers work, so she can identify what might make them investigate, and so stay away. Ragnar's a dwarf, so if anyone is going to be easily able to navigate twisted tunnels and caves to stay under the radar, it's him. And Aelara has her Earth magic. As long as they don't literally bump into a patrol, she should be able to hide them. And with Nova there to feel farther than the others can see, I don't think that's going to happen.

Oh, that reminds me!

"Hmm?"

Nova's been working on sculpting! Aelara made her a beautiful obsidian rose from some of Nova's meltings, and she's been inspired. She's still got a ways to go to reach Aelara's level, but simpler flowers are within her skill set. They look cool, too. Since she can still only manipulate the magma, they look a little melted. I think it's a neat effect, but Nova is a bit self-conscious about it.

Teemo laughs. "That sounds like Nova, yeah! I'll have to ask her for one when she gets back."

Yeah. I'm also hopeful she'll be able to expand her affinities to get Earth from her sculpting, too. Magma is just really hot earth, after all. I'm sure she'll figure it out, even if only from trying to add some finishing touches as it solidifies.

"Oh, hey, that reminds *me*."

Yeah?

"How come you have all kinds of suggestions for the weirder affinities, but not a lot for the simple ones? Water, Earth, Air, and such. I'd say Fire, but you know a lot about fire."

Well . . . I dunno. Maybe the others are just so well defined? There are a lot of things in just Earth, for example, so I don't know where to start. Maybe once Nova gets it, she can explain. I get the feeling Rocky won't be able to expand to Earth just by using kinetics to toss around boulders.

Teemo nods at that, and we slip into a companionable silence for a few minutes before I continue to try to bring Teemo up-to-date with the situation at home.

Oh, Jello got her title for metalworking!

"Oh yeah! I heard you when it happened, but I completely forgot about that! I'm gonna have to go visit her after the denizens are settled and congratulate her!"

There's also the local haberdasher helping keep the spiderkin and ratkin warm on their trip. Did you know a haberdasher is basically just a tailor that specializes in men's clothing, not just hats?

"Huh." Teemo pauses in directing the returning denizens to let that sink in before resuming his work. "Did he actually show the spiderkin a new way to weave silk?"

Nah, he has access to wool. I think Thing wants to try playing around with some heating and insulating spells to make it even better, but as it is right now, the dwellers are basically ready to march once you and Rocky are.

"I'd like a day or two before heading back out, please?"

Hah, no problem. It'll give the new basilisks time to spawn some more, too.

Teemo smirks at that. "I wonder if you'll ever get anything that looks like the dragons you were expecting, Boss."

I hope so. I'm liking my weird ones too, though. It makes me wonder what else they might look like. Maybe I won't get any *normal dragons, and just get the weird ones!*

Teemo smirks again. "It'd fit you, at least. You weirdo."

We both laugh at that and continue to chat as my denizens come home. I'm pretty sure we could talk like this even when he's out on expedition, but it just feels right to hang out here, chatting and laughing.

Chapter 61

I'm feeling a lot better about things after chatting with Teemo. He's good at cutting to the heart of what's bothering me and reminding me what's important. It also helps that he's more than happy to point out mistakes, so when he says something is good, it rings true instead of just hollow praise.

I like to think I help calm him down some, too. I'm not the only one worried about everyone, and both of us being able to vent those worries to each other really helps. It's technically nothing we haven't said nor heard before, but it just clicks better, I suppose.

Whatever the reason, we're both feeling refreshed and ready to get back into the action.

Looking at my dwellers as they prepare, I realize something I've managed to miss. They should be all right like this, but the idea of them going without it makes me reject the notion that they should. I'm Thedeim, the weird dungeon! If anyone can pull a technical war crime out of thin air, it's me!

While I accept it won't be ready by the time they march, I refuse to accept that I can't have it ready by the time the fighting starts! It's going to take a lot of effort from everyone, though.

I can feel my denizens reacting to my resolve, and Teemo is more than happy to help explain and get this project moving yesterday.

First hurdle: manpower. It's almost enough to tempt me into making the Ant Enclave, but they'd have to finish their transformation, and we just don't have the time for that, so it's going to have to rest on the backs of my magmyrm. My ratlings and aranea will probably help, too, but they have their places in me already. My magmyrm have still been searching for something to contribute, and this idea resonates *deep* in them. It's not going to be easy, but they are willing to give it their best effort.

The only potential problem with them is their temperature. They're kinda made from magma, or at least don't seem to care about the very high temperatures closer to the volcanic area. Then again, they've been able to deliver sleeping potions to people who lose in the labyrinth without melting the glass or igniting the cork, and can carry people out, too. I guess they can handle their temperature well, which is a huge relief.

I get a group of them headed toward Thing's private lab in the Sanctum while Teemo explains the idea to him. He looks as eager to do it as I've seen him before, and gets the magmyrm to clear a space for him to teach. I can feel there's a lot he wants to impart on them, but he's also not going to be their only teacher.

Queen is already organizing her own lab, setting up stations for the magmyrm to learn her trade as well. Alchemy is going to be a vital part of this plan, too. I don't know how much Queen can teach them on such short notice, but she can probably squeeze at least a few basic recipes into them, as well as a bit of herbalism to be able to gather the herbs they'll need, too.

My ratlings take to the forges, working on the fine, delicate instruments we'll need. I'm not completely sure if they'll be needed, or if the magmyrm will even have the expertise to use what my ratlings are making, but I'd rather have it and not need it, than need it and not have it. Some of the delvers might actually have the skills for this, come to think of it. I'll have to have Teemo ask them once he's back on the front lines.

The aranea get to work weaving silk overtime, and even process some of the wool and mycelia fabric the enclaves have offered to my warehouse. We're going to need a *lot* of fabric, both for uniforms and for the actual work.

For the uniform, I make a few alterations to the robes we made for Yvonne and Aranya . . . Well, I *would* say so long ago, but it's only been a couple months. How time flies. Anyway, the uniform. I go with what looks a lot like sweatpants and hoodies. I think they look a little cooler than the fabric those usually use, but I'm mostly going for utility, not fashion.

Elastic silk at every opening in the fabric will allow for easy fitting without letting loose sleeves and legs get in the way and snag on things. Even the bottom of the shirt has the elastic silk, to try to keep any mess confined to the fabric. The work can get more than a little messy, so the combination of a good fit and ease of changing will help keep things running smoothly.

I do need to adjust again after the first batch is made, once I remember the magmyrm are going to be the first ones wearing it, not taller bipeds. I think it'll go well as long as they can cool themselves enough not to set the clothes on fire. Considering Thing has them looking at his books, I don't think it's going to be an issue.

I even get the bees contributing, with Teemo helping to direct them. I think they're a bit confused as to why I want some empty honeycombs, but they're not bothered with complying. Oh, actually, I bet having some honey would be really helpful, too!

It's a bit of a mess to get everything organized, but Queen's ants are a big help in getting the honey out of the combs and into clean vials.

I smile as I watch everyone working. There's still a lot to go, but I think we'll be able to make this work before the fighting starts.

"Hey, Boss? Why're you calling this a war crime? It seems like a good thing to me?"

I chuckle at his confusion. *It's mostly me being silly, though it really is technically a crime. See, in a war, people always get hurt, right? There are classes that can or even specialize in minimizing that, but it still happens. There are also uniforms in just about any war, so people know who's on what side. Wearing the wrong one can be a big problem. I'm going to be stealing a uniform, basically.*

"But we don't know what that other dungeon dresses people as. And it probably doesn't even have magmyrm, anyway."

I'm not stealing the uniform of that dungeon; I'm stealing a different one. One of the people who don't do any fighting, yet are always on the front line. Their duty isn't to fight but to heal. They don't carry weapons; they don't even differentiate sides. Their only duty is to gather the people who are too injured to fight and make sure they don't die, no matter which side they were fighting for.

Teemo dons a confused look. "That's one of your weirdest ideas yet, Boss."

Yeah, but it's an important one. Honestly, it's one I should have remembered much earlier. I guess magic healing makes it easy to forget, but even with a few clerics mixed in with the fighters, there are going to be people who get injured too badly to fight but can't get a magical heal before the front line moves on.

There's gonna be people just trying not to die, and even after a battle, there's going to be injured enemies. While I've heard stories of ancient armies going around after a battle to finish off any foes not quite dead, I'm not going to do that.

I watch an aranea stitch some red fabric to the front and back of the shirt, as well as the top and bottom of the ant pants, and smile to myself at the old symbol. The red cross. It's an old symbol of healing, and a war crime to wear or even display if you're not actually part of them.

I pause as I see Grim step out of a shortcut and into the work area, his scythe free of grass and trimmings. He runs his skeletal hand along the edge before moving to help cut bandages and dip them into the sealing wax to help keep them clean.

So yeah, I want to bring them here, to make them a symbol of help. If battles are anything like I've heard they are, wounded can outnumber the dead, or even the living! If I don't want to add more bodies, I need to do something about it, and this will be that something.

Teemo chuckles as he watches Grim. "You know the enclaves are going to be all over this once they find out, right?"

Yeah, I know. The only reason I didn't already include them is—

"Lord Thedeim?" comes the surprised voice of my High Priestess as she sees all the activity in the Sanctum. She stays well out of the way of my denizens and scions as they work, and her confusion gives way to a wide smile.

"More healing, of course! The dwellers will be relieved to see you taking an even more active role in keeping them safe."

"Not just them," corrects Teemo as he hops onto her shoulder, earning a confused look. "It's a bit complicated, but it's not just for our dwellers. They're going to heal every injured person they can get their hands on; ours and the other dungeon's."

She still looks confused at that, but smiles as she turns to walk toward my core and place a hand on me. "That does sound like the kind of crazy idea you'd come up with."

Hah, I wish it was my idea. I'm not above borrowing the really good ones, though.

Chapter 62

It's time for the next wave to move out, which includes the dwellers. While I'd rather they stay back and maybe go with the medics, I'd just come up with another excuse to try to keep them back when the healers head on out. There's nothing I can think of to actually keep them home, or at least not anything I haven't expressed already.

My denizens are ready to go. This batch of reinforcements mostly has tundra wolves and basilisks, with a smattering of more arcane hands, too. A few of my other denizens are preparing to head out, including a twinsnake that really wants to go, but I don't think they'll manage it. They're having trouble just exiting the mausoleum with how cold it is outside right now.

Rocky is looking reinvigorated, and I'm pretending I don't notice he has his gloves hidden inside his lich robe. He's had a few more challengers to play with in the arena, but nobody has put up the kind of fight the kids did. I think partially because they don't think they can win. The kids were pretty sure they'd lose, but they had that youthful optimism to still give it their all.

The other delvers haven't been digging as deep, so Rocky hasn't been digging as deep for their rewards, either. Still, he's been enjoying the fights, and I think the delvers have, too.

My dwellers are having just one last hiccup before they can get going. While Larx has grudgingly accepted he can't go off to war and potentially leave the ratkin leaderless, my spiderkin happen to have three leaders, two of whom are very good in a fight. Norloke doesn't want either Folarn nor Vernew to go, but they've outvoted her on that front. She was, however, able to get them both to accept that only one can go.

It's kinda getting to the point where I wonder if she'll actually have success in keeping them both home. She continues siding with the other to keep them there. If they can't actually decide soon, they're going to miss the boat, which I'm sure is all according to Norloke's plan.

Right now, they're outside a mausoleum, watching the army muster and arguing. Sorry, *debating*.

"Why can't you both just stay?" asks the matronly spiderkin, not bothering to pretend at this point. Folarn sighs and speaks up as Vernew stumbles over herself to try to answer.

"Because we can't send them off without one of us. Even with the guidance of the Weaver and Warden Leo, it smacks of callousness and cowardice to not have either myself or Vernew there."

The huntress nods and folds her arms as she finally secures her verbal footing.

"Yeah, if we don't go, it'll look like we don't *want* to go. It's one thing to tell someone to do something you can't do on your own, but it's just laziness to send someone to do something you can do but just don't want to. Lots of my new hunters act like gutting a fresh hunt is optional and they only get assigned to it as punishment, at least until they see me dressing my own kills. They need to know it's important by seeing us do it, not just being told to."

Norloke sighs and reluctantly nods. "I know. While my weavers don't get as messy, some of the process is incredibly tedious, and they only ever accept it as necessary after seeing me do it personally. I just . . ."

Folarn smiles and pats her fellow triumvirate member's shoulder. "I know. And you're not wrong that we can't both go."

"You guys really should just let me go," speaks up Vernew, earning a flat look from them both. She doesn't let that stop her, however, and barrels forward. "I'm serious! I even have good reasons! It basically boils down to them not actually needing you in this fight, Folarn."

At the large spiderkin's frown, Vernew quickly continues. "I mean, sure, you're good at military planning, but that's Warden Leo's job. You'd need Teemo there to be able to actually try to make plans together. He'll probably be there, but I don't think he's going just to translate for you two.

"I'm not good at planning, but I know how to listen on a hunt. I don't need to try to make a plan; I just need to stick to the one they give me. And I can help scout, at least until it's time to actually fight!" She pauses and glances away, looking uncomfortable for a moment, but not shying away from her reasoning.

"And . . . we need you here, Folarn. The outsiders—the delvers and townsfolk—they know you. You're good at talking to them and getting them to listen. If the worst happens . . . we'd be in a lot more trouble without you than without me."

"No!" object the other two, but Vernew isn't backing down just yet.

"I'm not putting myself down, okay! I'm just . . . just looking at the whole web. If we lost Norloke, the enclave itself would be in shambles as we tried to learn how you can juggle all those domestic problems without losing a stitch! And if Folarn was gone, the townspeople wouldn't know who to talk to. There'd be no big, gruff, secret softy to approach for negotiations.

"But without me . . . you guys would be sad, I know, and the hunting might be a bit lean, but my hunters would be able to step up. There'd probably be some drama, but nothing you two couldn't handle."

Now it's Norloke and Folarn's turn to look uncomfortable. While Vernew is of course more than the hole she'd leave behind should the worse happen, they're all close enough to be honest with each other, so it's difficult to argue against her logic, heartless as that logic is.

And, like the master huntress she is, she has a finishing blow to land. "I just . . . I want to show Him I've gotten better. I failed to stop the kids. Sure, it worked out, but I still failed. I need this."

Folarn rests a hand on her shoulder now, too, though she doesn't put too much of her weight on it. "You know that, if you go, the only way you could fail Him would be by not returning, right?"

Vernew inhales deeply and nods. "Yeah, I know. I know it's not just me out there. If Leo says the best way I can contribute is to dig latrines the entire time, I'll do it with a smile on my face." She pauses for a moment. "Okay, not a smile, but I wouldn't try to weasel out of it, at least." She takes another few seconds to straighten herself. "So, that said: I call for a vote on allowing me to join our forces and march under the Weaver's banner. I vote aye."

Norloke looks to Folarn, who crosses her arms as she considers the vote seriously. "Aye . . ."

The weaver deflates a bit and nods. "Aye. I'm still worried, but aye. The decision is unanimous. Huntsmistress Vernew will accompany our forces, rendering whatever aid the Weaver and His scions ask."

All three nod, and the officious air remains for a few moments before Vernew moves forward and hugs Norloke, with Folarn joining in not long after.

"I'll be careful, don't worry. I hope they'll have me scout, but I really will do whatever they tell me to. Uh . . . I'll probably suggest they don't have me cook, though."

That earns her a laugh from them both, with Folarn recovering first to speak. "I still don't understand how you managed to burn tea!"

"I thought I'd only need a cupful of water! And I like it strong! So I tossed in the leaves and only turned my back for a few minutes!" she exclaims, trying to defend herself, but that only earns another laugh.

"Well, make sure you have all your stuff, Vernew. The vote is one thing, but I don't know if the Weaver will delay the whole army just for you," points out Norloke, earning a scoff from the small spiderkin.

"He'd probably love the excuse, but yeah, I shouldn't tempt Him. I brought my whole kit, but I'll check it now and hope I haven't forgotten anything." She heads back into the mausoleum to go over her gear, leaving the other two outside. I nudge Teemo, who points Aranya and Larx toward the spiderkin, all three wearing encouraging smiles.

"Boss says you finally decided on who will go?"

"Yes. I'd still prefer it was me . . . but she's not wrong in her reasoning. Somehow, that makes me feel worse about it," grumbles Folarn as Norloke nods.

"I still wish she didn't need to go. It's one thing to watch the others prepare to go, but another to watch a close friend do it."

Larx nods at that. "Indeed. I don't like letting them go, and I don't like not getting to go with them, but I can't change either of those facts."

My Voice smirks at the unhappy faces. "Sounds like you guys know what the Boss is feeling, then. He's gonna do his best to bring everyone back safe, even though he knows that's not a reasonable goal."

That earns a laugh from Aranya. "Since when has a goal being unreasonable kept Him from striving for it anyway?"

Teemo chuckles, as do I. "Yeah. If anyone can pull it off, it'd be him. Still . . ."

Norloke sighs and nods. "Better to be prepared for the worst than to be ambushed by it."

The somber mood is waylaid as Vernew rejoins everyone, carrying a large pack and wearing her warm gear. "Alright, I should have everything! Oh, Teemo!" She raps her right hand against her spear in a salute. "Vernew, reporting for duty!"

He smirks at her. "It's about time! I think everyone is about ready to go, too. The Boss says you volunteered for latrine duty, right?"

That earns grins from everyone except Vernew, who is trying to hide her horror at the idea. "Uh . . . I guess?"

"Good! It's important work, you know?" Teemo hops to her shoulder and points her toward the rest of the dwellers as they prepare to move out, extolling the virtues of the unpleasant task.

I wonder how long he'll string her along? He probably can't manage it for the entire march, right?

From the gleam in his eyes, I get the feeling he just might try.

Chapter 63

Nova

As the Wyrm Scion quietly glides through the earth, she reflects on just how strange scouting duty is. While she's finding she quite enjoys it, that doesn't make the duty any less strange. It's the juxtaposition of heightened awareness with lessened need to actually do anything that makes it so strange. Feeling for vibrations keeps her mind active enough to pay attention, but not so active that her mind doesn't start to wander.

She's certainly had a lot of things for her mind to wander to lately. Take magic, for example. She knows affinities can be expanded, but knowing and seeing are two different things. The way Rocky taught the Stag to embrace fire . . . it seems so obvious after, but so impossible before. While she can't use the specifics of light, she has been trying to focus more on her Magma affinity to see what she can do.

From the vague hints through the bond with the Guide, he seems to think she could expand to Earth affinity, but her own efforts are leading her toward Fire, she thinks. She feels more attuned to the heat than the magma itself. On the other mandible, her work with sculpting might lead her to Earth affinity after all.

She rumbles happily at the memory of the elf making a beautiful flower from her unnoticed obsidian. She had never thought about the molten rock she leaves behind, or the cooled rock that comes eventually after. She also hadn't thought that an affinity could be used to make something like that. It would be basically no use in a fight, it probably wouldn't take any interesting enchantments, and it can't even be eaten by most things. She took a little nibble, but it tasted like any other obsidian.

And yet, that little flower made from volcanic glass has captivated her like nothing else really has. She's been trying to make one of her own, but her first try was such a failure that she almost gave the entire idea up. But she changed her focus to simpler flowers, and she thinks she's making good progress. She doesn't like how they always come out looking a little melted, even though she can feel the Guide's happiness at each one.

Her thoughts are interrupted as she hears footsteps that don't belong to the Guide's chosen party. They've been dodging rangers and scouts for a day or two now, but this is the first group they've found!

She retreats a bit before waving a bit of magma through the earth behind her, letting the Earth mage of the party feel the moving absence of her element as the signal to hide.

She's been trying to listen in on the people they've been avoiding, but they were all solo, so they didn't say much. This feels like a group of four, so hopefully, they'll talk among themselves and she can get some information.

She feels the chosen party hide themselves, so she glides ahead, being careful not to get too close, lest one of them is another Earth mage.

She stays back, far enough to get an idea of the group's composition before trying to get close enough to listen in. They're almost certainly from the dungeon, as they seem to be two pale elves and two pale dwarves. An elf with a spear is in the lead, with a dwarf with either a thick wand or a thin mace clanking on his belt behind them. Behind those two are the other elf and dwarf, who seem to be trying to keep an eye out.

While Nova isn't an expert, she's pretty sure an actual scouting party would be quieter, and probably not wear as much armor as some of them. The dwarf in the back has armor to rival Ragnar!

After a few minutes of them not seeming to notice her, Nova slowly drifts closer, letting her finally pick out words from the indistinct noise of their conversation.

"What about this spot, Jayle?" asks the spear elf at the front, sounding like they've asked the question many times before. The dwarf nearby seems to be looking in a book and glances around before speaking.

"Maybe? We're definitely far enough away now. The field guide says we should try to find clean water, and I see a little trickle out of the wall there."

"It's a bit cramped," speaks up the elf in the back. Nova agrees with his estimation. They're in more of a tunnel than a cave at the moment. As she understands it, a good camp should let wildlife easily go around. If they camp here, they'll have to deal with local things having to wander through their camp, and some might be more ornery about it than others.

"I'll mark it on the map. If we can't find anything better in an hour, we'll come back," suggests the armored dwarf, which seems agreeable to the others. Nova is a little less confident in that, since the nearest actual cave is the one the chosen party is hiding in. While they are sure to have their camp fully sealed off, she doesn't know how well they will handle needing to stay there and stay quiet.

"I'm glad you two got cleared from recovering enough to be able to come," speaks up the spear elf after a few minutes as the bookish dwarf nods.

"Yeah, if it was just me and Dergol, we would have had to stay home and probably just keep doing drills."

"I'd rather get impaled through the shoulder again than spend a week doing drills," dryly answers the other elf, who Nova is suspecting is some kind of caster. He walks much lighter than the others. Or maybe he's some kind of rogue?

"If it's one or the other, I think I'd rather do drills," snarks back the spear elf before he continues with a bit less sarcasm. "So, how was it in the enclave? I've always wanted to sneak in and get a look at the kobolds, but Mom always said she'd round my ears if I tried it."

The book dwarf snorts. "She'd probably do it, and be in the right, too. You shouldn't mess with the Great Maw's kobolds. They're busy."

"I know! But they're so mysterious! I only ever get to see them at the sacrifices!"

"Well, I wouldn't suggest going and getting yourself injured if you want to look at them," answers the armored dwarf, pulling the conversation back on track. "I only saw one a couple minutes a day, and that's partially because he was also checking on Merrik."

"Being in the same room as one is still closer than I've ever been! What're they like?"

The group continues walking in silence as the two who were injured consider their answers. The possible caster, Merrik, comes up with his first.

"Special. There's a certain weight to what they do, even when it's something as simple as changing a bandage."

"Like they know the weight of their . . . purpose," adds the armored dwarf. Nova realizes she's a she, or at least sounds like one. She can't exactly surface right now and take a look.

"That's so cool. Oh, the tunnel's opening up." The group quiets as they enter the cave and see another small pool of water near the wall.

"Ah, that should do! The field guide says multiple water sources will help keep wildlife away. Even if we camp right next to one, the other is right there and can be used instead of trying to contest us." Nova can hear the book being consulted as the dwarf double-checks, and soon, the group sets about deciding specifically where to set up.

"Think you two can handle this part? Me and Merrik should probably make sure there's nothing too nasty nearby before we get too settled," speaks up the armored dwarf.

"Sure, I think we can handle it. Hang on a sec though, Lechula. I got us all a little treat! You and Merrik can snack on yours while 'securing the perimeter.'" The spear elf—Dergol, Nova reminds herself—digs through his pack for a few moments before exclaiming in victory.

"Yes, they're still sealed! Catch!"

"What is this?" asks Jayle, the bookish dwarf. Nova tries to keep the names straight, just in case it's important with her report.

"A cheese kobold," answers the caster elf Merrik, earning a gasp from Dergol.

"You know?"

Lechula answers. "Yeah. They gave us some at the enclave. They're . . . really good cheese."

"Aw, I wanted to surprise you. Oh well, at least I know the cheese is good now. The guy I paid for these said it was good, but he was trying to get my money. Anyway, go secure, shoo."

The two leave, and Nova slowly moves to follow, though she catches a bit more from the two who are staying.

"The field guide says we shouldn't split up."

"Pfft, it's fine. If we had to follow it to the letter, the Great Maw would have sent denizens instead of us. We'll just need to keep an eye out until they get back."

"We still shouldn't split up."

"Jayle, give them a little privacy. I think they want to spend a little time together. They're acting a little different after the stay at the healers'. I think they finally hooked up!"

Chapter 64

Nova

The Wyrm Scion does her best to stay calm as the two dwellers head deeper into the cave, unknowingly getting closer and closer to her party. She sighs in relief when they finally stop. They're close, but at least not directly outside her friends' hidden camp.

She can actually join them while still listening in, which she happily does. She doesn't feel very qualified for this kind of thing, so hopefully the delvers will have some idea of what to do about the other dungeon's dwellers.

She tries to split her attention between listening to those two as she does her best to sculpt some magma to let the party know what's going on. There are quiet sounds of surprise when she first makes a little magma puddle, but with the rough outline of the cave and little teardrops of magma marking the positions, the Guide's chosen delvers mostly stay quiet.

Nova's very glad for that, as the two hostile dwellers are speaking in hushed tones.

"Should we just . . . leave?" asks the armored one, sounding very nervous. Nova can hear her fidgeting and shifting her feet, clearly ill at ease.

The other hums in thought for a few moments. "Perhaps? I'm not sure how much longer we can keep them in the dark."

"You're still sure they won't see our side of it?"

"Yes. Jayle is devout. I'm actually surprised the clergy haven't claimed him yet. Or maybe they already have, and he's their eyes and ears into Master Harbinger's training. Dergol is . . . not exactly devoted to the Great Maw, but he doesn't see. He'd try to convince us to just drop it. And he's known Jayle longer than he's known us. If it came to blows, he'd side with Jayle just to keep him from being outnumbered."

Nova can hear more shifting from the armored dwarf before Merrik continues. "I know, Lechula. I want to try to convince them too, but I don't think this is the place for it. Even if we convinced Dergol, we'd never convince Jayle. And if Jayle caught a whiff of what we're trying to cook, he'd rat us out if given the chance."

Lechula sighs. "Yeah . . . if he found out, we couldn't let him get back. I don't think I can do something like that."

The two stand in silence for a few more moments before Lechula continues. "Let's just finish securing the cave for now. I don't even know if leaving is a good idea. Silvervein doesn't feel like home anymore . . . but I don't know where else to go."

"I've tried to subtly get a look at maps to try to go somewhere else, but either they're all redacted or there really aren't any other settlements within a couple days. The Great Maw has been eating well, I suppose."

With that, the two resume moving, and Nova surfaces in the hidden camp. While she moves the two drops to coincide with the dwellers' position, she quickly notices her party has not been sitting idle. She tilts her head at a recreation of the cave shape, with lines drawn all around and in it. She tilts her head at the gathered delvers, and Aelara is eager to quietly explain.

"We want to try to capture them. I know you were listening to them, so they must know something. Even if they're just regular soldiers, they'd know more about what's happening than we do. We just need to keep them from alerting the others."

"We're thinkin' a luring them t' a spot an' caving it in behind 'em. We'll need you fer that, Nova," Ragnar briefly summarizes as Nova starts understanding the scribbles on the earthen floor. She nods over to her own little magma map and produces two extra drops before having them pop in a fake landslide, then she rushes the other two dots at the camp over.

Yvonne nods. "They'll know something happened, but cave-ins are a natural danger. If their friends never return from scouting the cave, they'll have to assume they were caught in it. An obvious answer helps keep questions at bay."

Nova supposes that makes sense. She still has another question, though, and tries to mime it with her little magma drops. She multiplies them, having them all wander around the cave and taking different routes back to the camp. Ragnar and Aelara look confused, but Yvonne seems to understand.

"How will we know where to ambush them? We'll try to lure them in. If the other dungeon really is sending out patrols this far, we can make a more permanent hidden camp for ourselves, so we don't even have to capture these two. As for how to lure them, that's where you come in."

Yvonne motions to Aelara, letting the elf explain.

"I'll be busy with setting our thin wall to crumble, as well as preparing a cave-in. You can make a little magma flower to try to draw them in. The light should get their attention even without direct line of sight, and unless they're trained, and hardened scouts, a little solidified magma flower will make them curious enough to get closer. Once we drop the cave-in and reveal ourselves, we should have them at our mercy before they can do anything, and they should know it."

"An' if they don't notice, we'll jus' try again wi' th' next batch o' scouts," finishes Ragnar.

Nova isn't sure about this plan. On the one hand, the Guide would love to get more information. That's what this entire scouting expedition is for, after all. Still, it seems dangerous. Although . . . the delvers seem pretty confident. And it doesn't even need to happen right now. If they can't get ready, or if they can't lure the dwellers to the right spot, they'll try again later.

She nods, and the party smiles wide.

"Perfect!" exclaims Aelara with a clap of her hands. "If you'd keep your magma map of their position up-to-date, I'll focus on preparing the ambush site. Just outside seems good; I'll need to make some subtle adjustments to help funnel them."

Nova does as asked, quietly moving the magma drops on her map as the others prepare. Yvonne and Ragnar both check their weapons and armor, making little adjustments as they prepare for the ambush. Aelara faces the wall, slowly moving her arms and waving her fingers as she shapes the stone as she pleases. Nova wishes she could actually watch her work. Once this is done, she's going to need to try to expand her affinities. Earth affinity would just be so useful to have!

"Looks like they're coming back this way to head back to camp. Is everything ready, or are we waiting for next time?" asks Yvonne.

"I'm ready. It won't be quite as clean as I might like, but if we can get them into position, it'll work."

Ragnar readies his weapon and nods at Nova, who understands it as her queue to try a lure. She slips under the surface and creates a pool of magma, which she then starts to sculpt. She goes a little off the script for the lure. Instead of making a flower, she decides to try something a little different. The dwellers mentioned kobolds as something important. Maybe she could make a sculpture of Aranya?

She's glad the Guide's High Priestess usually wears that robe, as it's a lot easier to keep the form stable and she can pretend the slightly melted look is just the fabric flowing with her motions. Of course, she's not making the pose particularly dynamic. Instead, she has the kobold kneeling, hands clasped in prayer, like she's seen her do so many times before.

She almost drops her focus and lets the magma slump when Aelara sends her a pulse, and Nova realizes she stopped keeping the position of the dwellers up-to-date. She quickly remedies that. They get closer, and she wonders if they'll notice the soft glow of the molten rock. For a moment, it seems like they don't, but then they pause before slowly approaching.

Letting the magma start cooling, she puts her attention more on keeping their positions on the map accurate than on her sculpture. She thinks it came out pretty good, but now is not the time for preening over her work. She can feel Aelara stiffen as the footsteps get close enough for the elven Earth mage to detect, and soon, the two dwellers get close enough to see Nova's art.

"Did you drop your cheese kobold?" asks Merrik as he spots the small sculpture, sounding incredulous.

"No . . . I put it in my bag. How did this get here?" The footsteps slow, and though Nova can tell they're looking around with their heads, their feet are still slowly following where their curiosity demands.

"In position," whispers Aelara. "Three. Two. One. Now!"

The ceiling rumbles, and the fake wall crumbles to sand, revealing the two dwellers looking up like the impending cave-in is impossible. They don't see Ragnar and Yvonne rushing forward. The birdwoman grabs Merrik and hurls him behind her, while Ragnar does similar to Lechula, putting them both on the ground, dazed, as the view of the cave vanishes behind falling rubble.

Nova surfaces, adding her glow to the darkness, letting the two dwellers see they were not necessarily saved from danger. Yvonne has her mandible sword pointed at Merrik's neck, while Ragnar has a foot on Lechula's armored chest, hammer raised in case she tries anything.

Aelara takes a few moments to ensure the hidden campsite isn't going to collapse before turning her attention to the two on the ground.

"As long as you cooperate, you won't be harmed. We will be taking you with us, however," she informs the two. Merrik frowns with tight lips, but Lechula must have been more rattled from the ambush than him, as she can't keep her silence.

"Well, at least now we don't have to try to run away."

Chapter 65

Watching, or rather *listening* through Nova is an odd experience. I'd checked in on her a few times while she and the others were scouting, but her spike in anxiety drew my attention. I can't really blame her for being so nervous. That group was plainly different from the very start.

I'm glad the ambush went so well. I just wish I was better able to communicate with Nova so she could ask what I want to know. Of course, she doesn't talk so good, so I'd need to wish for that, too. Ragnar, Yvonne, and Aelara are doing great, though. The two new prisoners don't try to resist as they're stripped of their gear, and Nova even does her part to help make sure they're not too cold. I'm just glad she's above the surface so I can actually see, no matter how poor her actual eyesight is.

My Wyrm Scion rumbles at Ragnar as he ties their hands in a weird way. He gives her a curious look before glancing back at what he's doing, then nods in sudden understanding.

"Ah'm ropin' their fingers. Weave it between, see?" He angles Merrik's hand for Nova to get a better look, and the pale elf sighs with a nod.

"It won't fully stop me from casting, but it makes it a lot more awkward. By the time I can manage anything, they'll be able to react and . . . *discourage* me from trying again."

"Aye, lad, ye've got it. Y' two keep behavin' an' we may not need dem bindings soon."

"So . . . who *are* you?" asks Lechula as she sits not far from Nova.

Yvonne and Aelara look up from the map and exchange glances with Ragnar before my birb resident answers. "Enemies of a certain hostile dungeon down here, though not necessarily enemies of you two. It sounded like you were looking for an excuse to get away from something."

Lechula's eyes widen at that, and even the stoic Merrik raises an eyebrow in surprise. "You're from the surface, then."

Ragnar nods with a grin and finishes tying Merrik's fingers. "Aye, lad. An' yer from th' dungeon we dinnae like."

"Actually . . . we're from Silvervein, but the Maw emancipated us so long ago that it's just history," corrects Lechula.

The Maw? That sounds like a dungeon that would have something like that Harbinger and would treat Aranya's people like dirt.

"So, you two were looking to get away from this Maw?" asks Aelara, stepping forward to let Ragnar take her place at the map.

"Yes," states Merrik simply. He lets the silence continue for a few long seconds until Lechula nudges his foot with her own. He gives her a flat look, which she meets with an encouraging smile, causing him to sigh and relent.

"Fine. If they're inquisitors, they already know enough that we'd be sacrificed anyway. I've been growing more and more dissatisfied with the Great . . . the Maw and Silvervein for a while now, but I've kept quiet about it. Lechula and I got injured in training, and the time healing seems to have opened her eyes, too. I've been looking for a way to get us out since. Lechula wouldn't be able to keep herself hidden for very long."

"Hey!"

"Am I wrong?"

Lechula pouts as Aelara chuckles and motions for Merrik to continue.

"We are on assignment from the Harbinger to help guard and secure the area around the G—the Maw. Our friends were setting up camp while we scouted." He pauses and looks a bit uncomfortable. "What are you going to do with them?"

"Nothing," assures Aelara. "The caved-in section is thick enough they won't be able to hear us, and as long as neither of them has Earth or Wind affinity, they won't be able to detect us, either."

Merrik relaxes slightly at that. "They don't."

"You'll really let them go?" asks Lechula with a mix of hope and fear, and Aelara nods.

"We really will. We're not here to just slaughter. We're going to stop that dungeon, that Maw, with as little pain as possible."

"How?" asks Merrik, a skeptical eyebrow raised, earning himself a laugh from Yvonne.

Looks like she and Ragnar have settled on a route.

"With our own dungeon. Several, really. Thedeim is getting to be something of an expert in fighting other dungeons."

"It'll need to be. The Harbinger killed two scions before the third was able to fell it, and the Redcap is at least as dangerous," warns Merrik.

"Redcap? You'll need to tell us more about that. Later, though; let's get moving. You two have a good path out?" asks Aelara, to the nods of Yvonne and Ragnar.

"Aye. We'll need you t' cut through a few tunnels, but it'll put a' least a mile a passages b'tween us."

"Then we can parallel the graveled path back to the surface. Should take us only a couple days."

"The surface?" asks Lechula with wide eyes, looking like she was just promised a pony.

"The surface," confirms Yvonne. "You'll probably need a couple of days to adjust to the sun and the sky . . . and maybe the cold. It's winter right now, but spring isn't all that far away anymore."

The prisoners clearly want to know more, but the party wants to get moving. With Nova's hearing, I can tell the other two members of the little guard are on the other side of the cave-in trying to figure out what happened.

I wonder if they'll immediately jump to the conclusion their friends were caught in it, or if they'll try not to. I'm thinking they'll come to the conclusion that they are under the rubble pretty soon. Their scouts should come running to a disturbance like that quickly, yeah?

It's about another hour of marching before they break for camp, electing to make a hidden cold camp, though *cold* is relative with Nova there to provide heat and light. As everyone settles in, waiting for the stew to cook, Merrik breaks his silence.

"You're not dwellers. You work like you've all been together a long time, and I doubt your dungeon has three enclaves."

Yvonne smirks and nods. "We're not dwellers, no. What can you tell us about that Redcap?"

Merrik keeps a blank face, but Lechula's shows several emotions before her friend starts speaking. "He's a Metal affinity Fey Scion. Fighting him would be like fighting an army of blades, except an army takes up a lot more room. He likes to make gruesome headwear from his victims. Traitors to the Maw get sentenced to be hatted."

Lechula looks a bit green as she nods, the party all wearing deep frowns. Yvonne speaks up first.

"What other scions does the Maw have?"

"The Harbinger," answers Lechula. "Did it really kill two scions before it could be stopped? Everyone says it was on the brink of total victory before a lucky surprise attack knocked it off-balance enough for it to get overwhelmed."

Nova rumbles with her weird smile. Does having a triple-mandible mouth let her smile three times at once? The frowns of concern from the others flip to grins as Aelara corrects the record.

"The two scions the Harbinger killed were not frontline fighters. Rocky is, and he obliterated the Harbinger after it hurt his friends."

"A Conduit, then. The Redcap is probably one as well. The Maw has consumed other, weaker dungeons, though it hasn't had the chance since the Harbinger came. Can your Rocky withstand the Harbinger and another Conduit?" asks Merrik, though he looks confused when the grins don't vanish.

"Rocky's not the Conduit—Fluffles is. In a straight fight, I can't imagine hardly anything standing up to them working together."

Merrik's eyebrows rise in surprise. "A fourth scion? From the same dungeon?"

He grumbles to himself and his fingers twitch, causing the party to tense. Thankfully, it seems like he's just running some numbers, not trying to cast anything. His thoughtful frown turns into a more ordinary unhappy frown as he finishes his theorycrafting. "Even with a dungeon strong enough to field four scions, distance will make it difficult to strike. If it takes days for your dungeon to react, the Maw will still have the advantage."

"It might take days for him to send more denizens, but it won't take him long to *react* at all. Besides, your numbers are off," corrects Yvonne, glancing at Nova significantly.

Merrik looks doubtful, but Lechula just comes out and says it. "That's not your familiar, then?"

Yvonne laughs and shakes her head. "I've never been especially good with animals nor denizens. Nova there is Thedeim's newest scion."

"Five?" responds Merrik, his fingers twitching again. Yvonne doesn't let him run those numbers for long.

"That's not even half of them."

The two prisoners just stare, Lechula's mouth hanging open in shock while Merrik tries to come to grips with that statement. "Then . . . why not just roll in and subsume the Maw?"

"We said we're not here to slaughter. We need to stop the Maw, but we don't want to just kill everything. We also want to save the kobolds. With a technically independent town nearby, we'll want to minimize collateral damage, too. Right now, we're trying to get as much information as possible while giving as little to this Maw as we can," explains Aelara, causing Merrik's frown to deepen.

"That's . . . going to be difficult. While I'm pretty sure Lechula and I aren't the only ones with doubts, there's a lot of people who actively worship and revere the Maw, and a lot more people who go through the motions just to live. If it comes to fighting, I think most people will side with the Maw, if only because their friends will."

Aelara sighs as the other two grimace. "That's what we're afraid of. But that kind of situation can't be allowed to continue just because it'll be too big of a mess to fix. And the Maw and its Harbinger are too big of a threat to ignore."

Most everyone slumps a bit at the unfortunate reality before us, but one looks filled with determination.

"I want to help," states Lechula, earning looks of confusion and shock from the others. "I don't know how, but I want to help. The people don't know what's going on; the kobolds are slaves and sacrifices . . . We just need to open everyone's eyes, like mine were."

Hmm . . . a propaganda campaign? Difficult to do in a war, but maybe in a siege? Ugh, I really hope it doesn't come down to a siege.

I start tinkering with a few vague ideas as Yvonne smiles and rests a hand on Lechula's shoulder.

"Then please tell us everything you can. The more we know, the more we can do to keep the town out of it. Take some time to try to organize your thoughts, too. We have a few days to get to the surface, and then a few days more to get to Thedeim."

Merrik sighs and speaks up. "I want to help, too. I think we're going to need a lot of information to be able to give you the info you need, though. It sounds like the surface works a lot different than the Maw does."

Yvonne chuckles. "It does, and Thedeim works a lot different than the surface in general, too."

Chapter 66

Down in the tunnels somewhere around that Maw's territory, Nova watches as the party sleeps. The prisoners are sleeping, too, but I think their status will pretty quickly change to defectors, or maybe refugees, after Teemo and Leo get a chance to talk with them. I'd say interrogate, and while that'd technically be accurate, the pale elf and dwarf seem pretty relaxed and accepting of their situation.

It could be a trick, but the kind of paranoid fishing trip they would have to have been sent on is way beyond reason. The Maw would have had to send out a bunch of newbies with directions to split up and make themselves targets, and somehow expect all of them to be good enough actors to fool my scouts. The kind of zeal it'd take to follow that kind of plan is at odds with how Lechula and Merrik are acting.

Merrik might have pulled it off on his own, but Lechula is an open book. Merrik had to wean himself off calling the Maw *Great*, but Lechula had already dropped it. It's probably not the kind of thing to earn yourself a trip to the reeducation camp, but it'd certainly get eyes on her that she wouldn't want.

The way they've been talking about how Silvervein and the Maw work, I'm more convinced than ever that we need to deal with this problem, even if they've confirmed the . . . like fifth-worst-case scenario? I haven't done a hard list, but having a lot more scions and having mutant scythemaw denizens would have definitely made the situation worse. The situation with civilians pretty much is my worst-case scenario, though.

Some fanatic followers, some sympathetic followers, some neutral, but basically everyone believing anything outside is a threat. Counterpropaganda is going to be difficult, if it's possible at all.

"Everything okay, Boss?" asks Teemo from Vernew's shoulder as the two relax. My forces are making great time through the shortcut, and they're all camped out right now.

Teemo's question earns a curious look from the Huntsmistress.

"Hmm?"

"The Boss is just worrying."

. . . Maybe a little. Just processing what we're learning about the Maw.

"That's the dungeon, yeah? I can hear you reacting to what you're hearing through Nova, but I can't hear what she's hearing. I'm only getting like half the conversation."

"Can't imagine what that's like," snarks Vernew with a wide grin, which helps lighten my mood a bit.

Well, the short version is that Yvonne, Ragnar, and Aelara have captured a few people from Silvervein, the town outside the Maw, which is the dungeon we're after. They're technically POWs right now, but they're probably going to be refugees here real quick. I don't think they want to go back.

The town is . . . Well, I'd call it a communist state, but it's probably more a theocratic dictatorship. Less "it belongs to everyone, and I get first pick," and more "it belongs to the Maw, appreciate the scraps you get to keep."

Teemo grunts at the weight of the words I dump on him, but waves off my concern before I can apologize. "That doesn't sound great, but now Leo can actually plan for that, yeah?"

Yeah. I just wish I had advice for what he should try. I'm not exactly a student of history, but I'm pretty sure a society like that will be difficult to change without a lot of growing pains.

"Anything I can help with?" asks Vernew, getting a smile from Teemo.

"Nah, but I might need to leave the comfort of your shoulder and go on ahead to meet with Leo. Yvonne's group captured a few people, and while the Boss can hear what they're saying thanks to Nova, he can't really tell Leo the details on his own. The report should be moving through the rockslides quickly, but I can get there even faster."

"I'm fast! I can help!" she insists, getting to her feet. I consider for a few seconds before giving Teemo the verdict.

"Sorry, Vernew, the Boss needs you here with everyone. Rocky is friendly enough, but he's not going to be able to organize setting up and taking down camp. If you went on ahead and I stayed, you wouldn't be able to give Leo the details. The Boss needs you to make sure everyone gets to the Southwood quickly and safely. The pace today should be good, so mostly try to keep that for everyone, okay?"

"But . . ." she starts, before closing her eyes and taking a deep breath. "Yeah . . . yeah, okay. It'll be like leading a huge hunting party." Her eyes drift over all the dwellers and denizens. "A *really* huge hunting party."

"Hey, it beats latrine duty!"

She gives him a flat look. "Digging it wasn't that bad. Covering it will probably be a bit less fun, but probably better than having to keep track of everyone. There's a reason I leave that kind of stuff to Norloke and Folarn."

Teemo pats her shoulder. "You'll be fine. Rocky'll be here to make sure everyone understands you're in charge with me gone."

A bit of her tension eases at that, and she looks over at the zombie as he tries mixing his Sonic and Fire affinities. It looks really cool, especially with the standing wave he's conjured around himself. I don't think he's going to get to

Lightning with that, but it's cool enough that I don't think he's bothered. If nothing else, it helps him train what he already has.

"Right, Rocky. Not on my own, at least."

Teemo pokes her chitinous cheek. "You alright?"

She tenses up and looks ready to deflect before deflating instead. "I think so? I'm just . . . trying to do better. I don't want to disappoint Him again."

"Hey, Vernew. Look at me." She obeys, getting to see one of the few times Teemo has a serious look instead of the casual smile or smirk he usually wears. "The Boss isn't after perfection, okay? Failing to stop the kids wasn't the problem. Failing to take them seriously was."

Vernew's eyes flick away, and I nudge Rocky to come over for a second as Teemo continues.

"You need to be a proper web as a person, yeah? Too much tension, and you'll snap when an opportunity comes along. Too loose, and the opportunity will slip through instead. Don't overcompensate and snap, okay?" Vernew dejectedly nods before her eyes snap to Teemo in confusion. Rocky grunts a chuckle as he hugs the smol spider, and Teemo smiles.

"Boss says you looked like you could use a hug, and I'm a bit small for that. Thanks, Rocky."

My Zombie Scion grunts and nods, giving Vernew another squeeze before releasing her. She looks a little overwhelmed and a lot relieved as she sinks down into a sitting position, meeting Rocky's eyes as he sits beside her.

"I . . . I think I did need a hug, yeah. Thanks, Rocky. And thank You, Weaver," she finishes quietly, closing her eyes for a few moments. She takes a deep breath and opens her eyes, looking a lot better. "Then . . . I guess you should get going, Teemo? The Weaver is always busy."

Teemo laughs at that and hops to the ground. "You're telling me! You kids be good! I'll see you in about two days!" He gives them a wave, which they both return, before he scurries off down the shortcut. I can feel him working his affinity as he goes, compressing the distance even further than it already is and letting it snap back as he passes.

I watch Vernew through Rocky's eyes. She looks a lot more comfortable now, after that little pep talk.

Never underestimate the power of a hug.

"Think a hug might stop the Maw?" asks Teemo, and I laugh at the idea.

I seriously doubt it. You can suggest it to Leo, though.

"Yeah, but I gotta get there first. Got any advice for humble little Teemo, oh mysterious Weaver?"

Don't make me figure out a way to smack you. Teemo chuckles at my empty threat as I consider his question.

Well, there are a couple things to potentially try. I think you're close to something fundamental with your Spatial affinity, but trying to play with that is something to do while sitting down, I think. Not when you're trying to make good time. Right now, you're just compressing the space around you, right?

"Yeah. It's a lot like making a shortcut or a trail, but those last a lot longer."

Yeah, I can feel it snapping back into place behind you, which is a weird thing to sense. Anyway . . . how about not fully compressing the space around you?

Teemo stops and scrunches his face as he tries to picture it. "What?"

Well, right now, you're making it so you just have to travel less distance, yeah? But if you can unwarp around your feet, I think you can increase your speed, too. Instead of each step being like an inch apart, you could effectively have them be yards apart.

Teemo folds his arms as he tries to wrap his head around that, and I do my best not to think about the math very hard. "That . . . might work? I'm gonna go slow; I don't want to accidentally leave a foot behind or something."

Yeah, that would make it a bit difficult to go fast.

Teemo smirks before concentrating, moving slowly at first. It feels *really* weird when he starts reaching outside of his compressed bubble, but it doesn't seem like it's hurting him. I mentally step back, letting him focus while also letting my mind wander a bit. I make sure to keep my thoughts distant from Teemo, not wanting to hurt him.

I realized like halfway through what exactly I was explaining to him; I'm just glad I could keep my thoughts from running away before I could give him the very basics of the idea. I don't know how well it'll actually work, but I wouldn't want to pop Teemo's head with the full concept of an Alcubierre drive.

Chapter 67

It takes Teemo about a day to get to Leo, which gives him about a day to prep him for the two refugees; I don't see much point in pretending they're anything else at this point. Yvonne and company have already undone Merrik's hand binds. I think the two young adults are a bit too marveled by the stories of the surface to try anything.

It also helps that Lechula is likable. I wouldn't go so far as to call her adorkable, but there is a bit of that thirst for knowledge combined with a bit of awkward innocence. She's mostly interested in getting defense advice from Ragnar, though she'll answer questions for Aelara or Yvonne when they ask.

Merrik is a lot more subdued than Lechula, but there's an intense hunger for knowledge in him, too. He tends to alternate between asking Aelara about magic and asking Yvonne about ranged attacks. Lechula let it slip that he's a Steel mage, and after a deep sigh and a shake of his head, he agreed to give a little demonstration. I was expecting him to be very similar to Berdol, but aside from sharing an affinity, they seem to work a lot differently.

Berdol needs metal around to control, but Merrik basically summons it. He says he technically can manipulate metal that already exists, but it's much easier for him to conjure it. I don't know if that makes him a summoner or what, but whatever he technically is, his techniques sure look effective to me.

He has a couple simple attacks that call a short-lived weapon that appears near his target, swings (or stabs), then vanishes. He also has what I like to think of as a blender attack that fills an area with slashing metal. He calls it a BladeWall; I'd probably call it an unbound blender, but the effect is the same: don't go in.

Ragnar, of course, waded in with a wide smile while Aelara just gave him an "oh you" look and Yvonne shook her head at him. Lechula and Merrik about panicked, but after he dismissed the wall, they saw his beard wasn't even trimmed from the damage. I'm not sure if that makes Lechula and Merrik low level or Ragnar and crew high. Possibly a bit of both, even.

I'm feeling confident in them being refugees after that. If they were spies, they'd probably be a bit nervous after that show, even if only for themselves. The two, instead, seem to be even more relaxed. I'm pretty sure they feel like they have some actual protection from the Maw now. Nova has been noticing them sleeping better, at least.

As for Lechula's class, Ragnar said she was a pretty standard shield bearer without her even saying so. Her look of surprise and his laugh pretty much confirmed it. It's a bit different from his class in that it relies on heavier armor to not take damage in the first place, instead of regenerating a lot of it like Ragnar does. She even asked him about it, though he was pretty sparse on the details.

I get the feeling it's less that he doesn't want to help her and more that he doesn't want to inflict his particular fighting style on anyone else. It sure seems effective, just as it seems like he takes at least a bit of a beating with each fight. It must be sustainable somehow, but I'm not surprised if the guy who works to take all the hits doesn't want to see someone else shoulder all that pain.

I relay all of that through Teemo once he gets to Leo, which takes a good chunk of the night for him to do. Honey takes notes, because of course she does.

Teemo meets Leo's eyes once he finishes regaling him with all the info.

"So, what do you think?"

Leo stands and paces, his ears flicking as he thinks. After a few minutes, Honey buzzes, which seems to pull him from his thoughts, and he gives a tired growl.

"Yeah, 'complicated' is about how the Boss feels, too. Let's break it down a bit, yeah? First, I guess, is: does it change any of the plans for dealing with the Maw?"

Honey does a little mocking dance, and Leo grins and woofs. Teemo snorts before translating.

"They say there needs to be a plan in the first place before it can change." Leo gives a grumble, looking a bit more serious with his reply.

"Still not enough for a real plan yet, hmm? Well, just be careful and don't get caught, but you already know that. Anything in specific you want to ask the two when they get here?"

This time it's mostly Honey who answers, giving a dance and pointing at a sheaf of papers that I'm certain already have a ton of questions. Teemo smirks at my reply and relays it.

"The Boss says to ease up, or else they'll be wanting to seek refuge from us, too. What do you two think of taking them in?"

Leo tilts his head as Honey buzzes in a question mark.

"I mean, not literally. The Boss isn't going to make residents of strangers, no matter how upstanding they seem to be."

Leo nods and sits, his ears flicking for a moment before he gives a quiet bark.

"Fair enough. It's not like anyone is going to try to just send them back. The enclaves might adopt them or something, but otherwise, I guess they'll move into Fourdock and maybe join the adventurers' guild?"

Maybe they'll become cooks instead. They have lots of turns of phrase and idioms involving food.

"Huh." Leo and Honey both give Teemo expectant looks, so he explains after a few moments. "Boss says they might become chefs or something. Lots of food-based sayings."

Honey notes that, while Leo looks thoughtful.

"That give you any ideas, Leo?" My Warden shrugs and chuffs.

"Need to talk to them first? Fair. How about the reinforcements? The basilisks are looking pretty strong. And there's the dwellers . . ."

All three scions look a bit uncomfortable at that, but Teemo powers on. "You can't just leave them here at Southwood. They'll go off on their own."

Leo whines at that and reluctantly nods, causing Honey to droop a bit in the air. Leo *wuffs* and nods at the pile of maps, getting a nod from Teemo.

"Ah. He says he won't know exactly what to do with them until they have a better idea of the cave systems down there. If the battlefield is going to be some big, open cave, that's one thing, but a series of tight tunnels would be another."

Eew, I never considered the possibility of narrow tunnels. It'd be like urban fighting and give the defenders a huge leg up. I don't think the idea of a carbine would really work with something like a crossbow. Bow skills might make the compound bows effective. Either way, it'd probably be a good idea to have them train in tight quarters once they get here.

Teemo relays that, with Leo and Honey both nodding. "They say that's their basic idea until they can make an actual attack plan. It'll also depend on how much the Maw and its forces can shape the battlefield. If they have Earth mages, things could get ugly fast."

Yeah. And if they're not completely stupid, they'll protect any Earth mages with all they've got. Underground, having a monopoly on Earth magic would be like having air superiority: not a whole lot a foe can do if you have it.

My Voice echoes me again, and again, the two planning scions nod. "At least we should have a better idea of what the Maw has access to once they get here and can answer some more directed questions instead of just idle chatter."

Any plans for dealing with that Redcap? I'd suggest cold iron, but nobody seems to consider that a thing.

Teemo shrugs. "Probably need to throw Fluffles at it, especially if it's a Conduit like you said they said."

Leo grunts and *wuffs* as Honey dances in the air, making Teemo tap his chin in thought. "That's a good point. We'll probably want to be ready to face him and the Harbinger at the same time. Fluffles and Rocky could probably take them, but it'd also be a messy fight. Leo suggests keeping Slash with them. The most skeletal outline of a plan is to use those three as part of our main force to keep the Maw's attention, then use a sneakier force to try to head straight for the core."

Oh, that reminds me: should we ask Southwood if he wants to make the Stag a Conduit, send him after the core?

"Hmm. I mean, he'd probably like to, but the Stag isn't exactly . . . sneaky." Leo nods and Honey bobs in the air in agreement.

We can ask. I don't think Hullbreak or Violet are ready for a Conduit right now. Hullbreak would only be able to send the Quartermaster, who isn't exactly built like Solid Snake. Violet might send Onyx, but that'd be a long way from home. She hasn't shown much interest in this fight either, so I think she's wanting to focus on growing and securing what she has instead of trying to get a Conduit.

"Who were you considering, Boss?"

Probably you or Nova. I don't know how sneaky someone would have to be to get all the way to the Maw's core, or if it's even an option. Honestly, if anyone gets the chance, they should take it. Anyone could use the power boost, and I just want to have that dungeon dealt with. It's probably going to be too much of a fight for us to be able to actually decide who gets to do it.

"Me?!" exclaims Teemo, missing the rest of what I said. Leo and Honey nod a third time, and he gives them a glare. "Don't pretend like that's your plan, too!" Leo just grins as Honey digs out a scrap of paper with a list of likely Conduits. She even has Teemo at the top, followed by Nova.

I pat the bond with Honey, glad to have a second opinion for who will likely be the one to take the core. *Did you catch the rest of what I said, Teemo?*

"Yeah, I got it. Hopefully Nova will be the one to get it, but it makes sense that whoever gets a good chance should just take it. The Maw probably won't make it easy on us."

"Does that include me?" asks the Stag as he enters the little clearing Leo and Honey have been using as their base of operations. Teemo smiles and nods.

"If you're gonna be there, yeah! The Boss was considering trying to sneak you in."

The Stag looks a bit surprised at that, tilting his head as he listens to the Southwood. He doesn't look too happy about what he's hearing, but he relays it anyway.

"My Lord says I should remain here, in case this Maw manages to sneak something through. I'd rather go and fight . . . but my Lord is not wrong. I am ill-suited for fighting in caves, especially if they're as tight as you've indicated they could be. He's considered making a second scion for the task, but the mana He'd need to spend to raise it to a decent level would be . . . considerable."

Yeah, probably even by my standards.

Teemo gives an understanding nod. "Still, you want to send some of your illusion foxes along, at least? They won't be as quick as a scion, but having extra sneakiness wouldn't be a bad thing. Maybe they'll even meet the requirement for a Conduit if you make them a scion after they drain the Maw."

The Stag smiles. "My Lord is willing to help, and will happily take what He can from the Maw, but He expects it will be one of yours to finish it. Whatever forces you may wish, my Lord is willing to commit, within reason."

"Cool. Right now, I don't think we have anything set in stone, but the bears and the foxes will probably have good uses in there."

Leo nods at that, earning another smile from the Stag. "Then I shall return to my duties, though my Lord would request I be present at the interrogation of the prisoners. He may have His own insights and questions."

"Probably a good idea, yeah. We could even practice a technique the Boss knows."

"Oh?" asks the Stag, looking interested as my Voice grins.

"It probably won't be too necessary for these two, but good cop/bad cop is supposed to be a good way to get info out of someone. You'd make a good bad cop."

The Stag frowns at that for a moment before his ear flicks, and he sighs. "Explain. My Lord is interested, though the term makes little sense."

Teemo's smile widens, and he hops onto the Stag's head. "This is going to be great, just you wait."

Chapter 68

As the party closes the distance to the surface, Teemo explains the general tone for good cop/bad cop. The Stag still looks confused about the whole idea, but he's willing to try. Teemo even tries to get a few of the illusion foxes to fake an interrogation room like on TV, with a one-way mirror and everything, but I have to shoot the idea down.

Even if the idea of the Stag and Teemo giving significant glances to the mirror and grabbing the hanging lamp to shine in their eyes is funny, I don't think it'll work. For one: light in the eyes might actually hurt the two cave dwellers.

The classic dynamic should work, though with a little tweaking. The two aren't actually in any trouble, so slamming tables and demanding answers probably won't make too much sense. We can still have the Stag play more stoic and suspicious, with Teemo being more friendly; a bit more chaos/lawful than good/bad.

While Teemo and the Stag go over their roles and get set up in the cave Honey did the dissection in, Leo and Honey are occupied with the reinforcements arriving. Rocky and Vernew are at the fore, and my scion takes the chance to catch up with the Warden and Librarian as Vernew does her best to help keep everyone organized.

The denizens are pretty simple to handle, with Leo giving a few sharp barks and a howl to direct them where to go. The dwellers are a bit more difficult, but with the Stag busy, it's kinda up to Vernew to get everyone settled. She's pretty uncertain at first, but with an encouraging squeeze to her shoulder from Rocky, she gets her many feet under herself.

"Alright! Let's get deep enough that we can get this warm gear off, but don't get too comfortable. The Southwood might want us somewhere else."

The other dwellers accept that, and soon, they march off deeper into the Southwood. I poke Fluffles to grab some warm gear to take to the tunnel's entrance, and make sure he knows to get some good hoods, too. Some sunglasses would also be great, but I don't have any of those available.

I might be able to have Teemo explain the concept of polarized light to one of the illusion foxes, but that'd probably take too long. For now, the cave dwellers will have to deal with the cold and the brightness with mundane methods.

Even with a bit of cloud cover today, Nova can see them squinting and shielding their eyes even before they get out of the cave, so I nudge the bond to have her suggest they stop for a few minutes while Fluffles gets there.

"Why is it so bright? And so cold?" asks Lechula as she tries to figure out how to deal with both issues. She wants a hand to shield her eyes with, but she also needs both arms to wrap around herself. Merrik closes his own eyes, deciding full blindness is better than effective blindness. It's probably warmer, as he's not shivering as much as Lechula is.

"That's the surface," supplies Yvonne. "Looks like Nova wants us to wait here?"

My shy little dragon nods, making a little magma image of Fluffles as she scoots a bit closer to Merrik and Lechula.

"Feels like a cold one today," observes Aelara. "Think it'll snow?"

Ragnar shrugs as Yvonne answers. "Maybe, but probably not much. It looks merely overcast out there, instead of there being deep snow clouds."

"I still don't get how ice falling from the ceiling isn't something to worry about," grumps Lechula, earning smiles from the party.

"Aye, was strange t' me, too. Y' git used ta it."

The pale prisoners don't look too convinced, but Fluffles making his entrance keeps their questions in check. His shadow falls over the group, even as his wings make the walls of the cave shine in a multitude of colors. His majestic aura doesn't last too long, however, as he drops the winter gear on the two gobsmacked newcomers.

He hisses a chuckle as they clear their faces, and the party does its best to suppress its mirth. Nova rumbles at him in greeting, earning a bob of the head from Fluffles before he slithers beside her.

"Go ahead and get those on," suggests Yvonne. It takes a few moments for Merrik and Lechula to realize the cloth is clothing and not just blankets or something, then a few seconds to organize everything, and a few more minutes to put everything on, but they're looking a lot more comfortable by the time the march resumes.

Fluffles and Nova chat as everyone walks, Nova even showing him the little sculpture she made of him, now cooled and solidified. I can feel Fluffles's interest and appreciation through the bond, just as I can feel Nova's embarrassment at the praise.

Once everyone enters the Southwood, the two prisoners stiffen a bit and look around, clearly aware they're in a dungeon, and looking a bit nervous about that.

"This is the Southwood, not Thedeim. It's a bit out of the way, but a good example of one of the dungeon varieties," reassures Yvonne. "Fluffles? Where should we take them?"

Fluffles hisses and motions for them to follow, though Nova heads off toward Rocky and the others. It's weird to see Merrik and Lechula both looking so nervous and amazed at the woods around them, but it makes sense. There's a lot of new things going on. They still look a little relieved to see the small cave ahead, though the relief vanishes as Yvonne and the others wave and go their own way, too.

They look at my wingnoodle with apprehension, and even Merrik jumps a bit as Teemo calls from within the shadows of the cave.

"Come along, you two! It's all right; we just want to talk, and we figured this cave would be the best place for it. Outside seems to be a bit distracting for you two, yeah?"

The two steel their resolve and stride into the cave, looking confused once they turn the bend and find it empty. The voice of the Stag comes from behind, one of Teemo's shortcuts letting them get between the two and the exit. Not the most subtle of implications, but getting them a bit off-balance is kind of the point.

"Take a seat wherever is comfortable. My Lord and His ally have much to ask."

Merrik has his emotions mostly in check, but Lechula swallows heavily as she moves to sit near the far wall. The heavy atmosphere shatters as Teemo pops up from the Stag's mane and hops to the end of his muzzle.

"Don't mind him. Well, maybe mind him a bit. This *is* his dungeon. I'm Teemo, Voice of Thedeim, and he's the Stag, Voice of the Southwood."

Lechula looks confused, while Merrik looks suspicious. "A rat? They mentioned a rat Voice, but . . ."

Teemo grins. "You were expecting maybe a dire rat? A plague rat? A swarm? Maybe a giant rat, or one made of lightning that farts tornados?"

The Stag's stoic look cracks slightly as the corner of his mouth twitches upward. The two prisoners look confused.

"Lightning?"

"Tornados?" they ask at the same time. Teemo deflates a little.

"I knew I should have gone with metal and earthquakes. Anyway, Stag, you wanna tell them what kind of situation they're in?"

The Stag regally nods. "You two are prisoners of war in the care of my Lord, the Southwood. While you will not be harmed, you will not necessarily be *helped*, either."

"He means you'll be fed and kept safe, but probably kept in the dark. If you two can give us info, though . . ." Teemo gives the Stag a pleading look. The larger scion sighs and leans into the role as he finishes the sentence.

"If you two can give us information that will help in this war, Lord Thedeim is willing to grant you asylum or refugee status. My Lord is not against offering similar, but he has no enclaves to house you."

"What if we want to go back?" asks Lechula. The scions exchange a look before Teemo answers.

"I mean, after the war is over, sure. But that might not be a good idea, and it definitely won't be a good idea until after the fighting is over."

"What if we wish to simply leave?" asks Merrik.

The Stag answers.

"You will be taken to Fourdock and released, though the winter will likely keep you there for another month at least."

"Not released back into the underground?"

Teemo shakes his head. "Nope. Again, once the fighting is over, you're free to go wherever you like, including back to the depths. But you know too much to be given a chance of getting back to the Maw. Even if you swear not to say anything, the Harbinger has mental stuff. That's a major security risk."

Merrik doesn't look happy, though that seems to be his default look. Lechula, however, looks disappointed.

"But how are we supposed to help?"

"By giving us as much information as possible," answers the Stag. "My Lord prefers to minimize bloodshed, as does Lord Thedeim. The Maw must be dealt with harshly, but the people may yet be salvaged. It will depend on you two telling us what we need to know to be able to maximize our effect against the Maw and minimize it against the dwellers . . . townsfolk."

"But . . . I don't think we know anything too important. We've seen a little more than average, but nothing big."

"I've researched and investigated, but I only have slightly more knowledge than Lechula," admits Merrik.

Teemo just smiles and pulls out Honey's big list of questions. "Even common knowledge can imply a lot. Just knowing where the main Maw cultists congregate will give us a place to start."

"And you're sure that'll help?" asks Lechula, looking uncertain.

"Yes," answers the Stag, with Teemo nodding.

"Definitely. The Boss says knowledge is power. Even the simplest question, the simplest answer, could be what tips the scales for us."

Lechula and Merrik exchange a look, then nod before the pale dwarf speaks. "We'll do it."

"Great! Let's get to it, then!" Teemo shuffles the sheets as Honey and Leo enter, with the latter bringing a lot of blank paper for the former to take notes with. "Let me see . . . Ah, here's the start." Teemo pauses as he reads it, looking to the Librarian. "Really, Honey?"

She bobs up and down in affirmative, causing Teemo to shake his head. "You're the one with Knowledge affinity. Alright. So . . . what did you two have for breakfast before heading out into the caves?"

The pair from the Deeps look confused, but take a few moments to think back. I think it's a weird question to start with, too, but as the questions flow, their memories seem to naturally follow, bringing more details than I would have expected. Honey dutifully takes notes as Leo gives her more paper.

The war has truly begun, whether the Maw knows it or not.

Chapter 69

The Redcap

The unsettling Fey Scion oversees the excavation, his placid blue eyes at odds with the gruesome thing atop his head. He likes the shadow it casts over his face, though he needs to refresh it soon. This hat was a singular masterpiece, in his opinion, but time marches on, and it is spoiled now. Such is the ephemeralness of art, he supposes.

His eyes wander the workers, wondering if one of them would make a suitable hat. Unfortunately for the macabre artist, while the work goes slowly, none of the workers are slacking. He could make a hat anyway, but the Master would punish him for it. Wasting food, plucking it before it's ripe, would be an affront. He could hardly plead ignorance, especially not after dressing down the Harbinger not long ago for wasting food so wantonly.

Perhaps after the cave-in is cleared? His lips curl into a smile at that. Yes, the material will no longer have an urgent task to do.

He eyes the rubble and flicks a few blades to where the workers have marked. Some cleave through the stone like it's mere flesh, while others spear in to provide support. The workers resume their tasks, clearing what is now loose and figuring out how to quickly and safely clear what is still supported.

It's not the worker's safety that the Redcap is concerned about, however. It is the safety of whatever the rubble has buried. The trainees have started their scout training, and two are missing. The Harbinger declared them dead, crushed beneath the stone, after personally examining the memories of the other two scouts. The warning about wastefulness was at least heeded, as neither had to be sent to the enclave for healing, but the Redcap thinks the two scouts are wrong.

He smells no blood here. Even through the rubble, he should be able to detect *something*, yet all is clean. The Harbinger, of course, argues they are buried too deeply, pulverized and perhaps turned to mud from mixing with the debris. But the Master is uncertain, so has allowed the Redcap to dig for the remains.

He hopes to find nothing, and so prove the Harbinger's incompetence once again. First, it failed to take the surface, even after petitioning to only use its vaunted least for the campaign. How it expected to be victorious while leading things literally called *least*, the Redcap will never understand. Second: it wasted the potential of the first trainees, not even doing anything with the bodies. Such a waste for them to all be relegated to fertilizer, none of them having the opportunity to become a new hat.

If the Harbinger has failed here, it will be a third time the transferred scion failed the Master in a short period. While even the Redcap admits he probably won't be permitted to make a hat of the scion, he can still lower the influence it has on the Master.

When the outsider first arrived, the Redcap was all too happy to have a proper challenge! Oh, that day . . . He should recreate another scene from the battle with his new hat, once he makes it. His current one was a monument to suffering, which was an interesting challenge, but he should never forget his roots.

White teeth show in the shadows of the Redcap's face, encouraging the workers to remain diligent, though he hardly notices them. Forcing the Harbinger to help with his new hat would be a good start for the punishment it deserves. Its advice was excellent at first, giving the Master such wonderful power. Now, however, the Harbinger seems determined to squander that power.

The Redcap thinks the scion just wants to steal the Master's power, like rot stealing away food; like time stealing away the glory of a good hat. It is slow and insidious, taking just a little here and there, and once you realize it's ruined, it's too late to do anything meaningful. The rot has spread too far; nothing can be salvaged.

The Harbinger insists the Redcap is just being jealous. It's not wrong, but he's not blind to what the other scion does. If he can find evidence of another failure, the Master will have to recognize the Harbinger is fallible, and maybe even consume it. Then maybe the Master will raise a Metal elemental scion instead of the Harbinger.

He's pulled from his imagination by one of the workers, the lead, nervously approaching. "Yes?" he asks with a smooth voice, yet the worker flinches anyway. It's no matter; artists are never understood.

"Uh . . . M-Master Redcap? We've found something, but we don't know what it means. We can take more time to clear the area, or you can come take a look now? You said you wanted to be informed as soon as we found anything."

"Good. Take me to it, and explain on the way."

The worker takes him to a tunnel through the rubble that forces him to almost crawl. Even the dwarf has to bend low to get through, though he explains as ordered.

"This team has been trying to get through the rubble so we have a better idea of how large the cave-in was. We haven't found the wall nor the other side, but we did find . . . well, a kobold."

The blue eyes of the Redcap show confusion at that. "A kobold was crushed? How did it get out? Why don't I smell the blood?"

"Ah . . . sorry, not a real one. A sculpture, or maybe a carving of one? It seems to be part of the cave floor, though the stone is a different type than the rest of the cave."

A carving? Somehow, that makes even less sense than an actual kobold being caught in the collapse. A real kobold would be easily explained: it escaped. It doesn't happen often, but it's possible. Someone carving a kobold into the cave floor makes no sense. He needs to see it.

"How much farther?"

"Just up ahead, Master Redcap. I'll let you go first. There's not much room for me to try to get out of your way once in there."

The dwarf presses himself into a divot, and the Redcap can soon see the truth in the worker's words. The opening is hardly enough for a cupboard, let alone both a dwarf and the Redcap himself. He also sees the confusion the worker had about it being a sculpture or a carving. It's a small statuette of a praying kobold, looking at first like it's simply sitting on the stone of the cave floor.

Looking closer, the robe flows smoothly into the floor, and a gentle tap confirms it is firmly attached. If it was carved, it was from a stalagmite.

As he takes in the piece, he starts doubting it was carved. He sees no toolmarks, though there are a few chips from the ceiling collapsing on it. He's surprised it managed to survive the cave-in.

He's also growing to appreciate the artistry involved. Whoever did it seems to be new, inexperienced. They attempted to capture detail, but lacked the practice to truly bring them into focus. The imperfections draw his eye, and he wonders if they're deliberate choices or some limitation of the medium or the artist. It's like it was dripped on, and the drips were then captured.

Perhaps it was a stalagmite, after all? While that would explain the odd blemishes, it would also make it even less likely to have survived the collapse. It would have had a matching stalactite above it, primed to fall with the rest of the ceiling.

He ponders the mystery for a few more seconds before pulling out a blade and slicing the odd piece of art from the floor, turning to the dwarf in the divot.

"You said this is a different stone than the cave's?"

"Uh . . . yes, Master Redcap," he answers with a gulp, his eyes on the blade used to free the statuette. "The cave is fairly soft, but that stone is much harder. I have a worker with Earth affinity, if you'd like more detail?"

The Redcap shakes his head and motions for the dwarf to lead the way out. "No. Just knowing it is different is all I need. It was deliberately done by an artist with talent but little practice. It's also of a foreign kobold," he states, having noticed the lack of chains. He doesn't bother explaining to the worker about that, instead opting to think while he's led back to the cave at large.

He will need to know more about the stone, after all.

"Bring the Earth-affinity worker. I need to know if these imperfections would be an unavoidable part of shaping stone with magic." He doesn't hear the reply as he resumes studying the enigmatic piece of art in his hands. Perhaps it's a shrine or an offering to the Master? Most would carve a feast instead. On the other hand, kobolds are the Master's favorite.

No chains, though . . . a sacrifice from outside? It's been some time since outsiders were seen in these tunnels, which would explain the drips. Ah, but didn't the worker say it was different from the stone of a stalagmite?

"Y-You wished to see me, M-Master Redcap?" The pale dwarf goes even paler as the blue eyes lock onto her.

"Yes. This is all one variety of stone, correct? And not the type stalagmites are made of?"

"C-Correct, Master Redcap. The stone of this cave is much more susceptible to erosion. The stone of that sculpture is usually deeper than this layer."

"Hmm. These imperfections"—he leans forward to point out with a small blade, causing the worker to flinch away for a moment—"are they a byproduct of working earth directly with magic?"

The worker tries to keep her fear in check as she looks, and confusion starts to slowly erode her terror. "N-No, Master Redcap. I've never tried to sculpt like that, but texture is very easy to control. It really does look like stalactite drip, but that stone wouldn't do that . . ."

"Hmm," he repeats and stands, the blade vanishing. "Resume the excavation and keep an eye out for stones that don't belong, as well as corpses." The dwarf nods and scurries off while the Redcap turns the statuette over in his hands. He still feels it's the work of an amateur, but there is definitely a spark of talent in it. Perhaps one of the workers made it?

He snorts at that idea. It's possible, but if any of them had the talent and desire to craft like this, they'd be employed as a carver, not a simple worker. It's possible they've slipped through the cracks, but he doubts it.

He needs to meet this artist, even if they are an outsider like he thinks they would be. Finding them is not as important as damaging the Harbinger in the Master's eyes, but it's not too far behind.

It's so rare he gets a chance to trade techniques and tips with an artist.

Chapter 70

The Harbinger

The amorphous mass of eyes, teeth, and tentacles glowers as it stalks the tunnels, making itself look even more unpleasant than usual. That's fitting, as it's feeling rather unpleasant at the moment, and the last thing it needs is someone trying to engage with it right now.

It had thought things couldn't get any worse after being saddled with the responsibility of training the applicants for the Maw's army. Oh, to be so blissfully ignorant again.

It had actually started enjoying the training, much to its own surprise. While it takes so much longer than simply dominating the minds and forcing the body to do as it's told, the Harbinger has to admit the trainees last longer when they use their own will to carry out the instructions.

Most of the trainees are doing well. There was really only one group having any difficulties with the Harbinger's training: Lechula's group.

It growls and slams a tentacle into the wall in frustration as it continues to prowl the tunnels. It should have snuffed her when it had the chance. Potential is one thing, but to have the audacity to try to *escape*?! She even took a Steel mage with her!

The cave-in was a brilliant move on her part, it has to admit. Only someone as spiteful as the Redcap would try to recover the body—or bodies, if one counts the Steel mage—so now the Harbinger is being blamed for two defectors! It can even feel the Maw weighing if it should consume it or not!

It wouldn't be so simple, but the very idea proves the Harbinger needs to do something soon to prove its usefulness.

Capturing the defectors would be a good start, but the Harbinger knows they're long gone by now. It's not roaming the tunnels to find them. No, it's roaming to think. Not to sulk, like the Redcap suggested—think! But what can it do? It convinced the Maw to upgrade the spawner for lessers before this whole debacle, but there are not enough spawned yet to do anything significant.

Its many mouths frown as it fails to come up with anything. There are no other dungeons nearby to quickly raid, nor other settlements. The Maw has kept its territory rather clean. The only thing the Harbinger can come up with is to send an expedition deep to bring back something powerful for the Maw to consume. But that will take time, and the Harbinger isn't certain how much it has to play with right now.

Its frustration is interrupted by the feel of a mind nearby. It pauses in its patrol to make sure it knows where it is. There should be no elves nor dwarves in this area. That's part of the reason the Harbinger chose this section of tunnels to think in. Some invader? There shouldn't be any with enough of a mind for it to notice like that.

Curious and cautious, the Harbinger makes its way toward the mind it senses. As it gets closer, it's more and more confident it is not one of the followers of the Maw. It feels too simple for that.

It's also difficult to pinpoint. The Harbinger could snuff it out, but presenting whatever it is to the Maw could get it back in its good graces. Whatever it is, it doesn't seem to notice the Harbinger closing in.

After several minutes, the Harbinger realizes it's not that it's not been noticed but that the intruder thinks itself safe. It's buried within the rock. It can feel the intruder's apprehension as it gets nearer, but not the kind of panic the intruder should have if it thought the Harbinger could actually get to it.

Well, it's time to stop playing.

The Harbinger seizes the mind before growling in frustration as it simply collapses. Too much force, of course. A weak mind like that can't withstand a firm grip like the Harbinger's. It will need to be gentler. It didn't get much out of the mind before it succumbed, but the Harbinger doubts it was alone. It resumes moving through the tunnels, now actively seeking minds.

It doesn't take it long to find another, and the Harbinger is more careful as it stalks this particular prey. It wouldn't do to lose it because it sensed the death of the first. Thankfully, it seems to be unaware or uncaring about what happened to the other one.

This time, the Harbinger slams a cage around the mind instead of directly grabbing for it. The mind, of course, panics, slamming itself against the unbreakable bars.

The Harbinger lets it struggle as it moves closer, once again finding the mind to be inside the stone. What a strange invader. The Harbinger constricts the cage carefully, restraining the mind more and more, slowly removing its ability to meaningfully resist.

Surface, it orders, then immediately sighs. The mind shattered from the order. It snuffs the pathetic thing to ensure it can't warn any of its fellows should it somehow slip the Harbinger's grasp, and resumes seeking.

The next one is caged and restrained properly, and the Harbinger considers how to proceed. An order will simply overwhelm it like the other.

Well, as a simple mind, a little encouragement might be all the Harbinger needs. It considers trying pain to force compliance, but suspects that would just break this mind like the other two. Instead, it takes the time to craft a desire for the simple mind. The Harbinger is no threat to it. It should surface and meet a new potential companion.

It is careful not to make the compulsion too strong so as not to break the fragile little mind. It can't take too long with crafting the desire, though. Take too long, and the mind will break itself in its attempts at escape.

It introduces the desire to the mind, and is surprised how quickly and utterly it rejects it. Fierce loyalty and a sense of betrayal radiate from the mind at the concept, firmly repudiating the idea that the Harbinger could possibly be a friend. The Harbinger snuffs it before it can tear itself apart. It doesn't need that kind of distraction while it thinks.

It considers the Harbinger a threat on a fundamental level. It must know what the Harbinger is, at least in part. If it *actually* knew how much of a threat it can be, it wouldn't happily sit in the wall while it nears. It also doesn't want to associate with the Harbinger, as that'd be a betrayal on a fundamental level as well. So the Harbinger is a threat not only to the mind but to what the mind holds dear.

It goes over the possible threats that would fit that profile, but it has the same problem as trying to find something useful for the lessers to do. The only thing that could even possibly know the power of the Harbinger . . .

Ah. Of course. The surface isn't as shortsighted as it seemed. A denizen would have exactly the kind of loyalty the Harbinger felt. It'd also explain how such a simple mind could be working for some great purpose.

Its mouths open wide in grins, profane tongues licking at nonexistent lips.

The surface dungeons are searching for the Maw. They may have even found it by now. This is the Harbinger's chance to reestablish itself.

It swiftly continues down the tunnels and cages the next mind it finds, this time in the ceiling. It takes its time, studying it and learning what it can. While the mind is properly terrified the entire time, it doesn't understand what the Harbinger is doing. If it did, it'd break itself rather than suffer what the Harbinger will do to it.

It studies and notes the connections from the mind to the body, figuring out and separating motor functions from higher thought, bodily processes from desires. Once the mind is mapped, the Harbinger makes its move. The mind is severed from the body and quickly snuffed. Ordinarily, the Harbinger would relish in the torment of sensory deprivation, but it has more pressing concerns right now.

Piloting a body is always awkward at first, especially when the Harbinger doesn't quite know what it looks like. It can make some guesses, thanks to the connections, but they are unlike anything it's seen before. It wills the body to surface, letting the muscle memory drive it. It learned long ago to let things like that guide its puppets.

It moves slowly, but soon, a small pile of rubble falls from the ceiling, and the Harbinger can see what it's captured. A living rockslide? Hmm . . . a type of Earth elemental.

It tries to get a feel for the essence of the dungeon it came from, but it's a lot harder to do with a denizen than with a scion.

The Harbinger grins as it moves back down the tunnel, toward the first of the corpses. It should be able to use the puppet to get the bodies to use as proof, and then take the Redcap down a notch or two. The surface is coming for them, and if not for the tireless efforts of the Harbinger, they might have been taken completely unawares! But now the Harbinger knows what to look for, it can make sure the spies only report back what it wants them to.

Chapter 71

I let my attention wander as Lechula and Merrik are questioned. The two have really loosened up, though it's a bit more difficult to tell with the elf than the dwarf. Lechula happily talks about life in Silvervein, though she gets significantly less happy whenever she notices another disturbing fact about life there. Merrik gives his own stories as well, and adds wry commentary on Lechula's accounts, too.

Honey takes diligent notes the whole time, gleaning tidbits from the innocuous talk. Silvervein seems to be pretty similar in size to Fourdock, for example, but they don't have anything like the adventurers' guild. Most townspeople are craftspeople or other working classes, with only the guard and the clergy having any really appreciable levels, or at least any appreciable fighting ability.

Unsurprisingly, a lot of people have food-related professions. Food is pretty big for the Maw, which probably shouldn't be too surprising either. What is a bit surprising is that the Maw and its clergy seem to follow the rules for food. They don't just stuff their faces, definitely liking to take their time with a good meal. The Maw also seems to take it as a personal affront if anyone starves, so I guess it gets a single mark in the positive column.

The clergy are fanatical to the Maw and seem eager to feed it anything they can, including townsfolk that don't pay their taxes. So . . . yeah, the Maw isn't getting any more positive marks, I expect. Maybe if it has chocolate, but I seriously doubt that.

From Honey's notes, it sounds like we're looking at a lot of cramped tunnels rather than a few open caverns. That's . . . going to be a problem, if true. It'd make sense, too, considering the leech-headed things. In open ground, they weren't too difficult to pick off at range. In a tunnel, though, they'd be a nightmare. With how they can dig, they'd even make decent sappers to collapse the tunnels enemies are in.

It also might make it more difficult to sneak in. My wyrms will have to weave around tunnels to get where they want to be, and any enemy Earth mages will be able to spot them. Teemo's shortcuts might be our best bet for getting inside their guard.

On the other hand, it could make it easier to attack. A couple basilisks would be real tough for even a swarm of those abominations to get past. They don't even have any metal in them, so the soldiers, guards, clergy, or whatever will have few options to deal with them. I might need to get a bigger group of tunnelbores up here so we can make our own tunnels.

The Metal affinity is going to make things difficult for my dwellers. From how the two talk, nobody is going to be pulling a Magneto, but the metal gear my dwellers have will still be a lot less effective than I might have hoped. The Maw apparently has Metal affinity, so all the denizens are going to have it. It'd probably be a very bad idea to send my dwellers to try to face them.

Unfortunately, that means my dwellers will probably have to fight the guards and such, who will only *mostly* be Metal affinity. I'm sure Teemo will explain the problem to my dwellers, and I'm almost positive they'll still insist on fighting.

I'm glad Leo will be figuring out where they should go, because I have no idea. I should probably have Teemo give him some ear scritches or something as thanks for shouldering that particular burden, too. I know he's the best for the job, but that still makes me feel like I'm just dodging responsibility.

Yvonne

"So, wha' next?" asks Ragnar as he relaxes against a tree. He looks pretty happy there, but Yvonne and Aelara both know he's a bit anxious to do more. Yvonne feels the same way, and she'd wager Aelara does, too. The birdwoman glances over to Nova, who is still following them around, but she doesn't seem like she has any ideas, either.

"I don't know," sighs Aelara once the silence stretches on too far for her liking. "We should probably take some time to recover and resupply, but after that . . ." She trails off.

"We could scout more?" suggests Yvonne, but nobody really acknowledges the idea. By the time they get back to being near the Maw, the other adventurers should start returning. They could get more information, but the rockslides should soon be in position to relay reports much quicker.

Ragnar grunts, expressing a bit of everyone's frustration as he closes his eyes, looking like he's going to try to catch a nap. After a few moments, he gives a thoughtful hum and opens one eye.

"We could organize th' returnin' adventurers."

"That's a good idea," compliments Aelara with a smile, and Yvonne nods in agreement.

"If we can organize their reports, we can tell Thedeim and either send a copy to the guild with whoever doesn't want to go back down there, or take it back ourselves," she reasons, then glances at Nova. "Do you think Thedeim would give us whatever information his rockslides are gathering, too?"

The wyrm rumbles in thought as she toys with a blob of magma, doodling with the molten rock as she considers. She gives an uncertain nod after a few seconds.

"We'll need t' bug Teemo fer the details anyway. An' fer paper."

Aelara takes a moment to dig through her pack before agreeing. "Yeah. I have some soft leather for maps, but not nearly enough for all the adventurers' reports."

"I'll go ask after sunset. I'd imagine they'll take a break with the questions around then. In the meantime, we should see if any of the other adventurers have come back yet. We returned pretty quickly, but we also went pretty deep. There could be a couple groups around."

Yvonne thinks back to the many adventurers that came along, wondering which groups could have returned early. She remembers at least a few were planning to explore the shallower caves, so they might be back already.

Ragnar gets to his feet and stretches. "Then le's go!"

With nothing else to do, they set out. It doesn't take long for Yvonne to smell the smoke of several campfires, and soon, the party exits into a large clearing. Yet, instead of adventurers, they find Thedeim's dwellers.

"Oh, they're already here?" slips from Aelara in surprise. They all knew the dwellers would be coming eventually, but it's still a bit of a shock to see the spiderkin and ratkin milling about. They're all trying to put on a brave face, but their nerves are obvious to the experienced band of adventurers. The camp looks in good condition, at least, and even with nerves, morale seems high.

"Lady Yvonne! Ragnar! Aelara!" Three heads turn to see the familiar form of Vernew leaping through the air toward them, clearly happy to see them. "I heard you were participating, but I didn't expect to see you all! How's everything going?"

"Please, just Yvonne," starts the undead birdwoman, just as she does every time Vernew or the other denizens call her a lady. "And things seem to be going well. We just came back from scouting, and we found a couple sympathizers. The scions are talking with them right now."

"Ooh, sympathizers? Do you think they know some secret entrance we can all slip through and take the dungeon without a fight?"

Ragnar chuckles and shakes his head. "Nay, lass. They're no elites, jus' soldiers, really."

"Though they still know a lot more than we did," admits Aelara. "The dungeon is called the Maw, for example. It's also Metal affinity, which will make things a bit difficult."

Vernew takes a moment to absorb that before quietly swearing. "Tangled web . . . Do you think Lord Thedeim will tell us to go home?" she nervously asks. Yvonne considers what she knows about him before responding.

"I'd imagine he'll try to give you the option to, but he won't try to force you. It'll be more dangerous than expected, but I don't think anyone really came here expecting everything to be safe."

Vernew sighs and sags a bit in relief. "Good. Good. So, anything I can help you with?"

"Have any other adventurers come by? We're going to try to organize their reports so they can get back out quicker," explains Aelara.

“They’ll probably be attracted by the smoke from your campfires,” Yvonne follows up.

Vernew folds a set of arms as she taps her spear on the ground in thought. “None that I’m aware of. Are you three going to stick around here for a while, then?”

“If y’ don’ mind?”

Vernew smiles wide. “I don’t mind at all! You’re Lord Thedeim’s chosen party! We’d all be happy to have you share our fires, especially if you share some stories in return!”

Yvonne smiles at that, deciding to ignore being called Thedeim’s chosen party. “Then we’d be delighted. I know Ragnar is always looking for new vict—I mean, a new audience for his stories and jokes.”

“Har har,” the dwarf deadpans, but he can only keep the act up for a few seconds before the facade cracks.

“Just don’t accept any of his challenges, be they fighting or drinking,” warns Aelara, earning an indignant “Oi!” from Ragnar.

Vernew grins wide and lays an arm over his shoulder. “I won’t, but I know a few suckers who’d leap at a challenge. Cut me in, and I’ll encourage a few of them.”

Ragnar grins wide as Yvonne and Aelara exchange a worried glance. There’s no hope of avoiding shenanigans now. All the two can try to do is minimize the impending disaster.

Chapter 72

Teemo gives me a mental poke to get my attention, pulling my focus out and away from toying with some composite ideas. I've seen Queen working on what looks like one using spider silk and lacquer, and I've been doodling ideas for how to get some carbon fiber going. I'm pretty sure that'd all be on Queen to manage, anyway.

"You probably want to hear this part, Boss."

Sorry, right. What do I need to hear?

"The Maw's denizens."

That certainly gets my attention, and Teemo chuckles as he motions to Lechula and Merrik. "Could you repeat that? The Boss was busy with something else, but now you have his full attention."

The female dwarf looks a bit uncomfortable at that, reaching toward her beard for a moment before forcing it down. "Uh . . . the Maw's denizens. Well, almost everyone in Silvervein has fought at least a couple of them. They pretty much need to, to get their class, right? Even the crafters. It has two types of spawners, and I think multiple of them, too? It has fey and elemental, and at least one of each is maxed out."

Merrik speaks up to give a bit more information. "I have personally seen at least three spawners, and I don't think they're maxed. I'm not an expert, though. I saw two elementals and one fey, but from the numbers in and around the Maw, I'd expect at least one more for fey. The Redcap was his first scion, and I don't imagine it would invest in a fey spawner like that and not keep its numbers on par with the elemental ones."

"They keep a lot of the details pretty secret," admits Lechula. "I'm pretty sure I saw a different fey spawner than Merrik, but we didn't get our classes together, so it's hard to say." She pauses as Honey scribbles, letting my Librarian catch up. She soon moves to a new sheet and buzzes her readiness, and Lechula continues.

"I'm pretty sure the weakest of the fey are needleslinks. They always make me think of weird beetles, but . . . there's not much resemblance. They have four legs and one little weird arm thing, with their needlelike head on a long neck. They have a smooth, shiny body, but stepping on them is usually enough to finish one off.

"They don't do much damage on their own, but they like to smear the needle with dirt and other things. They're usually not dangerous immediately, but it can take days to recover from a delve if you encounter a swarm of them, and they do usually swarm. They don't fly, at least.

"Bladesprites do. They have small, thin bodies, and one weird foot/hand thing. On their backs, they have bladed wings, shaped kinda like axes, but a lot thinner. The whole thing is about hand sized. They sometimes swarm, but I think a swarm is one of the higher spawns.

"They like to charge at targets, flying in a straight line, then close their wings and flip over, hitting like a throwing hatchet. The swarms sometimes try to surround someone and slice them up like that, but I think they tend to get in each other's way when they do that. Or they weren't trying too hard to kill anyone when I delved."

Lechula gets lost in thought at that for a few moments, wondering if the Maw was being magnanimous or if the bladesprites are just kinda stupid. I'm going to assume any bladesprite swarm will be similar in power to that BladeWall spell Merrik showed off, and from Honey's notes, I think she's on the same page.

My bee finishes her scribblings and buzzes to get Lechula back on track.

"Oh! Sorry. Uh . . . I think the bolties would come next?" she asks, looking to Merrik. He shrugs in response.

"In rough order of estimated power, I'd say so."

Lechula nods at that and returns her focus to Honey and the other scions. "Bolties, then. I'm pretty sure they're a type of brownie? I don't know enough about fey in general to really say. They're around two feet tall and are pretty thin and wiry, but with oversized, clawed hands. Instead of getting into melee to slash, they launch their claws like darts. They sometimes will taint them like the needleslinks, but they're big enough to be dangerous even without that."

She pauses again to think.

"I only fought a couple. They're thin enough to be able to hide in cracks and crevices and stuff, but tend to just stand there and shoot if they have the option once the fighting starts. Then . . . I'd put the bladesprite swarms . . ." She shudders as her thoughts land on the next threat.

"Then the pricklethorns. They're only a little shorter than a dwarf, but just as stocky. They're covered in small hooks and barbs, and have weird, wide forearms, like small shields. Their hands are too stubby to really hold a weapon, but they make good fists. I've never fought one, but I heard about a couple people who tried. It, uh . . . It sounded like you should try to keep your distance.

"The last ones are the thinlinks. They look like a really lanky elf covered head to toe in chains. I've only ever seen the chains, but I've only seen one once, and I didn't want to get its attention by staring. Rumors say they use the chains to grab and choke, or sometimes pull, and just one can be a threat to a full party."

Honey scribbles as I take that in, comparing it to my own spawners. It sounds a bit like the progression for my spiders, and they're probably physically focused like mine. I consider my potential countermeasures as Lechula leans back against the wall, letting Merrik step forward with what he knows.

"I've dealt more with the elementals than the fey. The weakest, easily, are the living caltrops. They like to lie in wait rather than actively attack, though they will sometimes try to trip someone to make them fall onto the little spikes. Metal boots don't hinder them much.

"After those . . . the lodewisps. They're floating, rough spheres of metal and can attract or repel metal at will. They probably won't see much use in this fight, though. When I encountered them, they were always alone. I believe they can't exclude anyone or anything from their influence, so deploying them in the fight would disrupt the Maw's forces at least as much as your own.

"Rust elementals I would put next. They look like a roiling mass of scrap, and while they can hit hard if given the opportunity, their main threat is in their ability to rust metals with a touch. The guards are always complaining about their new sword getting ruined after encountering a rust elemental. If you don't have anything metallic, they're not much to worry about." He pauses and frowns before moving on to the next elemental.

"Sliverstorms *are* a threat. They look like a gnashing maelstrom of needles and razors, and if that's all they were, that'd be bad enough. But they feed on metal, making themselves bigger. An armored opponent would find himself minced as his own armor unraveled like a cheap cloak to feed the sliverstorm. Keeping them away from metal will lessen the threat, but they are still dangerous even without making themselves bigger.

"Then there are the iron maidens. I don't think they'll be on the battlefield, but they will be abundant within the Maw itself. As far as I know, they can't move around, but they can be exceptionally dangerous. They will camouflage themselves to look like the floor or wall, or something else innocent, and usually leave a bit of gold or other valuable metal as bait.

"When a hapless delver thinks they've found a nice treat, they instead *become* the treat as the maiden snaps around them. They come in a lot of varieties, too, and I've heard them sometimes called steel mimics. I've heard of ones that disguise themselves as chandeliers, or even as chairs or doors, only to rapidly engulf their victim when they reveal themselves."

He sighs before continuing. "But I think the most dangerous of the Maw's denizens are the forgemasters. They look like crude statues of dwarves, or maybe dwarves in crude metal armor. They are Metal-affinity mages, and tough to kill.

"They will support and repair the denizens, manipulating the metal directly, without needing any fire. They will also hinder or even kill opponents wearing anything metal, twisting armor and weapons to terrible effect. They are rare, but the Maw will certainly use every single one it has if a fight comes to it."

I digest that as Honey scribbles, but Teemo has a question before either I or Honey can come up with a response.

"What about the weird leech-headed things?"

Merrik and Lechula exchange a glance, with Lechula looking a bit embarrassed and Merrik looking uncertain as he answers.

"I've only heard rumors. Everyone knows the Harbinger has a spawner, but I don't know anyone who's actually tried to fight what it produces. The rumors call them least, but don't say much. Dergol said a friend of his heard a drunk ranting about 'monstrous lessers,' but the guards showed up before he could give any details. I don't know how much I'd trust that as a source, but there you go."

That doesn't sound good. The rest of the info sounds great, though. Most of my denizens shouldn't be outright countered by anything, and I think the wyrms and basilisks will be a great counter to the swarmy things.

I'll need to watch through Leo's eyes as he and Honey start working on our plan to deal with everything. Those pricklethorns and sliverstorms both sound pretty nasty, especially if they have forgemaster backup. We'll also need to be aware of the least getting used as sappers and tunnelers to get behind our positions or collapse them outright.

Before all that planning, though, I think it's time to officially change the status of Lechula and Merrik.

Teemo hops onto the Stag's head to whisper to him, and he nods.

"I and my Lord agree, Voice Teemo. While it would be wise to await confirmation from other sources, these two have been very cooperative. My Lord would like to offer them the chance to stay as delvers for as long as they wish."

Teemo smiles at that. "Sounds like about what the Boss would like, too." He turns his focus to the two refugees. "If you're up for it, I'll lead you out to the Boss's dwellers and the adventurers. I'm sure they'll love to chat and maybe fill you in on what your options are now.

"You can stay here with the Southwood if you really want, or maybe try to join one of the enclaves back with the Boss. We can even try to get in touch with the mayor of Fourdock if you want to seek refuge somewhere that's not a dungeon. I'd ask you stick around somewhat close for a bit before taking off to explore the whole continent, though. We wouldn't want the Maw to somehow find you."

I mentally nod at that, glad Teemo left the other reason unsaid. I like the two, but I can't give them my full trust just yet. If it were just me, I might give them the full benefit of the doubt, but there's a lot more people than just me involved in this.

One source is good to start, but I want as many as possible before I actually begin making any decisions. And if they're an unreliable source, I'll need to be able to ask them more questions to see if they're deliberately lying or just wrong about the Maw's forces.

Chapter 73

The rockslides are slowly getting into position and actually sending reports back now, so Honey and Leo are turning their attention more toward that than trying to wring more information from Merrik and Lechula. Not only do they get to go through the scout findings, but they also have adventurer reports to organize, too.

Teemo is more than happy to help be an interpreter, and not just because it lets him hang out with Yvonne. Fluffles wanders by a few times, getting a few more pointers on Fate magic from Teemo when there are no reports to be made. I make sure Teemo tells him to spend whatever he needs to practice. Something like Teemo's Butterfly Effect could be great in the chaos of a pitched battle.

When Fluffles isn't getting pointers from Teemo, he's practicing with Rocky, Slash, and Nova. Rocky is having a lot of fun sparring in general, but especially trading blows with Slash. My Earth elemental still prefers playing his axe to swinging it, but I didn't make it an axe just to look cool. Even if I do think it looks really cool.

Rocky is helping him look cool swinging it around, too. My Boxer might be more focused on punches, but he still understands melee fighting. It probably also helps that he has Kinetic affinity. I wouldn't be surprised if Slash picks it up by the time we make our move, too. Rocky seems to be trying to hammer into Slash's head the idea of momentum, and how much more an axe has than a sword.

He's also getting Slash to take advantage of his unique biology with his swings. A human can only bend in so many ways, but Slash's joints are basically an illusion. His hip bones aren't connected to his leg bones, because neither technically exists.

Slash toyed with just spinning his wrist like a helicopter at one point, which earned him a lot of grunts and a big lecture. I don't think he was quite in trouble, but he hasn't tried that again. No, now he's starting to turn his entire torso around when he swings.

It's like in a lot of movies where the fighters spin to get more force on an attack, but it's a really stupid thing to do for a person. Never turn your back on a foe, after all. But Slash doesn't really have a back, and he can keep his head locked on target as he swings a full rotation to really build up steam.

He's tried doing his best top impersonation, but he can't quite go quickly enough to make it viable. While he's a big pile of rocks, the rotation still leaves him open to hits, so he needs to save that trick to take advantage of someone being off-balance. He can miss with a swing and a foe can move in, only to be taken by surprise as the axe comes around full circle to hit even harder.

Slash only landed it on Rocky when they were working it out, but it'll still be a good ace for him to have up his sleeve. Nova is also having some interesting progress.

She's been trying to hone her ambush techniques, but my gathered scions are too experienced for her. Slash can feel her in the earth, as can Rocky, and Fluffles can just stay high enough to be out of her reach, so my shy little wyrm has had to get creative, and I'm liking her creativity.

She's been making little magma sculptures of the other denizens, practicing her art. She seems really interested in the basilisks, too, which I don't blame her for. I wonder if she'll change into them as she gets stronger, or if she'll mostly stay as a wyrm if she doesn't get some title that causes her to ascend like Fluffles. She's been trying to make her little figures move around instead of just being still, and after toying with a few while watching Fluffles and Rocky, she seemed to get an idea.

She pulled up a lot of magma and formed it around herself, managing to look like an even more intimidating basilisk. Rocky, of course, was all about sparring her new form, and has been grunting advice to her between bouts. He's still able to pick her magma apart with sheer kinetic force, but Nova is improving quickly. She's moving the magma quicker, recovering more of what's lost instead of having to melt new stone, and generally making a really cool fighting style that's all her own.

I wonder if she'll get Fire or Earth affinity first. I think one will follow the other pretty quickly, but I still don't know which will happen first. Magma has a lot of heat in it, and with how much she must be throwing around to melt the stone, she's gotta be close. On the other hand, Rocky pressing her has been forcing her to keep ahold of her magma for as long as possible, especially when he starts using his thermodynamic techniques to pull the heat right out of her element.

Back on the home front, things are proceeding apace, which is great. I haven't been paying too much attention to the quarry in a while, but taking a peek, it might become my busiest section! The lighthouse is going up quickly, now that the kinks have been ironed out, and I think Rezlar is working to stockpile as much limestone as he can while the winter stays mild.

It feels like Hullbreak is expecting a big storm, but I can't get much detail without Teemo to go ask. It might be a blizzard, it might be some nasty ice storm or something blowing in from the ocean, or it might even just be me not understanding the feeling through the bond.

I'm inclined to think something will be on the horizon, though. The civilian delvers have a certain urgency to their movements that the adventuring ones don't.

What adventurers didn't head out to go poke the Maw are instead having a ball in the labyrinth. It's my strongest section yet, and a lot of groups have been defeated either by the traps or the denizens. The basilisks are not easy to beat. Being beaten and taken back to the entrance just seems to encourage them, though.

I think, for my next expansion, I'll aim for a classic crawl: lots of tough fights, chests to find, things like that. The special attractions are all well and good, but a classic room-by-room slugfest is a classic for a reason. The manor is the closest I have to that right now, and that's definitely aimed to newbies. The more experienced delvers are going to want a tougher version of that to go along with the other delving activities.

That means my next expansion will probably be out past the cemetery into the woods surrounding the town. Considering I want to get my Ant Enclave up and running closer to the volcanic area, it'd work out well for everyone. My ants will be able to develop without delvers constantly running around, and the delvers will get to have a more normal experience without having to worry about terrain hazards.

Of course, I doubt a forest expansion will give me a proper structure with rooms and such. I idly consider a tower, or maybe a castle, and rub the bond with Coda to see if he has any ideas. I get a few vague notions back from him, but I don't press. He still has the lighthouse to finish, and I'm not going to be expanding until after dealing with the Maw anyway. It's a good idea to be prepared, though.

What would I put in a classic dungeon crawl? I'd definitely like a variety. I might even try to design it to let me theme sections of it, though that might be a bit ambitious. I already have themed sections; I don't know how well it'd work to condense them enough to fit into a crawl.

Eh, I can run the numbers later. I should first see if I even have enough denizens to make theming worth it. Sure, I have a lot of them, but not a lot of them are specialized toward fighting.

Let me see . . . the widows and the twinsnakes would be easy inclusions. They're both pretty significant encounters. While I kinda think of them as wandering minibosses in the tunnels and caverns, they could be more regular encounters in the crawl. Ah, the classic RPG staple of a boss later becoming an ordinary encounter. Definitely going to have them there.

The basilisks would have a home there too, just need to make sure the structure is fireproof. My wyrms will probably be sticking mostly to the labyrinth so they can easily tunnel wherever they need to go. While I'm sure the crawl will be littered with shortcuts so my denizens can travel to whatever rooms they need, I think the wyrms will feel better burrowing than crawling through one.

Tundra wolves . . . might be decent in there? They've been great scouts in the winter, but I don't know how well they actually fare in fights. They seem tough enough, but they just haven't had enough encounters with delvers for me to get a good feel yet. They're a definite maybe, and probably near the top of my list of spawners to enhance for something like a crawl.

What about my undead? I haven't upgraded them in a while. The zombies and skeletons are focused for resources, not fighting, though. Tougher versions could be a good thing to put in, however; what kind of dungeon crawl doesn't have at least a few undead to slog through? The hands would probably be good after another upgrade. I'm pretty sure I'll get stronger magical hands with the next one, and they'll be great to mix in with everything else.

Oh man, theming will be a lot easier once I get that climate control option from the Southwood, too. Make the hot section hot, the cold section cold, the undead section dark and foreboding . . . I'll need to try to save up enough to be able to expand and get the upgrade at once, if I can. Hopefully the Maw will have plenty of mana for me to take, even after sharing a bunch into the ally fund. I'll also need to budget extra for whatever spawner I get, too.

Maybe I'll get a plant denizen of some kind? Creeping vines, lumbering treants, things like that.

I let my mind flit through a couple possibilities, though I don't chase the threads far. The Southwood has a bunch of different things, even if the foxes and bears are the most useful in this situation. Heh, maybe I'll get regular old worms. I could even focus them for combat, just to play against the type and be weird with them.

Teemo chuckles at my musings, but he doesn't comment. It'd be pretty unlikely for me to get regular worms as denizens at this point, I'd think, but who knows? All I know is it's fun to imagine several large worms poking out of the ground, one with a shield, one with a sword, and one with a helmet, the three acting like a single fighter. I even poke Teemo with the idea to see if Nova or Slash would be able to do something like that with their affinity.

Probably not, but you never know until you try. Weird innovations come from weird experiments like that, and can be the sort of thing to ensure we win the war against the Maw.

Chapter 74

Information is starting to flow like . . . Hmm, what is it flowing like? Water flows nicely, but my information isn't nearly that swift nor clear. Honey and Leo are receiving and organizing the reports from the field, which makes me very glad to have both my Warden and Librarian on the case. When a report gets to them, I get a rush of information, but it's not especially organized.

It takes me a bit of effort to focus on what's new, arrange it in a way that is actually helpful, digest it, and finally mull over what it means. With Leo and Honey receiving them and making their own, however, everything feels nice and tidy, easy to interpret, and easy to pick out the important pieces. It's the difference between getting the messy notes from someone versus getting a succinct presentation.

The problem is what the reports are saying. My denizens on expedition are relaying some pretty concerning things. They say there are a lot more strong denizens than Lechula and Merrik were expecting, as well as an organized army of guards and clergy. Were the two wrong, or lying? I can't really see either of those options being the case, though.

Those kinds of numbers should be pretty obvious even to civilians, and as basically initiates into the military, the elf and dwarf should have had at least a basic understanding of the numbers in the force.

Lying doesn't really track, either. Not only would it require the Maw to have planned for them to get kidnapped but they would have had to plan exactly what to say and be good enough actors to pull it off around the clock. The Southwood has been watching them pretty closely, and from what the Stag has shared with Teemo, they don't act any different when alone.

Additionally, the adventurers are starting to come back and giving their reports, which Teemo is helping Yvonne and the others organize and consolidate. Honey would like to stop by to see what they're doing, I'm sure, but she's a bit busy with the denizens' own reports.

From what the adventurers are saying, things seem closer to what Merrik and Lechula said: lots of civilian classes, a smattering of denizens around outside, etc. They haven't been able to get close enough to overhear any conversations yet, but they paint a different picture than what my rockslides are creating.

So yeah, my information is more flowing like mud, and I need to figure out how to clarify it before trying to act on it. Could my rockslides be peeking into secretive locations, spying behind a false facade of normalcy and seeing the beating heart of darkness?

Poetic and impressive as that sounds, I'm doubtful. Still, it can't hurt to check.

Hey, Teemo, does Aelara have a map from the areas the adventurers are reporting on? I'd like to compare it with Honey and the information the rockslides are giving.

"Lemme check," he answers from Yvonne's shoulder. Said shoulder, along with the rest of her, is perched on a branch high in a tree, feigning relaxation like a jungle cat as she keeps watch.

"Hmm?" perks up my undead birb resident, giving my Voice a curious look.

"You know where Aelara is? The Boss wants to compare maps, and she'd be the one with one, yeah?"

Yvonne nods. "She should be. She and Ragnar have been working on it, consolidating the info the adventurers have with our own. I think Ragnar is still fleecing his way through the denizens and newer adventurers with Vernew, but I believe Aelara is relaxing in our tent. We haven't had any new reports since this morning, so she should be free."

"Cool." With that, he hops off her shoulder and through a shortcut, quickly popping up in the tent with Aelara. She doesn't notice him yet, as she's taking the chance to check on her gear and perform a little maintenance while she has a few moments to spare, humming to herself as she works.

"Heya, Aelara."

She jumps a bit at his voice but quickly realizes who's snuck up on her. "Teemo! You startled me!"

He chuckles and gives a little dip of his head in apology. "Didn't mean to. The Boss wanted to see if you had an updated map. He wants to make sure everyone is on the same page on how things look like down there."

The elf nods and picks up a rolled piece of soft leather. "This is what I have so far. Ragnar was helping with it before he went out with Vernew to try to scam a few more people, so it should be as accurate as we can get."

"Perfect! I'll compare it with Honey and Leo, and get this back to you soon. I'll bring one with what we have, too." He accepts the map as Aelara smiles.

"I'm glad to hear it. I think most of the adventurers are wanting to stick around, but one of the lower-leveled groups is planning to head back soon, so they can take this to the guild."

"Sweet. Oh, do you think any guild members will want to come for the actual fighting? I think the Boss is going to bring up the medics—and probably Aranya—soon, so that'd be a great time for them to join in."

"I think there will be a lot of interest. From what the adventurers are saying, there will be a lot of tight tunnels, which means strong parties will be able to shine and hold back or push through forces without getting overwhelmed."

"Sounds about right. Leo will need to brief them on the overall plan once they get here, but the plan itself is still being drawn up, so there's no rush. I'll get you something like a formal request when I bring back the map?"

Aelara smiles at that and nods. "It would be appreciated. Even with that basic outline, I think a lot of adventurers will happily join the fight. Thedeim has a pretty good reputation, so I doubt anyone will try to act completely independently."

"Awesome. I'll bring this to Honey, and maybe get it back by tonight? Probably tomorrow."

Aelara nods and waves goodbye, so my Voice slips through another shortcut to deliver the map to Leo and Honey.

"Hey, guys," he says with nonchalance as he appears in their cave, earning a buzz from Honey and a grunt from Leo. When the wolf spots what Teemo has, he pays more attention and woofs where Teemo should set it.

"Alright, let's see what we've got . . ." mutters my Voice to himself as he rolls out the map.

It's pretty quickly clear there are a lot of discrepancies.

Tunnels the rockslides say should lead to caches and other strategic valuables seem to only lead to dead ends, according to the adventurers. The location of the main temple complex is also different, with my scouts saying it should be almost in the center of the town, while the adventurers seem to think it's more to the south, closer to where they estimate the actual dungeon to be.

I mentally frown, and can feel and see similar unhappiness from my gathered scions. "Where are the rockslides hiding? The Boss was wondering if they're just a lot deeper and able to see more detail than the adventurers."

Honey buzzes around the map while Leo makes nondescript wolf sounds.

"Hmm . . . it looks like they're a bit deeper than the adventurers got, but there are reports on the same areas. They don't match up. What's going on?"

Leo gives a tired growl, sounding like he doesn't have any ideas. Honey buzzes in a little dance, though, which Teemo nods to.

"Yeah, they can't both be correct, so which is wrong, and why?"

All of us try to think of something, but I'm stumped. My rockslides have been great scouts in the past, practically mapping out Hullbreak before we headed in, so I can't imagine how they'd get so much incorrect information.

On the other hand, I can't imagine why the adventurers would be wrong, or even be lying. Sure, not all of them are cartographers, but being able to make an accurate map is a vital skill in their line of work. Sometimes just to make sure they don't get lost, and others so they can come back and pick up some more loot that they just couldn't carry all at once.

And them lying wouldn't make any sense, either. I'm pretty sure them helping and bringing a map back to the guild is an actual quest. I don't think they'd fail something like that just to mess with me.

As far as I can tell, most of them are at least professional acquaintances of mine and wouldn't want to make me actually upset with them. It'd be hard for them to do any delving if I banned them, especially since Hullbreak would most likely follow suit, and probably not be as gentle as I would be about keeping them out.

So what's going on?

My musing is interrupted as Honey darts upward into the air and calls a few more of her bees to her. I watch through Teemo and Leo's eyes as her swarm descends on the maps like they're a small patch of delicious flowers.

I can feel thoughts zipping through Honey's mind via the bond, and it takes me a few seconds to realize what she's doing: She's embraced her Seeker of Truth title and is working her affinity over the two maps, trying to piece together the truth between the two.

It's interesting to watch her work, and I can only guess as to the actual thought process running through my Bee Scion and her swarm. As the minutes pass, they start to shift, more of them congregating on Aelara's map than the one from my own scouts. It starts with just a few bees migrating over, but before long, the entire swarm is covering only Aelara's map.

A few moments later, they disperse, leaving a confused and tired-looking Honey sitting on the middle of the map from the adventurers' reports. She gives Teemo a confused buzz, which he translates after a few seconds to process the information himself.

"She says our map is wrong."

Chapter 75

Honey

Some small part of the Bee Scion was worried the Emperor might reject her verdict, but he seems to accept it more easily than even she is willing to.

How can her map be wrong? She and Leo worked together on it with the reports from the rockslides, and while her affinity is certain it's accurate to those reports, it is also certain the adventurer's map is much closer to the actual truth than her own, now that she has something to compare it with.

She lets her legs sprawl out beneath her, physical fatigue matching the mental one from working her affinity and title so hard.

Leo gives her a concerned look. "Are you alright?"

"Just tired," she buzzes, not bothering with any dance right now. Teemo comes over and scoops her up to plop her on his head, earning an indignant buzz from her, but she doesn't fight it. Lying on the map isn't exactly helping figure things out.

Teemo taps his foot as he stands on his hind legs, looking at the map with a frown. Honey can feel his ear twitch as the Emperor speaks to him, and soon, the Voice relays the message.

"Boss says we have a couple of facts, and we should try to break things down to figure out what could possibly be going on here. So . . . we have our two refugees, the adventurers, and even Honey all saying this map is the more accurate of the two. The Boss trusts Honey, and he says having three sources agree either means the truth is with them or there's a major conspiracy.

"Considering how many things would have to happen for all those sources to actively lie, we can basically count that option out. That means we will need to plan using the map and the info we've gotten from the others."

Leo nods at that and gives a sigh. "But what about the rockslides?"

"That's the big question. Boss says they're a single point of failure, so there must be something wrong. Maybe some kind of weird dungeon option, like the Southwood's climate control? Something that would confuse rival dungeons but not adventurers?"

Teemo doesn't sound very convinced, Leo doesn't look very convinced, and Honey definitely isn't convinced. "Maybe," she buzzes, "but that seems highly unlikely. We could ask the Southwood if it has any advanced options like that, but I don't think he does. Some kind of illusion doesn't sound like what the Maw would have access to. It's a Metal-affinity dungeon, not Illusion."

Teemo nods, making Honey cling to his head, which in turn earns a chuckle from both him and Leo before the Voice speaks. "Yeah, the Boss isn't so sure about it, but we can try to ask. Any other ideas that might sound absurd but at least a little less absurd than that?"

Leo grumbles as he slowly stalks his logic. "The rockslides are either wrong . . . or lying for some reason. Both seem impossible, but it has to be one or the other." He quietly growls as he considers, then gets an idea. "Whatever the reason, they're compromised, but to what extent? Is it all of them?"

Honey buzzes and gets to her feet, determination helping her fight back the fatigue. "We can cross-reference the information to see. They each have their own reports, so we can see which ones are giving the truth, and which aren't. Teemo, can you please get the records from the adventurers?" She takes to her wings as he salutes, ordering her swarm to get out the rockslides' reports as he slips into a shortcut.

With Leo's help, she gets the papers organized by both date and depth, and as they start going through them, she can already start seeing inconsistencies. Most of them seem accurate, with the rockslides reporting on the broken road, as the Emperor seems to call the clear path from the surface to the dungeon. It's not inaccurate, as the road has been torn up by monsters traveling through.

As of several days ago, the reports of even the deepest rockslides seemed to still be accurate, with their locations still remote enough that they didn't have much besides topography to relay back.

The new reports, however, raise her suspicions. They speak of a marked increase in patrols and sightings of strong denizens and high-level guards and other followers of the Maw. When they first received the reports, she and Leo simply took it to mean the dungeon was mustering its forces to make a more concentrated effort to breach the surface, but now, she notices little details missing.

Perhaps the largest error, and one she and Leo probably should have spotted earlier, is a significant lack of logistical support. They had originally chalked it up to the dungeon not being especially experienced with moving around people at that kind of scale. Denizens don't really eat, but people do. The Emperor knew what that meant, and so his denizens marched with wagons full of supplies, but the rockslides have only reported soldiers, not wagons and support staff.

With the information about the Maw being so concerned with food, there's no way it would send soldiers off without at least basic provisions.

She's so focused on the task at hand, she hardly slows down when Teemo returns with the elf from the Emperor's chosen party. No, she instead has the Voice explain the situation quickly and gets the elf to help with the flow of information.

Aelara looks a little overwhelmed, but Honey is too focused to worry about that. Teemo and Leo help guide her through the buzzing swarm of a good research project, and Honey lets her affinity guide her through the shaded meadow of information.

The flowers are shy, but she and her bees know how to get the nectar and the pollen with efficient ease, and before long, she puts the final period on the updated report.

Teemo looks it over. Honey can feel the Emperor assimilating the information with ease thanks to the combined efforts of the three scions and the elven adventurer. Said elf is looking at the information as well, baffled.

"A couple days ago, the rockslides started giving false reports? But why? How?" she asks as she looks over not only the simple written words but also the attached map that shows the rockslides that are giving false information.

"Those are the questions we want to answer," replies Teemo.

"Does . . . Does the Maw have rockslides?" she asks. Teemo shakes his head.

The question sticks in Honey's mind, though. Could it? Could it have a secret Earth elemental spawner? Her intuition says no, but she also feels like the elf is on the right track.

"How many rockslides does the Emperor have on expedition?" Honey asks, her swarm moving to tabulate how many are currently under her and Leo's command.

Teemo looks like he doesn't understand where Honey is going with this, but dutifully relays her question. "Hey, Boss? How many rockslides are out right now?" Honey can feel the Emperor's confusion as he considers the question, then a bit of surprise. Teemo shakes his head and smiles as he gives the answer. "Boss is surprised he had so many out. Two hundred and thirty-six."

Honey buzzes in triumph as she gets the number from her own swarm: two hundred and sixty-three rockslides are under her and Leo's direction!

Her jubilation turns to confusion as she checks her numbers and sees that each and every rockslide is confirmed to have left from the Emperor's domain, meaning no sneaky spawner from the Maw.

Then how has it subverted twenty-seven rockslides?! It's Metal, not—!

She almost falls out of the air as the realization hits, Leo's bark of concern only just pushing through her shock.

"No, I'm fine. It's just . . . I know what's going on." She lands on the map and points out the compromised rockslides. "We have twenty-seven more rockslides than the Emperor has on expedition. They're not secret spawns from the Maw, though. They all have a trail of reports linking them back to the Emperor."

She pauses and looks up at Teemo, Leo, and Aelara, meeting their eyes as well as she can. She can feel the Emperor's confusion before it gives way to shock as he comes to the same conclusion she has, at least if the anger and feeling of self-disappointment are anything to go by.

She feels a bit stupid for not putting it together earlier, too.

"The Harbinger has Mental affinity. It's taken over the slides closest to the Maw. They no longer belong to the Emperor, which is why his number doesn't match ours."

Aelara gasps at that while Teemo and Leo look grim.

"Mental? I need to warn the adventurers before they head out!"

She gets up to go, though she pauses when Teemo speaks up. "Have them swing by before they go, if any of them are still willing!" Aelara nods before running out of the cave.

Leo growls as he looks at the map. "They know we're coming, then. They'll fortify their position now that we've lost the element of surprise." The Warden's hackles rise with his frustration, and Honey buzzes in grim solidarity with her fellow scion. Teemo looks more confused than upset for a few moments before he grins wide.

"Boss says we might be able to use this." Leo and Honey both look confused, so Teemo elaborates. "They know we're coming, but they think we don't know they know. But we *do* know, so we can leverage knowing we know they know without letting them know we know they know, you know?"

"What," states Leo, Honey right there with him. Even with her affinity, that all sounded like nonsense. Teemo keeps smiling.

"Boss calls it counter-counterintel. We make it look like we're taking the bait, but we're actually preparing to ambush the ambush!"

Leo blinks at that before grinning wide, and Honey's wings start to buzz as she understands. Each of the false points of interest would be a perfect place to ambush their forces, but there are only a few places the enemy could launch an ambush *from* on those locations!

"Don't send any more rockslides in there, though," says Teemo, knocking Honey's train of thought off the tracks. "Tell the suborned ones to get into a better position to keep an eye on the fake points of interest, but don't send any fresh ones in. The Boss doesn't want to send them on a deliberate suicide mission. Danger is one thing, but any others sent in there would be being deliberately sent to their death."

Honey and Leo both nod at that.

Honey has to admit she was vaguely pondering sending in a few more to try to lure out further ambush positions. The Emperor is right, though. It's one thing to send them into a dangerous location with little information when there's little to give. But knowing they'll be attacked by the Harbinger without giving them some means of protecting themselves?

Honey shudders at the thought. She knows how twisted the Harbinger is. Even with respawning, it's not an experience she'd wish on anyone.

Chapter 76

Lechula

The pale dwarf warily peeks out from the cave she and Merrik have been staying in. The surface is . . . nothing like she had expected. She would take consolation in the fact that Merrik has been blindsided too, but he hasn't been having a great time of it either.

The first day, they could hardly see anything for how bright it all was. It only made her and Merrik more concerned when the group of adventurers said it was a dim day, and the trees provided even more shade! It was a relief to be questioned at the back of that other cave, shallow as it was. It was a little bright, but much better than being outside.

After night fell, it was much easier to walk around and explore the dungeon, the Southwood. While it was much colder than she's ever experienced before, it was actually dark, so her eyes didn't hurt! She and Merrik had encountered a few other people, mostly ratkin and spiderkin, but mostly kept to themselves, eventually finding another cave to sleep in.

It was a bit concerning when a large bear came in, but the Stag followed behind and explained he would be their bed for the night. It was weird to consider sleeping near such an imposing denizen, but as the temperature continued to drop, she and Merrik both were more than happy to cozy up to the bear.

But now it's late morning, and the big, warm, fuzzy bed has wandered off to do denizen things. The light is still bright, but somewhat more bearable than yesterday, which Lechula will eagerly accept.

"Do you think we could defeat that bear and get ourselves some bedding that won't wander off in the morning?" asks her pale elven friend as he joins her, squinting out into the daylight.

"Maybe? But that might be a bit rude, and maybe not as warm. We could make a fire, but . . ." she trails off.

"An open fire like that would be a bit bright to comfortably sleep near," he finishes for her. He doesn't look happy about it, but Lechula has been around him enough to know he's not being grumpy; rather, he's thinking about how to fix the problem. He doesn't look like he's coming up with much, so Lechula makes her own suggestion.

"We could find the dwellers and ask how they handle all this? It sounded like they're mostly underground too, so maybe they have advice they'd be willing to share?"

Merrik sighs and nods, lifting a hand to shield his eyes as he leaves the cave. "And we can attempt to get some kind of hat to help protect us from this light. After the Redcap, I thought I'd never want to wear anything on my head. I'm not quite ready to wear one of his, but I would be very happy to try to work for something much less . . . drippy."

Lechula shudders and nods as she follows her friend. "Maybe we can help prepare some meals? I think we're a bit late for breakfast, but should be right on time to help make brunch for the late risers and the late shift before they go to sleep."

The pale elf nods, and the two make their way to the dweller camp. Lechula can't help but let her eyes wander around their surroundings, though she resists looking up for too long. The night sky felt so full, like a cavern ceiling high above filled with sparkling gems.

The daytime sky, though, just feels . . . empty, almost hungry. It's also a bit painful to look at, even when not looking at the sun. Just another reason not to stare at the uncomfortable expanse stretching away above them.

She shakes her head, trying not to think about it too hard, but her traitorous eyes keep wandering toward the skyline. At least that makes it easy to spot the smoke from the dwellers' fires.

The camp takes up the entirety of a large clearing. The two of them just stand at the edge for a few moments, considering what they should actually do, where they should go. After a few moments, they both close their eyes and inhale. When looking for food, look for the kitchen. When looking for the kitchen, follow the scent of food.

Lechula lifts her hand and points before opening her eyes. Merrik doesn't look like he's got anything, so she nudges him with her elbow to get him to look. "I think I smell something that way. Some kind of bread, maybe?" Merrik frowns but doesn't argue as she leads the way.

They get a few looks from the dwellers as they walk through the camp, but nobody bothers stopping them. The scent of fruits tickles Lechula's nose, and she has to fight increasing her pace. Whatever it is, it smells good already.

Soon, they exit from the small alleyways between tents and onto more of a road, though it's hardly paved. The tracks from wagon wheels split the mass of tents roughly in half, and to the east, the two can see their destination. One of the wagons looks to be a mobile kitchen, and is handing out food in the form of some kind of pancake.

As they approach, they see a male spiderkin inside; one of the smaller jumping varieties, if Lechula understands correctly. His face looks a bit more insectile than the women spiderkin's, and the smaller stature is also usually a good indicator, but she wouldn't want to give insult by getting something so simple wrong.

While trying to figure out how to introduce herself and Merrik, the spiderkin spots them and waves, his pedipalps twitching.

"Ah, you two are the ones from that other dungeon, yeah?" His voice at least confirms he's a he, though the content of his greeting has Lechula looking around nervously. Back in Silvervein, something like that would get the guards' attention *very* quickly.

Instead of glares and drawn weapons, the dwellers glance at them with curiosity before returning to whatever they were doing.

"Yes, that's us," replies Merrik. "Is there anything we can do to earn a few of your pancakes? We haven't eaten yet."

The spiderkin's pedipalps twitch as he thinks. "Hmm . . . Well . . ."

A mammalian hand reaches from elsewhere inside the wagon and pushes him across the counter, letting a wide ratkin take his place at the counter. "No charge for the pancakes. We don't even have a till. We might get one once we get back, though. I bet we could make a killing selling these at the arena."

The spiderkin bristles and ineffectually slaps at the hand keeping him at bay. "Bron! That's no way to run a business!"

Bron just rolls his eyes. "Donny, we're not running a business. We're helping feed our people so they have the strength to drive back the evil dungeon," he says plainly before realizing the two people waiting for food are from the evil dungeon. "Er . . . no offense?"

Lechula blushes. "None . . . Well, maybe a little taken. It really is evil, but it's still weird to wrap my head around," she admits.

"How're you only just figuring that out? Whoa!" Donny scrambles to keep his footing, but his rather rude question has Bron pushing him fully off the counter and onto the floor inside the wagon. Despite the apologetic look from the fat ratkin, Lechula tries to answer.

"Well . . . I never knew anything else. The outside was supposed to be full of danger, and the public sacrifices always reinforced that. Monsters, enemies, sometimes traitors. They always said it was justice. But . . ."

As she explains, Donny climbs back onto the counter, looking guilty as her answer continues. "Sorry. Forget I asked. Uh . . . Oh! You're hungry, right?" He tries to change the subject, and Lechula is all too happy to let him. She silently nods, and he puts on an exaggerated smile . . . at least she thinks it's a smile. She's not quite used to spiderkin facial features.

"Then you've come to the right place! Do you like your pancakes sweet or savory?"

"What's the difference?" asks Merrik, curious about potentially new cuisine.

Bron turns back inside the wagon as Donny explains. "Sweet ones get berries, while savory gets cave lobster bits. We're still hammering out the best combination of taste and portability, but just adding them into the batter and then cooking works well enough."

"Can we have one of each?" asks the pale elf. The spiderkin nods.

"Yeah, that'll be fine. Hey, Bron, two sweet, two savory!"

"I'm right behind you. I can hear you just fine," complains the cook from out of sight. Despite the tone signifying a long-standing argument, the two can hear the sound of batter on a hot pan and smell the scent of food cooking.

"What kind of flour are you using?" asks Lechula, the scent not matching quite right with the flour she's used to. Maybe it's a new grain?

"It's a mix of sporeflour and wheat. The Weaver says military food should pack a lot of energy and protein, so we use a mix. The texture and taste is a little different, but they're filling and definitely not bad. Kinda weird, if you're used to normal flour, but you'll get over it," explains Donny as he relaxes on the counter. His eyes focus behind Lechula and he hops off the counter, causing her to look around, curious what could have caused that.

"Hey, Bron, are these all the empty sacks? Filcy's on her way," comes the muffled voice of the spiderkin. Lechula ignores the sounds of rummaging from inside the wagon as she tries to figure out who Filcy is. It doesn't take her long to notice the large tarantulakin woman making a beeline toward the food wagon. She diverts her attention to the two pale outsiders as she approaches, eyeing them before speaking.

"You're the two refugees, then?"

Lechula is feeling a bit intimidated by the large woman, but Merrik seems to be taking her presence in stride. "We are. I'm Merrik, and she's Lechula."

"Filcy. Have you two eaten, or are you here for seconds?"

Merrik shakes his head. "We got a late start, so this will be our breakfast."

The gruff woman nods at that, her eyes flicking to the wagon as Donny hops back onto the counter, a bulging bag in his hands. "Hey, Filcy! Got the empties here for you!" He looks to Merrik and Lechula as he holds out the bag for the tarantulakin woman. "It'll be just a couple more minutes. I'll get you two something you can use for a plate or something, too."

Filcy silently accepts the bag, then turns her attention to the two outsiders as well. "Pale elf and pale dwarf, right?"

Lechula slowly nods. "Yeees?"

Filcy nods at that. "After you eat, head to the other end of the camp, to the infirmary. And try to stay in the shade. You probably don't know what sunburn is, but you two are already looking like cooked sea lobsters. They'll help you with that."

Lechula and Merrik both look confused, but Donny's eyes go wide with concern at her statement. "Move around to the back, into the shade! I'll bring your food out in just a sec!"

Merrik looks like he wants details, but Lechula is willing to take things at face value. Donny doesn't seem like the most sensitive of people, so if even he is looking worried, she thinks they should move first and ask questions later.

It's only later that she and Merrik both learn that was probably the correct choice.

Chapter 77

Lechula

As far as Lechula is concerned, the surface dwellers can keep the place. It's bright, it's cold, the sky is *terrifying*, and even if that massive void up there won't swallow you up, it'll still cook you medium rare if given the chance!

The healing salve helps, but she still has no intention of leaving the cave until she stops being as red as one of the Redcap's hats. Merrik seems to have avoided the worst of the sunburn, as the surfacers call it, so he's taken to slipping outside occasionally, but even he is mostly staying inside until night.

"The sun really did do a number on you, Lechula. Even your temperament is inflamed," he teases as he returns with dinner. The reddened pale dwarf would grump at him, but it's just not the same without crossing her arms, and that would involve far too much of her skin touching anything besides air. Still, he's not wrong about how sour her mood is right now.

"I think I had a better time recovering from the Harbinger speaking to me." She sighs and leans back against the blessedly cool cave wall. She would say the caves wouldn't betray her, but a cave-in is why she and Merrik are here. The pale elf nods as he sits beside her, taking a moment to enjoy the cool cave wall as well. Just because he didn't get it as bad doesn't mean he's not also suffering.

"The spear was a lot more painful, but at least it was just in one spot. I'm not certain which I'd prefer." Lechula grunts in sympathy. She'd much rather a spear in the shoulder than this, but probably because she's trained to take a spear wound. This sunburn . . .

"Do you think the surface folk could win just by retreating and letting the sun cook the Maw's forces?" she asks in a weak joke. Merrik at least chuckles, making her feel a little better.

"I actually asked a similar question to the healers. While the sunburns can get even worse than what you got, they're mostly painful, not incapacitating. In a long campaign, the Maw's forces would lose a lot of morale, but it wouldn't be enough to actually stop them. And I don't know if the denizens would be affected at all."

Lechula sighs and rests her head against the wall, trying not to think about her burning skin, nor about the idea of the Maw's denizens attacking the surface without fear of the sun overhead. Thankfully, the scent of the meal Merrik brought is a good distraction from things she'd rather not think about. "What'd you get?" she asks, nodding at the wooden boxes.

He hands her one as he explains. "Mushroom bread, with a venison and vegetable stew. I saw some of the dwellers loading everything onto the bread to make messy sandwiches, but I think I'm going to eat it as it is."

Lechula tests the meal with her fork and takes a small bite of the bread, letting the flavors mingle. It's not the most balanced profile, but it's definitely edible. "I don't think I want to make that much of a mess. And having some of the stew drip out onto my arm right now would probably hurt a lot," she agrees, and soon, the two settle into a nice, quiet meal.

They both seem to be hungrier than they thought, or the stew was tastier than initially expected, because by the end, they both use the last of their bread to mop up the final bit of thickened liquid, setting the boxes aside after finishing. There's plenty of time to return them. For now, they both want to relax and not move too much so as not to anger the sunburn.

Before long, though, a small spiderkin peers into the cave, smiling as she sees the two. "Ah, you're the ones from below, yeah?" she asks as she walks in like she owns the cave. From the light armor and odd spear, Lechula can tell she's one of the fighters, but the way she carries herself makes her suspect she's one of the better ones.

"Oh, yes. I'm Lechula, and he's Merrik. I don't think we've met?"

The spiderkin nods as she settles on a large rock nearby.

"Nah, we haven't. I hear you two got burned pretty bad. Makes it kinda hard to go be social. The ratkin sometimes get it bad on their tails if they stay underground too long. Anyway, I'm Vernew, Huntsmistress and leader of the dwellers; at least this batch." She offers a hand to each of them to shake, and Lechula nervously accepts hers. Merrik looks a bit more confident, or at least less nervous about it, as they both shake.

"So . . . I'd ask how the surface is treating you, but it's kinda obvious. How're you two holding up?"

Merrik takes time to consider his response, but Lechula answers pretty quickly. "Sunburn aside, we're doing well. There's . . . Everything is just so *different* here! Not just the environment but the people. Even the dungeon is different than I was expecting!"

Vernew chuckles at that and nods. "Yeah, heh. We're still figuring out how to work with outsiders. The Weaver only gave us an enclave a few months ago. We're still figuring ourselves out, honestly. He helps a lot."

"The Weaver?" asks Merrik. Vernew nods as she fishes out a little amulet from under her armor. The string is simple leather, with a lacquered orange disk attached to it.

"The Weaver of the Threads, Lord Thedeim. Our home, our Sanctuary," she says with a smile, looking at what Lechula can only assume is a holy symbol. She and Merrik are both put a bit on guard at that, remembering how fanatical the clergy of the Maw could be.

"I . . . thought this was the Southwood?" Lechula tries gently digging for information, hoping to not offend.

Vernew doesn't look offended in the slightest. "We're currently in the Southwood, yeah, but he's Lord Thedeim's ally. He's a good four days' journey away, I think? Even with Teemo's shortcuts."

Ally? That sounds nice, but . . .

Vernew smirks at the two sunburned subterranean people. "From your looks, I take it the Maw doesn't play well with others?"

"Not . . . really . . ." replies Merrik, understating the situation significantly.

"Well, the Weaver's pretty friendly. You've seen the adventurers, yeah? Not just the dwellers? The Weaver is friendly enough with the guild that their guildmaster is encouraging them to come help, and they're happy to do it, too. According to them, He's the best delve Fourdock has had in . . . ever!"

Merrik gives her a curious look at that. "Are they really so close to a dungeon? Even though he kills some of them?"

Vernew grins wide at that. "They sure are! Probably because He doesn't kill them. Almost a year now, and still no delver deaths. Well, except a few scythemaws, but those don't count."

"Still, only a year. That's not especially long," argues Merrik as Lechula pipes up.

"That seems like a pretty long streak to me. Accidents happen. Even after he got chastised for it, a few people have still died in the Harbinger's training. What was his record for no deaths before?" she asks Vernew, earning an even wider grin.

"He only has the one record. He's never killed a delver since he started, not quite a year ago."

Lechula looks confused at that. Merrik processes it quicker than she can. "He's not even a year old?! That's not even *remotely* possible! How can a dungeon not even a year old have an ally, an enclave, and over a dozen scions?!"

Vernew just looks smug as she settles onto her rock. "He has two enclaves, as well as a protégée and a vassal, too. Lord Thedeim isn't any ordinary Sanctuary. I don't know how He does half the things He does, but He does them just the same. I've met the local inspector from the Dungeoneer's, and even he doesn't know how the Weaver does it. He just fills out the paperwork."

"How often does he demand sacrifices?" asks Lechula, trying to wrap her head around how any dungeon could afford that kind of insane growth.

"Sacrifices?" echoes Vernew, looking confused for a moment, then furious, before she takes a deep breath and continues. "The Weaver of the Threads doesn't need nor want sacrifices. He grows like He does because He does things differently."

Her rigid demeanor softens as her anger truly subsides, and she meets their eyes. "Look, I know most enclaves worship their dungeon. High Priestess Aranya even said so, and I've talked to the High Priest of Hullbreak, too. But the Weaver . . . He's more than that.

"It's more than the fact He made us. He *cares* for us. He cares for practically everyone! That's why He doesn't just kill delvers! That's why He didn't want any of us to come join this fight! But we want to help Him, even though some of us probably won't be coming back from this. He's always trying to help . . . so we want to help, too."

Lechula and Merrik both stare at her for several long seconds, each trying to process what the spiderkin woman just said. "He really didn't tell you to come fight?" asks Lechula in shock. Vernew's snort helps cut through her confusion.

"He even asked us to stay out of it. When we insisted, He started making us things to try to keep us safe." Vernew looks at her spear, smiling at the strange head on it.

"Can . . . Can you explain more?" asks Lechula.

"It's a lot different than the Maw, that's for certain," Merrik follows up. "He demands sacrifices, demands we fight . . ."

Vernew nods at that. "Yeah, I can help you try to understand Him a bit better. I'm not exactly Aranya, but I do my best. Heh, that's the closest to anything He demands of us: our best. So . . . where to begin . . ."

Chapter 78

I'm surprised any of the adventurers are willing to go back and try to keep scouting the Maw. I mostly had Teemo suggest they come talk to us on the off chance, but there are three groups willing to get a closer look. That doesn't include Yvonne's group, who will be setting up a forward base camp, and the couple other teams who will be ferrying the reports back.

The No-Longer-Terrible Trio is there, though they're going to be running messages and providing a bit of security for the base camp. They don't have any specific mental defenses, but they're apparently strong enough to have a good shot of resisting the more dangerous mental attacks.

For the scouts, there's a group of . . . scouts. They look like the kind of people I'd expect to be rangers instead of adventurers. The trio of elves look comfortable among the trees, and give assurances they'll be just as comfortable in the caves and tunnels.

I'm a bit unsure about letting them go down there, but they say they specialize in getting information without being noticed. I don't know if they'll have what they need to avoid the Harbinger, but they're confident, and I have even less authority to try to stop them than I do with my dwellers.

The next is a solo adventurer, a changeling with some kind of rogue class. She says she can literally hide in shadows, and implied she doesn't do all her work inside dungeons. While I don't know the exact countermeasures nobles and such might use to stop thieves, I have to imagine the changeling has something to get around mental detection. She's hoping she can actually infiltrate the town. I'm *real* nervous about that idea, but I still don't really have many options for actually stopping her.

The last is a group I didn't expect to see: a party of Crystal Shield followers. I didn't even realize any of them were participating in all this! They don't strike me as particularly stealthy, but the priest leading the small group is confident the Shield will be able to keep their minds safe, secure, and secret behind its protection.

Teemo keeps pestering them for more information, and I'm happier about their plan once they give a few more details. They have a ratkin member—not one of mine—who is actually sneaky. The wolfkin is usually their frontline fighter, and he'll mostly be staying back to help keep the base camp secure. The elven priest will bless the ratkin, and he'll go scout and return.

Once Teemo gets that bit of info out of him, the other two teams ask for a similar blessing for their own efforts, which the priest is more than happy to provide once they're actually out there and doing the job. He'll also be helping secure the base camp, since he won't be out and about doing the scouting. I bet Aranya will be joining them all and helping ease the burden of keeping the place magically secure once she gets here.

Which means I should probably get Teemo back home one last time before all this gets going. The healing brigade needs to be brought up, and I'd like for Teemo to ask Tarl about any weaknesses the known denizens might have. A rusting attack could be nice, but I don't think anyone here has an ability like that.

Rezlar might, but no way is he going to be joining this particular fight, at least not directly. Even if he wasn't the lord mayor of Fourdock, he's still pretty young and inexperienced. Even the weakest adventurers here, I'm pretty sure, have quite a few levels on him. Crazy as the adventurers are, even they are being careful around a Mental affinity as strong as the Harbinger's.

Careful is a relative term, though. None of them, not even Yvonne's group, really wants to wait for the medics to get here before they go. At least they'll have a chance to set up the camp before Aranya arrives. Nova is pretty insistent on going with them, too. I can feel Rocky and Fluffles are also tempted, but they're going to resist for now. One scion will be easier to keep secret than three, especially with the kind of power those two have.

I don't know if that kind of thing would make them more obvious; probably not, but stealth is vital here. The only one sneakier than Nova is Teemo, and even he can't just hide deep inside the rock of the tunnels.

Of course, that didn't keep the rockslides safe, but I'm also not going to let Nova get any closer than the camp until I'm fully ready to assault the Maw. And speaking of, Honey and Leo are starting to flesh out a plan for doing just that.

There's a *ton* of tunnels into and out of Silvervein, but so far, not many of them allow for bypassing the town to strike into the Maw directly. Earlier into the information gathering, I was expecting to be able to pretty easily go around the town to get to the Maw, but now that we have a more complete picture, it looks pretty deliberate. There're still a few potential direct-access tunnels to the Maw, and I'm betting the forces the suborned rockslides are reporting are way lower than what's actually there.

Most of my more ordinary denizens are going to be assaulting those tunnels. Yeah, they're the obvious entry points, but they'll also be perfect places to launch further attacks into the Maw. Which also means they'll be the most well guarded. I don't think Leo expects to be able to take those points easily, but putting pressure there will force the Maw to keep a lot of its denizens committed to its defense.

It'll probably be a grinder for both of us, but it should at least keep as many of the Maw's forces occupied as possible, and away from my dwellers and the adventurers.

The adventurers will be tripping the traps, assuming enough of them come from the guild for the real fighting. Yvonne and everyone else seem to think it's a foregone conclusion that basically everyone will want to come, but don't go counting your chickens before they hatch.

Anyway, assuming they want to play ball, they should be able to cripple the Maw's numbers outside the dungeon itself, leaving the adventurers free to either help with the messy business of securing the town, or to come try their hands at breaking through to the Maw.

I think the best option for them, after tripping the traps, is to try to strike through the temple complex of the Maw's clergy and force the dungeon to spread itself thin trying to keep everyone out. If we can't slip behind their lines somehow, it'll probably devolve into a careful siege.

The medics will be busy making sure as few of my forces die as possible, and so try to starve the Maw of mana. The adventurers and dwellers will want to play it safe, too. While I'm confident my dwellers will be careful, the adventurers are going to be a bit more of a wild card. Still, the ones at the levels that will be needed aren't going to be so stupid as to think they can spend their loot if they're dead.

If we're lucky, we won't have to deal with a protracted siege. Leo and Honey are making plans for if it comes to that, but plan A is to sneak a decapitating strike past the Maw's defenses while it's distracted.

With the denizens pressing the obvious entrances, and the adventurers wreaking havoc, a strike force of my scions will try to break through. There are a few options for that, with the simplest being to use a few tunnelbores to open my own holes into the Maw's territory. It'll definitely notice them eventually, so we'll have as many as we can digging, forcing the Maw to try to swat them down before they can get too close.

I imagine a few of the adventurer teams will want to go with the tunnelbores, and possibly a few of my dwellers, too, and I'm torn about it. The adventurers are one thing; they know the risks as well as they can. But I'm still protective of my dwellers. I don't want them to get hurt, so is there anything I can do about it? Any way I can try to discourage them?

I pull the brakes on that train of thought, not letting myself think in circles, getting nowhere. Hullbreak is a good lesson on how poorly that goes. If they decide they want to join the tunnelbore teams, I can't stop them. All I can do is try to make each strike team a threat, and hope for safety in numbers to minimize casualties. And mixed in with the various tunneling teams will be my scions.

Once they take the field, especially if they manage to get into the Maw's territory, I think the dungeon will have more important things to worry about than my dwellers. Once inside, Rocky and Fluffles will be trying to cause enough of a ruckus to draw the attention of the Redcap and the Harbinger. With Slash's help, they'll defeat or at least distract those two, letting Nova and Teemo try to sneak off to claim the core.

That'll be the real goal: to subsume the Maw.

Well, the *real* goal is to protect the kobolds, which isn't looking like an easy task. So far, the scouts have gotten exactly nothing on their location. On the one hand, that's probably a good sign. Any rockslides close enough to try to find them have been suborned, so if they're not trying to bait a location for the Kobold Enclave, they don't know that's the real goal.

On the other hand, that still leaves us with very few actual leads. From the lack of info, I'm thinking they're inside the Maw's territory proper, and might even be very close to the core, like with Hullbreak's enclave.

We need to get a bead on where they are and their status before we can really make any move. Not only will we want to make sure they're safe to be able to free them, but tactically, we need to keep them unharmed, too. The Maw likes to sacrifice them, and it must get some mana from that. They could be an emergency mana bank, so we need to secure them before the Maw can try to cash them in.

Once we do that, *then* we can move on the core itself. If we're lucky, they'll be far enough away that we can do one, then the other. If it's like Hullbreak, we'll have to do both at once. If it comes to that . . . Teemo will probably be in charge of evacuating them, possibly with Nova protecting them from whatever else the Maw might throw at the kobolds to kill them for mana. My other scions will be there too, but in that situation, they'll probably be busy fighting the enemy scions.

We'll have to play it by ear, even if we get a good look at the enclave and core. Stealth might be an option, and we'll give it a try, but I expect the whole thing will be a mess.

Stealth will be plan A, with blitzing for the core being plan B. C will be the messy fight—probably the most likely outcome, I expect. Either way, taking the core leaves me with a few questions that I don't think will be answered until after we do it.

I'm not quite sure what'll happen when we subsume the Maw, at least with its territory and spawners. With Neverrest, basically everything just transferred to me. The scions vanished, but any denizens that weren't dead became mine. Even the scions vanishing might be more because they were dead at the time Fluffles took the core.

If I don't get the Maw's territory, will the denizens just be freed?

That'd be a mess, especially if the Redcap and Harbinger are also released. They'd be lower on power, but what if they slip away?

Those two on the loose could be even worse than them working for the Maw.

Chapter 79

Rezlar

Winter is a strangely busy time for the lord mayor of Fourdock, especially now that he's decided to actually step up and do his job rather than just let the guild leaders do it for him. Winter is usually a time of relaxation for the citizenry, as the cold and snow make it difficult for them to do much work. But for the people at the top, the ones who are supposed to direct that work, it is a vital time for planning.

The first phase of any plan is to make sure you understand where you stand, what your resources are, how full your coffers are, who will properly do the job you need them to do, and who is looking for a chance to drain you.

Thankfully, none of the local guild heads seem to be completely in the latter category. The head of the merchant's comes closest, but she seems to just be trying to wring every last coin out of every deal as she can rather than actually trying to swindle any business partners. Her costs are high, but contracts are clear, even if Rezlar sometimes suspects it's because Karn somehow abused a loophole or two to teach her a lesson.

Whatever the reason, her people have proven to be worth the high price, with the carts and wagons usually used for caravans showing they can easily move goods around inside the city, too. Ms. Silverwheat's people are punctual and professional, and the miners' and masons' guilds speak well of them. The adventures don't have much to say, which is a good sign. They don't meet often, but being able to remain professionally courteous is an excellent way to keep things running smoothly.

And smooth they have been. The limestone quarry in Thedeim has been averaging close to ten large blocks of limestone a day. Once the lighthouse for Hullbreak is finished, that number could double!

The numbers for the labyrinth are less rosy, and Rezlar should try to talk with Thedeim about creating a proper iron vein once he's done with that business to the north. A more exotic vein would be even better, but Rezlar has no idea what that would actually entail for the friendly dungeon. He's been pretty happy to scale up the more mundane resources like the limestone and timber, but keeps the more interesting things behind challenges for the adventurers.

As much as he'd love to have a massive orichalcum mine for Fourdock, even Ms. Silverwheat has cautioned against upsetting the market for rare materials. Still, he can ask. If he says no, it should be within his budget to ship iron—ore or ingots—as reinforcement for the hold he and Thedeim promised the town before winter set in. Hullbreak might be able to use the transmuted spider silk, but a hold for the entire town will require more than the denizens can produce, both in silk and the actual transmutation potion.

The rough design Coda produced for the hold is very interesting, and he often looks over it again, thinking of improvements. The basic concept is very simple: lots of arches and domes. They're hardly new concepts, but the concrete makes it so much easier to accomplish the rounded shapes! And the efficiency of volume to surface area lets them get the most room out of the least material. The actual living spaces will be simple enough to make, but the utility space will be a bit more difficult.

Rezlar hopes he can convince Teemo to create a network of shortcuts for things like plumbing, but he's not holding his breath. He had originally hoped to use Thedeim's smaller ants to dig the pipes for that sort of thing, but the first time something clogged, it'd be a disaster if there was no access path. Smaller tunnels would be best for something like that . . . The local dwarves and halflings might end up cornering the career market for plumbers.

Air ventilation will also be important, which leads him down an interesting path of research. The obvious solution would be bellows to force airflow, but that just isn't tenable for a hold of the planned size. There're two potential solutions, and Rezlar suspects it will end up having both, if they each work. When it comes to air, there's no such thing as too much access.

The first solution is one the dwarven holds seem to use.

Heat rises, bringing air with it. If you want fresh air, heat the old and let it vent, making room for new. The ductwork is a bit beyond him, but the theory is pretty understandable: put the forges, smiths, and other crafting professions that need heat near the bottom of the hold, and provide chimneys for the fires they use. Put air vents all around the hold, with a few clever fluid traps to keep siegers from being able to pour anything nasty down them, and you have fresh air circulating! Not as fresh as actually being on the surface, but better than nothing.

The other solution is one included in the concept designs from Coda, the bat artificer having a lot of interesting ideas to use old things in new ways, like waterwheels. Grain has been milled via waterpower for ages, but Rezlar hasn't seen anyone try to use it for anything else, at least until he saw these designs.

They'll need a lot of refinement, and Rezlar isn't sure they'll be viable for the entire hold, but much like the dwarven solution, the concept is pretty simple: use the rotation to turn fans to distribute fresh air. The ducting is just as complex as the dwarven version, so they'll probably be able to use the same system, which makes each a good backup for the other.

If neither works quite well enough, Rezlar is confident there are enough citizens with Wind affinity to keep everyone from suffocating.

The next major obstacle will be lighting. The only real solution to that is either enchanting or somehow cultivating the disparate glowing plants, lichens, fungi, and whatnot from Thedeim's underground segments. That will probably be something else to discuss with Coda, once Teemo is free to translate.

It would be simple enough to line the public spaces with the glowing flora and let them stay lit, but living spaces would need a way to dim them so people can sleep. The only thing Rezlar can think of for that is some kind of curtains to cover the glowing things. Shutters might be cheaper, or at least easier to source at the needed scale.

He can't help but smile at the idea of people needing to close their "windows" even when deep underground.

The last major obstacle will be making sure everyone can eat. Thankfully, the enclaves seem to have the solution to that. The ratkin have their sporeflour to take the place of a staple grain. It's strange, but not bad. They're still working out the best way to use it, the best recipes and methods of cooking. Miller even tells Rezlar that the owner of Cobble Bread, just across the street from Thedeim's manor, is working on making a version of the signature bread that only uses subterranean ingredients!

He wishes her luck, as a treat like that would definitely help with morale if everyone were stuck in the hold.

For meat, the Spiderkin Enclave is to the rescue with their cave lobsters. The crustaceans don't look like much, but they have a lot of meat in their tails and claws. Their innards can also somehow be made into a delicious and nutritious broth. He knows offal can be healthy to eat, but it's always been disgusting to him. Some people really like it, but he's never acquired the taste.

Other food needs should be able to be sourced from Thedeim directly, especially if he expands toward the hold. He talked with Tarl to try to figure out Thedeim's next move, and after having a laugh at the idea of predicting what the dungeon might do, he told him the most likely surface expansion is probably out past the cemetery.

Tarl said it would probably take a couple expansions to actually get to the hold, but with Teemo's shortcuts, it shouldn't be too difficult to get some kind of secret passage from there into the dungeon; it'd be a good plan for him and the city both, after all. The city would continue to get access to his resources, and he'd continue to get access to plenty of delvers.

The only thing stopping Teemo from doing it now is that they haven't surveyed to find the location for the hold's entrance . . . and the fact that Teemo is off to the Southwood again.

Rezlar hopes he comes back soon, just as he hopes he comes back with good news. He's seen the anatomical sketches of the strange invader, and that's definitely the kind of thing he doesn't want anywhere near his town. If he's lucky, the hostiles will be dealt with before they can be even more of a threat. It shouldn't come to that . . . probably.

While he saw the sketch and wanted no part of it, Karn looked eager to fight something like that. The adventurers can have it with Rezlar's blessing. He might be getting better with his rapier, but he just doesn't have the kind of adventuring drive as most of them. He's glad his friends and teammates have a similar attitude toward delving: it's fun, it's a good way to get stronger, but it's not the highest priority.

Rhonda wants to learn, Freddie wants to grow in his faith and inspire others, and Rezlar just wants to . . .

He pauses going over the reports and plans as he realizes he actually has something he wants. For the longest time, he just wanted to be left alone, to not create any waves, to not gain any attention. But those were mostly things he *didn't* want.

Now . . . he wants to build Fourdock to be prosperous and safe. It wasn't exactly poor and dangerous before, but it can be so much more.

He likes the people, even though their attention makes him uncomfortable. The thought of walking down the street with everyone waving at him still makes his stomach twinge, but the idea of walking down the street as his adventurer identity, with people just talking, laughing, being loud, and living happily . . . that's the kind of thing that he could strive for.

Chapter 80

Teemo's on his way back home to get the medics and whoever else wants to come for the actual assault. Most of the adventurers are going with him, either just to go back home or to get a few last-minute things so they'll be prepared for the attack. The scouting teams are already back out, setting up the base camp.

I'm still nervous about it, but they're as prepared as they can be, and are all pretty experienced delvers. It's easy to forget that I'm a bit of an anomaly with how I treat my delvers, but a hostile dungeon like the Maw is what they are used to dealing with. They've only just started setting up, so no excursions just yet. I imagine they'll wait for the reinforcements to make any real effort of getting a closer look, but who knows with adventurers.

As for my dwellers, they're all making their own preparations for the upcoming fight. It pains me to see, but they're probably right to ditch the metal armor and weapons. The compound bows are still going to be used, since they should be at the rear, and so out of range of anyone trying to take control of them. If any hostiles get close enough to actually make use of their Metal affinity, the archers are going to be in trouble anyway.

That doesn't mean the melee fighters are going in empty-handed. The nets for the tarantulakin aren't metal, so they should still be able to ensnare foes like that. They're also swapping out their tridents for oversize bolas, reminding me of . . . I forget the name, but that ninja weapon with a weight on one end and a hook on the other. Except they're putting weights on both ends.

They're using rocks and ensnaring them in a big monkey's fist knot, which looks cool, and I don't doubt could be used to devastating effect as a blunt weapon.

The jumping spiders are making do in their own way, too. The adjusting metal heads of the spears are gone, but the quick-swap mechanism is still being used. They managed to convince Nova to stay behind and help create obsidian, and they've been making a ton of volcanic glass spearheads attached to the quick swap.

While there are apparently skills to help them penetrate metal armor, they'll still break pretty often. But with the quick swap, they can just change out a broken head on the fly. Not how I expected the spears to work, but I'm proud of my dwellers for thinking on their feet and coming up with a solution like that.

Leo and Honey are having the dwellers drill with the denizens when they're not adjusting their gear, my scions wanting to make sure as many kinks in the system are worked out here instead of getting blindsided on the battlefield. They're also working on changing their formation in tight quarters, letting whoever needs to get to the front get there with minimal hassle while also not just creating a huge hole for the enemy to take advantage of.

They first tried swapping out half at a time, but that left too much of a gap. Thirds work better, and I think the new drills are trying a quarter at a time. I think thirds will be the best option, since I don't think the tunnels will allow for eight fighters to stand side to side. They might work with four, but I think six is going to be most common.

Still, narrower will probably be four, and wider could be eight. Learning to change positions in thirds and quarters will give them options for how to handle the actual fighting.

While my dwellers' offensive needs are being handled, their defenses are suffering. They're experimenting with wooden and silk armor, but it's really clunky with what tools they have available in the field. Queen is hoping to fix that, at least partially. Her work with lacquer-and-silk composite armor is impressive, but I don't think it's as good as metal armor yet. Still, it'll be better than nothing.

She's working on standardizing the process and making it work with what she can get in the Southwood. I'm pretty sure tree sap is a major part of resin, and silk will be easy enough to source from the dwellers, too. She's still refining it as quickly as she can and preparing to take part of her lab on the road. She's intending to come with the medics, and I'm not going to complain.

Not only will she be able to try to outfit the dwellers in composite armor, but she could also help with any alchemical healing that might be required, too.

Thing may or may not come along. He's been experimenting with how well the composite takes enchantments. So far, it doesn't seem to do so easily, but even a simple durability increase would be great. I'm pretty sure most metal armor uses a lot of enchanting to make them lighter, but the composite is already nicely light. A durability boost would be perfect.

He still hasn't perfected it yet, and if I understand the problem right, I don't blame him. Most armors are engraved, etched, or inlaid with enchantments because that works best on metal. I'd imagine it works decently with wood, too, but not a whole lot of people wander around in wooden armor. Robes and cloth have the enchantments woven into them. Thing's been trying to use the metal methods, but they aren't working.

I poke the bond with him with the notion to try weaving the enchantment before the resin/lacquer sets, to see if that would work better. He might even be able to inlay something into the lacquer as it dries, too. Maybe composite materials require composite solutions.

He freezes in his work as he listens to the bond, then scrambles off the table to go find Queen. I can feel inspiration practically boiling off him, so I have a good feeling in regard to what he'll be able to accomplish with Queen's help.

I wonder if it'll actually let him enchant it even more than a more traditional material. If so, we're going to have to try figuring out how to make metallic honeycomb.

I eye Honey's bees before mentally shaking my head. No, I think it'll be on Jello to try to make something like that.

In normal composites, a metal honeycomb is . . . well, just that, with the walls usually only a little thicker than foil. I'm pretty sure it's usually used in vehicle armor, often sandwiched between carbon fiber or other ones. Maybe they run the fibers through the comb, too? I have no idea, but that'd be pretty cool, and probably a pain to manufacture by hand.

Still, if it'd allow for enchanting the fiber, the metal, and even inlaying something into the resin, we could have some serious enchantment density.

That's probably why Thing is signing at Queen like a madhand.

Oh, maybe we should try using chain or ring mail instead of a honeycomb, at least for the first prototype. It'll end up being a bit bulky, but probably not worse than some of the full plate I've seen people wear.

I just wish we had some good weapons that aren't metal. It's definitely too late to whip anything up right now, but it's absolutely something to try to prepare so we'll be ready if anything else with Metal affinity shows up. So . . . what are the options?

Classic weapons do one or a mix of three things: bash, cut, stab. Bash is pretty easy to do without metal. Practically any rock can be carved into a good smashing shape, though they tend to crumble if you hit them too hard. A durability enchantment will probably help with that . . . probably.

Cutting and stabbing are a bit more difficult. Stone and wood can be used for stabbing, but wood doesn't hold a point very well without some magical shenanigan, and rock weakens a lot when carved to a point. Composites don't offer much in the way of help, or at least normal ones don't. No matter how refined, it's still just tree sap and silk. Those can only be sharpened so much.

Is there anything weird that might work as a composite? It'll be difficult, because metal really does have all the properties a good weapon wants: it'll hold an edge, so it's hard, but it's also strong enough to not shatter when under a high force.

Even when it breaks, it tends toward bending rather than breaking. A bent sword isn't great, but probably a little better than just having an empty hilt, and a bent hammer doesn't really care, while a bent spearhead can be forced back into shape for a couple more thrusts.

So we need flexibility and hardness, which are not quite mutually exclusive, but they're not far off. Magic might be able to help some . . .

Maybe a take on a macuahuitl? I've heard them called obsidian swords, which is pretty far off. They're practically a cricket bat with shards of obsidian along the sides. I'm pretty sure they were more for maiming than actually killing, but refining the idea might work: softer core, harder edge.

So . . . silk and lacquer for the main body of the weapon, and maybe some kind of ceramic edge? I think I've seen swords that were basically a razor-thin bit of steel set into a carbon fiber blade. I don't know how well that'd actually work, and it'd also still have some metal in it. I don't really like the idea of trying a ceramic or glass edge, though. Maybe a thin bit of metal wouldn't give someone with the affinity enough to actually get a grip on it?

I'll have to ask Berdol once Teemo gets back. I want him to ask Tarl about the known denizens of the Maw, anyway. I should also touch base with Rezlar, too. I don't know if he'll be able to contribute much to the fight, but there's more going on than just dealing with the Maw.

With the lighthouse getting close to finishing, he'll probably want to get started on the vault. Coda seems to be looking forward to that, too. The lighthouse gave him some unique challenges, and the vault will, too. I just need to make sure there are no crazy social experiments going on in there.

It'll probably be fine, as long as Queen doesn't run the place.

Chapter 81

The problem of a bladed weapon helps distract me until Teemo gets here. At least I have a good idea for a sharp weapon that's not metallic, even if we'll only really have a supply after the fighting: the blade limbs of the least monsters.

If I had thought of it earlier, we could have harvested them from the battlefield outside the Southwood, but they've long since dispersed into mana at this point. But a properly field-dressed limb with a durability enchantment would probably make a perfect short sword.

Or maybe a pick. Hard to say. Either way, Teemo's back, and there's not really time to let him relax. At least he knows my plans, so it's not like I'm blindsiding him with work. No matter how much he jokingly complains.

"You're a slave driver, Boss. Poor Teemo, making shortcuts with no moment to rest before he has to go meet with people. Poor Teemo." His grin and tone give away the game, but it's fun to play along.

Yes, Evil Thedeim! I shall work my Voice to the bone! No rest for you!

"Oh, cruel fate! To be the Voice of such a dungeon!"

We go back and forth a few times until Teemo pops into the ODA and does an Igor impersonation. "Tarl! The Master needs your brain!" he exclaims, dragging one of his feet.

The elf just gives my Voice a confused look from behind his desk. It looks like he's planning out his inspections for the spring. "Teemo? Are you alright?"

My Voice bursts into laughter and nods, taking a few seconds to gather himself enough to reply. "Yeah, I'm fine! Me and the Boss are just joking around, though we really do need your brain for this. We've got a list of the denizens the Maw should have, so the Boss wants to know if there are any easy weaknesses or special synergies we need to keep in mind."

Tarl looks over to Telar at her desk, who perks up at the mention of a list and pulls out a scroll. She uncaps her inkwell and readies her pen, then locks her focus onto hopefully her favorite rat. "I'll make an official note of it. I've been preparing a dossier on this Maw, even if it's going to soon be subsumed. The guild will want the information regardless."

Teemo nods and takes a moment to organize his thoughts. "Alright, let me see . . . The Maw has two types of spawners, three if you count the least monsters—those are the weird leech-headed things. Anyway, two main spawner types, with several of each. We're estimating between three and five of each fey and elemental. The Maw is Metal affinity, and the spawners match."

Tarl groans at that but doesn't otherwise interrupt as Telar scribbles. Teemo lets her catch up before continuing.

"It only has a scion from the fey spawners, as well as the Harbinger. Want to guess what the scion is, Tarl?"

"A redcap," he answers with no hesitation. "Probably its Voice, too. That many spawners mean it should have upgraded by now."

Teemo nods at that. "Yep, a redcap, and it's the Voice, according to the two refugees we found. It maxed out the spawners, too, so it had an Elf and Dwarf Enclave, but they got emancipated?" he asks, looking to Tarl for a bit more information on that. Telar is still scribbling, so Tarl indulges my and Teemo's curiosities.

"Emancipating enclaves is more common for older dungeons out in the wilderness. Having an enclave gives a dungeon good bonuses and can more easily let it develop its territory, but an emancipated enclave allows for more mana generation. When still an enclave, the dwellers are usually a net neutral on mana and resources. But once emancipated and technically fully independent, they can generate mana for the dungeon by ordinary delving."

Teemo snorts. "Technically independent is right. They're independent in name only, especially with the Maw's clergy practically running the town."

Tarl and Telar both nod, with the latter pausing her scribbling to give her opinion. "Dungeon worship is quite common among dwellers and the recently emancipated, letting dungeons get mana both from the worship and from the delving. I've heard some inspectors say it's only a short-term gain, with people often moving away after a couple generations if the dungeon treats them poorly."

"I mean, they're not wrong about that. But it's a pretty good mana boost, as far as we can tell, and just because dungeons *can* live for generations, doesn't mean many actually do," supplements Tarl. "Like with Thedeim's own dwellers. With how he treats them, I doubt they'd leave of their own accord.

"The only real argument against him emancipating them is political. The principalities would want to claim them as beastkin, the kingdom would want to claim them because they're in our territory, and the holds might even try to claim them as being below the surface. It'd be a pretty weak claim, but they could try it just to have better access to the ores in the labyrinth.

"As long as Thedeim doesn't need more mana income, there's no need to emancipate them directly into a big political mess."

Teemo and I both chuckle at that. The idea of giving my dwellers true freedom has crossed my mind, but the political ramifications have kept the idea deep in the fridge, not even close to on the back burner. "Yeah, the Boss is aware. Not about the dwarves maybe making a claim, but about the big mess it'd cause politically. He's got ideas for cleaning up a lot of messes, but politics is not one of them."

Smirks are shared before Telar taps the scroll with a finger. "You said you had the list of denizens?"

"Right, right. The weird spawner has least and maybe lessers. The Boss thinks they'll probably go into normals or standards, then to greaters and greatest, but that's just names. We have no idea what anything beyond the least would look like.

"The fey are needleslinks, bladesprites, bolties, bladesprite swarms, pricklethorns, and thinlinks. For the elementals there are living caltrops, lodewisps, rust elementals, sliverstorms, iron maidens, and forgemasters."

Tarl whistles at the list as Telar jots it down. "Those are some ugly denizens. The bladesprites and sliverstorms work similarly to deny movement and will both be very dangerous when combined with the caltrops. You're going to need some good area attacks to deal with those.

"Try to minimize the amount of metal your dwellers bring to the battlefield. Only the lodewisps and the forgemasters can really turn it back against you, but the sliverstorms can tear up any they get ahold of and make the swarm bigger.

"I wouldn't imagine they'll want to use the lodewisps too much, however. They're very good at controlling nearby metal, but they don't discriminate between friend and foe. They can act a lot like a sliverstorm if they get the chance, but with all the other metal denizens, you can probably not worry too much about them.

"The rust elementals are going to be the biggest threat to anyone using metal, though. The elementals are pretty weak on their own, but they can relieve someone of their armor and weapon really quickly, and then they're vulnerable to attacks from the others. They'll probably be on the front lines, hoping to devastate anyone wearing armor, then either fall into battle or retreat to make room for the fighters.

"The iron maidens will be ambushers, not actual fighters. They'll be guarding any side passages, hoping to pick off scouts and other sneaky attacks. I'd expect them to mostly be in the dungeon itself. The real nastiness will come from the last three working together."

Tarl leans back in his chair, folding his arms as he thinks.

"Pricklethorns, thinlinks, and forgemasters. Those are going to be nasty. Pricklethorns like to grapple and are tough to take down quickly. Usually, grapplers would make it difficult for others to help fight, but thinlinks have enough control over their chains to be able to do just that, no matter how hectic the melee gets. And forgemasters will be buffing them both, as well as tossing around offensive magics too.

"An overwhelming magic attack would be the best option, but that's easier said than done. In a tight tunnel . . . I think the main priority will be not to let the front line descend into anarchy from the pricklethorns. That's also a lot easier to say than do, though."

Tarl looks thoughtful, trying to puzzle out a solution, before Teemo gives them our rough plan for the fights. "For our denizens, we're going to use as many basilisks as possible to try to deal with the caltrops, sprites, and storms. We'll also be able to use the wyrms to get around them if we need to, and they can play their own havoc with the enemy lines of prickles, thinlinks, and forgemasters. Arcane hands can bring some magical pain to bear, too, to try to keep things in our favor.

"For the dwellers . . . they're swapping away from metal right now, and the Boss is working on replacements. I dunno what the adventurers are doing, but I'm sure they all have some kind of plan, at least if they're going. Against the area-denial denizens, they'll be waiting on the basilisks to clear them out, and against the enemy denizen parties . . . they'll probably rely heavily on using silk to ensnare what they can and hopefully keep the fights from getting too messy."

Tarl nods to himself. "That sounds workable, though I'd suggest trying to keep as many adventuring groups handy as possible to help deal with area denial. Basilisks are good and strong, but they're still obvious targets. Having adventurers supplement them will make progress a lot smoother."

"Then we'll pass that along. I think Karn is our next stop. The adventurers are going to be needed soon, so the Boss would like to get a head count."

"I'll work with Telar to get a primer on those denizens written, then. Metal-affinity dungeons are pretty rare, so I doubt many of them have had the pleasure of fighting those particular monsters before. We'll still need to charge them, but it shouldn't dent anyone's coin bag." Tarl looks a little uncomfortable about that, so Telar speaks up.

"It's against guild policy to give information for free, but with your contribution and the situation, we can put the payment for your information toward that. And speaking of guild policy . . . can we purchase any additional information about the Maw, once this is over? Even subsumed dungeon information can be valuable to the guild."

Teemo echoes my smirk as he nods. "I think we can do that. Honey will probably write an entire encyclopedia on the thing by the time we're done."

Tarl looks indifferent to that answer, but Telar looks a bit conflicted. I'd say she's trying to decide if the boost to her prestige in the guild will be worth trying to organize that much information, which only makes me laugh harder.

As if Honey's standards aren't stricter than the guild's.

Chapter 82

Teemo chats with Tarl and Telar for a few more minutes before taking his leave. I was hoping we'd be able to ask Berdol a couple questions about Metal affinity, but it seems he's delving right now.

I take a few minutes to search for him while Teemo heads to the adventurers' guild, and I only just spot him before Teemo pops out of a shortcut. The catkin is exploring the lava labyrinth, so I think we'll have plenty of time to finish with the guild before trying to catch up to him to ask our questions.

My Voice scurries through the door and weaves through a variety of feet as he makes for the bar. To Teemo's ears, the bar is pretty loud, and it seems a lot busier than I was expecting it to be. He climbs up next to a hyenakin . . . or is she a gnoll? Is there a difference?

My confusion doesn't distract Teemo as he gets Karn's attention.

"Hey, Karn!"

"Oh hey, Teemo! I'll get to you after this round, unless it's important?" he asks as he gathers a double fistful of mugs.

"It's important, but not really time sensitive." Karn quickly fills the mugs and slams them on the bar.

"Six ales! Come get it yourself; I got stuff to do!" Chuckles resound as a large party gets up to grab their refreshments as Karn comes over to Teemo's end of the bar. "So, what's up? Or do you want to head to my office?"

I think it'll be fine to speak here. There isn't really anything we need to keep secret from the adventurers.

"Here's fine. The Boss finally has a better idea of when to strike the Maw."

Karn raises an eyebrow. "The Maw? Is that what the dungeon is calling itself?"

"Yeah, and it's quite a piece of work. It's Metal affinity and has the Harbinger, which is a Mental-affinity monstrosity."

The thin orc whistles at that. "A nasty combination. What kind of level?"

Teemo shrugs. "Pretty strong, but Rocky was able to obliterate it on his own, so a pretty far step from him."

The guildmaster rubs his chin as he considers that. Teemo can see several of the bar patrons looking thoughtful as well. If they're thinking, might as well give them more information. "We talked to Tarl about the denizens too, and he didn't seem too worried. Some of the combinations will be nasty, but he didn't seem to think it was anything insurmountable."

"Yeah? What's the worst of the denizens?"

"Thinlinks, pricklethorns, and forgemasters. He thinks they'll probably form groups, but the tunnels should hopefully keep them from getting too overwhelming."

Karn frowns at the list. "Hmm . . . that *is* pretty nasty, but there should be more than a few groups who ought to be able to handle something like that. Anything else?"

"Well, we don't expect the Harbinger to be on the front lines, but it's possible. There's also a Redcap Scion that seems to be a real nasty one, too. Oh, and you should be getting groups coming back with info on the dungeon and the caves and such soon. A couple groups are helping with better intel gathering. We're hoping to be able to attack in as soon as a week, if we can find the Kobold Enclave."

"Aranya doesn't know where it is?" asks the orc, looking surprised.

Teemo sighs and shakes his head. "No. Inside the Maw itself, but aside from that, she doesn't remember. She wasn't one of the ones allowed out into the dungeon and the town outside. When she fled, she wasn't exactly making a map, either. All she really knows is the core isn't inside the enclave, or at least not visibly so."

"Hmm. A town, you said?"

"Yeah. Emancipated dwellers; worship the Maw. Most of them are civilians. The Boss isn't sure if he should try to leave securing it to you guys or try to do that himself."

"Fair, that kind of thing can get real messy. My guilders are great at their jobs, but any mistake can lead to a tragedy. I'll try asking the Shieldies if they want to join for that part of the mission. They're a lot better at being organized, and they are used to having the defenses to be able to react instead of having to act first like most adventurers do."

"Yeah, that'd probably be for the best. You guys are a lot more used to just kicking butt, but the Shield followers actively train in public relations. It'd probably be a good idea to have a few groups of adventurers around to help them out, though. Boss was hoping to use the rest to potentially attack the Maw itself; try to open a route for his heavy-hitting scions to come and actually bring the fight to it."

Karn nods, looking like he's mentally sorting a couple lists. "The newer groups will be good to help the Shieldies. Not the kids; they don't need to get mixed up in this. I have a few groups transitioning away from being mercs that should be able to do what might need to be done . . ." He trails off for a few moments before his eyes latch back onto Teemo.

"For the assault, I think basically any of my established parties should be good. Did Vnarl's group say what they were going to do?"

"Yeah, they're helping with a forward base for spying. They're not especially good at being sneaky, but if anything nasty manages to find the base, they'll make sure everyone gets out. For the actual attack, they haven't said, but I can't imagine them wanting to be anywhere besides the front line."

Karn chuckles at that. "Yeah, I don't think they'd let that kind of opportunity slip by. How are you going to keep the adventurers from giving the Maw a whole bunch of mana from killing the denizens?"

"We're going to be pairing them up with some of the Boss's denizens. I don't know if that'll let the entire group count as invaders or not, but it should at least make the Maw take some kind of a loss on each encounter."

"Hmm, experience splitting is complicated enough without adding that kind of variable in. The Maw only getting half the return is probably a reasonable assumption?"

Teemo nods. "That's what the Boss is figuring, yeah. The exact numbers vary a bit, but only getting half the payback of mana from a lost denizen should be a net loss for the Maw. If we're lucky, it'll count the entire group as invaders and it'll get nothing, but we'll have to see."

"Anything else?"

"Oh, Tarl said he's working on a primer pamphlet thing for how to handle the Maw's denizens, and he says anyone interested in going should buy one."

Karn smiles at that. "I'll make sure everyone knows, and probably buy a couple copies for the library, too. That Maw probably won't stick around for much longer, but I'm always looking to make the guild bestiary more complete."

"How many adventurers do you think will want to come and help?"

Karn laughs at that and raises his voice. "If any of you were somehow *not* eavesdropping, Thedeim is putting out a call for adventurers to help put a stop to a hostile dungeon calling itself the Maw. The delve is going to be a tough one, but you'll have at least a few of Thedeim's own denizens to tag along with each party! There will also be a need for some help in securing a town, and probably room for runners and other logistics work!"

The bar goes silent at his proclamation, and Karn smirks at Teemo before he continues. "Who wants to go?"

Every hand in the guild rises. Teemo can even hear the sounds of boots up the stairs scrambling to get down to signal their own desire to come fight. Karn's grin only widens as he sees the expected response.

"I'm gonna have to force a lottery to keep someone behind with me. Not only are you offering a new adventure to a guild founded to find things like that, but you're also the best delve anyone here has ever had, Thedeim. You might not be an adventurer, but you're still practically family to a lot of the people here.

"Aranya's one of us, too. Her people are in trouble. Adventurers might have a reputation for being flighty or unreliable, but we protect our own. You saved Yvonne; don't think any of us have forgotten that. We can't buy you a round as thanks, but we can definitely go kick some butt to show our appreciation."

His wide smile softens to one of pride in his guild as everyone raises a glass. He raises an empty mug as well. "Besides, this is going to be an adventure nobody is going to want to miss. The Slim Chance guild always defies the odds!"

The hall erupts in a cheer as Teemo and I are both a bit dumbfounded. I've always tried to treat the adventurers right, but I somehow never expected them to reciprocate, especially not with a situation as dangerous as this.

I guess . . . that kind of attitude, of doing what needs doing no matter the danger, is just what makes an adventurer an adventurer.

Chapter 83

After all that with the adventurers, I'm feeling more motivated than ever to make the fight with the Maw a quick and decisive one, if at all possible. The adventurers probably would prefer a bit more of a fight, but I'd rather have them disappointed and all coming home. The frustrating part is that there's probably not a lot more I can do to try to influence that particular outcome.

I've done a lot of planning, and my denizens, scions, and dwellers have been executing a lot of those plans. There are a few last-minute things to do, and who knows, maybe the final bit of scouting will reveal some fatal flaw to exploit in the Maw, but I doubt it.

The Maw is big and old, so if it had some fundamental flaw in its defenses, something would have gotten through by now, I'd imagine. Maybe it'd be something only I would notice and be able to exploit, but I feel like magic makes having any weakness like that difficult to sustain over a long period.

"You okay, Boss?" squeaks my Voice while in the middle of a shortcut.

Hmm? Oh, sorry. I'm just . . .

"Just running around in circles in that big mind of yours. Try to relax or something, Boss. Everyone and everything is about as prepared as we can make them now. Don't go stressing out over something you can't really do anything about."

I take a deep mental breath and nod. *Yeah . . . you're right. It's just easier to say than to do, you know?*

Teemo barks a laugh at that. "Yeah, I know. Go watch the delvers or something. I'm gonna check if Rezlar is available for a meeting later. Go unwind, Boss. Waiting is hard, but it's all we can really do right now."

I let my attention wander over my territory, watching everything going on. People are mining, gathering, fighting, looting, chatting, crafting . . . The life just makes me happy to see. I don't focus on anyone in specific, instead just kinda soaking in the atmosphere. My attention eventually drifts toward the Ratkin Enclave, where I notice Aranya with a mixed group of dwellers around her.

Usually, that'd mean she's giving or about to give a sermon, but the mood feels a little different for that. It's like just before a movie starts rather than right before the pastor comes in. Aranya smiles as my attention falls on the group and speaks up over the murmurs of the crowd.

"It feels like Lord Thedeim is interested in today's legend, too."

The murmurings shift to have a mix of surprise and reverence, but I'm feeling a bit more confused. She's been telling legends? About what?

The red kobold smiles as she feels my confusion.

"Kobold legends, passed down from before the Maw captured us. Today, I'm going to tell our creation legend."

Ooh, a creation myth? Those are fun. I settle in to listen, and Aranya takes a few more moments to prepare herself for the tale.

"At first, all was still. The earth, the waters, the air . . . the mana. Nothing moved, and though it was very stable, there was no life. Then, there was a disturbance in the mana, causing it to ripple like a tapped bowl of water. The movement was slight and small compared to all the mana, but it was still there.

"The ripples expanded—bouncing, reflecting—until finally, chance brought enough of the ripples together to coalesce. This coalescence was the First Sanctuary, born from the confluence of still and moving mana. The First Sanctuary marveled at everything around it, observing and examining everything it could sense.

"The earth was hard and unmoving, stable and secure. It had interesting shapes and structure, but it didn't hold the Sanctuary's attention for too long. The air and water held its attention for even less time. This is partially because the mana was so much more interesting. The mana *moved*. The ripples were there, creating interesting and intriguing interactions, as fascinating as they were fleeting.

"It looked out and saw that some mana wasn't moving. In truth, most of it was still and boring. There was so much stillness, with such a small island of motion. It started to fear the ripples would stop altogether, but looking closer relieved the First Sanctuary. It was helping move the mana, sending out its own ripples to keep it interesting.

"But is it fair for the mana to be the only interesting thing? If the Sanctuary can move the mana, can it move the earth? It tried, but earth is stubborn; far too stubborn for the Sanctuary to move. Perhaps it should start with something easier? The water is probably easier, but the air would be even easier still! Water likes to sit in its ponds, lakes, and oceans, but air seems to be happy anywhere. Not wanting to be anywhere in specific should make it easy to move, right?

"The Sanctuary tried to shift the air, tried to use mana to make it react. It succeeded! Making the air move was easy! It shifted the air for a time, enjoying how it could even coax the water to do the same, at least a little. It even enjoyed how stubbornly the earth would stay still as the air whirled around it. But there was a problem: the air would only shift when the Sanctuary itself made it do it. Could it make the air move on its own?

"This was far more difficult. Air doesn't mind moving, but it also doesn't mind being still. It needs a will, a reason to move! And so, the First Sanctuary wove mana into the air, trying to make it understand how much more interesting motion was! The mana slipped away from the First Sanctuary, and it thought it had failed, but then, it noticed a small swirl of air, going about on its own. It worked! The First Sanctuary had created the first Air elemental!

"It made more, and eventually, the Air elementals learned to make more of themselves. The First Sanctuary watched them dance and frolic, their motions disrupting even the still mana! Now the First Sanctuary could truly enjoy movement without having to make it all on its own.

"With its success fresh in its mind, the First Sanctuary set about making a new elemental. It learned with the air how to make movement, and though water was more resistant, the First Sanctuary could get the waters to make waves, to move in rivers, to fall from clouds.

"And with it now used to motion, the First could weave will into it just like with the air. This time, the mana didn't slip away at the end, instead flowing smoothly into the small drop of water. The Air elementals welcomed their new brethren, and the two groups worked to keep their elements in motion. The First relished in the camaraderie and wished to bring in the earth as well.

"With all the movement, even stubborn earth would sometimes try to shift, though it found it much more difficult. Sand would ride the winds, but rarely moved on its own. Rain could relocate some of the mountains, but once it had slid down far enough, the earth went still again. This would be much more difficult.

"The First worked hard to make the earth move, and though it didn't seem against the idea anymore, it still refused to! It tried harder, even creating an earthquake, but the rumbling quickly subsided. Perhaps the Sanctuary should try making the elemental and let it work it out?

"Making a single piece of earth move quickly seemed to be impossible, as any large rock would shatter instead of flow like the water or air. The First was concerned, but the broken bits of earth didn't seem to mind. Uncertainly, it tried again, gathering the broken pieces to suffuse with will and mana, and to the Sanctuary's surprise, it worked!

"The small Earth elemental was happy to move, though it didn't do so like the other two elements. They would dance and glide, while the earth would rumble along. The Sanctuary tried to ask it why, but the Earth elemental was confused. It was moving, as was its element. Wasn't that what the First Sanctuary wanted?

"Of course, but the earth wasn't moving at all! Then the small Earth elemental told the Sanctuary to just pay more attention. The earth all around was moving, inspired by the air and water, but moving in its own way. It moved slowly, deliberately. It didn't need to move at the speed of the others. It would take its time.

"This was strange to the First Sanctuary, but after watching for a time, it came to appreciate the earth's movements, as well as those of the air and water. And yet . . . it felt like there could be more to it. But what else was there? The mana? It was already moving that.

"It thought as it watched the elements, and eventually noticed something interesting. The air's movement brought cold air and froze some shallow water.

Could ice move? It felt very different from regular water, so perhaps? The First tried to make the ice move, and immediately felt like something was wrong. It was very different from the others; not really stubborn, but . . . missing *something*. What could it be?

"It thought and observed some more until an Earth elemental brought something interesting it had found deep below: liquid rock! Very *hot* liquid rock! The Earth elemental called it fire but didn't know what it was. Once it left the liquid rock, the rock became regular earth again.

"Seeing the fire inspired the First Sanctuary, and it realized what the ice was missing. It needed something to move with! The other elements might be happy to dance with each other, but these two would need an opposite to move properly!

"It still needed some of the other elements to move well, however. The ice needed water, and the fire needed the stone, but stone was so difficult to work with! The First Sanctuary tried to get the water to take both of the new elements, but while it didn't mind the ice, it refused the fire. Air, however, was eager to be included, and so took the fire and burst into a brilliant orange color.

"The Sanctuary was happy at that, but could see it needed to work quickly. The fire and ice were suffused with will and mana, each opposing the other, yet also somehow bolstering them. The First Sanctuary released the two, and they spun off in a beautiful dance across the earth, the air, and the water!

"The First Sanctuary reveled in the new motion, seeing so many things moving, and coaxing more of the mana to move with it. The endless stillness was being beaten back. After a time, a Water elemental came to the Sanctuary with something new. It was a lot like water, but green, and could move on its own despite not being an elemental!

"The Water elemental left it with the Sanctuary, and the First Sanctuary watched. It saw the green move toward the light, away from the shadow, and it saw another pair to release into the world. At this point, it was used to creating them, and so the first Light and Shadow elementals were created.

"It continued to watch the green with its strange movements, and eventually saw some of it stop. Something about its movement, and lack of movement, felt fundamentally *different* than the difference between moving and still mana, and after watching closely, the First Sanctuary saw another pair to unleash: life and death. While the others had created some motion with their release, the Life and Death elementals created the biggest difference of all!

"New green appeared across the land, some standing tall to get more of the light it needed. Things appeared to eat the green, and things appeared to eat what ate the green."

Aranya finally pauses and smiles at the gathered dwellers. "And that is how everything came to be. Mostly. The creation of kobolds and thinking life is a different legend." Her smile grows mischievous as she glances toward my core, despite the buildings, caves, and stone between her and it. "Maybe I'll tell that one tomorrow?"

Aw, but I wanna hear it now!

Chapter 84

I spend most of the rest of the day watching the enclaves, letting Teemo catch Rezlar up on what's going on. He doesn't really have anything new to add to the plans, though he does have a few questions about resources.

A full-on iron vein would be pretty cool, and I don't doubt it'll be sustainable. Just the limestone quarry is pumping out tons of mana from how much the people want it. Making an iron vein won't exactly be cheap, but the upkeep is pretty minimal. I'm confident it'll be a good mana printer.

I'll be waiting until after the fight, though. I'm sitting on a lot of mana, which I fully intend to let Fluffles leverage for the fight. He and Teemo have been working on something interesting, and I get the feeling it's going to need boatloads of mana to be able to actually pull off.

I check for cheaper veins, and while copper and tin wouldn't be too bad, some of the more interesting minerals just flat out don't show up. Mythril and orichalcum do, but those are stupid expensive. Meanwhile, more normal things like sulfur or salt don't. I dunno if it's because of where I'm located or if they're just not options for veins. If they're quarries, I don't see them yet, either.

So yeah, I'll be adding an iron vein to my to-do list, alongside expanding into the forest and making the Ant Enclave. But all that aside, my dwellers are doing great. The spiderkin have been working hard to make more winter wear, and so they've been wandering around a bit more on the surface. I'm always a little nervous when they leave my view, but they're grown-ups, and the town is safe, so I do my best not to dwell on it.

I'm also keeping an eye on where Aranya told that legend yesterday. She promised another one today, and I don't want to miss it. If I didn't know better, I'd say she's deliberately taking her time preparing and doing other errands; I wouldn't put it past her to tease me like that. At least being focused on the story keeps me from obsessing over the upcoming fight.

I kinda wish she wasn't joining the next group going that way, if only to get more legends out of her. I bet she was on her way to a Historian class or something before stumbling into me. Maybe she actually was one? I think classes can change or upgrade or something? Nobody really talks about it much, at least not where I can hear.

My mind idly chews on the idea of classes advancing and how before I notice Aranya making her way to the . . . pulpit, I guess? She smiles as I settle in to listen, and the gathered ratkin and spiderkin glance around. I wonder if they can feel me like Aranya can. Tarl said he could sense when I was paying attention, but is that just having good perception, or is it an inspector thing?

"Yes, Lord Thedeim is listening today," says Aranya to the gathered dwellers, leading to the murmuring growing a bit more excited before she continues and they fall into a respectful quiet.

"I promised the legend of how kobolds came to be, but it's really how all intelligent life came to be. Oh, people argue their own legends, of course, but this is the one my people tell.

"The First Sanctuary, after creating so much, was not satisfied to stop now. I can only assume spawning was different so long ago, because I never said anything about a spawner for the elementals, did I? Sometimes they would make more of themselves, and sometimes the First Sanctuary would make them itself, but there was no spawner for them.

"The First Sanctuary never imagined the need for something like that, and so merrily kept creating and sending the creations out into the stagnant mana. Some would die, but that was simply part of life. The First Dungeon experimented with life, trying to weave all new and wonderful varieties. The fey came first.

"Did you think a kobold legend would start with kobolds?" she asks the crowd with a smile. "Though I say the fey came first, it would be more accurate to say plants and beasts came first, but they were part of the last legend, so they don't count.

"Anyway, the fey. They were different from the beasts. Most of the beasts had little use for mana, at least in any complex form. They would use some, but their manner of use was not far from what many today would consider to be martial. They would hit harder rather than throw a fireball.

"The fey were inclined to wield mana more directly. The First Sanctuary even looked back at the elementals and was intrigued to discover they were rather balanced in their mana usage. With three different ways of handling mana, the First Sanctuary wanted to see if the different varieties of life could handle more.

"It took time, but progress was steady. Stronger beasts were created, stronger elementals, stronger fey. They would impact the stagnant mana more and more, and yet, the First Sanctuary felt there was still room for improvement. Finer manipulators, greater intellects, things to better guide and better understand mana were needed.

"The First decided to focus on the fey for this new idea. The beasts saw little difference between mana and muscle, and the elementals had difficulty understanding there was a difference between themselves and mana. But the fey actively tried to manipulate it. That would make the process much easier to start with!

"And so, after much effort and a great multitude of lesser fey being created, the First Sanctuary created the first elf. The Sanctuary was beside itself with joy, and quickly made many more. The new life naturally brought mana to motion, making the Sanctuary's desire all the easier.

"The elves were grateful, and though they stayed with the Sanctuary for a time, they were curious about the lands of stagnant mana. The First Sanctuary warned them of the dangers, of the strange, twisted versions of so many of its creations that would come back mad with bloodlust.

"But the elves needed to go, so the Sanctuary wouldn't stop them. Once they left its territory, it was shocked to see just what kind of impact they had on fully stagnant mana. While it could feel them moving it within its borders, the mana almost heaved and frothed with what the elves would make it do!

"The Sanctuary worried it may have made a mistake until the stagnant mana tried to resist the movement, and the opposing forces created a new Sanctuary. The First was ecstatic to have another of its kind. It guided the newborn, and the two worked to bring even more intelligent life into the world. With the success of the elves, the First set about replicating it with the beasts, while the second decided to create different elves based on different affinities.

"The First created beastkin, apparently many at once. I don't know which kin was first. I personally suspect birdkin, but that might just be from me listening to some of Yvonne's legends of the goldenwings." She titters at a few memories before continuing.

"Which was first wasn't important. The important part was that they were, as a whole, much more able to expand into the stagnant mana than the elves. A single elf is versatile, sure, but will not thrive in any particular niche as well as a kin in the perfect environment.

"After the kin came the dwarves—elementals. The surface was well populated, but the tunnels of the deep were still stagnant, and the dwarves were perfectly suited to the tight confines. The second dungeon was even inspired by the dwarves to create gnomes, having had difficulties with certain affinities to base an elf on.

"Life flourished, and new Sanctuaries were born, new intelligence created. The First continued to learn and grow, observing what made the fey different from the elementals different from the beasts. As it watched and learned, it found something new; some other variety of life. It wasn't quite tied to the elementals, but to something very similar. It was a strange piece of existence, and so the First decided to weave will and mana into it, if only to see what it was.

"It created a gremlin—a primal spirit of Shadow affinity. I've heard some rangers call them nature or natural spirits, not to be confused with incorporeal undead. This new variety of life was just as wonderful to the First as the others, and soon, orcs and goblins spread across the surface and below it.

"But still, where are we? Where are the kobolds? I'm getting to that," she answers her own question with a smile.

"The First wanted to create more, but felt it had almost run out of things. It searched and found no new life like with the primal spirits. It briefly wondered if the stagnant mana could be a life, but every interaction with it showed it antithetical to it. So what could it create?

"Maybe it could weave life together, like with mana affinities? It sounded difficult, maybe impossible, but the First was eager for a challenge. It wanted to weave life together, but how? There is so much to life, in all its varieties. Where to even begin?

"Well, much like with starting with the elemental affinities, it should start with the simplest forms, the most obvious things.

"Elementals, fey, beasts, spirits. The beasts were strong and incredibly varied; surely at least one of them would provide a proper base? Muscle and bone, but the First wanted more. The elementals had such trouble differentiating themselves from raw mana because they were suffused with so much of it. Could that strength be infused into a form like a beast's? The fey were great with manipulating mana, second only to the Sanctuaries themselves, so if the First wanted the best aspect of them, it would be that mana control.

"But what of the spirits? Perhaps it didn't need them? It tried to weave the new life, and could immediately see a terrible imbalance before the whole weave fell apart. It needed more, but could a primal spirit give what was needed? The First understood the spirits the least, but it had a feeling they would prove a vital part of this new creation.

"It tried again, this time with the ephemeral traits of the spirits in the mix. They proved to be the last ingredient, though not the most vital. All parts were imperative to the whole, each needed to strike the balance and create stability. It was difficult, so very difficult. Easily the most difficult thing the First had ever done, but it finally succeeded!

"No, not the first kobold. The first *dragon*. A wyrm." Aranya smirks and continues. "After that, the creation of my people was almost an afterthought. With a new variety of life, all the Sanctuaries set about creating dragons with different affinities, and making them stronger, wiser. The First created us. Some of the other Sanctuaries were not impressed. The intelligent form of the new life, one built from the best of all the others, and it's just some short lizardkin?"

She smiles fondly. "But the First loved us as much as all of its creations. That's why we kobolds call them Sanctuaries rather than dungeons. They are our home. We don't begrudge the others for moving away and moving on. Perhaps, if given time, we would have done the same. But before we could, the Great Catastrophe befell the Sanctuaries, sparked by one that even the most devout kobold would readily call a dungeon."

She stretches and looks around the gathered dwellers, then nods to herself. "But that is another legend as well. Maybe I'll tell that one after I come back. I need to prepare to sojourn to the Southwood with the adventurers and Lord Thedeim's denizens. Be safe and be well, all of you." She smiles as everyone stands, making some small talk while I digest the legend.

There's a lot to unpack, even without how far it's probably drifted from the truth over the years. I think the biggest oddity is that I don't hear anything about the system, or whatever they call it here. Were dungeons a lot more free-form way back when? Or was the system so obvious that nobody thought to explicitly mention it? There was no mention of Voices either, despite the dungeons communicating.

At least I'll have something to occupy myself with while Aranya and everyone travels. Maybe the system was always there but only started imposing rules after that Great Catastrophe? It's too bad it sounds like there are no dungeons from that time left to ask.

Chapter 85

As everyone gathers on the far side of the cemetery wall, I watch through Teemo's eyes the growing throng in the predawn light. Every last basilisk of mine is there, and I'll probably keep sending them as they spawn. It's still pretty slow, and I'm tempted to upgrade the dragon spawner again to increase the speed, but I hold off. A couple dozen more basilisks could be nice, but I want to make sure Fluffles has plenty of my mana to throw around when the time comes.

My own denizens and scions are the first to show up, unsurprisingly. Queen has her lab packed up and secured to several tunnelbore ants, and I watch through her eyes occasionally to make sure things are going well. Sensing her pheromones is kinda weird, but she's calm and collected throughout the apparent chaos of the ants moving around. Thing's senses are even weirder; I don't even know how to describe it. Maybe touch, but at a distance? Anyhow, his lab is also strapped to several tunnelbores.

I think he and Queen are trying to see if they can make their labs functional on the go, but I wouldn't hold my breath, even if I still had any. The ants are pretty stable as they move, but there's still a bit of motion to them. I think they might be able to get used to working in that kind of conditions, but I don't think they want to waste the materials to learn. They don't have the most resin to play with right now, but they should have plenty once they get to the Southwood.

The medics gather as well, my magmyrms looking a bit nervous about being on the surface, yet eager to put their training to work. More tunnelbores carry their equipment, as well as empty baskets and bags for gathering. Quite a few aranea are riding along, too. I think some are hoping to give some quests in the Southwood. I don't know if that'll work, but I like the initiative. If it doesn't work, they can help make silk for the composite armor.

Aranya shows up at the same time the first couple adventurer groups do, and she happily chats with them. I wonder if the timing is an adventurer thing? I can't imagine them keeping to a rigid schedule, but I *can* imagine them having a rough idea of the best time and way to prepare to go on a long journey.

As dawn nears, I think the entire guild is here, except for Karn. There's probably some unlucky group staying with him, but it's not one I recognize as absent.

The Shield worshipers start showing up only slightly later, and they mingle with the adventurers. I think everyone is a bit nervous but looking forward to doing their part. They all know it will be messy, but they also know the mess won't clean itself. Teemo chats with a few as he wanders, checking in on everyone and relaying info to Aranya when needed.

Just as the sun is getting ready to actually rise, I see two people I wasn't expecting to show up. The birds in the cemetery do their best to give them the appropriate welcome, but there are just more around the manor than the cemetery. I don't even need to poke Teemo for him to dart through a shortcut to greet the surprise guests.

"Tarl! Berdol! The Boss didn't think you guys would be coming!" exclaims my Voice from a bush before hurrying out.

Tarl smirks at my scion. "Really? Did he actually think I wouldn't want to do an inspection of the Maw? Besides, a hostile inspection will be good training for Berdol. Facing a matching affinity can help lessen the danger for a first run."

While Tarl looks confident, the tabby catkin looks a bit more nervous. I'd probably be nervous, too, bringing that much metal to this particular fight.

"Yeah? Is he strong enough to resist the influence of the nastier denizens, then?" asks Teemo, eyeing Berdol. The apprentice gives a small shrug.

"Matched affinities are pretty complicated, especially when they try to directly control the same piece of their element. It's usually too much of a hassle to try to directly grab something under someone else's control. It's better to just use your own blade to engage, like a sword fight."

Teemo doesn't look too convinced, mirroring my own worries for the catkin. "You're sure? I'm pretty sure Rhonda did that to Rocky to get her class."

Tarl snorts at that. "To get a very rare class that's all about examining magic. Berdol should be fine. I'd give details, but it's rude to give away the secrets of someone else's class."

Teemo looks to Berdol with curious eyes. I can practically feel him channeling Honey to get some more info out of the inspector in training. He can't stand against such an onslaught, and he soon elaborates.

"My personal style of Metal magic is . . . well, very personal. It works best with *my* stuff, and anyone else will have a hard time taking *my* stuff from me. Tarl's been talking about those denizens since you dropped the info on us, and I think the biggest threat to me will be the rust elementals. I won't quite be a counter to a sliverstorm or something, but I should be able to slow one down enough for someone else to finish it off."

"Which will be my job," interjects Tarl. "A friendly inspection should be done solo, so the inspector can better bond with a dungeon. But against a hostile dungeon, a partner is practically required. Metal is a little more difficult for me to deal with, but with Berdol able to interfere with the denizens, I should be able to land hits on weaknesses a lot easier than on my own."

Teemo nods at that. "Fair enough. Do you want to try some of Queen and Thing's new armor, Tarl? I'd offer some to you too, Berdol, but there's no metal in it. Heh, they'll probably want your input on a few designs that incorporate some, though."

They both look intrigued by that, the senior inspector speaking up first. "New armor? What madness has Thedeim cooked up this time?"

Teemo smirks and hops up onto Berdol's shoulder, then motions toward the gathered crowd, letting the two continue walking as he explains. "It's basically a thick silk weave encased in lacquer. It will scratch and gouge pretty easily, but getting fully through it is hard to do. The Boss is still working on improving it, but they should last for at least one battle, which is hopefully all we'll need for now."

"What does he want to know about adding metal to it?" asks Berdol as Tarl considers the benefits of a good ablative protector.

"He mostly wants to know how much metal you need to get a grip on something, and if that's a general limitation or a *you* limitation."

"That's . . . a bit complicated. I can pull metallic buttons off of someone's shirt, but I won't think to grab a hidden blade if I don't know it's there. I've met a few who could sense metal better than I can, but it's not very common."

"Can you grab thin metal? Like really thin?"

Berdol thinks it over as they join everyone else. "I've never had thin metal to test against, at least not thinner than a blade. Would metal that thin help with armor, though?"

Teemo nods. "It seems weird to me, but the Boss is pretty confident in it, so I'm not going to doubt him. Do you think you'd be able to tear metal out of a layer of lacquer and probably silk, too?"

Berdol slowly shakes his head. "Even if I knew it was there, I doubt it. If you, for some reason, put a bunch of blades into the armor, I might be able to get them to cut free, but with more blunt metal, it would be . . . pretty difficult to tear through something like that."

"Would you be able to immobilize someone wearing it?"

". . . Maybe? I'd have to try it. I don't think anyone has ever had to test it."

Poor guy, he just said the secret word. Every ant and hand within earshot looks at him, with the ones farther away turning their gaze on him like a tide of eyes and . . . fingers? I still don't understand how the hands sense things.

Berdol, at least, can sense the danger he's in, but he's in too deep now. Teemo gives him a sympathetic look before turning to Tarl.

"Queen and Thing want to borrow him for the trip, and probably for the entire time up until the attack."

Tarl solemnly nods, regretting having to give his assistant away like this, but he has no other choice. Poor Berdol. When they say curiosity killed the cat, I don't think they usually mean it like this.

I'm sure he'll be fine.

Chapter 86

The next couple days are almost a bit of a halfway point between waiting and doing, like packing your bags for a big trip. It doesn't feel like there's much to do, but you're also incredibly busy while doing it.

Berdol actually works great with Thing and Queen. They have him test all sorts of things for moving metal embedded in other materials, and he heads to bed with an eager tiredness each time—the kind of tired that makes you look forward to getting tired again, knowing you've actually done something.

The tests are looking pretty encouraging, too. It looks like the force Berdol can exert on metal inside materials is proportional to its strength. A stronger mage could probably do some damage, but even they would only be able to do so much with a bit of foil. A composite with metal also seems to be more resistant if it is a single piece instead of links in chain mail.

It looks like the layers can move a bit against each other, but with a single large piece embedded, it's difficult to get traction to do anything. And again, with the embedded foil, it's difficult to do much anyway.

I think a honeycomb will give a bit more to grab onto for a Metal-affinity user, but all the resin and silk in and around it will basically make it impossible to tear out of the armor. Other materials also seem to get in the way of noticing the metal in the first place, and I wouldn't be surprised if Thing can obfuscate it further with enchantments.

At the Southwood, we're starting to get reports back from the forward scouting base. They're pretty confident they've mapped out the Maw's borders, and have a few potential angles to try sending in the tunnelbores to dig our own way into the Maw. The team of scouts have successfully done a delve and are carefully mapping it out.

As far as Leo and Honey can tell, the information seems legit. The details contradict some of the suborned rockslides, so I'm cautiously optimistic they're as good as they said they are. It also hints that the Maw isn't more attentive than me, which is a relief.

I'd imagine it would have an easy time getting an exact number from the townsfolk or the clergy about how many are delving, but it hasn't bothered to cross-reference. Three people isn't enough to make it notice extra bodies, so it also probably has regular delvers.

From what Lechula and Merrik said, it probably has more delvers than usual right now, what with the recruits needing to train and gain levels.

The changeling lady has also started her infiltration of the town. She hasn't reported much back just yet, but she warned everyone that'd probably be the case. She can't be tracked back to the base if she doesn't go back. My other eyes and ears haven't noticed any significant change in the activities of the town and the Maw yet, so things are probably not a disaster yet, right?

Jen

She really hopes she hasn't bitten off more than she can chew. She told Thedeim she could sneak in and get information about the town, and she doesn't intend to make herself a liar.

Still, she's nervous. She's used to working solo, but even on her own, she always had the guild to retreat to, whether it was with the thieves or adventurers, it didn't matter. But here, she doesn't have anyone even theoretically nearby to try to pull her out of any mess she might get into. No safety net makes her a bit nervous, but just like any acrobat who might work without one, she's good enough to not need it.

Hopefully.

She crushes that small bit of doubt just as she crushes the urge to scratch her beard. She should have taken a pale elf form, but the best place she could find to slip in as an unnoticed worker was in an industry with mostly dwarves: hauling. Moving goods all over has enough turnover and crossover between different overseers that she had no trouble slipping into the role.

Well, maybe a little trouble. She had done some careful exploring to learn the tunnels, but changing her shape can only change her strength so much. Thankfully, she was able to shyly admit to her superior that she hadn't been hauling long. He just gave a deep sigh, clearly used to having sudden inexperienced people on his payroll.

She was assigned a regular route that's not too long, though the loads are heavy. She almost asked where they would even get milk down here, but managed to keep her silence and her cover intact. Seeing the caverns with rich, loamy soil didn't explain anything until a fat worm poked out and crawled over to a dwarf with a pail.

She couldn't hide her stare at the process of a worm getting milked, and the dwarf doing it chuckled before coming over to greet her.

"The worms never look like what people expect. First time seeing them in the flesh?" he asked with a friendly grin. She could only mutely nod, earning a guffaw at her expense.

"Milking them is harder than it looks, too! But you're not here to hear me jaw; you're here to bring Ol' Bessy's juice to the cheesemaker." Her reaction to him calling it *juice* earned another hearty laugh from the rancher, and he waved her and her cart over to the side of the pen, where canisters of milk awaited.

Her first couple deliveries, the cheesemaker was busy, so she just put the canisters in their place outside, gathered the empties, and returned them to the worm ranch. The deliveries took most of the day, and she'd take her pay to a tavern to drink and listen.

In her experience, taverns are the best place to gather information without arousing suspicion. *Everyone* talks in a tavern, and most people are not as subtle as they think they are. She heard lots of rumors, but nothing especially actionable. She did, however, start noticing an interesting trend.

The kobold cheese was getting more popular, which wasn't especially surprising. According to the two defectors, it was a campaign to reinforce the kobolds' place in their society as the Maw's chosen. Most of the townsfolk simply enjoyed their cheesy treats and moved on.

But some would take the time to examine the cheese, to see the details. Those ones often ended up looking a little conflicted before eating. Even more than that, the tavernkeeper seemed to notice those ones, and on subsequent nights, he would take their cheese from under the counter instead of from the large crate.

Jen only noticed thanks to her particular class and set of skills. It was like dealing from the bottom of the deck to guide a game where the dealer wished. Today, her mind chews on the possibilities as she makes her deliveries to and from the cheesemaker, wondering what the significance of the cheese could be.

She hadn't noticed any messages tucked into it, nor any particular differences on the outside. They seemed to be more kobolds in various positions, so why give those thoughtful ones special treats? Could there be some kind of magic involved? Maybe a bizarre cheese-based alchemy to shield their minds from the Harbinger?

She snorts at that thought as she rounds the last bend to the cheesemaker's shop. Weird alchemy isn't out of the question; she's had cobble bread before, so she knows effects can be put into food. No, the ridiculous idea is that just being sympathetic toward the kobolds would make someone a target for the Harbinger. That kind of paranoia—on the Harbinger's or the peoples' part—would cause the situation to eventually collapse without Thedeim doing anything.

As she nears the shop, the door opens, and a tall pale elf exits, his focus on the canisters by his shop. His pointed ears still work, though, and he turns at the sound of Jen's cart coming down the tunnel. He smiles and waves, speaking as she gets nearer.

"Ah, you're the new milk hauler! I've been hoping to catch you, but it looks like we've both been busy," he says with an amiable tone. Jen, for her part, grunts and sets her cart down, playing her role as a bit of a rough, businesslike dwarf.

"Catch me? What do you need?" she asks, giving the elf a wary eye.

Her suspicions don't seem to bother the elf, who reaches up to pat one of the milk canisters. "I actually wanted to ask if you could pour them instead of leaving the canisters here?"

She squints at him. "What, just dump it in front of your shop?"

He laughs and shakes his head, then leads her to what she mistook as a partially buried barrel. When he removes the lid, she can see she's not fully wrong about that. The barrel has a large hole in the bottom, with a pipe leading deeper. "My tank is buried, with my workshop in my cellar. I'm surprised nobody noticed you not bringing back the first set of canisters, but you're supposed to pour the milk and bring them straight back instead of leaving them here."

She looks surly at that information. "But there were empties outside that I brought back."

The elf just looks apologetic. "Those were decorative. You couldn't know. But now you do. Oh!" He brightens as he gets an idea. "Come with me, and I'll get you a bit of cheese as an apology. It's very popular."

She puts on a cautious look and nods. She's usually not too much of a cheese person, but the locals are pretty skilled at making it.

Even if the image of a worm getting milked will haunt her dreams.

She follows him to a large cellar door and down a wagon ramp.

"What's with the ramp? I didn't know you produced the kind of volume to need a full wagon instead of a hand cart."

He chuckles as they get to the main floor, where she can see the simple equipment required for making cheese. "I usually do bulk orders, but I've also been experimenting with new varieties. My latest one has been much more of a success than I could have ever hoped. If there's much more demand for it, I might not get to make simple wheels for much longer!"

He leads her to a rack of lumpy molds, and it's not until he upends one and hands her the contents that she realizes what she's looking at.

"*You're* making the cheese kobolds?" she asks, flashes of the tavernkeeper playing in her mind as he nods.

"I am! I thought it might be the perfect way to help."

She nods absently at that, her mind churning. There's something more to this cheesemaker than meets the eye. She's sure of that. She just doesn't know what. For now, she files his statement away and offers her hand.

"I'm Jen, by the way. Never introduced myself. I'm still getting used to hauling."

The elf smiles and shakes her hand. "I'm Serd."

The two make small talk as they head back up and pour the milk into the bottomless barrel. She's glad her current persona isn't exactly chatty; it gives her time to think about what Serd said.

He said he wanted to help, but never said whom. The townsfolk would assume he means the Maw, of course. She's starting to suspect otherwise. She'll need to be careful, though. If her suspicions are wrong, she could be captured as an ordinary rebel or heretic or something, rather than a spy. Although the end result probably wouldn't be much different.

But if she's right . . . she might have a valuable insider to find not only the Kobold Enclave but to keep the townsfolk from all attacking when the time comes.

Chapter 87

Jen

The next time she enters the tavern, she takes the time to appreciate the cheese kobold. It really is a good mold the cheesemaker is using. Or two molds, rather. Now that she takes the time to pay attention, she can see each figurine must have two molds: one for the cheese, and one for it to rest in once dipped in wax.

She takes careful note of the subtleties that transform a figure from looking peaceful and serene to looking weak and downtrodden, all while maintaining plausible deniability. The Maw's clergy might not notice it, but as a changeling, she can recognize subtle differences to influence perception.

It's definitely deliberate, she has no doubt now—not after getting one of the cheeses from under the counter instead of from the crate. These are a little less subtle, though still not crossing the line to be easily recognized. Now that she has a potential mastermind for undermining the Maw, she needs to discover how deep the plot goes.

Unfortunately for her, the threads are difficult to track. She probably shouldn't be surprised that people are exceptionally subtle with the Harbinger able to just rip secrets from whatever minds it fancies. Still, difficult is not impossible, and her next several days involve quite a lot of shadowing people, assuming temporary identities, and other quiet ways of gathering information. She even earns a level from her efforts, which already makes this all worth it.

Most of the people she follows don't seem to have anything subversive in mind, or at least don't make any moves to indicate they are. No checking on hidden stashes of weapons or potions, no disappearing down secret passages, no clandestine meetings in quiet alleyways or darkened corners of dive bars.

There are a few who catch her attention for the frequency she encounters them and what they are doing. It could be coincidence, as they're all involved in making, selling, and distributing food, but her instincts tell her there's more to it. Even with so many here occupied with food, she would have expected *someone* in this secretive web to be in some other industry.

She might have left it alone at that, taken it as some paranoid conspiracy theory, but every single one of them had two separate stores of cheese to give out, always giving most from the obvious spot, but sometimes slipping one from a more private stash when someone sympathetic would come by to purchase.

They're influencing public opinion and being careful about it. But why?

Why they're being careful is obvious, but why try to make people feel sorry for the kobolds? What's the next step in their plan? She doesn't know, but she suspects the cheesemaker, Serd, will be able to answer her questions.

So, come morning, she takes her route to deliver milk, hoping to catch the pale elf as he works. Unfortunately, he seems busy and doesn't exit his workshop while she makes her first delivery. He's nowhere to be seen for the second one that day, either. The third is more of the same, and she has no more deliveries for him today, but she can't just leave empty-handed!

She sets the last empty canister back in her cart with a hollow bang, trying to figure out how to get his attention. She could try all sorts of subtle things . . . but her current persona isn't exactly subtle. She nods to herself and pounds on the door to the house, getting no reply. She grumbles, not even needing to feign annoyance at this point, and tries the cellar doors, but pounding on those doesn't summon the cheesemaker either.

She tests the doors and finds them unlocked, so she bangs one open and shouts into the basement. "Hey! Serd! Are you down there or am I yelling at cheese!"

The silence makes her suspect the latter, but a shouted reply gives her hope. "Ah, Jen! Sorry, I was occupied with my work! Feel free to come down if you need to talk or if you just want some more of my work!"

She can't help but smile at that, and soon shouts her reply. "I need to return the cart and canisters, but can we talk after?"

"That's fine! I'm cutting the curd right now, so I'll probably have it packed away by the time you return!"

She grunts at that, not caring if he can't hear her, and closes the cellar door with more care than she opened it with before hauling her cart and canisters back where they belong. She resists hurrying, not wanting to draw any attention as she finishes up her work and collects her pay.

Before long, she returns to the cheesemaker's home and place of business, and tries knocking on the ordinary door, but it's as fruitful as the last time. Opening the cellar door earns her a shout before she can even announce herself.

"Ah, Jen! Perfect timing! I'll be waxing some cheese, but I can talk and work at the same time." His cheerful voice echoes up the ramp, and he gives her a friendly wave once she comes into view. She gives a grumpier wave in reply, but her surliness continues to go unnoticed or ignored by the genial elf.

"You need any help?" she asks, looking resigned to some menial task but also subtly not looking too upset about the idea. Grumpy friendliness is a difficult rope to walk.

"If it wouldn't be too much trouble? I need to do much of the work myself, but can you hand me the cheese and mold, then put them back after I'm done? It'll make it go much quicker."

She snorts but doesn't argue, and is even glad to see a rolling ladder attached to the rack of cheese that will be worked on. Getting closer, they seem to have a thin layer of wax on them, but not enough to protect them as they are moved around with carts and wagons.

His dipping vat is on wheels, so it must be simpler to move that than to move the racks. Considering just how much cheese is down here, she's not surprised. "You make a lot of cheese," she states as she grabs the bottommost occupied mold and hands it to him.

He laughs at the understatement and accepts her offering, smoothly freeing the contents as he replies. "I do! I'd even go so far as to say that if I stopped making cheese, the whole of Silvervein would quickly run out, used as they are to my rate of production!"

"What's your favorite?" she asks as they settle into a rhythm. She's going to be covered in wax by the end, but aside from that, the process is pretty simple.

"You may as well ask who's my favorite child! That said . . . my last batch of pepper cheddar came out especially well."

That does sound pretty good. She'll need to ask about it later. For now, though . . .

"I was expecting you to say the kobold cheese."

He smiles at that, but Jen can recognize the unease in his movements now, though his voice doesn't show it. "Ah, they are very popular. A lot more popular than I could have ever imagined, really."

"I'm not surprised. It's good cheese, and good craftsmanship on the molds, too."

"Thank you, Jen. I put a lot of work into them, but it's still surprising how well they're doing."

Jen grunts in reply, letting the conversation lapse as she considers how to proceed. Being too direct might scare him off, but she feels like she doesn't have the time to beat around the bush. She doesn't know when Thedeim wants to attack, but it can't be too far away now.

Direct it is. If he's on the Maw's side, she'll just have to bolt. If he's not, beating around the bush will only be against character right now.

"What's your next step for them, then?"

Serd shrugs. "Probably make more, maybe commission another set of molds to keep things fresh, and to keep up with demand."

"I mean the kobolds, not the cheese."

He freezes at that, though his eyes flick toward the ramp to the cellar doors. "What do you mean?"

"You're going through a lot of effort to make them sympathetic, so what are you going to do with the sympathy?" She holds out another mold of cheese for him like she's not suggesting he's a traitor to the powers at large.

He slowly takes it, trying to read her face, wondering if he should run or maybe attack. He decides on neither, instead dipping the cheese and handing it back. "I . . . I don't know. I want to help them, but I don't know how. I was hoping to get the people on their side and somehow just . . . convince the Great Maw to stop eating them."

"Do you think it'll work? Do you think it'll stop eating them?" she presses, still handing and taking cheese like their conversation is nothing out of the ordinary.

". . . Maybe? It'll be years before public sentiment will even support asking a question like that."

"Would you be interested in a faster way?"

He takes the offered cheese and sets it aside, turning his attention fully on Jen. "Like what? Try to free them? We'd get hatted for certain."

Jen's lips slowly curl into a smile. "Maybe not. It'd be a drastic change, but it's possible."

"How?" he asks, frustration clear in his voice. "The Great Maw cares too much for his favored delicacy; he won't let them go without a fight. What, do you think you can *fight* the Great Maw?"

Jen shakes her head. "Not me, no. But I know someone who can."

Serd freezes at that, his gaze locked on her. "Who?" he asks in a whisper, afraid to even entertain the idea of someone able to fight the Maw.

"Before I tell you, would you be willing to help? They're willing to deal with the Maw, but they don't want to have to fight all of Silvervein, too. Can you do anything to keep the city from trying to stop them?"

Serd leans on his vat for a moment, before the heat causes him to flinch away. "I . . . don't know. I'll try, but a lot of people will ignore me, especially if someone just charges through the tunnels to attack the Great Maw."

"Convincing anyone will mean fewer people they'll have to fight."

He sighs and looks at the racks of cheese kobolds. "Just like with them. I knew not everyone would see the kobolds in a new light, but even just a couple would make it worth it." He sighs and nods. "Alright, I'll help; at least as much as I can. So, who do you know?"

Jen smiles and steps back, giving herself a bit of room to slowly change her form as she speaks. "I know a lot of people from the surface, for starters. A whole guild of adventurers who don't appreciate the Maw making waves for their favorite dungeons."

Her body narrows and grows, her hair vanishing as her skin darkens slightly. Few would call changelings tanned, but compared to a pale dwarf, gray is darker than stark white.

Serd is dumbfounded by the change in the pale dwarf, but the dramatic reveal makes it difficult for him to argue that she's a fake, ironically enough. It's a tall tale, but when confronted with something impossible like her changing forms, it becomes easier to swallow.

"And I know a dungeon who has a personal stake in stopping the Maw. He has a resident who escaped from here, and he promised to free her people. He only needs two things before he can strike: a good way to keep the town from resisting too hard, and the location of the enclave."

She lets Serd slowly come to terms with what she said. It's a lot to take in, really. Emotions play across his face as he tries to comprehend the position he's in, as he tries to weigh the risks and rewards.

"Do . . . Do you think your dungeon can defeat the Great Maw?"

Jen grins. "He already did. He crushed the Maw's attempt at invading the surface, and now, he intends to make sure it won't get a second chance."

The pale elf looks surprised to hear that, but Jen's confidence in her statement is like a gentle breeze on the embers of hope. "Then . . . yes, I will help. I know where the enclave is."

Chapter 88

I can't believe the changeling actually found the enclave.

"Jen, Boss," absently corrects Teemo as he studies the updated map.

Right, Jen. Not only has she infiltrated the town, but she's found sympathizers! It doesn't seem like they're going to actively fight on our side, but they should be able to keep at least some of Silvervein from joining in the defense. Even more, we have not just the info for where the enclave is but where the core is, too.

The enclave is pretty much right in the center of the Maw's territory; the sneaky delving group is trying to verify that before we make our actual move. The other scouting parties have been carefully guiding the tunnelbore ants. We've been going slowly, not wanting to make too much noise and arise any suspicion. We also haven't gotten too close to the Maw's territory with them just yet, either.

We have a rough idea of the range the Harbinger can sense thoughts, so it's been a tricky thing to guide the ants to dig routes that stay far enough away from the known tunnels and passages. These are going to need to be a bit of a feint, I think, thanks to where the core is: the temple complex.

The main temple entrance is in Silvervein, but it's vast and sprawling, and has a section that goes well into the Maw's territory. I don't want to give the Maw credit, but it's pretty clever. Most dungeons will have their cores deep in their territory, or nearby a valued enclave, at least from the ones I've seen so far. The Maw's is actually not too far from its borders. It's also in a kind of place that I think a lot of dungeons wouldn't think to check.

I wasn't expecting it to be there, at least. But from that position, it can have not only the clergy protect it but easily bring denizens or even scions to bear for extra security. I'd also bet the lion's share of the iron maidens are going to be in there, along with a healthy dose of denizens to slow people down. The Maw has a lot of those types, so if it can bog down any hostiles, it can bring in other forces to destroy them.

The temple complex seems to be . . . well, pretty complex, with lots of rooms, passages, and probably lots of secret doors to let the clergy and denizens move around freely while confusing any would-be invaders. We know the rough way to where the core should be, but getting there is going to be easier said than done.

Leo, Honey, and Teemo are holding a bit of a briefing with the Stag, Aranya, and a few other adventurers, and we're all trying to figure out just what to do for the battle. We're looking at probably three major fronts: Silvervein, the temple complex, and the Kobold Enclave. The problem is the fronts are going to overlap a lot, and we could even consider the Maw's territory in general to be another wide front, too.

Teemo thinks out loud as I think in my own mind, trying to organize the information so far. "Alright . . . Silvervein itself will be mostly up to the Crystal Shield church, with some adventurer and denizen help. Their job is the messy one of urban combat, finding hostiles and eliminating them while protecting civilians.

"The adventurers are going to be attacking the temple complex and the ambush areas, generally sowing chaos and trying to keep the Maw from being able to mount any organized defensive effort. The dwellers and denizens, with some adventurer support, as well as Tarl and Berdol, will be going with the tunnelbores to make their own mess deeper in the Maw's area and try to secure the enclave."

Leo growls as the others present nod, with the Stag speaking up next. "What will the Maw try to do to stop us?"

Honey shuffles some notes while Leo growls and yips. After a few moments, Teemo translates.

"We can only guess right now, but the Maw should have two priorities: protect the enclave and protect itself. It will probably try to protect the town as well, but it will likely be much lower in priority than those.

"It also definitely knows we're snooping around, so a true surprise attack isn't going to be an option. If we attack the town, the Maw will be on alert for sneak attacks, especially if it thinks we're using only a token force there. We might be able to feign weakness at the start and get it to overcommit, sending denizens to try to flank or flood our forces in the town."

Honey gives a rude buzz to that idea, earning a chuckle from those who can understand her, before Teemo continues.

"Yeah, Honey isn't too sold on trying to do that, especially since the Harbinger would be really effective in that kind of fight. We don't know exactly how many least the Maw has spawned now, nor do we actually know what the lessers do, if they even exist. In the winding tunnels of Silvervein, the least would probably be able to flank and overrun our forces, so we shouldn't try to specifically draw any attacks there."

Teemo taps the map at the two major entrances to the Maw, the ones that are sure to be the most defended. "These are probably the best places for us to engage the Harbinger, or at least the least. They'll still have their potential large numbers, but they should only be able to attack from a few directions. This is probably where the Harbinger will be, if it's going to be commanding them. The scouts haven't mentioned the least much, so either they spawn a lot slower than expected or they're keeping them hidden. The other place the Harbinger will probably be is around the enclave."

My Voice gestures in the general vicinity of our target. "The whole area is basically a no-go zone, which would be a great place to keep the least. With how convoluted the tunnels in the area are, they would also give the least a huge advantage in fighting.

"The final place we expect the Harbinger to be is in the temple complex. Again, lots of convoluted passages, lots of ways for them to slip behind us—could be a very bad place to try to fight. That assumes the Harbinger will want to be with the least, but considering how much more effective they are when it's around, that's probably a safe bet."

Teemo grimaces as Leo continues. "The risky bet comes with the Redcap. It could be stationed anywhere. If we force the Maw onto the backfoot by assaulting from multiple directions, it'll probably have the Redcap protect either the core or the enclave, with the Harbinger at the other.

"The worst-case scenario would be them both at once place, most likely at the core. Rocky and Fluffles should be able to take them, especially with Slash's help, but that'd require correctly guessing where they'll be. Rocky should be able to deal with the Harbinger on his own, but even he isn't sure he could handle the Redcap solo. He's a Conduit, after all, so it's hard to put a number on how strong the Redcap is."

"Can we draw them to us?" asks the Stag. "If you reveal those three scions making a beeline for the core, the Maw would have to consolidate or be subsumed."

Leo *woofs*, looking unhappy, and I don't blame him as Teemo translates. "Probably, but if either is stationed around the enclave, they'll most likely kill the kobolds for mana before making for the core. We've got some heavy hitters, but the Maw has a lot of easy ways to delay us. If we make it clear we're going to reach the core, the Maw will probably have time to eat the enclave for the boost."

Everyone frowns at that information, taking a few seconds to digest it. Keeping the Maw occupied shouldn't be too difficult, and it would likely keep the scions at or near where we expect them to be. But if we make any actual progress toward the enclave or the core, it'll collapse its forces without us being able to do much, possibly killing the kobolds, too. Attacking the enclave might make it fight to protect them, or it might just kill them and turn the entire thing into a trap for us.

I have a vague idea, and though Teemo doesn't look like he likes it too much, he voices it to all gathered. "Do you think Nova and I could sneak into the enclave and evacuate them before the Maw notices? I'd need an enchantment from Thing to handle the heat from her magma, but I should be able to make a shortcut even through the rock."

Leo and Honey consider it as Aranya speaks up. "I'll need to come with you. They will be suspicious of just you and Nova, but they'll know me. They'll listen to me."

Leo *borks*, Honey buzzes, and Teemo translates. "We'll have to move them quickly, they say. The Maw will probably notice if their numbers start falling, so we won't have long before it responds. We'll have to gather everyone before taking the shortcut and hope we don't take so long the Maw notices us."

"So we siege the Maw on all sides as a diversion while Teemo, Nova, and Aranya make for the enclave. Once the kobolds are secure, Rocky, Fluffles, and Slash make for the core," summarizes the Stag, earning nods from my Warden and Librarian, with a minor correction from Teemo.

"We'll start the siege with Fluffles's new trick. He'll probably need all of the Boss's scions to help combo to make it work, too. Even if he'll be the main caster, me, Slash, Rocky, Thing, Nova, and Queen should help. It's an incredibly powerful concept from the Boss, so it'll need a lot of power to make it properly manifest."

"I think the dwellers and I can help, too. It's powerful but not especially complicated, if I'm hearing Him right. I think we can help channel our faith to aid into it," follows Aranya, her hand moving to the amulet at her neck.

Even with me still feeling a bit uncomfortable about being a focus for faith, I'm willing to take all the help I can get. The last thing I need is to fall to the very concept I'm hoping to hit the Maw with.

Chapter 89

I look through the eyes of my scions at everyone gathered, and can't help but feel humbled. Having everyone here puts the upcoming battle into perspective. There are a lot of people willing to risk everything for this, and that's only counting the ones actively present for this ceremony.

Every single one of my wayward dwellers is here, from support to combatants, but they're not the only ones. There are a surprising number of adventurers joining us, too. I didn't realize any had converted. Or maybe I didn't want to think about that. Probably the second option. I'd be trying to discourage them if I didn't need to get every iota of help for this that I can.

Everyone is gathered in a large cavern well outside the Maw's territory, with Aranya and my scions in a loose circle in the center. I can even feel Violet, Hullbreak, and the Southwood paying close attention through the various bonds with me, each lending their support in their own way.

Support isn't even limited to the people here, either. Even with the adventurers' guild waiting in the tunnels for their chance to join the fighting, there are plenty of other delvers back home. They're not exactly master combatants, but my denizens understand how to set a proper difficulty curve by now.

Rezlar has his guards helping escort crafting groups, with Rhonda and Freddie joining his Larrez disguise to give more support. Those three are currently tearing through the lava labyrinth, dealing with traps and encounters, generally having fun and helping keep my mana flowing.

It's intimidating, if I'm honest, having everyone raring to go. But it's way too late to get cold feet for this. *Teemo? Let's do it.*

My Voice nods from Aranya's shoulder. "Butterfly Effect." My gathered scions echo him in their own ways, using the same skill as my High Priestess opens her eyes and looks up at everyone gathered around her.

"In an ancient tale, a single nail leads to the downfall of a kingdom."

A lot of people take the butterfly effect to be a time travel thing. If you go back into the past and step on a butterfly, *oops*, humanity never existed. I always likened it to the metaphor of a butterfly flapping its wings on one side of the globe and causing hurricanes on the other. Whatever the origin, the basic principle is the same: small causes can have big effects.

"Butterfly Effect," repeats Teemo, my scions following up with their own uses of the skill.

"A blacksmith runs out of nails for horseshoes, and so the shoe is not as secure as it would need to be."

Combination skills are powerful. I've seen all kinds of groups bring attacks together to decisively end a fight in a spectacular way. I even wonder if Rocky is comboing with himself sometimes with his advanced moves. Teemo's Butterfly Effect is a weird skill, though, in that I think it combos with itself. With just one person, it takes a bit of setup. When multiple people contribute to it, though . . .

"Butterfly Effect."

"The horse throws the shoe at the worst possible time, creating a gap in a charge."

I can feel the air tingle with power already, though it's mostly through Thing's senses. He can feel not only the mana from my scions but also the faith of the gathered dwellers and adventurers. They know vaguely that we're doing something big, but I didn't give out the details of it just yet.

"Butterfly Effect."

"With the charge broken, the tide of battle is turned. It's only a matter of time before the army is routed."

The tension in the gathered believers slowly turns to confidence, as even they can feel that *something* is happening. Fluffles can feel the energy swirling and taps into his Conduit title to ensure he can manage the flow properly. My mana dips as he draws on it. It's just a drop in the bucket right now, but I don't think it's going to stay like that.

"Butterfly Effect."

"With no army to protect it, a vital supply route is captured."

Rocky reaches and helps Fluffles with the flow of energy. He might not be an expert in Fate affinity, but he's only been getting better and better at translating the stability of his boxing stance into stability in his magic. Fluffles must be the foundation of this, but Rocky helps ensure the growing structure can float like a butterfly before delivering a sting stronger than any bee.

Nova pitches in at this point, too, adding her burgeoning sense of art to Rocky's established martial sense, bringing a unique kind of structure and stability to the effort. The structure takes a bite out of my stockpiled mana instead of just a nibble. It's only going to get more expensive from here.

"Butterfly Effect."

"With the supply line lost, other armies find themselves wanting for far more than just nails. The whole front is unsustainable."

Queen and Thing assist now, each intimately familiar with complex magical constructs. They are used to working with physical media to impart their magical effect, but Rocky, Nova, and Fluffles are all more than willing to follow their guidance and hold the threads as they form. The threads thicken to ropes and cables as my mana rushes through them, intermingling with the faith of those gathered.

"Butterfly Effect."

"The front is a loss, and the cities of the kingdom fall, one by one . . . until only the capital remains."

The floodgates open as Honey, Slash, and Leo add their efforts to the brewing spell. Slash knows how to sense the earth and air, the vibrations of life echoing through each. It's so much information, far too much for Fluffles to handle on his own, but Honey is up to the task. It's sorted, categorized, and organized for Fluffles to understand.

While Honey is the mistress of understanding what is, Leo is a commander and comprehends how things will react. The thick cables of mana fray to tiny threads, spreading over the area and beyond, slowly encompassing the Maw and its territory in a delicate net of possibilities.

"Surrounded on all sides, the capital has no chance. When the fighting is over, it's razed to the ground."

"Butterfly Effect!"

Aranya's eyes glow orange as she helps direct the faith of the gathered dwellers and adventurers, Fluffles's eyes doing the same as he spreads his wings wide. My mana plummets from the draw, but it's too late to slow down now, let alone stop. I draw from the ally pool as my own mana almost bottoms out. I can *feel* the threads pulse in time with the flow from the shared pool.

Violet tries to contribute to the cause, her mana a trickle among raging rapids, but every mote matters. Hullbreak follows right behind her, his own flow not enough to stem the tide but at least enough to slow it, if only just. The Southwood opens his own mana holds, the initial influx actually enough to fight back the drain for a few moments before it too is swallowed by the ravenous spell we're casting.

I nervously watch as the shared mana drains away, uncertain what I'll do if all that's left is Violet's college fund. That's hers, not mine! The demarcation has really only been in my head, but I still can't go taking that from her!

And yet the stores dip and dip, wane and wane, before finally stopping. It took everything except for Violet's college fund. If this wasn't major Fate magic, I'd be suspicious about that. I don't really have a chance to focus on that, however, as the magic finally stabilizes. I realize all my scions have glowing orange eyes for a few moments before Aranya speaks up once more.

"Small causes can have big effects. Small mistakes can topple kingdoms. A single stroke of bad luck can devastate even the strongest foe. What can go wrong, will go wrong."

The threads burst into orange motes with the declaration, settling into everything in . . . I don't even know how big of an area. Combination skills seem to be more than the sum of their parts, and we had a *lot* of parts in this one: each of my scions, contributions from each of my dungeon friends, and the combined faith of probably a hundred people.

It all seems to just barely be enough, or maybe the effect is proportional to how much effort we put into it. Considering when the drain stopped, that's a distinct possibility. I feel the name of the attack before Teemo can utter it, and I'm equally relieved it worked and worried about what we've just unleashed.

Teemo's voice seems to reverberate through reality itself as he declares the combination attack finished.

"*Murphy's Law.*"

Chapter 90

The Maw

For once, the Maw is glad it has no mouth. It can only imagine how much it would be drooling at the prospect of what's happening. The surface alliance is finally making their move, and in the Maw's opinion, they're already making mistakes.

Even if the Harbinger hadn't suborned the rockslides around its territory, the surfacers are either ignoring the town or underestimating the impact they could have, as the Harbinger has found no other signs of surveillance. The Maw would have liked to station in torpor around the small city, but the odd denizens are too unpredictable to leave in that state around the delvers.

While that could earn it an influx of mana from the kills, it would lose out on mana in the long run. Better to keep them near the Harbinger, where it can easily control them.

There are a few handfuls of lessers now, and though they are very good at organizing the least, their influence doesn't extend especially far—only a hundred feet or so. More lessers would easily blanket a full army in their control, but the Maw just doesn't have that many of them. For now, it stations them near the ambush sites so they can rip apart whatever surface forces try to claim the false targets of opportunity.

They'll have their hands caught in the cookie jar and bitten clean off.

The Harbinger itself is stationed with the clergy, prepared to defend its core against whatever feeble attack the surfacers have planned. Its other scion is stationed at the primary entrance to the Maw. The Redcap could probably eliminate the approaching foes all on his own, but any true chef should have subordinates to mind the details of the meal. The Maw intends to feed the surface invaders a bitter feast of defeat.

Its forces move, and the Maw considers the powerful magic it felt wash over itself. It was an impressive display, but they must have spent themselves casting it. It doesn't appear to be any sort of subtle poison or massive scry, and the lack of effect has the Maw wondering if they actually failed to complete whatever they were trying to create. If so, they'll probably retreat and regroup.

It wishes its denizens were as sneaky as the rockslides . . . which it now technically owns, actually. It's far too late to make a spawner for them and get any use out of it, but the Maw can move them out to try to find the surface forces! It gleefully spends the mana to order them to do just that, eagerly awaiting what news they would have to give.

With things still quiet after the spell, the Maw takes a few moments to focus on its beloved pantry and the delicious kobolds within. They are such a wonderful variety, ranging from staunchly loyal to those young, rebellious ones who think it doesn't know their little plans for escape. The older ones keep the younger in check, mostly, not letting their youthful exuberance earn them a place on the Maw's plate.

Honestly, those are the ones least likely to catch one of the Maw's cravings. They are still delicious, as all kobolds are, but the mature kobolds are . . . "bland" isn't the right word. Just . . . the same. So little variety. Even the tastiest treat will grate without variety.

Speaking of treats; it should treat itself after this battle. The creamy caramel of a loyal one or two, or the spicy crunchiness of a few rebels?

Both, it decides. Definitely both. They'll pair perfectly together. A fitting dessert after the feast of consuming these invaders.

Ah, and here they come!

They focus on the two main entrances to the Maw, as expected. The others are too secret and too small to move any real forces into.

Sliverstorms and bladesprites turn the entrances into a flensing field of destruction for any invaders that try to press forward, with the living caltrops making it impossible to try to sprint through. The Maw is saddened that only a few invaders are minced before the others hang back, outside of the killing field.

Then a needleslink reports back from the expedition. Something is happening at the town. Ah, surface delvers are attacking from that direction. An interesting idea, but having the Harbinger in the temple makes it simple to send it forth to sweep through the twisting tunnels of the settlement.

Oh? More than just the surface invaders are making their move. It shouldn't be surprised that dissidents in the population are trying to take this chance to make their own move, but the Harbinger and a flood of least can sweep them aside just as easily.

The Maw prepares to spend the mana to order a counter before more reports start pouring in. The rockslides have found something concerning. There is something tunneling through the rock! A lot of somethings! They're large enough to leave room for other invaders behind!

It demands more information, taking advantage of the communication chain the slides naturally form, but the leading edge is now silent. Further demands for information only reveal more and more of the small spies are unable to respond anymore.

One manages to slip a name through shortly before there is a development at the main entrances.

The surface has a dragon spawner! It has wyrms *and* basilisks?! It's glad it has no mouth for a different reason now, as it would be clenching its teeth so hard they may shatter as the information continues to come in.

It vaguely recalls a few scattered wyrms from the Harbinger's reports, but the Maw had been more focused on the enticing delicacy of that lich!

The rockslides are wiped out by the wyrms, far more than were apparent in the battle on the surface, and the Maw can only guess what mischief those invaders will get up to now. At the main entrances, basilisks are spewing magma at the first line of defense, encasing or melting the sliverstorms, bladesprites, and caltrops!

It needs to do something about the rapid change in the battle, but what? The lessers are outside its reach now that they're on expedition to the ambush sites! And those tunnelers could let the surface dwellers make their own entrances into the Maw wherever they like! From the last of the rockslides' reports, it seemed the tunnelers were aiming to pierce the Maw's demesne from practically every angle!

A chill runs through the Maw as it realizes its delicious kobolds could even be a major target! Even if they don't know exactly where the enclave is, with all the potential breaches, *one* of them will stumble over it by pure luck!

It orders the Redcap to protect the enclave and leave the main entrances to the denizens to hold. Keeping them would be helpful, but if the tunnelers get through, the intended entrances won't matter!

It orders the Harbinger to tell the clergy to secure the town, then orders it to respond to the tunnelers. The least are probably its best option to counter them, either by collapsing the tunnels or meeting them with their own and forcing combat.

It moves its other denizens around, securing its own tunnels and passages as best it can. The iron maidens will work best around the enclave, where the Redcap can easily force invaders into the traps. Lodewisps will have to try to sense metal as the tunnelers get near, giving warning to other denizens so they can attack. Rust elementals are released into the town to counter the foreign delvers and traitor townsfolk at once.

The Maw's mood is thoroughly soured as it is forced to react to the complex attack. It's forced to spend mana on extensive expeditions of needleslinks and bladesprites, trying to get information about what's happening! It needs to know if the ambushes are going off properly or if they've vanished like the rockslides, probably even to the same infernal wyrms!

The Harbinger seems to echo the Maw's apprehension about the attack, and the Maw can feel it trying to figure out what that spell that seemed to be the signal to start was. Perhaps that's all it was: a signal? Something like that would not be as expensive as an actual attack, and it would explain the coordination of the attacks.

Yes . . . it must have been a signal. That would explain so much! The Maw's mood shifts from reflecting the Harbinger to reflecting the quiet confidence of its Voice. The attack is well planned, but the Maw's defenses should be more than enough to repel them. It will be messier than it had expected, but some meals are all the better for how much of a mess they make.

Its clergy and the Maw's own delvers will repel the foreigners and subdue what townsfolk are foolish enough to try to take the opportunity to rebel. The tunnels will be annoying to deal with but shouldn't prove anything worse than that. They'll be natural choke points, allowing its denizens to deal with the intruders with as much backup as the Maw can spawn! And with the Harbinger organizing the response with the least and some lessers, the invaders can be on the receiving end of a few coordinated attacks!

Let the invaders eat their fill of the simple bread of the Maw's denizens! It knows this meal will have many courses, and it will be fully prepared and hungry for when the entrée arrives.

Chapter 91

Vnarl

The troll reflects on the events of the last couple months, and not for the first time, has to admit getting captured by Thedeim was probably the best thing that's ever happened to him and his party. In the moment, it was painful and humiliating, but looking back, it really helped recenter them all.

They'd started out so idealistic, wanting to help people, but it didn't take long for the politics of a large guild to grind that notion away. It was all just for the money, and power was all that really mattered. Even Mlynda and Hark were growing colder, more callous. Much as he'd like to throw the blame at the feet of the old guild, he has to shoulder at least some of the blame as the leader.

Going through the punitive gauntlet was a reforging, a coming back to basics and gaining perspective, all of the things that make people take a step back and examine what they've been doing, and realize how far they've fallen.

His party . . . His *friends* are still cocky, confident, and rough, but there's a happiness and satisfaction in doing guild jobs now. And *right* now, all three of them are looking forward to this particular quest. Thedeim has been an amazing place to delve, but he still doesn't have any areas really designed for the really strong to let loose. This fight with the Maw, though . . . they can go nuts. Well, within reason.

The dungeon is smart enough not to try to tell the adventurers what to do, instead giving points of interest and setting them free. Vnarl's group is staying well away from the town, at least for the moment. They'll need to come back to hit the temple complex, but that can come after they spring a couple of the ambush sites.

He and his friends might not be as bad around civilians as they used to be, but none of them are stupid enough to think they're good with PR. Better to leave the Crystal Shield to that while he and his companions have some fun getting messy.

And oh, do they intend to make a mess. While most of the adventurers had to refit quickly to not be vulnerable to the Metal-affinity monsters and foes, Vnarl's group doesn't use much in the way of metal. The most significant amount were his swords, but a pair of unique wooden clubs from Thedeim's dwellers solved that easily. He heard the Voice call them cricket bats, though he doesn't see anything close to crickets or bats about them. Just another one of the weird things about Thedeim.

Whatever the reason for the names, they feel good in his hands, enough that he might keep them around as a backup.

"How close are we?" whispers Hark, drawing Vnarl from his reflections.

"Close," answers Mlynda, her eyes on the map.

Vnarl smiles and shifts his grip on the bats. "We'll go hard on this one. Thedeim wasn't sure just how tough things would be in here. I'd rather have this first target be boring than have to test out those weird ant healers."

Hark shrugs. "They're probably really good."

Mlynda nods and puts away the map. "Probably, but time spent healing is time not spent fighting. If the clergy is as tough as they're expecting, we won't want to miss any of that."

Vnarl nods at that as they near what should be the last corner. "Keep an eye out. Those least are supposed to be pretty nasty, and there are rumors of stronger versions. I bet if we can kill one without too much damage, the guild and the dungeon both will reward us for the body."

Mlynda agrees and acts casual, but uses hand signs to convey what she senses.

Danger in walls. Ambush around corner. Hark, focus on foes in the open down the tunnel. Vnarl on the ones that burst out.

Vnarl grins again. "Sounds like a plan to me. Who doesn't love getting credit for a quest twice?"

Hark hefts a boomerang as they near the corner, getting the ambush started in a way uniquely suited to himself: he arcs it around the bend. The trio hurries forward, rounding the corner as they hear the impact of the heavy throwing weapon. Their particular style of combat should work best if they can get ahead of the enemies in the wall, letting Vnarl handle one side and Hark the other, with Mlynda providing support as needed.

Around the corner, they see a group of five armored people, a mix of dwarves and elves, as well as a pair of thinlinks and a forgemaster. One of the elves looks to be out cold from the opening attack, and Hark seamlessly catches and throws the returning boomerang before following up with a few more. Behind Vnarl, the blades of the least stab through the wall, starting to tear it down as they try to salvage their ambush.

The troll grins and lays into the exposed blades with the clubs, striking at the sides and the few joints he can see, working to make it difficult for the concealed enemies to come out to join the fray.

Hark's projectiles bounce off shields or are swatted out of the air by the thinlinks, but his skill and choice of weapon make it simple for him to guide them back to be launched again. Fighting Hark is like fighting a deranged juggling act, and that's without Mlynda interfering.

"Strangle Grasp!" she shouts, slamming her staff into the cave floor, rapidly enhancing the growth of the fungus all around. Vnarl would have thought she'd have a harder time using fungi instead of normal plants, but from the tendrils of mycelia trying to tie up the thinlinks, it doesn't seem like she's having too much trouble.

Vnarl isn't having too much trouble just yet either. He pulps the first disturbing head that tries to get through the wall, but all that does is make it difficult for the thing to see. He'll probably have to crack its legs to incapacitate it, if he remembers the information about them right. Vitals mostly in the torso.

Without a good stab, he's not going to get at them easily, but if he breaks all the limbs, the things can't do anything anyway. Mlynda's work with the fungus also seems to be holding the wall together, further slowing the least's progress. Smashing another blade, he's pretty sure he's basically accomplished the same. Those sure look like four legs from a monster in the wall, with a smashed head, too. That's going to be a nice impediment.

Or not. The least suddenly vanishes before it bursts through the wall. He sidesteps and prepares to counter, but the thing looks like it was used as a ram to batter through, and now he has a breach in the wall to keep him occupied.

His bats lash out, crippling and cracking limbs, and crushing the disgusting heads of the least. Busy as he is, he doesn't miss when another stuck least is ripped from the wall, and his bats don't miss cracking its carapace as a tentacle hurls it through the opening. For a moment, he's worried they've managed to get the Harbinger's attention, but this tentacle seems to have a pretty defined form, for a tentacle.

"Mlynda! I think I just found a lesser! In the wall!"

"On it! Sporeburst!" The glowing fungi in the tunnel release countless fluorescing spores, lighting the breach for Vnarl, but he also knows they give Mlynda a lot more information than just sight.

"You good, Hark?" the troll shouts to his teammate, glancing over his shoulder. The enemy team is having trouble dealing with Hark's barrage, especially with Mlynda's mycelium tendrils impeding them. The frontliners are kept at bay by the lashing fungi, while the ranged attackers can't get a moment's respite to actually aim at the moving forest elf. Even worse for their foes, their thinlinks are slowly but surely getting tangled by the strangling grasp of the halfling's spell.

Honestly, in Vnarl's opinion, the only reason they're still going is the forgemaster working to keep armors from deforming too far, keeping blades straight and sharp, and even seeming to have some kind of fire attack to burn away some of the mycelia. It's not a very reliable attack, but it's probably the biggest thing keeping the forces of the Maw from being overwhelmed.

Vnarl focuses back on his own fight, ducking a tentacle as he brings both bats down on the back of a least. The carapace shatters and the thing goes limp as Mlynda finally gets a good look at the lesser.

"It's like a huge centipede! Sharp legs like the least, thicker carapace, segments look like they can break away. Each has a pair of legs and one tentacle coming out of the top. No head! Eyes on each segment!"

Vnarl curses at the information. Those tentacles aren't going to care much about his clubs, unless he can somehow catch it between them. He needs something sharp to deal with those, but he doesn't have any metal!

He catches a stab from a least on the flat side of the bat and twists, snapping the leg off at the joint before he follows up with a strike to the body. The least might be designed to take punishment, but there's only so much the things can do against blunt force trauma.

"Fungal Tendrils!" declares Mlynda as Vnarl suppresses a groan at what's coming. Spores dig into the flesh of his arms, and though painful, it's not what's making him groan. The vine whips are easy to control; it's like having longer limbs. Fungi are a bit more complex, though. Mlynda tried to explain it to him once, but it went well over his head. All he knows is the tendrils act like an extra set of limbs coming out of his elbows.

No matter how weird it feels, he's not going to pretend like it's not a very potent enhancement, especially right now.

"Disarm!" he shouts as the tendrils dart forward and wrap around the forelegs of the next least, his bats crashing down on its edge to neatly sever the limbs. He wanted something sharp, and now he has it. He uses the bats more like shields as he lays into the least with their own sharp limbs, smiling in triumph as he severs a tentacle that tries to slip through in the chaos.

Speaking of chaos, this battle is the epitome of it—just how Vnarl and his team like it. You keep an enemy guessing, and they won't know what to react to!

"Ricochet!" shouts Hark, and Vnarl hardly has to think as he follows.

"Guard Slip!" His bats and blades feint and slip past the raised weapons of the least, the bats smashing into the carapace as the blades fly toward the lesser behind them.

"Fluorescing Burst!" finishes Mlynda, the glowing spores suddenly strobing brightly as the three easily flow into the team attack.

"Blink and You'll Miss It!"

Hark's boomerangs swerve and bounce around the entire tunnel, striking the dwellers from impossible angles. The thinlinks are overwhelmed by a surge of fungal growth, immobilizing the tricky monsters. The forgemaster is pummeled to dented scrap under the assault, sounding like someone threw a suit of armor down a tall flight of stairs.

Vnarl's tendrils, armed with least scythes, strike where the segments meet on the lesser, slicing through repeatedly and spilling ichor in the ambush space. He would have expected more of a mess from dicing apart a monster like that, and he'd also expect the segments to simply collapse. Instead, they stay upright, though the coordination is severely lacking now. His bats crack the carapace of the least still nearby, the sheer force sending them barreling back into their hiding place.

Mlynda's spores settle on the foes, growing quickly and incapacitating them. Whatever makes the lesser somehow able to handle being severed like that, it doesn't help it against the invasive spores. The strobing stops, and the trio takes a few moments to take in the aftermath of the fight. Vnarl shakes off the tendrils, though he slips the least blades into his belt for later use.

"Anyone hurt?" asks Mlynda, with the other two shaking their heads.

"I got cut up a bit, but I'll be fine," says the troll.

"I don't think they're used to throwers; they didn't manage to land a hit. Might have gone worse if I didn't get lucky and hit what I'm pretty sure was their mage first."

"Survivors?" follows up the halfling, going down the quick after-battle checklist.

"None on my end, looks like. The least and lesser are hard to put down without outright killing them."

"Hard to say. Hits to the head can be a bit weird," admits Hark as he looks over the fallen dwellers. "Looks like they're all breathing, at least."

"Check for loot and leave them. We don't have room for prisoners. If Thedeim wants them, he can send the ant healers for them," says Vnarl. He gets no argument. They're not going to feel bad if any of the ambushers die before getting medical help, but they also don't want to go executing people after the fact. As long as they're not getting back up any time soon, that's fine by them.

Besides, they have more important things to do than worry about the health of people who attacked them. For example: hitting as many ambushes as possible before it's time to converge on the temple. Not only is this a chance to really let loose, but they'll also be helping out. It looks like Vnarl's group can handle the ambushes without too much problem, so taking more of them means less danger for their guildmates. And removing more danger here and now means less things to come and try to get them at the temple.

As fun as the ambush was, things will only get more difficult as they close in on the Maw.

Chapter 92

Vernew

If she weren't already devout toward the Weaver, watching that miracle be cast would have done it. His presence has always had a quiet power to it, a subtle surety of safety, making it easy to forget He is more than able to take a more proactive stance in protecting those He cares about.

She's not exactly a mage able to analyze magic, but even she could tell that was something *significant.* While watching and being a part of that spell made her want to go charging into the depths of the Maw, Leo and Teemo are still sticking to the basics of the plan. The concept of an actual Murphy may be a bit tongue in cheek, but the idea is clear.

"Just because we've turned Murphy's attention on the Maw doesn't mean he's going to fully ignore us. Keep careful, keep safe," said Teemo, and though Vernew still chafes at not getting to run rampant, the Voice has a point.

And so she sticks with the Crystal Shield followers as they enter the outskirts of Silvervein. Jen is with her, as well as most of the other dwellers, and even some of the healing magmyrm at the back. It's a pretty intimidating army, in her opinion, even if it's spread through several tunnels right now.

The bulk is moving for the main passage, the one that goes through the settlement's center. That's the one that will have the most resistance, most likely. Her group is heading for the cheesemaker, to see what he can do about ensuring as few of the citizenry resists as possible.

So far, it's going very well, but Vernew refuses to let that lull her into complacency. The worm farm is the official outskirt of the town, and the worm ranchers look on with nervous curiosity as she and the large group enter the cavern.

"Stay on the path," orders the lead paladin, a grizzled wolfkin in shining plate named Unsil. The others easily follow the order, marching by the farm and only sparing the farmers enough attention to ensure they don't come running at the group with pitchforks or whatever a worm rancher would use as a weapon. A manure fork? Do worms make manure, or is it topsoil?

Whatever they make, it's not important right now. Jen currently looks like a pale dwarf, and she moves toward the fence when she recognizes one of the ranchers. She shouts and waves him forward, which he nervously does.

"Uh . . . Jen? What's going on?"

"You felt that magic, yeah?"

"I wouldn't be surprised if the dead felt it. What *was* that?!" he almost yells, but reigns himself in as he looks over the gathered army.

"It was aimed at the Maw and its forces. Just hunker down and stay safe. The Maw's going to be gone before the day's out."

"Gone?" he asks incredulously, eyeing the fighters for a few moments before shrugging. "Well, if you're going after the Great Maw, and if you cast that thing, it's not like I can warn them any more than they've already been. Now, get a move on before someone shows up and your fighting makes a mess of my field!"

Jen chuckles before running back to rejoin us, and the rancher goes to gather his people and his worms.

"It sounded like they're staying out of it?" asks Unsil. Jen nods.

"Yeah, I think they will. Anti-Maw sentiment is probably the biggest in this area thanks to my contact. Once we get to him, he should be able to get us some more locals to help give us legitimacy about not wanting to attack the townsfolk."

"Then let's go. The sooner we can get his help, the sooner we can start securing the town."

Vernew keeps her eyes open on the way to the cheesemaker, though she still doesn't spot any of the Maw's forces. Are they focused elsewhere? Maybe they don't really care too much about the outskirts? Maybe the tunnelers are making the Maw pull back to deal with them? Or maybe the Maw was just not ready for a wide attack like this?

Whatever the reason, she's glad that things are going so smoothly, even as she grows more nervous about the lack of response. The cheesemaker is actually standing outside his cheesery, looking nervous as Vernew's group approaches.

"Serd, these are some of my allies!" assures Jen, though Serd still looks a bit jumpy. Vernew can't blame him. He probably doesn't have a combat class, so any kind of fight would be new to him.

"Did they do . . . whatever that was?"

Jen grins. "Some of them. That was Thedeim's opening move. It targets the Maw and its forces. The ordinary people won't have anything to worry about from it."

"I hope not. That was . . ." He trails off before shaking his head. "Sorry. Uh . . . you want to get to taking over the town, right? Let's go to the bar. We should be able to find more of my friends there, and they can go with you to prove you're not after the townsfolk."

They hurry down the tunnel for the bar and finally make contact with some of the Maw's forces. At least, Vernew is pretty sure the people outside the bar are working for the Maw. Once they spot the group, they rush inside before anyone can stop them.

"Inquisitors?!" gasps Serd, confirming Vernew's hunch.

"Vernew, Jen, slip in through the side. We'll go through the front and keep their attention. If the patrons are still alive, they're probably hostages now. I need you two to keep them safe if it's not too late."

Jen and Vernew both nod, with Jen's features shifting back to her changeling form. She places a hand on Vernew's shoulder. "I'd say this will be weird, but it's not too far from one of Teemo's shortcuts. Shadow Step!"

It really does feel like going through one of Teemo's shortcuts, except she can't see anything. Thankfully, they soon emerge in an unused bedroom. Though there's no lights in the room, it's still somehow brighter than the shortcut was. Jen gives a nod before melting into the shadows, leaving Vernew a few moments to ready herself.

She can do this. It's another hunt. Don't get spotted before it's time to strike.

She quietly opens the door and slinks down the hall, where she can hear raised voices.

"Invaders! What do we do!"

"Quiet! They're clearly working with these . . . *sympathizers*. They'll try to negotiate for their allies. We just have to buy time for more people to arrive and catch them by surprise! Get them lined up!"

Vernew carefully makes her way into the main bar area, where she sees a good dozen inquisitors, and a good dozen or so civilians, too. A guy with a lumpy red hat stands centered behind the civilians, and Vernew thinks it must be the Redcap! A few seconds of observation put that fear aside, thankfully. The hat is definitely made of fabric, not . . . people. And he looks more like a dwarf than a tall fey.

That doesn't make him any less dangerous. He has a holy symbol in his hands, an oval with triangles lining the interior—a toothy maw. It softly glows silver, along with a multitude of blades, each floating at the necks of the hostages.

The door to the outside slowly opens, and Unsil's voice carries through. "Forces of the Maw! Lay down your arms, and blood will not have to be shed today!"

The Maw priest sneers. "Blood feeds the Great Maw, and we shall see it feast! If you enter, you'll get to watch it consume these traitors before it consumes you!"

A helmed head peers past the doorway before vanishing, and Vernew would bet her best spear they're trying to figure out what to do. She doesn't have much in the way of ideas, either. She could probably skewer the priest before he notices, but she doesn't know if she can kill him before he can mortally wound the civilians!

Maybe she can take her own hostage? She discards that idea quickly. Even if it did work, it'd just add another layer to the standoff, except without her being able to act freely like she can now.

Act freely? She hasn't used that on a person before, but it should work. It's gotten a few of her newer hunters out of a jam before. It's not like she has any better ideas right now.

"Lone Hunt . . ." she whispers, feeling the magic take hold of her and the priest. Judging by the way he tenses, he feels it too. The blades move but find no purchase on the victims.

"Move! The priest is mine!" shouts Vernew, and havoc erupts in the bar. The Shield followers burst in as a blade of shadow swipes at the priest's neck, but it has no effect either. She *said* the priest is hers, and she wasn't kidding. She doesn't bother trying to dodge a mace that swings at her as she slips forward, letting it skid along her cheek as her magic enforces her skill. Everyone else can have a brawl, but her and the priest are the only ones who can harm the other now.

Unfortunately for the priest, he doesn't know that just yet, and he's still trying to attack the civilians. She doesn't trust her obsidian spearhead to pierce his body armor, but she has skills for taking down a strong opponent.

"Hamstring!" she shouts as she stabs the back of his leg, and though the head shatters, it does so *after* piercing the armor. The priest yelps and falls over, screaming in rage and pain before his eyes land on the spider.

"Maw Consume You!" he bellows, his symbol flaring and ripping the blades away from the civilians to lash at Vernew. She scurries away, jumping over and off of the various Maw loyalists in her effort to escape the blades. She might not be able to harm them, but she can distract them, and the forces of the Shield take advantage of any openings they can get.

She uses one pair of arms to change the spearhead as her other works with some silk, trying to ignore the flashes of pain when the blades find the gaps in her armor and chitin. She powers through, though she suffers a few more deeper gashes when she has to close back in on the priest.

She gets a loop over the foot of his injured leg before leaping straight up, momentarily avoiding the levitating blades as she takes an angle he wasn't expecting. He's quickly in an angle he wasn't expecting, too, as Vernew hops over a crossbeam in the rafters, where lights were hanging. "Snare!" is the priest's only clue as to what happened as his world goes upside down and his leg explodes in pain.

"Piercing Fangs!" he manages to gasp out, two of the larger blades darting toward Vernew. She drops the silk as she feels the two impacts, as well as two sharp pains in her chest.

She grunts but stays stable on the crossbeam for the moment, focusing on the priest and trying to ignore the damage he just did. "Cornered Beast," she manages as she hops down, putting all her momentum behind the move designed to return at least as much injury as was sustained.

The priest can't dodge and can't even maneuver his blades to intercept her before the obsidian spearhead pierces his armor and his heart. He gasps, trying to hold on for a few more moments, his blades wavering in the air as he tries one last attack, but the light leaves his eyes before he can manage anything.

Vernew slumps to her side, wondering if her armor was always so slick inside, before remembering the two blades stuck in her chest. She looks around the room, glad to see that not only the civilians are alright but the Shield's people are finishing off the last of the Maw's.

She closes her eyes, so tired, only barely registering Jen's shout.

"Medic!"

Chapter 93

Queen

The Ant Scion wonders if maybe she should step out of her lab more often. Working with the catkin on the way gave her so much information to work with! If only she could have another month to really iterate on the armor designs . . . But no, the Emperor was right in striking now.

Prepare too much, and opportunity will pass you by. Jumping too quickly is just as dangerous, but she suspects the Emperor was closer to the former than the latter. But oh, how that preparation has borne fruit!

She had been aware for some time that Fluffles was working on a variation of the Voice's Butterfly Effect, but even she couldn't have guessed at the complexity of the final product! Helping command the vast energies was, in some ways, like commanding her personal ants, and in others, it was so much *more.*

She would love nothing more than to explore the technique and new possibilities, but there is more pressing business to attend to. The Emperor wages war, so she can't just sit in her mobile lab and tease out the secrets of reality. She needs to contribute, even if he doesn't demand it. *Especially because* he doesn't demand it!

She and Thing work in tandem with the magmyrm, working to keep alive whoever the volcanic ants bring back from the battle. She still isn't so sure about healing the enemy, but the Emperor was clear, even without the Voice needing to spell it out: Any who are brought in will be healed. If you can't commit to that, get out of the medics area.

It's rare for him to be so vehement with something, so she is willing to bow to his unusual wisdom. It's shown itself invaluable before, so she has no reason to doubt it will show its worth again by the end of all this.

Pheromones fly through the air as treatments are administered, some giving diagnoses, and some giving information on the battle. Honey has her bees everywhere, and while they occasionally get conscripted to help with a particularly difficult injury, they are mostly here to get information about how the battles are going.

Despite how busy the medical ward is, the fighting is going well. If Queen hadn't been part of that spell, she would say it's going impossibly well. The delvers are outnumbered approximately three to one, even with the defecting townsfolk on their side. The counter-ambushes went exceptionally well, with the delvers either handling the attacks on their own or with the help of the wyrms.

The fighting in the town is the messiest, and she wonders just how bad it would be without Murphy's Law aimed at their foe. While it is not a perfect protection, the misfortunes of battle are certainly weighing more on the enemies than her allies.

Though that doesn't mean her allies are immune to it. The magmyrm have brought in over a dozen bodies now, along with tales of their misfortunes. That Crystal Shield acolyte was distracted and never saw the flying blade that took his life. This adventurer spotted an ambush early enough to warn her allies, but not early enough to save herself.

The dwellers, though, hurt Queen the most. This ratkin was too good with the compound bow, and the Maw's clergy decided to destroy him, even at the cost of their lives. That tarantulakin held a narrow tunnel so civilians could escape, buying time for backup to keep them safe and avenge her.

Her only solace is that the dead were brought in dead. So far, not a single living delver or dweller has entered her ward and been lost. But the fighting is still ongoing, and growing more brutal as the Maw's forces grow desperate.

She puts her musings aside as more magmyrm rush in, pheromones thick with alarm. Their charge is alive, but they don't know how much longer that will be the case. She directs them to her personal station and freezes for a moment when she sees who it is.

Vernew.

The spiderkin is usually so brash and vibrant; it seems so . . . so *wrong* to see her so still, even without her having two jagged blades in her chest. Another thick wave of pheromones kicks her out of her thoughts, and she replies with her own. Emperor as her witness, she will *not* lose her friend this day!

She embraces her titles, for she is not simply an Alchemist but the Wielder of Secret Knowledge. Let Honey hoard information—Queen will set each grain of truth as a scalpel for her ants to bear. A bee hoards; an ant uses. She knows spiderkin anatomy. Her compound eyes take in every detail as she orders ants and hands alike.

One lung is certainly punctured, with the other blade being dangerously close to Vernew's heart. Her ants swarm around the offending weapons, carefully digging away the armor without allowing the blades to move. They're jagged, serrated. If not removed carefully, they'll do more damage on the way out. They are also restricting bleeding, so removing them now would be a mistake.

The hands release the latches of the composite clamshell, freeing the two pieces. The holes are wide enough now, allowing the hands to carefully levitate the chest piece free.

So much ichor. She pushes the thought aside, needing to focus. If Vernew had a true exoskeleton, she'd already be dead. But having actual bones allows for a proper circulatory system, which helps minimize bleeding, no matter how much it might look otherwise.

She orders resin and bandages, as well as potions. This is beyond what a simple healing slime can help with. Her ants carefully enter the wound, her metal-mandible majors working to blunt the sharp serrations. Her smaller alchemical ants transport potion exactly where it needs to go, carefully bringing vessels back together, knitting lung tissue whole.

The blade near her heart is the easier task, more needing to prevent further damage than actively repair anything. While there are a lot of vessels in and around the beating muscle, her ants are able to navigate far more nimbly than something so large and crude as a scalpel.

The intrusion near her heart is removed first, and even with her ants managing the blood vessels, they could only get to so many of them with the blade still in the wound. She does her best to ignore the spurt of precious fluid, instead ordering the ants back as the hands bring forward the bandage.

She pauses for a brief moment when she sees it, immediately able to tell it's no ordinary one. She never made special bandages! What is . . . ?

Her mandibles twitch in an ant smile as she realizes what it is. She orders it applied to the wound, and resin applied as well, even as the events of the bandage's existence play through her mind.

She and Thing were not the only ones working on medical supplies, back in the safety of the Emperor's territory. At the time, she thought Grim was simply helping in a more mundane manner. His size and simply having hands were already an immense help in making bandages. His sanitized scythe made cutting them easier, and he could seal them in wax without worrying about burning his fingers.

But of course, the Grounds Reaper would help in his own subtle way. Queen wonders if other healers would apply a bandage so suffused with Death magic, even with all the Fate and Life in it as well. Other healers don't truly understand what infections are, and so wouldn't understand how important a little bit of death is to ensure proper life.

Other healers probably wouldn't apply resin overtop a bandage, but other healers don't often work with spiderkin. Even if her chitin isn't a true exoskeleton like Queen's, it will still provide an excellent surface to seal with resin, without little things like hairs to make removing it later difficult.

Other healers might not know how a lung is put together, and other healers certainly wouldn't have the delicate and precise mandibles of her ants to align everything properly. Other healers might be able to just brute force health with raw magic power, but Queen doesn't have the luxury of having Life affinity.

But she has her secret knowledge, and as the Emperor likes to say: knowledge is power. And power is more than just the ability to destroy dangers: it is the ability to protect. Her power can save and improve lives, not just end them.

The work is painstaking, but she cannot afford to just slather her friend in healing potions, nor toss her into a healing slime. The slimes are effective, but they really need all the important pieces to be roughly where they should be in order to work. The potions are effective, but she only has so much of a supply, even with her ants brewing more as she works. She needs to be efficient.

The blade in Vernew's lung is finally removed, and another bandage is applied and resined in place, with a dose of healing potion administered to help stabilize her friend. Queen would like to do more, but she can't waste materials. She can already scent more emergency pheromones from the magmyrm outside.

Vernew is not going to be the only dire case she deals with today. While she can't do anything for the ones that arrive too late, she *will* do her best to not let any slip away who make it to her in time.

Chapter 94

Aranya

The red kobold can't help but keep a hand at her pendant as she, Ragnar, Aelara, and Yvonne follow Teemo and Nova. She should be confident, especially after that miracle from Lord Thedeim and his scions, but she can't keep her nerves fully in check.

Should she have tried to insist her friends stay behind? What if they get hurt because of her? Not for the first time, she crushes that line of thought. Not only is it pointless to worry about that now—it's also insulting to her friends to even consider taking credit for their agency. No, they chose to come along, and if she's honest with herself, she's glad they did.

Even if she worries for their safety.

She does her best to set that cart on a quiet path in the back of her mind. Their safety is her concern; she *is* their primary support now, but she can't make their choices for them.

She turns her attention to the shortcut they're currently in, both to try to calm herself but also to appreciate just how skilled Teemo's become. The trail feels comfortably spacious, but she's pretty sure an ordinary worm would make more of a disturbance than the combined efforts of Teemo and Nova. The Voice hurries alongside the wyrm, manipulating distance as she melts through the rock.

Aranya suspects he's manipulating the space around Nova, too, as she watches the shy scion slowly add more and more magma to her form. She's pretty sure Nova is mimicking more advanced forms of dragon, currently what she would consider a drake, with four legs and a tail.

She suspects Teemo is shrinking her, because she's seen little ripples in the magma construct, hinting at Nova moving underneath. She doesn't know how significantly space is compressed there, but she's confident Nova wouldn't fit through any of those legs if they're actually the size they look to be.

"Nervous?" asks Ragnar at her side, looking more serious than usual.

"Yes," she admits, turning her head to look at her other two companions. "I don't know which of the scions would be worse to face."

"Th' Redcap," answers Ragnar without hesitation, earning confused looks all around.

"The Redcap?" repeats Aelara. "I would have thought you'd be more concerned about facing the Harbinger."

Ragnar shakes his head. "Nah. It'll be nasty, aye, bu' I c'n handle a headache. A Conduit's a whole other vein t' mine."

"Even without your usual armor?" asks Yvonne, earning a laugh from the dwarf.

"Are y' daft, woman? It's no cragplate, but it'll take as good a beatin' fer a while, and weighs nothin'!"

"What about your shield? Isn't it dangerous?" asks Aranya, still a little confused about why he kept it.

Ragnar smiles and reaches to pat the shield slung on his back. "Even a Conduit'll 'ave a 'ard time takin' m' shield. It's an heirloom an' 'as th' weight a mountains. Tha' Redcap *could* take it, but he'd bottom out th' Maw t' do it."

"But your axe would have been easier?" Aelara nods at the weighty stone hammer at Ragnar's hip replacing his usual weapon.

"Aye. B'sides, I figure we could do interestin' things together wi' an Earth mage an' an earth hammer!"

"Personally, I hope we all stay bored and beneath notice the entire time," admits Aranya, her mind focusing on what they're really here for: the kobolds.

"It'd be nice," affirms Yvonne. "How long do you think it'll take to convince them to come with us?"

"I . . . I don't know. I don't know if I'll even be *able* to. A lot of them worship the Maw, and as far as I can tell, it's genuine. Though a lot of them try to oppose it, too. But mostly . . . I think the majority will just be scared of changing the status quo. It's not a good life, but it's still *life*, and change doesn't guarantee anything better."

"What do we do about the ones who don't want to leave? Will they try to fight us?" asks Aelara with a small frown.

"It's . . . possible. The Maw fanatics might just laugh and watch, expecting it to immediately stop us or drag us back in a couple hours. That's how most escape attempts would go. But with two scions and us . . . they might try something."

Nobody looks happy about that, but before anyone can reply, Teemo speaks up.

"We're almost there. Aranya, you're up. Nova says she can feel a large cavern ahead, with a lot of smaller tunnels that don't meet up with the mess of a maze we're sneaking through. She doesn't feel anything that doesn't seem to be a kobold, but there's no way at least one of the scions isn't here. How do you want to do this?"

"Surface in the cavern. The tunnels are to the sleeping areas. Most of the people should be in there, and anyone who isn't should get there pretty quickly." She takes a moment to touch her holy symbol once again, her other hand resting on the hilt of the scythemaw blade Lord Thedeim gave her. She's still no expert, but she should at least be able to avoid embarrassing herself should she need to use it.

"Got it. I'll poke my head up to see if we're expected, then let you all in if we're good. If we're not good . . . we run."

Aranya winces at that but doesn't argue. A significant part of this plan hinges on being able to make progress before having to fight. Starting with a fight would go poorly. And if they're too late . . . she'd rather not see the remains of the enclave after the Maw decided to consume everyone.

Teemo pops his head through a tiny crack in the ceiling, soon pulling back with a smile. "Looks good. We'll head on up. Nova, if you want, you can leave the magma here so you can sneak through the rock, or you can wait until we need you to throw your weight around."

Nova rumbles from somewhere inside the magma drake, which soon collapses into a pile of molten stone. The magma itself vanishes as Teemo twists space around it, muttering, "Spatial Thermos," as he does. The others look confused at the wording, with Aelara giving their curiosity words.

"What's that?"

"It's one of Lord Thedeim's concepts—a powerful one, despite it having such a mundane use," explains Aranya. "It's a kind of wineskin that keeps the contents at the temperature you put them in. It's surrounded by nothingness, only having a thin lip around the spout that gives the heat or cold any chance to escape."

Teemo nods at that. "And this is a spatial version of that. There's only one way in or out of there right now, and it opens to solid rock . . . Well, more magma, since Nova went through. Either way, the heat has nowhere to escape."

"Think ye' c'n get a scion intae one?"

"Maybe, but the way out would be pretty obvious. It looks very weird in there, with the only normal bit being the exit. Anyhow, let's do this, yeah?"

Aranya inhales and nods as the floor slopes up to the crack in the ceiling, where Teemo waves her forward. He even hops on her shoulder as she steps through into a familiar nightmare.

The air is thick with the scent of bodies; thankfully the scent of living bodies, at least. Breath, waste, and shed scales fill her nostrils as the sight of confused kobolds greets her. Most have ragged clothes, with only the Maw fanatics having anything clean. Even their chains are shiny, which is much more than can be said of the others.

While the fanatics have thin, practically decorative links, the ordinary ones have thicker manacles and bindings. Despite them being loose enough to let a kobold move around, the chains serve two purposes. The first is a reminder of their place; they breathe only because the Maw allows it. The second is so there is an easy source of metal to punish any who get too uppity.

The gathered kobolds murmur before a fanatic cautiously approaches Aranya. "Who are you?!" he demands, relying on the threat of the Maw to get an answer rather than any weapon to give his question weight.

Oddly, her nerves seem to melt away instead of spiking. This is the time for action, not for second-guessing. She speaks loudly and clearly as she steps aside, letting her friends join her from seemingly nowhere.

"I am Aranya, resident and High Priestess of Lord Thedeim. He has come to free our people."

The fanatic sneers even as he seems to relax. "What makes you think you can stand before the Great Maw?"

"Jello's Embrace," she answers, a wave of orange engulfing the fanatic and holding him still. She directs the magic toward other fanatics, with Aelara soon bringing her own magic to entomb fanatics up to their necks. The commotion draws the eyes of everyone in the enclave, with even the tunnels filling with curious, nervous eyes.

She inhales to repeat herself but is interrupted by a wizened old kobold with dusty red scales leaning on a cane as he steps toward her. "Aranya? Is it truly you?"

She smiles and rushes forward, embracing him. "It's me, Grandfather! I'm back, and I've come to bring everyone with me."

"But . . . how?" he asks with wonder, his eyes wandering over her companions and eventually landing on Teemo, still sitting on her shoulder.

"There are a lot of hows in that one question, hmm?" he answers, only making her grandfather even more confused.

"There's too much to explain right now, Grandfather. Just please, get everyone here so we can go. Teemo here has made a shortcut for us all. We need to take it before the Maw notices."

"How would it not notice?" he asks before a crash of metal on metal sounds from just behind Aranya. She quickly turns, seeing Ragnar in a full defensive stance, staring at the entrance to the enclave . . . at the Redcap.

"So, the Master was right. You thieves wanted the Master's precious kobolds." The lanky fey slowly stands to his full height in the tall cavern, his blue eyes looking disinterested as he takes in the scene. "I should thank you, I suppose. I haven't had a chance to make a fresh hat in a while."

Chapter 95

The Redcap

The lanky fey takes in the details of the central kobold chamber, not especially concerned about the invaders currently in it. The pantry has been breached, but the kobolds are still safe. He can see the loyal ones incapacitated in several ways, but they're in no danger. If they're lucky, the Redcap will be allowed to make one of them a hat, though come to think of it, he has plenty of material in the invaders.

A dwarf, an elf, some strange fluffy biped, apparently an escaped kobold, and a rat. Not exactly the most intimidating group, even if he can tell the rat is a Voice. What kind of pathetic dungeon has an ordinary rat as their Voice?

They all wear a strange make of armor, and though the Redcap can feel metal inside it, there's not enough to get a grip on. He probably *could*, if he really tried, but it'd be like trying to grab a fistful of water. On the opposite end of the spectrum, the dwarf's shield sings to him of strength and durability. He lets his affinity caress it, and is surprised to discover how staunchly it ignores him.

He doesn't know what kind of magic could do that, and he tests it carefully as he stares at the invaders. He could claim it, but he would cost the Great Maw too much for it to be worthwhile, especially with the interesting swords at the hips of the kobold and fluffy thing.

The scimitars are oddly thick, with deep serrations on their backs. What kind of swords are those? They are interesting, different from the other blades the Redcap has forged. He wills the swords to himself, frowning as they fail to react at all.

He can plainly *see* they're metal, but his affinity finds no purchase in them?

"What interesting swords. I'll have to take a good look at them later."

"I don't suppose you'd let the kobolds go?" asks the rat, and the Redcap considers just ignoring it. However, the Great Maw is spending more mana than it's recovering, so a windfall would be nice.

"No," he answers simply, a hand flicking as he releases a long, sharp needle to sail through the air toward the enemy scion. That one was inspired by an old elf he once saw. He doesn't know why hers were so dull or covered in thread, but he feels he's improved on the design significantly.

The rat doesn't even blink as the needle drifts to the side, missing both it and the kobold it's perched on, eventually embedding itself in the wall some distance behind them. The Redcap frowns as the rat smirks. He guided the needle perfectly straight, yet it drifted? If he had hurled a stone, he might believe he was mistaken, but he could feel the trajectory of the needle. It flew straight; it should have impaled the smiling rodent lengthwise.

He frowns as he is forced to shift his estimation of the invaders. They're trickier than they appear. "Return to your burrows, kobolds," he orders, his mind going over his armory of blades. Which to summon first?

His musing is interrupted by the enemy Voice. "Nova, now!"

The Redcap is already moving, expecting some strange attack from the rat Voice, but the danger comes from the very cave beneath his feet. Heat! So much heat! He calls forth a spiked chain, inspired by the thinlinks, and harpoons the nearest wall, letting him yank himself to safety. He would have tried attacking one of the invaders, but he doesn't want to have his escape thwarted by the same thing that ruined his opening attack.

The floor he once stood upon explodes into heat and magma, causing the gathered kobolds to finally remember he ordered them to their hovels. They quickly flee as magma floods into the chamber, and the Redcap wonders if the invaders simply intend to completely fill it to kill the kobolds, and probably himself, too.

It's not that simple, it seems, as the magma starts to mound up and form into a long, powerful shape. Four limbs lift a hulking body, two more limbs spreading wide above it, while one more whips around from behind. A long, thick neck takes shape, a head sprouting details as the Redcap watches with rapt attention. It roars like a volcano, and the Redcap is stunned by the realization of what it is.

It's the mystery sculptor! It works with magma, not stone, so perhaps he should call it a molder instead? He ducks under a swipe from a wing, his eyes wide instead of half-closed with disinterest.

"You're the sculptor. I have your small kobold statuette. It looks like you've improved since you made that." A flicker of motion has him summon a kite shield just in time to intercept an obsidian-headed arrow. It shatters on the shield, though he can feel the weight of the skill behind it.

He'll need to admire the dragon's work later, it seems. The other invaders require his attention. He summons and releases a wide fan of knives, once again feeling the trajectories differ from what his eyes see. Some illusion, perhaps? Illusion affinity can be so bothersome, though it would explain the metal swords that ignore him. Why create them, though? Surely an illusionist would make them look like something other than what the Redcap has mastery over.

He may need to take this fight seriously. Unfortunately, the Great Maw doesn't have the mana for him to *truly* take the fight seriously. It needs mana for orders, for spawning, for a multitude of things. It may be able to consume some nodes or possibly even a spawner, but such desperate moves should be beneath the Great Maw.

Fine. He shall test these illusions, starting with what may be an attempt to mask the metal in the dwarf's armor. That he's charging with a stone hammer held high makes no difference. He can feel the traces of metal in the odd armor he's wearing. Trusting more in his ability to direct his affinity than in his eyes, he pulls more of the Great Maw's mana to attempt to crush the cackling dwarf.

He can feel the metal shear under his command, confirming it exists. Unfortunately, it lacks the strength to actually hamper the invader. As it nears him, he summons his own hammer, leveraging it around in a brutal, powerful arc . . . an arc that somehow feels longer than it should. His balance is off, and the head seems smaller than it should, but his attack still stops the dwarf cold.

Of course, it should have smeared the bearded nuisance across the floor. Wild eyes gaze from over the shield as the stone hammer crashes into the Redcap's hand. It stings, but isn't seriously damaging. In fact, he would say the words from the dwarf's mouth are more painful.

"An' 'ere I 'eard scions were scary!"

Blue eyes in the blackness under a grisly hat narrow for a moment before the Redcap recognizes an unexpected affinity. The dwarf clearly wants the Redcap's attention, and even if that would be playing into the annoyance's hand, he doesn't have much other option. He has some resistance to mental attacks thanks to the Harbinger, but he can't let this dwarf build up an offense with that variety of magic.

"I will carve a masterpiece of pain into you, dwarf." He doesn't usually like abstract art, but for this opponent, he's willing to make an exception. Summoning a bladed chain—all the better to hinder and dice the armored beardy thing—he swings it in a few loops before bringing it down on his foe.

"Flay."

The dwarf calmly steps back as a curtain of magma intercepts the chain. It digs deep into the sudden intrusion, and the Redcap can even feel it grab and pull at his weapon! He can feel the metal melt beyond his control as it sinks into the wing of the magma dragon, and he's soon forced to relinquish the weapon so he won't be sucked in, too.

Even worse, a glowing orange arrow seems to simply sprout from his shoulder, pain echoing through his arm as a cry of "Trick Shot!" echoes around the chamber. He frowns at the arrow before pulling it free and snapping it. These invaders are much more difficult than he first thought. In his defense, he didn't first think they'd have a dragon with them, nor that it would be the mysterious creator of the kobold statuette.

Hmm. The kobolds. He could win this battle if he drew deep on the Great Maw's mana, but that may end up costing it the war. Though, if he loses, the Great Maw may lose, too.

"Great Maw, I need mana." The dungeon is offended for a moment before grudging understanding washes through it. A wide, jagged smile splits the darkness below the Redcap's blue eyes as he nods.

"Of course, Great Maw. I'll leave a breeding population. I'll even make sure to return this wayward one to you, either to carry on her line or for you to savor after we win."

He feels for the nearby kobolds, for their chains. Most of them are down the tunnels and beyond his reach, but there are some with their hovels close enough for him to find them. He'd like to take his time, give each kobold his individual attention, but the invaders are already moving to press their attack.

They know precisely how precious the kobolds are. They're here to steal them away, after all.

Chapter 96

Nova

Nova isn't so sure she's cut out for fighting, no matter how potent her name is. Voice Teemo smoothly deflected the Redcap's opening attack like it was nothing, and he's supposed to be bad in a fight! When he called for her, she rushed to help but only made a mess, at least at first.

A lot of magma would keep the Redcap at bay, right? But he didn't sound worried, didn't stagger back or gasp in surprise. He just calmly watched. She needed to do more than just mound a bunch of magma if she wanted to achieve anything!

Her first idea seemed silly, but she didn't see anything else to do, so she shaped the magma like she had in the shortcut. She hadn't expected to bring a sculpture to battle, but the approval from the Guide encouraged her. It was unorthodox, and the Guide embraced the unorthodox!

She loomed dramatically, only for the Redcap to compliment her kobold statuette? What was he even talking about? Whatever his intention, he still didn't seem intimidated! Then Ragnar charged, and the scion produced some wicked-looking chain, and she had to intercept it!

With her and Ragnar acting as distractions, Voice Teemo, Aranya, and Yvonne were able to team up for an attack. It even hit home! When he pulled out the arrow and stepped back, she thought the Redcap was on the ropes, as Rocky might put it. But Rocky always warned about situations like that. A foe could be about to lose, or they could be preparing something nasty. A rope-a-dope, if she remembered right.

Then the Redcap spoke, and now she knows he's up to something bad. She can hear a rattle of chains from one of the nearby little kobold homes, which seems odd. They should be staying still. Then a snap. Then a thud. Then stillness.

It takes her a moment to realize what's happened, and Teemo can hear her cry. What can she do?

"Nova, push him back! We need to keep him away from the kobolds!" shouts Voice Teemo as the delvers withdraw, having to leave the fight to her if they're going to save anyone.

Her?! She can't face the Redcap! She barely has her first title, and what's an Artist supposed to do against a Conduit?!

"Y' got this, lass," encourages Ragnar as he withdraws. She can even feel the Guide's warmth trying to give her hope. But what—?

Rattle.

Snap!

Thud.

Another one! Indecision and uncertainty plague her as she tries to come up with something to stop the Redcap.

Rattle.

Snap!

Thud.

Do *something*! Anything is better than nothing! She's just glad she doesn't actually have knees to knock together in fear as she charges her magma sculpture forward. Heat pours off her from her fear, but that at least gives her easier access to more magma! She opens her wings wide, physically blocking the enemy scion from advancing, and tries to ignore the gruesome cadence playing out in the hidey-holes nearby.

The Redcap shifts his weight, and she can hear something heavy and metallic scrape the floor before a huge axe takes off one of her sculpture's forelegs. She manages to keep it together and stumble forward instead of just collapsing into a loose flow again. The axe swings a second time, removing the other foreleg and dropping the thick neck of her creation near the metal fey.

Nova gets an idea as her sculpture falls. The axe follows behind it, dropping blade first like a guillotine. Now, it's the Redcap who is at a loss. She could melt that wicked chain and claim it, so why not this axe? And whoever said her sculpture had to be static in form? The neck seems to catch the weapon, deforming and slowing it until it sticks instead of slicing cleanly through.

She regathers the removed magma limbs, reforming her creation and standing tall once more.

The Redcap chuckles. "A very impressive piece. But you are not the only artist here. Let me show you some of my work."

Two swords plunge into the eyes of her effigy, and though she jumps in surprise, Nova is quick enough to engulf the weapons. Then more start plunging into her, and she swims through her work. She's pretty sure the Redcap can't sense where she is, but a moving target is probably better than just sitting still, right?

"I know you're in there somewhere. I just need to find you." More large blades slash, opening brief fissures in the magma effigy before Nova closes them. She does her best to catch the weapons, making sure to spread their melted remains around. The Redcap hasn't shown any ability to manipulate molten metal yet, but she's not going to let it pool and give him a chance to try.

Then the weapons cease. Has she won? The hope is dashed as she feels a weight of mana descend on her, realizing the Redcap has fully embraced his

Conduit title. Even with that, her bond with the Guide still feels hopeful. He actually seems *happy* the Redcap is going all out!

Nova is not! Nova is the *opposite* of happy!

The onslaught resumes, with the metallic implements piercing deeper before they melt fully. He might actually hit her! She can't just stand there and take his attacks. She needs to attack back somehow. She only has one idea, and it doesn't seem like a good one, but nothing else is coming to mind right now.

Her creation leaps at the Redcap, the head scraping against the ceiling as she tries to get away from the probing attacks. He darts back, flinging more dangerous metal into her effigy as it lands, and she lets it collapse into a formless flow. The dragon sculpture is interesting, but the magma is easier to manipulate like this.

Now that there's no defined form, there are a lot more places she can hide, and it's a lot more difficult for the Redcap to try to dig to them! Not that he's against trying.

"Desperation, perhaps? Did I manage to hit you in there? It's difficult to tell, you know. I hope I can make a hat out of you, Sculptor. It seems I'll need to learn magma as a medium for that. No time like the present to learn . . ."

New weapons appear, though hardly traditional ones. As far as she can tell, he's summoned some kind of sharpened shovels, or maybe even wider axes? Whatever they are, he's able to scoop out a piece of magma and fling it aside, splattering the walls and quickly cooling it.

"Heavy and hot. Do you know how long it will take me to remake the blades I'm using for you? But I think you'll be worth the effort, Sculptor."

She redoubles her efforts, moving the magma faster, more desperately, trying to somehow corner the Redcap so she can actually hit him! But he's incredibly quick, dodging any tentacles she tries to make, avoiding any surges, and slipping past any blobs she might throw at him.

She's losing magma and starting to get low on mana, too. One last chance . . .

She hurls one last blob, and the Redcap doesn't even need to step back, as it falls short. She can practically hear him smile as he stands there, his attention squarely on her last large bit of magma.

"Nowhere else to hide, Sculptor. You weren't easy to best, I will give you that. I shall make a glorious hat of this battle, either from you or from your companions. Perhaps from that oddly furred one. I haven't seen something like her before. Goodbye, Sculptor."

Nova feels the magma part around three huge blades, or possibly just one moving incredibly fast. Her last hiding place is sliced into eight even pieces. A few more blades are summoned to further dice and separate the magma as the Redcap looks for his prize.

"Hmm . . . were you a slime instead of a dragon? I'm not sure if that would be more impressive, or les—*Agh?!*"

Nova grins to herself as her supposedly failed projectile finally hits its mark. With his attention on the larger pile, she could slowly inch it closer until there was no way for him to dodge!

The smaller blob pounces on the Redcap's feet, encasing them and holding him fast. She bursts from the ceiling where she had hidden, having escaped through the head when it scraped against it. The Guide had likened her to a strange, flying bomb when he first saw her hit a Fire elemental like this. They never see it coming, and she's pretty sure the Redcap is the same.

The Redcap can't move his blades in time, and Nova hears his last word before her jaws close around his head, her momentum dragging them both through the floor as she melts the rock around them.

"Beautiful . . ."

Chapter 97

The Harbinger

Things have been going poorly, and the Harbinger would bet all its mana on that Fate spell being the culprit. When it first washed over it and the Maw, the Harbinger was concerned, and that concern only grew as nothing continued to happen. It hasn't seen Fate workings in . . . so very long, but it remembers that the more subtle a work, the more dangerous.

Then the surface dwellers made their move. It had to be the surfacers; who else would attack the Maw like this? The Harbinger actually felt that the Maw using the rockslides as scouts was clever, at least until they were all dispatched by the tunnelers of the surface. Once the wyrms and basilisks became known, it was easy to explain what destroyed them.

It wasn't happy news, but it did at least explain. Wyrms also explained how the surfacers had been able to turn the ambushes around on the least and lessers. Their existence had slipped its mind in the hectic battle on the surface. Can it be blamed for the devastating attack of the lich seeming to be more important than a few wyrms? That particular failing galled the Harbinger.

Either the surface dwellers were much stronger than expected, or the Fate spell had something to do with it. The least, backed by a lesser, should have been organized and clever enough to obliterate a dozen or more surfacers! Yet even the modularity of the lessers didn't seem to slow down their opponents for long.

The Harbinger blames the invaders being well prepared for the unexpected difficulties. Blades really only slow down the lessers, as the severed segments can still mentally link together and guide the least. But their foes had been clever and changed from metallic blades to cruder crushing and impaling weapons; things that could be made without metal. Standards could have withstood such an improvised change of attacks, but the lessers seemed like they could only be crushed and stabbed to uselessness.

And speaking of uselessness, the emancipated enclaves could only dream of merely being *useless* in this fight! No, so many of the dwellers are actively *helping* the attackers! Even with the clergy moving in force, the tide is turning against the

Harbinger and the Maw. Only now are they close enough for the Harbinger to guide the least, now that they're close to breaching the temple complex.

But as it loses more and more monsters to the attackers, the Harbinger grows more and more concerned. It segments its mind, leaving the portion with the bond to worry, and freeing most of itself to consider what to actually do.

The surfacers are strong, even stronger than in their previous battle! Could they actually be victorious? The notion should be ludicrous, but with the Maw's forces consistently being pushed back, it's not outside the realm of possibility. And, loath as the Harbinger is to put that possibility on the table, it must acknowledge it and be prepared.

It can't fall here. If the Maw is subsumed, the Harbinger will be destroyed along with it. It must prepare to escape, but its options are dwindling rapidly. If it faces that lich once again . . . escape will not be an option. And if it stays here, it will very likely face the lich. Information is difficult to obtain, but a strong group of scions is not easy to hide.

Which isn't to say it's impossible.

The invaders have somehow gotten three scions to the entrance of the complex without being spotted, and the lich is among them. There is also an odd Earth elemental with a hat and axe, and a coatl that positively radiates mana. The Harbinger just hopes that if the winged serpent is a Conduit, it will be low on mana after that Fate working earlier.

More invaders are gathering there, too, though it's difficult to get scouts in the area to know more, and they're still too far away for the Harbinger to be able to get much of a read on them yet; however, more information won't help the Harbinger at this point. That lich obliterated it on the surface, and it very much doubts a second fight would go any better. If they move in, the Harbinger will need to mo—

Its thoughts are interrupted by abject panic from the Maw and a hammer-blow of mana ordering it to protect its core.

That's what it's pretending to do right now! What is it so . . . Where is the Redcap? It can usually feel that smug scion through their mutual bond with the Maw, but it's not reacting properly. It's almost as if . . . *Oh.*

The Redcap has been defeated and is respawning. Was it the lich?! No . . . the lich is still outside, as far as the scouts can tell. That must mean the surfacers were able to sneak even more scions into the enclave to kill the Redcap. It's no longer just possible the Maw will be subsumed, but *likely*. That changes things, almost as much as the group outside the temple complex making their move.

The Harbinger's course is clear.

It extrudes a thin part of itself near the core as the rest heaves forward.

Seal the core chamber, it orders the gathered priests, even moving some of its mass to help close the thick metal doors. It's not a perfect seal, but the Harbinger can fix that with its own mass. And none too soon, as the Harbinger can feel another significant working of mana beginning. But instead of Fate this time, it's . . . Thunder?

A simple series of notes seem to come from every surface outside the core chamber, impossible to ignore as they set the tempo for the battle through the complex. Heavy beats soon follow, the entire place seeming to vibrate at the whim of whatever enemy scion is doing this. The Harbinger fears it may be too late, that the entire complex may collapse, but the rumblings don't seek to tear the structure asunder.

A harsher melody barges into the budding song, and the Harbinger finally realizes it *is* a song. A Bardic working? With the power behind the music, the Harbinger can only imagine how the enemy scions are wreaking havoc throughout the complex. It can feel them getting closer, but once it springs its plan, it should be well able to handle the lich and its companions.

It shields the minds of the nearby clergy as the harsh notes continue to build, glad it did as a thrum of *intent* bears down through the music. *Say Your Prayers, Little One*, a challenge, a declaration of how feeble the faith of the Maw's followers is. Even the Harbinger is surprised at its weight. It's not enough to break its protection, but it is enough to make the Harbinger worry that, perhaps, the lich is not the only powerful scion coming for it.

It bolsters the will of the clergy as they call on their faith, preparing their most potent spells to unleash on the invaders when they show their faces. It's no longer a question of if, but that realization doesn't faze the priesthood of the Maw. The High Priest stands tall, chanting in defiance of the imposing music.

The Harbinger maneuvers tentacles into position to lash at anything that comes through the door to the Sanctum. The song continues to build as the scions get closer, promising doom and despair for the Maw and its forces. The Harbinger is surprised once again as it's forced to allow some of the intent through the shielding of the clergy so it can keep enough energy for itself.

If it gets much stronger, the Harbinger will have to make its move earlier than it wishes.

The music reaches a crescendo as the doors are flung open. For a terrible moment, the Harbinger and the clergy can see what they are up against. The lich has strange wrappings on its fists now, its staff lying on the floor at its feet, along with its black robe. It has something between its teeth, and bright shorts around its hips. One fist is forward, as if the lich had simply *punched* the doors open!

If it weren't for the intense magical energy around it, the Harbinger would think it a different scion, but it will never forget that signature.

Behind it, a long silver serpent floats, iridescent wings spread wide as it gazes into the room. Where the lich's energy is complex, the serpent's is like an ocean. The Harbinger suspects it doesn't have as much mana at it could have, but it still has the undeniable feel of a Conduit.

Behind them both is the Earth Elemental Scion and the source of the intense song. Lightning flashes around its strange hat, and it holds the axe oddly. It's some kind of instrument, from what the Harbinger can tell by how it's holding the device.

Then the moment is gone, and the spells fly and tentacles lash. Iron teeth, steel-biting jaws, howls of hunger, dissolving acid, and more descend on the trio of scions. Lightning and thunder flare, fire and ice erupt, and raw telekinetic might meet the incoming onslaught. The variety of affinities is more than enough to dismantle each varied attack. The Harbinger can even feel its tentacles being *parried* somehow, but its attention is elsewhere.

As it is, there is no defeating those scions. Even this plan contains some risk in fighting those three, but it has little other option. In the worst case, it should at least be able to force its way past them and flee with only a wounded pride to show for it.

Confusion comes through the bond with the Maw before the Harbinger grins with many mouths and finally ends the charade.

Abandon Dungeon? Yes/No?

The Maw's alarm is cut off as the connection is severed. The Harbinger, now an invader instead of a scion, engulfs the Maw's core.

Chapter 98

Rocky

He hadn't expected it to feel so *right* to be back in his boxing gear. He does feel a little bad about just dropping the nice staff Thing made, but the feeling is overwhelmed by finally not having to pretend. Coach said this room would probably lead to the Sanctum, and from the cultists and Harbinger inside, Rocky would say he was right on the money.

Working together with Fluffles and Slash is also going to be something he'll probably relish and look back on with happiness. Fluffles is incredibly precise with his mana, with *Coach's* mana, spending exactly what's needed to counter the incoming attacks. Rocky, on the other hand, likes to put out a good chunk at the start of a fight and use what he has left to manipulate and transform it as needed, making it look like his reserves are almost as deep.

And Slash . . . Well, Rocky isn't sure his heart can technically get pumping to the beat, but he's definitely buoyed by the music. He remembers the boss music from his fight with the young party, and this song is even more inspiring!

Which makes it all the more disappointing when the Harbinger turns tail and flees through a set of even heavier doors to what can only be the core room. He'll have to give chase soon, but there's the small issue of sorting the clergy first.

"Quickly," hisses Fluffles, and Rocky grunts in agreement. They'll need a moment to recover from that barrage, so he, Fluffles, and Slash need to deal with them before they can take a second swing.

Sharp icicles and compressed fireballs form, blades of wind and crackles of lightning telling of a building of their own attacks, but before they can fly, the clergy of the Maw look shocked, then they start screaming and falling to their knees.

Even Coach Thedeim seems confused before alarm spikes through the bond with a concept so clear that none of the scions need to be a Voice to understand what has Coach so shocked: *Consumed.*

Fluffles tastes the mana flow, and Rocky can feel it now, too. It's all being drawn into the core room! *Something* is draining the Maw's mana. Rocky can feel a pressure starting to build behind his eyes. He mentally ducks, relieved that he's got it right still. The pressure lessens but doesn't vanish, and he turns his attention to his fellow scions.

A little slap gets them both to focus, and Slash takes a few seconds to choose a new song. Rocky can feel Coach's approval as it starts, a song of not only fighting back the hordes of evil but chasing them to their twisted homes and ensuring they understand they are not indestructible.

Still, the gates of this particular doom are well and truly closed. For now. Rocky and the others hurry past the fallen clergy, some already gone, and some wishing they were so lucky. Even the High Priest can only whimper from the floor as they pass.

Fluffles starts circulating the air around the doors as Rocky starts working on them, the Conduit trusting the Affinity Savant to hasten their plan. The doors are thick, but they're still metal. No matter how thick, no matter how strong, metal eventually succumbs to cold. Melting instead of freezing would be an option—in theory—but it'd take a lot of energy. No, this way, Rocky and Fluffles can gain energy as they go instead of expending it.

Grabbing the heat within the doors, Rocky brings it toward him, letting Fluffles's moving air steal away the energy. It's a lot easier to let convection do the final job. Once it's under Fluffles's control, he passes it back to Rocky to hold, at least for now.

Ice tries to form, but Rocky denies it, not letting it insulate the metal from Fluffles's ruthless convection. Almost there . . . *now.*

Fluffles halts the air as Rocky brings a fist forward, carrying all the heat stolen. He's not aiming to melt the doors, no. He has a more destructive option at hand: thermal shock. Heat rushes back into the thick metal, which squeals as it warps before a deafening bang signals its structural failure. Jagged diagonal cracks lead from the center of the doors upward. Fluffles seizes the freed metal in his telekinesis and hurls it into the room, hopefully injuring the Harbinger.

With the door compromised, Rocky gives it a kick and grunts as pressure builds behind his eyes much more quickly this time. He moves on instinct, ducking even as his gloved fists flash out, dodging the attack on himself and parrying the mental onslaught aimed at his companions.

The rush of mana around them finally ceases as insane laughter echoes through the former Sanctuary. The Harbinger's mass has increased significantly, hardly able to fit inside the room the Maw's core once resided in. The three scions dart back as toothed tentacles lash out, needing more room to maneuver to avoid getting hit.

Distantly, Rocky can feel Coach reassure him that backup is on the way, but he keeps his attention on the supercharged Harbinger. He's still confident his group can deal with the monster, but having help is never a bad thing.

He grunts and harmonizes with Slash, flexing his Sonic affinity as he dashes forward. The Harbinger will have a different frequency now, but he's confident he and Slash can find it together, especially with Fluffles starting to build up a good and proper storm.

Lightning zaps at tentacles as they try to exit the core chamber, singeing and charring but not fully forcing them back as the Harbinger seeks to gain more room for itself, all the better to crush them. Rocky and Slash aren't just going to *let* it, though! The combination attack builds as Rocky and Slash prepare an even stronger Resonance Cascade for the beast, when three tentacles suddenly lash out.

Each scion is forced to drop the combination to try to defend themselves. Though none are wrapped by a tentacle, each bears a painful lash as unsettling laughter fills the room. The scions frown and pick up their attack again, trying a different tack this time.

Fluffles focuses on rain, gathering it with his telekinesis near Slash. The Earth elemental increases the tempo of his already fast-paced music, arcs of lightning engulfing the boiling water. But Rocky can feel the heat—or lack thereof. He keeps his eyes on the Harbinger, flash-freezing any tentacles that try to hinder the new team effort, letting him grow an inferno at the tip of one of his boxing gloves.

His eyes widen as he's forced to dodge, same as the other two, as three massive tentacles spear forward, once more interrupting the combined effort and injuring the three scions further.

Fluffles is forced to rely more on his wind to keep him aloft, thanks to the hole in his right wing. Slash is forced to stop playing as he reattaches his severed arm, his Earth-elemental body a bit better able to handle such an injury than most. Even Rocky has a new nasty gash in his side. He's glad he doesn't need that kidney.

Unfortunately, he can't take the time to properly recover as the Harbinger surges into the Sanctuary proper, fanged mouths grinning, eyes sparkling with sadistic glee at the injured scions around it. It takes its time gathering three more masses of its amorphous flesh, preparing three bigger tentacle spears to finish off the three fighters.

They don't just wait for the end, of course. If the monster is going to interrupt their combinations, they'll just have to attack on their own! Blades of wind, concussive bursts of sound, and lances of lightning fly at the Harbinger, even as it summons sacrificial tentacles from its writhing mass, letting the attacks impact those instead of what will be the kill shots.

Rocky dashes forward, his fists flying as he wades through a thickening bramble of lashing tentacles. He freezes, burns, and vibrates apart each in turn, but there are two more eager to take the place of each fallen limb.

He tries to increase his pace, tries to speed up, but he can see he's out of time. The Harbinger's many mouths open wide in mad glee as the tentacles spear toward the beleaguered scions, only to go silent in shock as all three somehow miss.

A Voice speaks up from the doorway to the Sanctum. "Whew, just in time."

Rocky grunts for Teemo to run as a tentacle lashes at the rodent, only for Coach's Voice to vanish down a shortcut and appear several feet away. "Eugh, that's a nasty one."

Rocky can feel the pressure behind his eyes spike as a mental attack barrels down on the Voice, powerless to stop it. He's too far away to deflect it!

He's not the only one surprised as he feels what should have been a tsunami of mental power have all the effect of a light breeze on Teemo's mind.

The Harbinger locks up for a moment, Teemo tilting his head at the amorphous monstrosity. "Is that all you've got?"

The Harbinger roils in rage as it launches a stronger mental attack at the Voice, Rocky getting a headache just from being near the powerful force. Teemo simply blinks as it hits.

"You've got nothing on the Boss, bud." Teemo strolls forward, occasionally darting through a shortcut as tentacles try to lash out at him. Rocky can feel a different mental attack brewing, and this time when it hits, Teemo actually pauses for a moment.

"Oh, hello. That's cute; you want to go mind to mind with me? Nah, I don't have Mental affinity. I'm just used to some pretty gnarly concepts thanks to the Boss. Here, try one on for size. Astronomical Unit."

The word doesn't make much sense to Rocky, but from the way the entire Harbinger flinches, he'd wager having the full understanding of it is something significant.

"Yeah, big doesn't even come close to doing it justice, hmm? Here, have one on the other end of the scale. Angstrom."

The Harbinger shrieks and starts to back away from Teemo, slamming itself toward a corner of the Sanctuary.

"I actually really like that one. I think it sounds cool. It was a lot to take in the first time, though. Kinda ironic, isn't it?" Teemo continues to walk forward, eyes on the undulating mass of flesh, mouths, and eyes looking frightened rather than confident before a simple rat. "You're starting to get it now, hmm? I'm not trapped in here with you. You're trapped in here with me, and those doors are your only escape," speaks the Voice of Thedeim, gesturing over his shoulder as he continues to menace toward the huge Harbinger. "Here, let me give you one that still gives even *me* a headache. Quant—"

With an unearthly shriek, the Harbinger bolts for the doors, tentacles tearing up the room as it dashes for escape in a blind panic. Teemo vanishes down another shortcut to land on Rocky's shoulder, grinning as he watches the Harbinger flee.

"Sucker. Mobius Trap." He closes a fist as the doorway *twists* just behind the last of the Harbinger, and the cacophonous shrieks of the former scion cut off. Teemo slumps on Rocky's shoulder, who is quick to take him into his gloved hands.

"I'm okay . . . just tired. Gimme . . . a few minutes. Boss says the fighting's basically done. Now comes the cleanup."

Chapter 99

That went better than I was afraid of, but worse than I had hoped. Of course, my hopes were pretty unreasonable. I was hoping to somehow not need to fight and get the kobolds out without any issue, and even have another ally after all was said and done. Not exactly a realistic hope, but it still counts!

If I keep to my actual expectations for how things went, trying to be reasonable, it's hard to think of a way it could have genuinely gone better. We still lost people, which hurts. Even if I don't know the names of them all just yet, I intend to give them all a special place in the empty mausoleum, unless they have some special burial wishes. I'll need to make a memorial or something for them, too.

But even being able to fit everyone into the mausoleum is a sign that there were a lot fewer casualties than there probably should have been. There were quite a few close calls, like with Vernew, but everyone who made it to the field hospital is expected to pull through, even the former followers of the Maw.

I didn't have any scions to spare to keep an eye on the takeover of the town, but reports are that they only had a few spots of hard opposition left by the time the Harbinger ate the Maw. When that happened, the worshipers basically all started screaming and fell down. Queen wants to do an autopsy, and Honey is right with her on that one. I'm pretty sure it was some kind of aneurysm, or something else indicating a mental attack.

I don't know exactly how closely connected the cultists were to the Maw, but it's not difficult to imagine the Harbinger being able to attack through that connection while consuming the dungeon.

As it is, most of the cultists are incapacitated, one way or the other. The living are mostly looking lost, though a few are raging and attacking as well as they can. Considering most of them were using Faith magic, and now their object of faith is gone, that mostly means punching, kicking, and biting, at least for now.

Most of those are tied up now, though a few more died while people tried to apprehend them. If someone is determined to fight and die trying, there's only so much that can be done. Cultists aside, we're occupying Silvervein for now, with the Shield's people keeping things stable while the rebels slowly come to terms with the fact they don't have to stay hidden anymore.

The ultimate plan is to get them back on their feet, maybe set up some trade convoys or something to the surface. It's a pretty long trek, but the Southwood is right there. His resources will help keep things stable down there and get him a lot of mana in the process, too.

Before I get too lost in thoughts of the future, I want to take a little more time to digest everything that happened. It's been pretty eventful. First came Murphy's Law, which worked even better than I could have hoped. We still had misfortunes, but the scales were definitely skewed against the Maw and its ilk.

Tripping the ambushes worked like a charm, and though nobody was able to capture a live lesser, lots of people brought back pieces. Queen and Honey want to dissect them after the autopsies, and I'm all for it. These things are nasty, and if we ever have to fight them again, I want all the information we can get.

The battle for the town itself was messy and is where most of the casualties came from, which isn't surprising. Everywhere else was mostly denizens and scions, with most people being in the town. Still, according to the Shield's people, it went relatively smoothly, so I'm willing to take their word for it and hope I never have to organize something like this again. If this was a *smooth* urban fight, I don't want to see a rough one.

The battles in the Maw were mostly as expected. My denizens did a great job of distracting the dungeon and keeping it from focusing where it should, which let Aranya's party, along with Teemo and Nova, sneak into the Kobold Enclave. Which is where things got a bit pear shaped.

We knew one of the scions would be there, but I honestly don't know if the Redcap or the Harbinger would have been better. Ragnar seemed pretty confident he could go toe to tentacle with the Harbinger, but if it could keep interrupting combination attacks like with my scions, I think we would have had trouble finishing the thing off.

And I think it might have been better able to kill the kobolds if it got desperate. Teemo did his best to warp space to try to keep them out of the Redcap's metallic reach, but even he could only do so much. Aranya's grandpa is fine, but a couple dozen were lost before Nova was able to strike the mad fey down.

The zealot kobolds were left alone, so at least the Redcap spared its allies, but they're suffering the same backlash the cultists are. Aranya and her grandpa are trying to get everyone used to their new reality, and working to get those chains off them.

The adventurers' guild is in pretty high spirits, even after the farewell toast they had to the fallen. Many levels have been gained, and though loot was a bit limited with the Maw getting eaten like that, there's still plenty of monster bits to field dress and take back as either trophies or things to sell or make into gear.

I haven't heard much from Tarl and Berdol yet, so I was starting to worry. Thankfully, a couple adventurers confirmed to Leo and Honey that they had seen the duo after the Maw collapsed. They're poking around where the Maw used to be, looking for clues about the specifics of how it worked. They're especially interested in finding where the spawner for the least and such was.

I'm sure, once things stabilize a bit more, Honey and Queen will send out whatever denizens they can convince to scour the territory for information, which we'll definitely share with the ODA.

It . . . It feels a bit weird, but we did it. The planning, the prep, everyone's hard work . . . it all paid off. The kobolds are being freed as I watch—well, listen through Nova. Her senses are still weird, but snapping chains, collars, and bands are pretty distinctive and a lot easier on the ears when there's no snapping of bones, not to mention the sounds of desperate gratitude and relief instead of deafening silence. It's slow going, but it's progress.

I think that just leaves dealing with the Harbinger now. Teemo says it's still running through the mobius trap. It has realized it's looping through the same space continuously, but it hasn't been able to find a way out yet.

"And it won't—not until I open it up. Trust me on this one, Boss. It took a bit of prep before revealing myself, but once it ran in, all I had to do was twist it and connect it."

And you can open it up whenever you want?

"Yeah, that shouldn't be hard. I figure we can just gather everyone up for a big attack and launch it as I open the way. It's not going to be able to interrupt anything this time."

How many people do you think it'll take to build up a strong-enough attack?

Teemo shrugs. "I think me, Nova, Rocky, Fluffles, and Slash should be enough."

I want overkill on this one. How many do you think can physically fit to contribute to the attack?

Teemo taps his chin while resting on Rocky's shoulder, who is relaxing in the former core chamber. "Probably . . . quite a few, especially if I concentrate on giving people plenty of room. Leo, Honey, Thing, and Queen should be able to lend a hand, and definitely Aranya's party, too. It'll be more complicated than Murphy's Law, though. That was basically all Fate, with a little of a few other affinities thrown into the mix. This will be . . . a lot more complicated with so many affinities."

Take some time to meet up and plan with everyone, then. Not only is the Harbinger incredibly dangerous but it's got a stupid amount of mana right now. Getting that will go a long way toward paying back my fellow dungeons for their participation in the ritual.

"I bet Queen and Thing are making a ton of mana with their hospital too. I dunno if saving a delver gives as much mana as killing one, but it's gotta at least be close, right?"

"Sometimes even more."

Poe? How did you get here? You should be . . . You are still in your nest by the chimney, organizing expeditions.

"Boss? What about Poe?"

I thought he was there in the core room with you, but he's back home still.

"Why do you think he's here? I don't see anything?"

How can you not see the huge . . . raven?

If I still had eyes, they'd be wide as saucers right now. All my scions tense up as concern floods across the bonds.

The bird tilts his head in an avian smirk at me, then nods before shaking and making an unhappy sound, puffing up his feathers. He focuses on something or someone I can't see before speaking.

"You're right; I shouldn't intrude on your domain. My apologies. I rarely get the chance to do this and was overeager." He pauses once more, letting his feathers settle as he nods. "Thank you. Now, it's time I tend to *my* domain."

Are you the Raven?

"The *what?!*" comes Teemo's shocked reply, though the mysterious bird doesn't seem to acknowledge my question.

"Bring your Voice to your hospital, Thedeim. I will allow him to see me. We have much to discuss."

Am . . . Am I about to die again?

Chapter 100

Is everything okay, Boss?" tensely asks Teemo from Rocky's shoulder even as I watch the Raven glide off through the wall without even a ripple. It's a bit weird seeing through their eyes, especially since they don't seem able to notice the big bird.

I . . . Maybe? I think he just wants to talk? I think if he were here to take me, he wouldn't really bother with a chat first, or ask to meet at the field hospital.

"The field hospital? Why?" echoes Teemo as Rocky puts up his dukes.

I don't think he's here for a fight. Besides, a fight would go pretty poorly for us. The more I think about it, the more I believe he just wants to talk. Maybe about Murphy's Law? I imagine there were a lot fewer deaths today than he was expecting.

I can still feel Teemo's uncertainty at that, but he accepts and pats Rocky's ear. "Easy, Rock. I think the Boss is right. If the Raven wanted a fight, we'd know it by now. You guys check on the cultists and make sure they can't cause any trouble, alright? I'm gonna go meet the VIP."

Rocky grunts unhappily but doesn't argue as Teemo makes a shortcut. "How bad do you think it'll be, Boss?"

I honestly don't know. He didn't seem upset. He might have even been happy? He started talking to me before someone I couldn't see got mad he wasn't talking to you instead.

"Why would he talk to me?" asks my Voice. My mental smirk gets him to put two and two together without me needing to spell it out. He facepalms once he gets it. "Right, talking for you is kinda my job. I didn't think even the Raven would have to stick to that."

I mentally shrug. *I guess even gods have to follow the rules.*

"Speaking of gods, what are you going to do about him? You've been pretty set on keeping a polite distance with even the Shield."

Oh. Uh . . . do you think it's too late to ask him to make an appointment for a later date?

This time, Teemo gets to smirk. "You want an official appointment with death?" I blanch at the idea while Teemo chuckles as we near the hospital.

Think we could just sneak away?

"I seriously doubt it, Boss. Also: are you actually more worried about him being a god than being death?"

Would you be surprised if I said yes?

Teemo shakes his head at me as he pops back into ordinary space just outside the field hospital. The magmyrm are still busily bringing in the wounded and occasionally the deceased, but Teemo has no trouble maneuvering between all the moving legs. He waves at Queen and Thing, but I don't know if they even notice him, since they both seem to be busy with the business of saving lives.

It's not difficult for Teemo to spot the Raven, as he's perched on a cot at the head of a covered body.

"He really does look a lot like Poe, huh?" comments Teemo before scurrying over to perch at the opposite end of the cot. He meets the Raven's eyes for a few moments as tension builds, then my Voice shrugs and holds out a hand. "I'm Teemo, Voice of Thedeim. He said you wanted to talk?"

The Raven quietly caws in a chuckle and holds out a wing, bringing a primary feather within reach for Teemo to shake. "I'm glad I'm not the only one uncertain about how to start."

Teemo shrugs again. "The Boss likes me to keep him grounded, so I don't really do pomp and circumstance."

"It is refreshing," admits the avianication of death. He preens for a moment, looking like he's gathering his thoughts, before he speaks again. "Do you know what it is to be a god?"

I've been trying very hard not to think about it.

Teemo snorts. "He's been trying to stay out of that kind of thing."

The Raven caws a short laugh at my expense. "For someone trying to avoid it, he's been checking off the list at a remarkable pace!"

There's a list?

"There's a list?" echoes Teemo, just as confused as I am.

The Raven nods. "There is, though it's not one that's been explicitly stated. We've simply come to recognize certain commonalities as the pantheons grow and shrink."

"And you said the Boss is checking them off?"

He nods again. "He has. A certain level of power is simple enough, though the threshold seems to be lower than most would expect. Having followers is another, though they don't need to be so organized as to have a High Priestess. Many leaders qualify for that prerequisite, as their followers believe in them and their ideals, even if they don't necessarily deify the leader.

"There are other requirements besides, but they're simple enough that many mortals can qualify for them. But you've also ticked a few boxes that are not so simple."

Teemo glances to the side as we try to share a look, the Raven giving us a moment to consider the implications. "Like what?"

"A great working of mana in your name, for one. You may have literally given the name to someone else, but Murphy's Law is all Thedeim. The vague concept has existed for as long as conflicts have, but none have understood and wielded it as you have before. You have also necessitated divine intervention, no matter how unintentional or minor."

The Raven chuckles and glances at empty space. "No, I'm not putting your work down. You've admitted it was a simple fix."

"A fix?" asks Teemo, the Raven setting a considering eye on him before speaking.

"Using libraries as signs to communicate before having a Voice. Not deliberately disruptive, and not difficult to fix, but it still seems to have counted."

"Why 'seems to'? And . . . I mean, not to be rude, but why you? Why now? Yvonne says you're usually pretty busy; way too busy to have a chat with a weird dungeon with a rat for a Voice."

"No objections to being called weird?" asks the Raven, and I can feel him somehow meeting my gaze through Teemo. "Hmm. Well, to clarify: Yes, I usually am far too busy to simply have a chat, as you put it. However, I was expecting a lot more work to be had here today." He pauses and nibbles at the bridge of a wing for a moment. "Maybe that counted, instead of the libraries?" He shakes his head and returns his focus to Teemo.

"Either way, now is a time where I find I have less work than expected. As for why me . . . Well, it's my work that requires this conversation."

"Boss says he's sorry about messing with your quotas, but he's not sorry about saving people."

The Raven caws in laughter again. "No, I imagine you're not! Tell me, are you aware of what my duties entail?"

You're the Reaper . . . you guide the dead where they need to go.

"You take the dead to where they're supposed to be."

The Raven nods. "I do. Across the pantheons, I deliver the souls of the departed where they must go: to their afterlife. Do you know what that entails?"

Uh . . .

"Not really?"

The Raven tilts his head in a smile. "Most mortals focus on what the experience of their promised afterlife will be. The Goldenplume, for example, promises to warm and protect the eggs that are her followers until they hatch. She will feed them what bitter truths they can handle, that they can grow, until they must be pushed from her nest. They will either take flight to whatever lies beyond, or fall back to the cycle of life and death, to gain more perspective, more understanding, more ability to accept the truths she offers and grow from them"

Reincarnation, but also with an out?

Teemo seems thoughtful before responding. "What lies beyond?"

The Raven stares right at me for a few moments before answering. "I don't know. I'm the god of death, not of the dead. Once they are where they should be, I have little power over them. So, where do you think I took the followers of the Maw, Thedeim and Teemo?"

"To the Maw?"

They certainly worshiped it, and with all the weirdness of the least and the Harbinger, I bet it qualified for those other checkboxes.

The Raven shakes his head. "No. The Maw lacked a single requirement, as I understand them. You also lack a single requirement, Thedeim, though a different one."

Wait, what? What?!

"What requirement did the Maw lack?" asks Teemo, taking the situation a bit better than I am.

The Raven smirks. "It was not where the souls of its followers belonged. It probably would have tried to eat them. Of all the requirements, this is the one I understand the least. I understand the truth of where souls belong, but I don't know exactly how it's determined."

I start to calm down a little at that as Teemo voices my reasoning. "So . . . you're telling the Boss he's not where his followers belong yet? I guess to try to help him be better?"

The Raven caws in a chuckle and shakes his head. Teemo's eyes widen as wisps of orange slowly take shape around us. They start as just little clouds, but eventually resolve into the forms of . . . of my fallen dwellers.

"No. That's not what he's missing. They belong with him. It's the first time I've seen this not be the final step, but it does seem to be one that truly starts apotheosis."

My calming concern shoots right up just shy of blind panic at that. My fallen dwellers look glad to hear they belong with me, and though that gives me a nice warm fuzzy feeling, the weight of that responsibility threatens to crush it and me.

The voice of the Raven feels like it pierces my very soul as he continues. "The prerequisite you are missing . . . is to define yourself. The Maw was insatiable. The Shield is a protector. The Goldenplume is a loving parent. I am a courier. What are you?"

His gaze and his question leave me . . . I'm not sure how to describe it. I can still feel the panic, the pressure, even the warm fuzziness, but it's all a bit muted as his question demands an answer.

What am I?

Honestly, it's a question I never really bothered to ask, even back on Earth. I never really saw the point, because I never could accept a singular answer. But it's a big question. I'm pretty sure midlife and existential crises stem from trying to find an answer to it.

There were answers that sometimes seemed to fit, but never for long. I was a kid. I was a grown-up. I was lonely. I was a friend. I was a student. I was an engineer. I was a gamer. I was a nerd. I'm a Christian. That's a lot, but that's still not quite *me*.

Am I a drifter? I tend to roll with the punches pretty well. But I'm also a dungeon now, and a dungeon drifter just sounds wrong. What else am I? Am I potential? If I claimed that, I think I'd also have to be pretentious.

I look at my emotions, taking advantage of the weird disconnect the Raven has me in right now, wondering if answers might lie there.

Am I scared? Well, yeah. I'm a lot of things, but I like to think stupid isn't one of them. I've never minded being a group leader, but it was always among peers—people I considered equals. Now I'm supposed to help prepare these people, these people who trust me deep enough that the Raven says I'm where they belong? I don't know how to prepare them! I don't even know what I'm supposed to prepare them *for*!

Who else?

Even with the disconnect I'm feeling right now, the thought hits me hard. I remember Teemo being worried about negotiating with the Southwood, not wanting to mess it up. There's been a lot of times where that simple question has helped cut away the nonsense, the fluff, all the unnecessary things and reveal the simple truth: Who else?

When faced with a difficulty, who else is going to deal with it? From a spilled drink to a wrecked car, am I going to just foist the unpleasant situation on someone else? Who else was going to help Hullbreak? Who else was going to stop the Maw? Maybe someone else, I can't know everything, but I didn't see anyone else able to step up.

And . . . after seeing my fallen dwellers, who else would I trust to help them? I can think of one, but He might already be on it. When asking why He doesn't do something, consider the possibility He already did, by making you.

That doesn't exactly relieve the pressure . . . but I tend to do pretty well under it. So . . . what am I?

Well, I'm feeling a bit better about all this, but that's a how, not a what.

I keep trying to figure it out, but I'm drawing a blank!

Alright . . . get out of your head and look around you. What am I? What does everyone say I am? Well, weird. I've never taken being called weird as an insult. It beats being boring, right? What else? Well, I've definitely flipped the table on a lot of people's understanding of a lot of things.

Am I chaos? It could certainly fit. Human history is full of chaos: wars, assassinations, genocides, famines, plagues, disasters . . .

But it doesn't feel right. Some people thrive in chaos, but I just don't accept that as humanity's natural state. But . . . what *is*, then?

I realize it just as I feel *something* happening, the realization feeding into it, and the apotheosis feeding into the realization. Whatever the Raven was doing to muffle my emotions fades quickly, and though I'm still nervous about what's happening, I try to embrace it. It's weird. It's new. It's scary! It's all that, and so much more.

There's only one constant in life. It's not going to be easy, but that's also life, isn't it? It's not easy, but it's less difficult once you accept it.

I am what all humans are. I am change.

Chapter 101

Things go orange, then go even more orange, quickly intensifying to a blinding white. I try to blink it away, hoping to clear my vision, before I remember that's not how my sight works anymore. I'm . . . in some kind of white void. It's weird how a white void can feel even emptier than a black one like space. It also feels more inviting, like a blank canvas just waiting for a painter's brush.

I look around in confusion before a thought hits me: Did I get *isekai'*d in my *isekai*?! Thankfully, it only takes a moment to reaffirm my connection to my scions, my territory, and even a thinner connection to . . . well, my followers, I guess. Outside of this white void, time seems to have slowed to a crawl . . . or time is weird here.

However *wibbly-wobbly* the time is acting, the connection to my dwellers and the few outside followers helps remind me what the Raven said about afterlives. Looking around, I don't think it'll be a bad one as it is, but it's definitely boring. So . . . what should I do?

When all you have is a hammer, your problems tend to look like nails, and when you've been a dungeon for almost a year now, empty spaces demand to be filled with interesting things. Should I just make a dungeon to adventure in for their afterlife? It'll be more interesting than this void, but that doesn't feel right. I want my followers to have a more peaceful afterlife than that.

I look around for a while, the endless possibilities making it difficult for me to even get started. I mentally shake my head and latch on to a simple idea I've seen work out countless times: rolling grassy hills. Will I keep the entire void like this? Probably not, but maybe so. Either way, it gives me *something* to work from. Blue sky, yellow sun, a few drifting clouds, a river there . . .

Before I know it, I have an area that looks like the starting area in every survival crafting game ever. That realization also gives me a good idea for what to make this afterlife be, and the goal for it. I start sprinkling around nodes for all sorts of resources, from things like stone, clay, or metals, to organics like fibers and wood, and more besides.

The placements are a bit all over the place, but from what the Raven was saying, it sounded like people need to put in a bit of effort to be properly prepared for what lies beyond. I start poking around, looking for animal nodes, when I hear a collective gasp and realize my fallen dwellers are here now.

At the moment, they're all just gazing around, eyes wide at the peaceful scenery around them. It doesn't take them long to notice me, and they start falling to their knees (or closest approximation) with looks of reverence on their faces.

"Whoa, easy there. You don't need to do that!"

They don't really listen, so I reach out with . . . I'm not sure what, actually, and help them to their feet. "Come on, you guys know I'm not looking for that sort of thing."

The ratkin and spiderkin slowly rise, all still looking a bit overwhelmed by everything, many with tears of joy wetting their cheeks. A ratkin steps forward, and I know his name is Emarlo before he opens his mouth. He dips like he intends to take a knee before remembering I just said I didn't want that sort of thing.

"L-Lord Thedeim. It's . . ." He struggles to find the words, so I pat him on the shoulder to try to help comfort him. In fact, I pat everyone—they all look like they could use a bit of guidance right now.

"Hello, everyone. I . . . Well, let me first apologize for . . ." I trail off, mentally shaking my head, chuckling. "No, I can't really apologize, can I? You all knew the risks of joining this battle. I won't downplay your struggles by trying to take credit with an apology. We all did our best, and we all knew some might not make it back home. So instead, let me say thank you. Thank you all for fighting for what you believe in, and for being willing to pay the price for it."

For a few seconds, the gathered dwellers keep it together, but then Cerli, an orb weaver spiderkin near the back of the crowd, slips free a sob. Then Nird, a ratkin, fails to stifle his own emotions. After that, the dam breaks, and I worry for a moment I've messed things up royally.

But they're not tears of regret. Every single one of them is crying tears of relief, the kind of breakdown at accepting that yes, things were bad, but things can also be better. I do my best to comfort them all, even as I feel a bit awkward doing it. I never feel like I know what to do when someone is crying, but sometimes, just being a shoulder for them to do it on is all they need.

It might have taken hours or maybe not even a moment, thanks to how weird time feels in here, but eventually everyone mostly processes everything, or at least enough to be functional again. I smile at them all, glad to see that even dying hasn't broken them.

"It's a bit overwhelming, hmm?" I ask, earning a few quiet chuckles at the understatement before I take a step back and bring their attention to their surroundings.

"This is . . . well, the afterlife. The one you get with me, at least. Take a good look around because it's not going to stay like this for long, I expect. If I'm change, I can't have my afterlife be something static, can I? And I think it's going to be on all of you to effect that change."

I motion for them to follow, which they do, rubbernecking around at all the scenery and nodes.

"The most positive of changes comes from people who plant trees whose shade they'll never sit under. You won't stay here forever; the Raven made that pretty clear. So, you'll make something here. Maybe you'll make a house, or a road, or a mine, or a pick, a sewing needle, a loom, a cart, a *something*. You'll make your change, probably only able to guess at the impact it will actually have.

"You all saw today how small things can have great consequences. You'll pour some of yourself into what you make, leaving behind something and gaining even more. When you're done, you'll either be ready to go into the beyond, or be eager to head back into life and experience more."

They all look excited at that, which is a relief. I'm not quite sure *how* what I said will work, but I somehow know it *will*, in fact, work.

"Work in groups or in one huge team or individually, whatever feels most appropriate. And do more than just work. Take some time to reflect, to chat, to relax. I'm not running a hell here, heh. Take your time and enjoy creating, and appreciate that you'll have more at the end than what you hold in your hands."

It takes them a few moments after that to start wandering around, exploring the area, and I wonder if I should make various workshops or allow them to make them on their own. I mull over the benefits of each for a while before a voice grabs my attention.

"Lord Thedeim?"

I focus on the same ratkin who spoke up first earlier. "What's up, Emarlo?"

He resists the urge to kneel once more before answering. "Um . . . what should we make?" he asks, and I see most of the dwellers around him also looking like they would like some guidance.

I smile at them before speaking. "Anything," I say, leaving the word hanging in the air for a few moments before continuing. "I know; it can be difficult to pick something with so many possibilities around. When you have everything to choose from, it's almost impossible to choose anything. I'm not going to make you make anything specific—that goes against the whole point. You can change your mind and make something else later, too, if you get a good idea. But if you want a suggestion . . ."

I gesture at the peaceful surroundings. "I would note a distinct lack of chairs around here."

"Chairs?" echoes Emarlo, looking confused.

I nod. "Chairs. While there's also a lack of rooms to put them in, everyone appreciates having a comfortable place to sit. Grass and rocks can only get so comfortable."

Emarlo still looks a bit confused, but the dwellers around him start talking about what to make, soon drawing him in. I listen to them discuss as I watch the others explore and poke at the nodes, unsurprised when most seem to want to make something other than a chair.

While I wasn't joking about the lack of places to sit, I'm hardly upset about them wanting to make something else. There are a lot of things that could make the afterlife a bit better, chairs are not specifically the point. It just helps ground their ideas, give them a point to start from, a way to look around for something to change for the better.

I pull my attention back to the world in time to see the wave of orange wash out from my core and through my territory. It also spreads out from Teemo over the hospital, and I know it's going to continue until it washes over probably all of Silvervein. I can feel my followers as the wave passes over and through them, bolstering them a little and reaffirming our victory.

Aranya feels like a beacon when the wave reaches her, and I can feel our connection strengthen considerably. I try to gently point her attention back to the kobolds around her, since they're probably going to need as much help as they can get. Their world has been pretty thoroughly turned upside down, and they'll need her to help right it once more.

In the hospital, everyone not one of my denizens is staring at Teemo, even the people from Silvervein. I guess the kobolds aren't the only ones who might appreciate a hand and an explanation.

The building realization of what happened is soon shattered as Teemo waves a hand in front of his nose.

"Whew, Boss! Really? Right in the hospital? You find some magic beans or something?"

I stare for a few moments before laughing. *Magic beans make beanstalks, not orange waves!*

"If you say so, Boss. Anyway. Everyone." Teemo pauses to look over the people in the hospital. "Yeah, jokes aside, you all know what happened. For the people from Silvervein, the Boss isn't big on ceremony. Besides, there's a big mess to clean up, so let's focus on that, yeah? So if you're in bed, focus on recovering. If you're walking around, focus on helping. That's what the Boss and I are gonna do."

I smile as Teemo slips into a shortcut, watching through the eyes of my scions as they help put back together the mess we made of Silvervein. It's going to be a lot different from how we found it, but that was kinda the point. Different doesn't always mean better, but I'm going to give it my best shot.

When I look at my territory, even peeking into the little slice of afterlife I control, and see how things are going, I can't help but feel confident that better isn't beyond reach.

About the Author

Khenal is the author of the Dungeon Life series. Born and raised in a small town in Northern California, he studied mechanical engineering but graduated from college in the middle of the Great Recession. Unable to find an engineering job, Khenal turned to content creation, streaming videos on Twitch and posting stories to Reddit and Royal Road.